TREASURES BEYOND IMAGINING AWAIT YOU

"The King of the Elves" by Philip K. Dick—He was only an old man running a broken-down gas station until the elves made him an offer he just couldn't resist. . . .

"Darby O'Gill and the Good People" by Herminie Templeton—He had been trapped inside the magic mountain, and only a woman's cunning might serve to set him free again. . . .

"The Long Night of Waiting" by Andre Norton—They were only children though they'd been born over a century and a half ago, but their escape from Faerieland might change the world forever. . . .

These are just some of the folk who, for better or worse, have crossed over into—

ISAAC ASIMOV'S MAGICAL WORLDS OF FANTASY

FAERIES

ISAAC ASIMOV'S MAGICAL WORLDS OF FANTASY

Edited by

Isaac Asimov
Martin H. Greenberg,
and Charles G. Waugh

A ROC BOOK

ROC
Published by the Penguin Group
Penguin Books USA Inc., 375 Hudson Street,
New York, New York 10014, U.S.A.
Penguin Books Ltd, 27 Wrights Lane,
London W8 5TZ, England
Penguin Books Australia Ltd, Ringwood,
Victoria, Australia
Penguin Books Canada Ltd, 2801 John Street,
Markham, Ontario, Canada L3R 1B4
Penguin Books (N.Z.) Ltd, 182–190 Wairau Road
Auckland 10, New Zealand

Penguin Books Ltd, Registered Offices:
Harmondsworth, Middlesex, England

First published by Roc, an imprint of New American Library,
a division of Penguin Books USA Inc.

First Printing, October, 1991
10 9 8 7 6 5 4 3 2 1

Acknowledgments
Introduction. Copyright © 1991 by Nightfall, Inc. Used by permission of the
author.

"The Manor of Roses" by Thomas Burnett Swann. Copyright © 1966 by
Mercury Press, Inc. First appeared in THE MAGAZINE OF FANTASY
AND SCIENCE FICTION. Reprinted by permission of Mrs. Margaret
Swann.

"The Fairy Prince" by H. C. Bailey. Copyright 1911 by H.C. Bailey
Reprinted by permission of the Tessa Sayle Agency, London.

"The Ugly Unicorn" by Jessica Amanda Salmonson. Copyright © 1991 by
Jessica Amanda Salmonson. An original story, used by arrangement with the
author.

"The Secret Place" by Richard McKenna. Copyright © 1966 by Eva Grice
McKenna for ORBIT. Reprinted by permission of Karl Edward Wagner,
Literary Executor for Eva Grice McKenna.

"The King of the Elves" by Philip K. Dick. Copyright © 1953 by Philip K.
Dick. Reprinted by permission of the agents for the author's estate, the Scott
Meredith Literary Agency, Inc., 845 Third Avenue, New York, NY 10022.

"Flying Pan" by Robert F. Young. Copyright © 1966 by Mercury Press,
Inc. First appeared in THE MAGAZINE OF FANTASY AND SCIENCE
FICTION. Reprinted by permission of the agents for the author's estate, the
Scott Meredith Literary Agency, Inc., 845 Third Avenue, New York, NY
10022.

Roc is a trademark of New American Library,
a division of Penguin Books USA Inc.

PRINTED IN THE UNITED STATES OF AMERICA

CONTENTS

FAIRYLAND

Isaac Asimov

Fantasies or folk tales thought to be suitable for children are often called "fairy tales," partly because the most famous of these stories involve entities of more-than-human powers, called fairies.

The most famous of all, for instance, is the "fairy godmother" who comes to the rescue of poor, persecuted Cinderella. This is a story that has filled countless children with the vague desire and the perceived need for a fairy godmother of their own. There are also evil fairies, such as the spiteful one who wasn't invited (through a mere oversight) to a princess's christening and who placed her under a curse that led her to becoming the Sleeping Beauty.

The result is that we have many pictures of fairies, some of them drawn from Disney cartoons. The good fairies look like kindly and rather bumbling housewives; the bad fairies like ugly crones, indistinguishable from witches. We have the Blue Fairy in *Pinocchio* and Titania in *A Midsummer Night's Dream* who look like beautiful actresses, as well as Titania's husband Oberon, who is a powerful (but fundamentally good-hearted) monarch. Most of all, we have a modern conception of fairies as tiny creatures, no bigger than a thumb, with gauzy little butterfly-wings, like Tinkerbell in *Peter Pan*. So strong is this particular version that earlier in this century some mischievous girls made paper representations of such diminutive fairies, took photographs of them, and fooled Arthur Conan Doyle into believing them to be authentic. (Conan Doyle wrote the Sherlock Holmes stories, but his hold on reality, at least in later life, was not very strong.)

But what *are* fairies? How did they get started?

To begin with, the original word had a form that was closest to our modern "fay." This word, fay, derives from Latin words meaning "faith" or "fate," so it bears a strong mystical connotation. We still say that someone is "fey" when they seem to have sense perceptions beyond the ordinary.

The land of the fays, the region in which they live, is "faerie," the "-rie" suffix being an archaic way of saying "land of." Because "faerie" has dropped out of consciousness these days, it has become "fairy." Nevertheless, this collection of stories is called *Faeries* because many of them are deliberately written in archaic fashion, and because "fairy" has gained a slang meaning these days that is far removed from what *we* are talking about.

Of course, "fairy" does not have any form that indicates it is referring to the place in which fays live; therefore it has become synonymous with fay, and the region in which fays, or fairies, live is now called "fairyland." This gives us two suffixes meaning the same thing, but we're stuck with that.

And what gave us the idea that fairies exist? The least dramatic explanation (and, therefore, the one most likely to be true) is that they are a holdover from the old nature spirits that filled the woods and fields—the nymphs and satyrs who represented the procreative powers of nature. In their place, we now have fairies, elves, brownies, trolls, kobolds, gnomes and other spirits that appear in various cultures and with powers and characteristics that vary from storyteller to storyteller.

Are there more dramatic explanations? Of course.

By and large, these spirits, whatever they are called, and we might as well lump them all together as fairies, are viewed as smaller than ordinary human beings, as hidden and elusive, as generally malignant, and frequently, as having longings to be human.

History is full of cases in which conquering invaders attack the natives of a region (sometimes of smaller size than the newcomers) and force them back into mountain fastnesses or hidden regions. In this way, the Celts beat

back the Picts in Scotland, the Saxons beat back the
Welsh, the Indo–Europeans beat back the Basques of
Spain, and so on. There would be a dim memory of the
time when the defeated people were not yet completely
eradicated; when they engaged in guerrilla activity, and
raided isolated outposts of the conquerors. The stories
of the "little people" arose and, of course, were fanta-
sized out of all recognition as time went on. Undoubt-
edly, Americans of European descent would have had
similar stories to tell about Native Americans, if the per-
secution and eradication of the latter had not happened
so recently, and, so to speak, in the full glare of written
history.

Perhaps the most dramatic version of this theory (and,
therefore, the least likely to be true) is that the tales
of fairies hark all the way back to the elimination of
Neanderthal man by "modern man," some thirty to fifty
thousand years ago. Neanderthals were smaller than ourselves in height but stronger in musculature, and perhaps
that is the source of the "little people" with their frightening power.

In any case, it is important to remember that the best-
known fairies of modern times are sanitized ones prepared for our children. Unlike these kindly fairy god-
mothers and flitting little Tinkerbells, fairies, in their
original conception, were dangerous and frightening entities, and faerie, or fairyland, was a place that mingled
wonder, awe, and terror in equal quantities.

Some of the stories in this collection are humorous;
notably the two by Kavanaugh and the one by Philip K.
Dick. Others are sentimental. Most, however, are grimly
powerful in their portrayal of different and fundamentally hostile cultures. I call your attention particularly to
Swann's "The Manor of Roses," which is the longest
story in the book and, in my opinion, the most riveting.
It is a medieval tale of authentic atmosphere, and its
description of the "mandrakes" is almost science fictional
in its intensity. Though I enjoyed that story the most, I
can say that each story offers to the reader rewards of
its own.

HOW THE FAIRIES CAME TO IRELAND

Herminie Templeton

The most lonesome bridle-path in all Ireland leads from Tom Healy's cottage down the sides of the hills, along the edge of the valley, till it raiches the highroad that skirts the great mountain, Sleive-na-mon.

One blusthering, unaisy night, Father Cassidy, on his way home from a sick call, rode over that same path. It wasn't strange that the priest, as his horse ambled along, should be thinking of that other night in Darby O'Gill's kitchen—the night when he met with the Good People; for there, off to the left, towered and threatened Sleive-na-mon, the home of the fairies.

The dismal ould mountain glowered toward his Riverence, its dark look saying, plain as spoken words:

"How dare ye come here; how dare ye?"

"I wondher," says Father Cassidy to himself, looking up at the black hill, "if the Good People are fallen angels, as some do be saying.

"Why were they banished from heaven? It must have been a great sin entirely they committed, at any rate, for at the same time they were banished the power to make a prayer was taken from them. That's why to say a pious word to a fairy is like trowing scalding wather on him. 'Tis a hard pinnance that's put on the poor crachures. I wisht I knew what 'twas for," he says.

He was goin' on pondherin' in that way, while Terror was picking his steps, narvous, among the stones of the road, whin suddenly a frowning, ugly rock seemed to jump up and stand ferninst them at a turn of the path.

Terror shied at it, stumbled wild, and thin the most

4

aggrewating of all bothersome things happened—the horse cast a shoe and wint stone lame.

In a second the priest had leaped to the ground and picked up the horseshoe.

"Wirra! Wirra!" says he, lifting the lame foot, "why did you do it, allannah? 'Tis five miles to a smith an' seven miles to your own warm stable."

The horse, for answer, raiched down an' touched with his soft nose the priest's cheek; but the good man looked rayproachful into the big brown eyes that turned sorrowful to his own.

With the shoe in his hand the priest was standin' fretting and helpless on the lonesome hillside, wondhering what he'd do at all at all, whin a sudden voice spoke up from somewhere near Terror's knees.

"The top of the avinin' to your Riverence," it said; "I'm sorry for your bad luck," says the voice.

Looking down, Father Cassidy saw a little cloaked figure, and caught the glint of a goold crown. 'Twas Brian Connors, the king of the fairies, himself, that was in it.

His words had so friendly a ring in them that the clargyman smiled in answering, "Why, thin, good fortune to you, King Brian Connors," says the good man, "an' save you kindly. What wind brought you here?" he says.

The king spoke back free an' pleasant. "The boys tould me you were comin' down the mountainy way, and I came up just in time to see your misfortune. I've sent for Shaun Rhue, our own farrier—there's no betther in Ireland; he'll be here in a minute, so don't worry," says the king.

The priest came so near saying "God bless ye," that the king's hair riz on his head. But Father Cassidy stopped in the nick of time, changed his coorse, an' steered as near a blessing as he could without hurting the Master of the Good People.

"Well, may you never hear of trouble," he says, "till you're wanted to its wake," says he.

"There's no trouble to-night at any rate," says the king, "for while Shaun is fixing the baste we'll sit in the shelter of that rock yonder; there we'll light our pipes and divart our minds with pleasant discoorsin' and wise convarsaytion."

While the king spoke, two green-cloaked little men were making a fire for the smith out of twigs. So quick did they work, that by the time the priest and the fairy man could walk over to the stone and sit themselves in the shelther, a thousand goold sparks were dancin' in the wind, and the glimmer of a foine blaze fought with the darkness.

Almost as soon, clear and purty, rang the cheerful sound of an anvil, and through the swaying shadows a dozen busy little figures were working about the horse. Some wore leather aprons and hilt up the horse's hoof whilst Shaun fitted the red hot shoe; others blew the bellows or piled fresh sticks on the fire; all joking, laughing, singing, or thrickin'; one couldn't tell whether 'twas playing or workin' they were.

Afther lighting their pipes and paying aich other an armful of complayments, the Master of Sleive-na-mon and the clargyman began a sayrious discoorse about the deloights of fox hunting, which led to the considheration of the wondherful wisdom of racing horses and the disgraceful day-ter-ray-roar-ation of the Skibberbeg hounds.

Father Cassidy related how whin Ned Blaze's steeplechasin' horse had been entered for the Connemarra Cup, an' found out at the last minute that Ned feared to lay a bet on him, the horse felt himself so stabbed to the heart with shame by his master's disthrust, that he trew his jockey, jumped the wall, an', head in the air, galloped home.

The king then tould how at a great hunting meet, whin three magisthrates an' two head excises officers were in the chase, that thief of the worruld, Let-Erin-Ray-mimber, the chief hound of the Skibberbeg pack, instead of follying the fox, led the whole hunt up over the mountain to Patrick McCaffrey's private still. The entire counthryside were dhry for a fornit afther.

Their talk in that way dhrifted from one pleasant subject to another, till Father Cassidy, the sly man, says aisy an' careless, "I've been tould," says he, "that before the Good People were banished from heaven yez were all angels," he says.

The king blew a long thin cloud from be wixt his lips, felt his whuskers thoughtful for a minute, and said:

"No," he says, "we were not exactly what you might call angels. A rale angel is taller nor your chapel."

"Will you tell me what they're like?" axed Father Cassidy, very curious.

"I'll give you an idee be comparison what they're like," the king says. "They're not like a chapel, and they're not like a three, an' they're not like the ocean," says he. "They're different from a goint—a great dale different—and they're dissembler to an aygle; in fact you'd not mistake one of them for anything you'd ever seen before in your whole life. Now you have a purty good ideeah what they're like," says he.

"While I think of it," says the fairy man, a vexed frown wrinkling over his forehead, "there's three young bachelors in your own parish that have a foolish habit of callin' their colleens angels whin they's not the laste likeness—not the laste. If I were you, I'd preach ag'in it," says he.

"Oh, I dunno about that!" says Father Cassidy, fitting a live coal on his pipe. "The crachures *must* say thim things. If a young bachelor only talks sensible to a sensible colleen he has a good chanst to stay a bachelor. An thin ag'in, a gossoon who'll talk to his sweetheart about the size of the petatie crop'll maybe bate her whin they're both married. But this has nothing to do with your historical obserwaytions. Go on, King," he says.

"Well, I hate foolishness, wherever it is," says the fairy. "Howsumever, as I was saying, up there in heaven they called us the Little People," he says; "millions of us flocked together, and I was the king of them all. We were happy with one another as birds of the same nest, till the ruction came on betwixt the black and the white angels.

"How it all started I never rightly knew, nor wouldn't ask for fear of getting implicayted. I bade all the Little People keep to themselves thin, because we had plenty of friends in both parties, and wanted throuble with nayther of them.

"I knew ould Nick well; a civiler, pleasanter spoken sowl you couldn't wish to meet—a little too sweet in his ways, maybe. He gave a thousand favors and civilities to my subjects, and now that he's down, the devil a word I'll say ag'in him."

"I'm ag'in him," says Father Cassidy, looking very stern; "I'm ag'in him an' all his pumps an' worruks. I'll go bail that in the ind he hurt yez more than he helped yez."

"Only one thing I blame him for," says the king; "he sajooced from the Little People my comrade and best friend, one Thaddeus Flynn be name. And the way that it was, was this. Thaddeus was a warm-hearted little man, but monsthrous high-spirited as well as quick-tempered. I can shut me eyes now, and in me mind see him thripping along, his head bent, his pipe in his mouth, his hands behind his back. He never wore a waistcoat, but kept always his green body-coat buttoned. A tall caubeen was set on the back of his head, with a sprig of green shamrock in the band. There was a thin rim of black whiskers undher his chin."

Father Cassidy, liftin' both hands in wondher, said: "If I hadn't baptized him, and buried his good father before him, I'd swear 'twas Michael Pether McGilligan of this parish you were dayscribin'," says he.

"The McGilligans ain't dacint enough, nor rayfined enough, nor proud enough to be fairies," says the king, wavin' his pipe scornful. "But to raysume and to continue," he says.

"Thaddeus and I used to frayquint a place they called the battlements or parypets—which was a great goold wall about the edge of heaven, and which had wide steps down on the outside face, where one could sit, pleasant avenings, and hang his feet over, or where one'd stand before going to take a fly in the fresh air for himself.

"Well, agra, the night before the great battle, Thady and I were sitting on the lowest step, looking down into league upon league of nothing, and talking about the world, which was suxty thousand miles below, and hell, which was tunty thousand miles below that ag'in, when who should come blusthering over us, his black wings hiding the sky, and a long streak of lightning for a spear in his fist, but Ould Nick.

" 'Brian Connors, how long are you going to be downthrodden and thrajooced and looked down upon—you and your subjects?' says he.

" 'Faix, thin, who's doing that to us?' asks Thady, standing up and growing excited.

" 'Why,' says Ould Nick, 'were you made little pigmies to be the laugh and the scorn and the mock of the whole world?' he says, very mad; 'why weren't you made into angels, like the rest of us?' he says.

" 'Musha,' cries Thady, 'I never thought of that.'

" 'Are you a man or a mouse; will you fight for your rights?' says Sattin. 'If so, come with me and be one of us. For we'll bate them black and blue to-morrow,' he says. Thady needed no second axing.

" 'I'll go with ye, Sattin, me dacent man,' cried he. 'Wirra! Wirra! To think of how downthrodden we are!' And with one spring Thady was on Ould Nick's chowlders, and the two flew away like a humming-bird riding on the back of an aygle.

" 'Take care of yerself, Brian,' says Thady, 'and come over to see the fight; I'm to be in it, and I extind you the inwitation,' he says.

"In the morning the battle opened; one line of black angels stretched clear across heaven, and faced another line of white angels, with a walley between.

"Every one had a spaking trumpet in his hand, like you see in the pictures, and they called aich other hard names across the walley. As the white angels couldn't swear or use bad langwidge, Ould Nick's army had at first in that way a great advantage. But when it came to hurling hills and shying tunderbolts at aich other, the black angels were bate from the first.

"Poor little Thaddeus Flynn stood amongst his own, in the dust and the crash and the roar, brave as a lion. He couldn't hurl mountains, nor was he much at flinging lightning bolts, but at calling hard names he was ayquil to the best.

"I saw him take off his coat, trow it on the ground, and shake his pipe at a thraymendous angel. 'You owdacious villain,' he cried. 'I dare you to come half way over,' he says."

"My, oh my, whin the armies met together in the rale handy grips, it must have been an illigent sight," says Father Cassidy. " 'Tis a wondher you kep' out of it," says he.

"I always belayved," says the king, "that if he can help it, no one should fight whin he's sure to get hurted, onless it's his juty to fight. To fight for the mere sport of it, when a throuncin' is sartin, is wasting your time and hurtin' your repitation. I know there's plenty thinks different," he says, p'inting his pipe. "I may be wrong, an' I won't argyfy the matther. 'Twould have been better for myself that day if I had acted on the other principle.

"Howsumever, be the time that everybody was side-stepping mountains and dodging tunderbolts, I says to myself, says I, 'This is no place fer you or the likes of you.' So I took all me own people out to the battlements and hid them out of the way whin—whish! a black angel shot through the air over our heads, and began falling down, down, and down, till he was out of sight. Then a score of his friends came tumbling over the battlements; imagetly hundreds of others came whirling, and purty soon it was raining black wings down into the gulf.

"In the midst of the turmile, who should come jumping down to me, all out of breath, but Thady.

" 'It's all over, Brian; we're bate scandalous,' he says, swinging his arms for a spring and balancing himself up and down on the edge of the steps. 'Maybe you wouldn't think it of me, Brian Connors; but I'm a fallen angel,' says he.

" 'Wait a bit, Thaddeus Flynn!' says I. 'Don't jump,' I says.

" 'I must jump,' he says, 'or I'll be trun,' says he.

"The next thing I knew he was swirling and darting and shooting a mile below me.

"And I know," says the king, wiping his eyes with his cloak, "that when the Day of Judgment comes I'll have at laste one friend waiting for me below to show me the coolest spots and the pleasant places.

"The next minute up came the white army with presners—angels, black and white, who had taken no side in the battle, but had stood apart like ourselves.

" 'A man,' says the Angel Gabriel, 'who, for fear of his skin, won't stand for the right when the right is in danger, may not desarve hell, but he's not fit for heaven.

Fill up the stars with these cowards and throw the lavin's into the say,' he ordhered.

"With that he swung a lad in the air, and gave him a fling that sent him ten miles out intil the sky. Every other good angel follyed shuit, and I watched thousands go, till they faded like a stretch of black smoke a hundred miles below.

"The Angel Gabriel turned and saw me, and I must confess I shivered.

" 'Well, King Brian Connors,' says he, 'I hope you see that there's such a thing as being too wise and too cute and too ticklish of yourself. I can't send you to the stars, bekase they're full, and I won't send you to the bottomless pit so long as I can help it. I'll send yez all down to the world. We're going to put human beans on it purty soon, though they're going to turn out to be blaggards, and at last we'll have to burn the place up. Afther that, if you're still there, you and yours must go to purdition, for it's the only place left for you.

" 'You're too hard on the little man,' says the Angel Michael, coming up—St. Michael was ever the outspoken, friendly person—'sure what harm, or what hurt, or what good could he have done us? And can you blame the poor little crachures for not interfering?'

" 'Maybe I was too harsh,' says the Angel Gabriel, 'but being saints, when we say a thing we must stick to it. Howsumever, I'll let him settle in any part of the world he likes, and I'll send there the kind of human beans he'd wish most for. Now, give your ordher,' he says to me, taking out his book and pencil, 'and I'll make for you the kind of people you'd like to live among.'

" 'Well,' says I, 'I'd like the men honest and brave, and the women good.'

" 'Very well,' he says, writing it down; 'I've got that—go on.'

" 'And I'd like them full of jollity and sport, fond of racing and singing and hunting and fighting, and all such innocent divarsions.'

" 'You'll have no complaint about that,' says he.

" 'And,' says I, 'I'd like them poor and parsecuted, bekase when a man gets rich, there's no more fun in him.'

" 'Yes, I'll fix that. Thrue for you,' says the Angel Gabriel, writing.

" 'And I don't want them to be Christians,' says I; 'make them Haythens or Pagans, for Christians are too much worried about the Day of Judgment.'

" 'Stop there! Say no more! If I make as fine a race of people as that I won't send them to hell to plaze you, Brian Connors,' says the saint, shutting up the book, 'go your ways; you have enough.'

"I clapped me hands, and all the Little People stood up and bent over the edge, their fingers pointed like swimmers going to dive. 'One, two, three,' I shouted; and with that we took the leap.

"We were two years and tunty-six days falling before we raiched the world. On the morning of the next day we began our sarch for a place to live. We thraveled from north to south and from ayst to west. Some grew tired and dhropped off in Spain, some in France, and others ag'in in different parts of the world. But the most of us thraveled ever and ever till we came to a lovely island that glimmered and laughed and sparkled in the middle of the say.

" 'We'll stop here,' I says; 'we needn't sarch farther, and we needn't go back to Italy or Swizzerland, for of all places on the earth, this island is the nearest like heaven; and in it the County Clare and the County Tipperary are the purtiest spots of all.' So we hollowed out the great mountain Sleive-na-mon for our home, and there we are till this day."

The king stopped a while, and sat houldin' his chin in his hands. "That's the thrue story," he says, sighing pitiful. "We took sides with nobody, we minded our own business, and we got trun out for it," says he.

So intherested was Father Cassidy in the talk of the king that the singing and hammering had died out without his knowing, and he hadn't noticed at all how the darkness had thickened in the valley and how the stillness had spread over the hillside. But now, whin the chief of the fairies stopped, the good man, half frightened at the silence, jumped to his feet and turned to look for his horse.

Beyond the dull glow of the dying fire a crowd of Little

People stood waiting, patient and quiet, houlding Terror, who champed restless at his bit, and bate impatient with his hoof on the hard ground.

As the priest looked toward them, two of the little men wearing leather aprons moved out from the others, leading the baste slow and careful over to where the good man stood beside the rock.

"You've done me a favyer this night," says the clargyman, gripping with his bridle hand the horse's mane, "an' all I have to pay it back with'd only harry you, an' make you oncomfortable, so I'll not say the words," he says.

"No favyer at all," says the king, "but before an hour there'll be lyin' on your own threshold a favyer in the shape of a bit of as fine bacon as ever laughed happy in the middle of biling turnips. We borryed it last night from a magisthrate named Blake, who lives up in the County Wexford," he says.

The clargyman had swung himself into the saddle.

"I'd be loath to say anything disrayspectful," he says quick, "or to hurt sensitive feelings, but on account of my soul's sake I couldn't ate anything that was come by dishonest," he says.

"Bother and botheration, look at that now!" says the king. "Every thrade has its drawbacks, but I never rayalized before the hardship of being a parish priest. Can't we manage it some way. Couldn't I put it some place where you might find it, or give it to a friend who'd send it to you?"

"Stop a minute," says Father Cassidy. "Up at Tim Healy's I think there's more hunger than sickness, more nade for petaties than for physic. Now, if you sent that same bit of bacon——"

"Oh, ho!" says the king, with a dhry cough, "the Healy's have no sowls to save, the same as parish priests have."

"I'm a poor, wake, miserable sinner," says the priest, hanging his head; "I fall at the first temptation. Don't send it," says he.

"Since you forbid me, I'll send it," says the king, chucklin'. "I'll not be ruled by you. To-morrow the Healy's'll have five tinder-hearted heads of cabbage, makin' love in a pot to the finest bit of bacon in Tipperary—

that is, unless you do your juty an' ride back to warn
them. Raymember their poor sowls," says he, "an' don't
forget your own," he says.

The priest sat unaisy in the saddle. "I'll put all the
raysponsibility on Terror," he says. "The baste has no
sowl to lose. I'll just drop the reins on his neck; if he
turns and goes back to Healy's I'll warn them; if he goes
home let it be on his own conscience."

He dhropped the reins, and the dishonest baste started
for home imagetly.

But afther a few steps Father Cassidy dhrew up an'
turned in the saddle. Not a sowl was in sight; there was
only the lonely road and the lonesome hillside; the last
glimmer of the fairy fire was gone, and a curtain of soft
blackness had fallen betwixt him an' where the blaze had
been.

"I bid you good night, Brian Connors," the priest
cried. From somewhere out of the darkness a woice
called back to him, "Good night, your Riverence."

THE MANOR OF ROSES

Thomas Burnett Swann

I

I am thirty-five, a woman of middle years, and yet in this time of pox and plague, of early death and the dying of beauty before the body dies, it is said that I am still as beautiful as a Byzantine Madonna, poised in the heaven of a gold mosaic and wearing sorrow like a robe of white petals. But sorrow is not a gown. It is a nakedness to the searching eye of the curious, to the magpie-tongued who love to pry out grief: She grieves too long . . . The Manor demands an heir . . . Who will defend us from the encroaching forest, the thieves and the Mandrake People?

It was eleven years ago, in the year 1202 of Our Lord, that my husband's comrade-in-arms, Edmund-the-Wolf, rode to me with the news of my husband's death and, as if for compensation, the riches captured before he had died in battle. Captured? Pillaged, I should say, in the sack of Constantinople. You see, it is a time when men are boys, rapacious and cruel, as ready to kill a Jew, a Hungarian, a Greek as an Infidel; happy so long as they wield a sword and claim to serve God. A time when boys who have not yet grown to their fathers' pride—Crusading, it is called—are the only true men.

And yet I loved my husband, a red-haired Norman, gay as the men of the South, and not like most of our stern northern people. I loved him for his gaiety, his hair the color of Roman bricks, and because he left me a son.

But the Crusader's code, like an evil demon of pox, also possesses children. Only last year in France and Germany, Stephen proclaimed his message from Christ, Nicholas piped his irresistible flute, and the children yearned to them as tides to the moon and flowed in a sea of white immaculate robes toward the shores of that greater sea, the Mediterranean.

Little of the madness crossed to England. Perhaps our children are not inclined to visions, perhaps they prefer the hunt to the drafty halls of a church and talks with God. But the madness, missing the thousands, somehow touched my son. He rode to London, astride his roan palfrey and dressed in a jerkin of sheepskin dyed to the yellow of gorse, with a leather belt at his waist and a fawn-colored pouch a-jingle with new-minted pennies. Ready to board a ship for Marseilles and join Stephen. But Stephen and most of his army were sold as slaves to the Infidel; Nicholas died of the plague before he reached the sea; and my son of fifteen summers, reaching London, stood on the banks of the Thames to choose what twin-castled ship would bear him across the channel, and fell to the blade of a common cut-purse. The Devil, I think, possessed the children, a jest to fling like a gauntlet in the teeth of God.

God is not blind, however. In less than a year, He sent me those other children, struck with the same madness: John, a dark-haired Norman; Stephen, a Saxon but named like the boy of France; and Ruth, whom they called their guardian angel (but no one knew if she came from Heaven or Hell.) God, I felt, had made me His instrument to preserve them from my own son's ruin. Was He wrong to trust me with so precious and difficult a task? I tried, Mother of God I tried! I sheltered them from the Mandrakes of the forest. Loved them, hurt them, and then at the last—

But you shall judge me . . .

He ran blinded by tears across the heath, startling birds into flight, pheasants and grouse enough to feast a king. Conies peered from their nests and submerged like frogs in a pond with a dull, simultaneous plop. Didn't they know that he, timorous John, who had lost his bow in the woods and scattered the arrows out of his quiver, was not a creature to fear? He had come from the hunt with his father, lord of Goshawk Castle, and the knights

Robert, Arthur, Edgar and the rest. The names of the knights were different, their features almost identical. Rough hands, calloused from wielding swords against the Infidel—and their fellow Englishmen. Cheeks ruddy with mead and not with the English climate. Odorous bodies enveloped by fur lined surcoats which they pridefully wore even in the flush of summer, instead of imitating the villeins with their simple breech-clouts or their trousers without tunics. Lank, sweat-dampened hair, long in the back and cut in a fringe across their foreheads.

John, the Baron's son, had been allowed the first shot at a stag beleaguered by hounds. He was not a good bowman, but the stag had been much too close to miss except by design. Once, gathering chestnuts with his friend Stephen, the shepherd, he had seen the same animal, a splendid beast with horns like wind-beaten trees along the North Sea.

"He isn't afraid of us," Stephen had whispered.

"Nor has he reason to be," said John. "We would never harm him. He's much too beautiful."

Now, the animal had turned and looked at him with recognition, it seemed, and resignation; harried by hounds, bemused in a clump of bracken. John had fired his arrow above the antlers. The stag had escaped, bursting out of the bracken as if the coarse ferns were blades of grass and leveling three dogs with his adamantine hooves.

"Girl!" his father had shouted, hoarse with rage at losing a feast and a pair of antlers to grace his barren hall. "I should get you a distaff instead of a bow!"

For punishment John was bladed. After the knights had downed a smaller animal, a young doe, they had stretched him across the warm, bloody carcass and each man had struck him with the flat of his sword. Most of the knights had softened their blows. After all, he was their liege-lord's son. But his father's blow had left him bleeding and biting his tongue to hold back shameful tears.

Then they had left him.

"Go to the kennels and get your friend Stephen to dry your tears," his father had sneered. A coarse guffaw greeted the taunt. Stephen was said to have lain with every villein's daughter between twelve and twenty, and men without daughters liked to jest: "Girls weep till Stephen dries their tears."

Alone in the woods, John forgot his shame; he was too frightened. Just turned twelve, he knew of desperate thieves, sentenced to die by the rope, who had taken refuge among the sycamores which remembered the Romans, and the oaks which had drunk the blood of Druid sacrifices. As for animals, there were wolves and bears and long-tusked boars, and amphisbaenas too, the twin-headed serpents, and griffins with scaly wings. Worst of all, there were the Mandrake People who, grown like roots, clambered out of the ground to join their kin in acts of cannibalism.

Where could he go? Not to the castle, certainly, where the hunters had doubtless climbed in a broad wooden tub to scrape the grime of weeks from each other's backs, while kitchen wenches doused them with buckets of steaming water and ogled their naked brawn. Once, the castle had held his mother. Its darkness had shone with the whiteness of her samite; its odors were masked with the cloves and the cinnamon, the mace and the musk of her kitchen; its bailey had bloomed with a damson tree whose seeds had come from the Holy Land, and delicate shallots, the "Onions of Ascalon," had reared their tender shoots around the tree, like little guardian gnomes.

"If there must be fruits of war," she had said, "we must see that they are living things, not dead; sweet things, not bitter; soft things, not hard. The verdure of earth and not the gold from dead men's coffers."

Six years ago she had died of the pox. Now, when he knelt on the stone floor of the chapel, he prayed to Father, Son, and Mary, but Mary was Mother.

No, he could not go to the castle. He could but he did not wish to visit the Abbot's cottage and face another lesson in logic and astrology, Lucan and Aristotle. He was a willing, indeed a brilliant scholar. But there were times to study and times to look for Stephen. In spite of his father's taunt, it was time to look for Stephen. It was not that his friend was soft or womanish like a sister. He was, in fact, as rough-swearing, ready-to-fight a boy as ever tumbled a girl in the hay. But he curbed his roughness with John, respected his learning, and ignored his weaknesses.

Stephen was a Saxon villein three years older than John. His forebears, he rightly claimed, had once been powerful earls. But the conquering Normans had reduced them to the status of serfs and attached them to their own former lands, which had once held a wooden hall surrounded by a palisade, but now a castle built by John's grandfather, a square stone keep encircled by curtain walls whose gatehouse was toothed with a rusty portcullis and guarded by archers in hidden embrasures. Stephen's parents were dead, killed by the Mandrake People in one of their swift forays out of the forest to steal sheep and hogs. It was on that very day, two years ago, that he and Stephen had become inseparable friends. John had found him crouching above his mother's body. John, who did not even know his name, had laid a tentative arm around his shoulders—an act of extraordinary boldness for one so shy—and half expected a snarled rebuff or even a blow. But Stephen had buried his head in the arms of his master's son and sobbed convulsively without tears. It was not long before they agreed to adopt each other as brothers and, cutting their forearms with a hunting knife, mingled their blood to cement the bond.

From that time till now, Stephen had lived in a loft above the kennels, dog-boy, shepherd, farmer, fighter with fists and cudgel second to none. He could not read English, much less French and Latin, but the wolves feared his cudgel and grown men his fists. How could you best describe him? Angry, sometimes, but angry *for* things and not against them. For the serfs and the squalor in which they lived; the dogs which were run too hard in the hunt and gored by wild boars; the animals killed for sport and not for food. Sometimes, too, he was glad: loudly, radiantly, exuberantly keen on things; drawing a bow, feeding his dogs, swinging a scythe.

At other times he was neither angry nor glad, but beyond anger and gladness; enraptured by dreams: of meeting an angel or finding Excalibur or, best of all, buying his freedom and becoming a Knight Hospitaler to succor pilgrims and slaughter Infidels ("But you would have to take an oath of chastity," John reminded him. "I'll think about that when the time comes," said Stephen). Furthermore, he was one of those rarest of rarities, a dreamer who acts on his dreams, and lately he had talked about the ill-fated Children's Crusade, and how it was time for other Stephens, other Nicholases, to follow the first children and, armed with swords instead of crosses, succeed where they had failed.

It was John's unspeakable fear that Stephen would leave for Jerusalem without him, and yet he did not know if he had the courage for such a journey, through the dark Weald to London and then by ship to Marseilles and the ports of Outre-Mer, the Outer Land, the Saracen Land. Now, he quickened his pace and thought of arguments with which to dissuade his friend. He met old Edward scything in the Common Meadow; a tattered breechclout around his loins, his face and shoulders as coarse and brown as a saddle ridden from London to Edinburgh. Edward did not look up from his task, nor miss a stroke of the scythe. "Why look at the sky?" he liked to mutter. "It belongs to angels, not to serfs."

"Have you seen Stephen?" John asked.

Swish, swish, swish went the scythe, and the weeds collapsed as if they had caught the plague.

"Have you seen Stephen?"

"I'm not deaf," the old man growled. "Your father's taken my youth, my pigs, and my corn, but not my ears. Not yet, anyway. Your friend'll be losing his, though, 'less he does his work. He oughta be here in the Meadow right now."

"But where *is* he?" cried John in desperation.

"Making for the Roman Place with that look in his eyes. That's where he hides, you know. Daydreams. Didn't even speak to me."

The Roman Place. The ruin where the Romans had worshipped their sun-god, Mithras, in an underground vault. Later, by way of apology to the Christian God, the Saxons had built a timber church to conceal the spot and turned the vault into a crypt for their dead. During the Norman Conquest, women and children had hidden in the church, and the Normans had set a torch to the roof and burned the building with all of its occupants.

The charred and mis-shapen remnants were almost concealed—healed, as it were—by flowering gorse, and a few blackened timbers, which thrust like seeking hands from the yellow flowers, summoned no worshippers to the buried gods.

A stranger would not suspect a vault beneath the gorse, but John parted the spiny branches and climbed through a narrow hole to a flight of stairs. A sacredness clung to the place, a sense of time, like that of a Druid stone which lichen had aged to a muted, mottled orange and which thrust at the stars as if to commune with them in cosmic loneliness. Here, the worshippers of Mithras had bathed themselves in the blood of the sacrificial bull and climbed through the seven stages of initiation to commune with the sun instead of the stars. A nasty pagan rite, said the Abbot, and John had asked him why Jehovah had ordered Abraham to sacrifice Isaac. "It was only a test," snapped the Abbot.

"But what about Jephthah's daughter? *She* wasn't a test." The Abbot had changed the subject.

Already, at twelve, John had begun to ask questions about the Bible, God, Christ, and the Holy Ghost. To Stephen, religion was feeling and not thought. God was a patriarch with a flowing beard, and angels were almost as real as the dogs in his kennel. With John it was different. Only the Virgin Mary was not a subject for doubts, arguments, but a beautiful, ageless woman robed in samite, dwelling in the high places of the air or almost at hand, outshining the sun and yet as simple as bread, grass, birds, and Stephen's love; invisible but never unreachable.

At the foot of the stairs he faced a long, narrow cave with earthen walls which contained the loculi of Christians buried in their cerements and which converged to the semi-circle of an apse. Now, the apse was empty of Mithras slaying the sacred bull and Mary holding the infant Christ. Stephen knelt in their place. He held a waxen candle which lit the frescoed roof: Jesus walking on water; multiplying loaves and fish; bidding the blind to see and the lame to walk.

"John," he gasped, "I have found—"

"A Madonna!"

She lay in a nest of bindweed shaped to a simple pallet. Her face was an ivory mask in the light of the candle. A carved Madonna, thought John, from the transept of a French cathedral, but flushed with the unmistakable ardors of life. No, he saw with a disappointment which approached dismay, she was much too young for the Virgin; a mere girl.

"An angel," said Stephen.

"An angel," sighed John, resenting her youthfulness. What did he need with a second angel, a girl at that? God (or the Virgin Mary) had sent him Stephen, angelic but not female and certainly not effeminate, his hair a riot instead of an aureole, his face more ruddy than pink: a Michael or Gabriel fit for sounding a trumpet instead of strumming a lyre.

The angel stirred and opened her eyes with a pretty fluttering; not with surprise or fright, but almost, thought John, with artful calculation, like some of the rustic lasses who flocked to Stephen's loft. Her teeth were as white as her linen robe, which was bound at the waist by a cord of cerulean silk. Her pointed slippers, unicorn leather trimmed with blue velvet, were such as might be worn in the soft pastures of heaven. She lacked only wings. Or had she concealed them under her robe? John was tempted to ask.

Stephen forestalled him. "Greet her," he whispered. "Welcome her!"

"In what language?" asked John sensibly. "I don't know the tongues of angels."

"Latin, I should think. She must know that, with all the priests muttering their Benedicites."

Stephen had a point. Rude English was out of the question, and also the French of the Normans, who, after all, had descended from barbarous Vikings.

"Quo Vadis?" asked John none too politely.

Her smile, though delectable, no doubt, to Stephen, did not answer the question.

"What are you doing here?" he repeated in Norman French.

Stephen, who understood some French, frantically nudged him. "You shouldn't question an angel. Welcome her! Worship her! Quote her a psalm or a proverb."

"We aren't sure she's an angel. She hasn't told us, has she?"

At last she spoke. "I do not know how I came here," she said in flawless Latin and, seeing the blankness on Stephen's face, repeated the words in English, but with a grave dignity which softened the rough tongue. At the same time, John noticed the crucifix which she held or rather clutched in her hands: a small Greek cross with arms of equal length, wrought of gold and encrusted with stones which he knew from his studies, though not from his father's castle, were the fabulous pearls of the East. "I remember only a darkness, and a falling, and a great forest. I wandered until I found the passage to this cave, and took shelter against the night. I must have been very tired. I feel as if I have slept for a long time." She lifted the cross and then, as if its weight had exhausted her slender hands, allowed it to sink becomingly against her breast.

"I suppose," said John with annoyance, "you're hungry."

Stephen sprang to his feet. "But angels don't eat! Can't you see, John? God has sent her to us as a sign! To lead us to the Holy Land! Stephen of France had his message from Christ. We have our angel."

"But look what happened to Stephen of France. Sold as a slave or drowned in the sea. Only the sharks know which."

"I don't think he's dead. And if he is, then he listened to the Devil's voice and not to God's. But we can *see* our angel."

"Indeed, you can see me," she said, "and you ought to see that I am famished. Angels do eat, I assure you—at least when they travel—and something more substantial than nectar and dew. Have you venison perhaps? Mead?"

"You must take her to the castle," said Stephen, clearly reluctant to part with his new-found angel. "I've nothing so fine in the kennels."

"No," said John. "I'm not taking anyone to the castle. I've decided to stay with you in the kennels."

"Because of your father?"

"Yes. He bladed me before all of his men, and then

he called me a ——" He could not bring himself to repeat the taunt, especially to Stephen. "He called me a churl. Because I missed a stag. *Our* stag. The one we promised never to harm."

Stephen nodded with understanding. "I'm glad you missed him. They say he's the oldest stag in the forest. They say"—and here he lowered his voice—"that he isn't a stag at all, but Merlin turned to a beast by Vivian. But John, how can you live with me in the kennels? It would wound your father's pride. A baron's son sharing a loft with a dog-boy! He'd give you more than a blading, and as for me! You mayn't remember he cut off my father's ears because he broke a scythe. And now with an angel on our hands, the only thing to do is—"

"Get the angel off our hands?"

"Leave at once for the Holy Land. I have a little food in the kennels, a change of wear. You needn't go back to the castle at all. We've only to follow the Roman Road through the Weald to London, and take ship to Marseilles, and from thence proceed to Outre-Mer."

"But Marseilles was where the French Stephen fell in the hands of slavers."

"But we have a guide!"

"If she isn't really an angel—"

"At least we'll have made our escape from the castle."

"You mean we should leave the castle *forever*?" The prospect of leaving his father exhilarated him; he would feel like a falcon with its hood removed. But the castle held all of his possessions, his codex, *The Kings of Britain*, written on the finest vellum and bound between ivory covers; and the parchment containing his favorite poem, "The Owl and the Nightingale," copied laboriously by his own precise hand. Much more important, it held his mother's ghost, his sum of remembering: stairs she had climbed, tapestries woven, garments mended; his mother living in song what she could not live in life and singing of noble warriors and deathless loves:

See, he who carved this wood commands me to ask
You to remember, oh treasure-adorned one,
The pledge of old . . .

"Leave my father's castle," he repeated, "and not come back? Ever?"

Stephen's face turned as red as the Oriflamme, the fiery banner of the French kings. "*Your father's castle?* This land belonged to my ancestors when yours were scurvy Vikings! You think I'll stay here forever as dogboy and shepherd? Serving a man who blades his own son? Giving him what I grow and what I hunt, and asking his leave to take a wife? John, John, there's nothing for either of us here. Ahead of us lies Jerusalem!"

To Stephen, the name was a trumpet blast; to John, a death knell. "But a forest stands in the way, and then a channel, and a rough sea swarming with Infidels. They have ships too, you know, swifter than ours and armed with Greek Fire."

But Stephen had gripped his shoulders and fixed him with his blue, relentless gaze. "You know I can't leave you."

"You know you won't have to," sighed John.

The angel interrupted them, looking a little peeved that in their exchange of pleas and protestations, of male endearments, they were neglecting their quest and their inspiration. "As for leading you to the Holy Land, I don't even know this forest through which you say you must pass. But here in the ground it is damp, and before I came here, I did not like the look of the castle. It seemed to me dark and fierce, with a dry ditch and a gloomy keep, and narrow windows without a pane of glass. A fortress and not a home. If indeed I am an angel, I hope to find dwellings more pleasant here on earth. Or else I shall quickly return to the sky. In the meantime, let us set off for London, and you shall lead *me* until I begin to remember."

The angel between them, they climbed the stairs to the sun and, skirting old Edward, who was still busily scything in the Common Meadow, came at last to the kennels. It was mid-day. The Baron and his knights had remained in the castle since the hunt. His villeins, trudging out of the fields, had gathered in the shade of the watermill to enjoy their gruel and bread. Had anyone noticed the quick, furtive passage of the would-be Crusaders, he would have thought them engaged in childish sports, or supposed that Stephen had found a young wench to share with his master's son and probably muttered, "It's high time."

While Stephen's greyhounds lapped at their heels, they climbed to his loft above the kennels to get his few belongings: two clover-green tunics with hoods for wintry days; wooden clogs and a pair of blue stockings which reached to the calf of the leg; a leather pouch bulging with wheaten bread and rounds of cheese; a flask of beer; and a knotted shepherd's crook.

"For wolves," said Stephen, pointing to the crook. "I've used it often."

"And Mandrakes," asked John wickedly, hoping to frighten the angel.

"But we have no change of clothes for a girl," said Stephen.

"Never mind," she smiled, guzzling Stephen's beer and munching his bread till she threatened to exhaust the supply before they began their journey. "When my robe grows soiled, I shall wash it in a stream and," she added archly, "the two of you may see if I am truly an angel."

The remark struck John as unangelic if not indelicate. As if they would spy on her while she bathed!

But Stephen reassured her. "We never doubted you were. And now—" A catch entered his voice. Quickly he turned his head and seemed to be setting the loft in order.

"We must leave him alone with his hounds," whispered John to the angel, leading her down the ladder.

A silent Stephen rejoined them in the Heath. His tunic was damp from friendly tongues and his face was wet, but whether from tongues or tears, it was hard to say.

"You don't suppose," he said, "we could take one or two of them with us? The little greyhound without any tail?"

"No," said John. "My father will stomp and shout when he finds us gone, but then he'll shrug: 'Worthless boys, both of them, and no loss to the castle.' But steal one of his hounds, and he'll have his knights on our trail."

"But our angel has no name," cried Stephen suddenly and angrily, as if to say: "As long as she's come to take me from my hounds, she might at least have brought a name."

"I *had* a name, I'm sure. It seems to have slipped my mind. What would you like to call me?"

"Why not Ruth?" said Stephen. "She was always going on journeys in the Bible, leading cousins and such, wasn't she?"

"A mother-in-law," corrected John, who felt that, what with a Crusade ahead of them, Stephen should know the Scriptures.

"Leading and *being* led," observed the angel, whose memory, it seemed, had begun to return. "By two strapping husbands. Though," she hurried to explain, "not at the same time. Yes, I think you should call me Ruth."

She is much too young for Ruth, thought John, who guessed her to be about fifteen (though of course as an angel she might be fifteen thousand). The same age as Stephen, whose thoughts were attuned to angelic visions but whose bodily urges were not in the least celestial. Unlike a Knight Templar, he had made no vow of chastity. The situation was not propitious for a crusade in the name of God.

But once they had entered the Weald, the largest forest in southern England, he thought of Mandrakes and griffins instead of Ruth. It was true that the Stane, an old Roman highway, crossed the Weald to join London and Chichester—they would meet it within the hour—but even the Stane was not immune to the forest.

II

At Ruth's suggestion, they carefully skirted the grounds of a neighboring castle, the Boar's Lair.

"Someone might recognize John," she said. "Send word to his father."

"Yes," John agreed, staring at the Norman tower, one of the black wooden keeps built by William the Conqueror to enforce his conquest. "My father and Philip the Boar were once friends. Philip used to dine with us on Michaelmas and other feast days, and I played the kettledrums for him. Since then, he and my father have fallen out about their boundaries. They both claim a certain grove of beechnut trees—pannage for their swine. Philip wouldn't be hospitable, I'm sure."

Deviously, circuitously, by way of a placid stream and an old water wheel whose power no longer turned mill-stones and ground wheat into flour, they reached the Roman Stane. Once a proud thoroughfare for uncon-querable legions, it had since resounded to Saxon, Vik-ing, and Norman, who had used it for commerce and war but, unlike the conscientious Romans, never repaired the ravages of wheels and weather. Now, it had shrunk in places to the width of a peasant's cart, but the smooth Roman blocks, set in concrete, still provided a path for riders and walkers and great ladies in litters between two horses.

"I feel like the Stane," sighed Ruth, "much-trodden and a trifle weedy." She had torn the edge of her robe on prickly sedges and muddied the white linen. She had lost the circlet which haloed her head, and her silken tresses, gold as the throats of convolvulus flowers, had spilled like their trailing leafage over her shoulders. As for John, he was hot, breathless, and moist with sweat, and wishing that like a serf he dared to remove his long-sleeved tunic and revel in his breechclout.

"Stephen," Ruth sighed, "now that we've found the road, can't we rest a little?" Her speech, though still melodious, had relaxed into easy, informal English.

"We've just begun!" he laughed. "London lies days away. We want to be leagues down the road before night."

"But it's already mid-afternoon. Why not rest till it gets a little cooler?"

"Very well," he smiled, reaching out to touch her in good-humored acquiescence. Stephen, who found diffi-culty with words, spoke with his hands, which were nests to warm a bird, balms to heal a dog, bows to extract the music from swinging a scythe, wielding an ax, gathering branches to build a fire. He could gesture or point or touch with the exquisite eloquence of a man who was deaf, dumb, and blind. When you said good morning to him, he clapped you on the shoulder. When you walked with him, he brushed against you or caught you by the arm. He liked to climb trees for the rough feel of the bark or swim in a winter stream and slap the icy currents until he warmed his body. But he saved his touch for things or the people he loved. Neither ugly things nor unkind people.

"We'll rest as long as you like," he said.

Ruth smiled. "I think I should borrow one of your tunics. You see how my robe keeps dragging the ground."

With a flutter of modesty she withdrew to a clump of bracken and changed to a tunic.

"Watch out for basilisks," John called after her. "Their bite is fatal, you know." He muttered under his breath to Stephen: "First she ate your food, and now she wears your clothes."

"*Our* food and clothes," reproved Stephen. "Remember, we're Crusaders together."

John was shamed into silence. He had to listen to Ruth as she bent branches, snapped twigs, and rustled cloth, almost as if she wished to advertise the various stages of her change. He thought of the wenches—ten? twenty?—who had disrobed for Stephen. The subject *love* confused him. The Aristotelian processes of his brain refused to sift, clarify, and evaluate the problem; in fact, they crumpled like windmills caught in a forest fire. He had loved his mother—what was the word?—filially; Stephen he loved fraternally. But as for the other thing, well, he had not been able to reconcile the courtly code as sung by the troubadours—roses and guerdons and troths of deathless fidelity—and the sight of Stephen, surprised last year in his loft with a naked wench and not in the least embarrassed. Stephen had grinned and said: "In a year or so, John, we can wench together!" The girl, snickering and making no effort to hide her nakedness, had seemed to him one of those Biblical harlots who ought to be shorn, or stoned. Who could blame poor Stephen for yielding to such allurements! As for himself, however, he had sworn the chivalric oath to practice poverty, chastity, and obedience to God. He had thought of a monastery but rather than part with Stephen, who was not in the least monastic, he was willing to try a life of action.

"Has a crow got your tongue?" smiled Stephen. "I

didn't mean to scold." He encircled John's shoulder with his arm. "You smell like cloves."

John stiffened, not at the touch but at what appeared to be an insinuation. He had not forgotten his father's taunt: "Girl!" According to custom, it was girls and women who packed their gowns in clove-scented chests, while the men of a castle hung their robes in the room called the *garderobe*, another name for the lavatory cut in the wall beside the stairs, with a round shaft dropping to the moat. The stench of the shaft protected the room—and the robes—from moths.

"They belonged to my mother," he stammered. "The cloves, I mean. I still use her chest."

"My mother put flowering mint with her clothes," said Stephen. "All two gowns! I like the cloves better, though. Maybe the scent will rub off on me. I haven't bathed for a week." He gave John's shoulder a squeeze, and John knew that his manhood had not been belittled. But then, Stephen had never belittled him, had he? Teased him, yes; hurt him in play; once knocked him down for stepping on the tail of a dog; but never made light of his manliness.

"It's not a dangerous road," Stephen continued, talkative for once, perhaps because John was silent. "The abbots of Chichester patrol it for brigands. They don't carry swords, but Gabriel help the thief who falls afoul of their staves!"

"But the forest," John said. "It's all around us like a pride of griffins. With green, scaly wings. They look as if they're going to eat up the road. They've already nibbled away the edges, and"—he lowered his voice—"she came out of the forest, didn't she?"

Stephen laughed. "She came out of the sky, simpleton! Didn't you hear her say she don't know nothing about the forest?"

Before John could lecture Stephen on his lapse in grammar, Ruth exploded between them, as green as a down in the tenderness of spring. She blazed in Stephen's tunic, its hood drawn over her head. She had bound her waist with the gold sash from her robe and, discarding her velvet slippers, donned his wooden clogs, whose very ugliness emphasized the delicacy of her bare feet. She had bundled her linen robe around her slippers and crucifix.

"No one would ever guess that I'm an angel," she smiled. "Or even a girl."

"Not an angel," said Stephen appreciatively. "But a girl, yes. You'd have to roughen your hands and hide your curls to pass for a boy."

She made a pretence of hiding her hair, but furtively shook additional curls from her hood the moment they resumed their journey, and began to sing a familiar song of the day:

In a valley of this restless mind,
I sought in mountain and in mead . . .

Though she sang about a man searching for Christ, the words rippled from her tongue as merrily as if she were singing a carol. John wished for his kettledrums and Stephen began to whistle. Thus, they forgot the desolation of the road, largely untraveled at such an hour and looking as if the griffin-scaly forest would soon complete its meal.

Then, swinging around a bend and almost trampling them, cantered a knight with a red cross painted on his shield—a Knight Templar, it seemed—and after him, on a large piebald palfrey, a lady riding pillion behind a servant who never raised his eyes from the road. The knight frowned at them; in spite of the vows demanded of his order, he looked more dedicated to war than to God. But the lady smiled and asked their destination.

"I live in a castle up the road," said John quickly in Norman French. Unlike his friends, he was dressed in the mode of a young gentleman, with a tunic of plum-colored linen instead of cheap muslin, and a samite belt brocaded with silver threads. Thus, he must be their spokesman. "I have come with my friends to search for chestnuts in the woods, and now we are going home."

The knight darkened his frown to a baleful glare and reined his steed, as if he suspected John of stealing a fine tunic to masquerade as the son of a gentleman. Boys of noble birth, even of twelve, did not as a rule go nutting with villeins whom they called their friends, and not at such an hour.

"We have passed no castle for many miles," he growled, laying a thick-veined hand on the hilt of his sword.

"My father's is well off the road, and the keep is low," answered John without hesitation. "In fact, it is called the Tortoise, and it is *very* hard to break, like a tortoise shell. Many a baron has tried!"

"Mind you get back to the Tortoise before dark," the lady admonished. "You haven't a shell yourself, and the Stane is dangerous after nightfall. My protector and I are bound for the castle of our friend, Philip the Boar. Is it far, do you know?"

"About two leagues," said John, and he gave her explicit directions in French so assured and polished that no one, not even the glowering knight, could doubt his Norman blood and his noble birth. It was always true of him that he was only frightened in anticipation. Now, with a wave and a courtly bow, he bade them God-speed to the castle of the Boar, received a smile from the lady, and led his friends toward the mythical Tortoise.

"Such a handsome lad," he heard the lady exclaim, "and manly as well."

"If I hadn't been so scared," said Stephen, once a comfortable distance separated them from the knight, his lady, and the unresponsive servant, "I'd have split my tunic when you said your castle was named the Tortoise. There isn't a castle for the next ten miles! It's the first fib I ever heard you tell."

"You were scared too?" asked John, surprised at such an admission.

"You can bet your belt I was! They were lovers, you know. Bound for a tryst at the castle of the Boar. He winks at such things, I hear. Runs a regular brothel for the gentry, including himself. That lady has a husband somewhere, and the Knight Templar might just have run us through to keep us from carrying tales."

With the fall of darkness, they selected a broad and voluminous oak tree, rather like a thicket set on the mast of a ship, and between them the boys helped Ruth to climb the trunk. With nimble hands, she prepared a nest of leaves and moss in the crook of the tree and, having removed her clogs and hidden them, along with her crucifix, settled herself with the comfort of perfect familiarity. She seemed to have a talent for nests, above or below the ground.

After she had eaten some bread and cheese and drunk beer, she returned to the ground, stubbornly refusing assistance from either boy, and showed herself a more than adept climber.

"Is she angry with us?" asked John.

"She drank all that beer," explained Stephen, "and while she's gone—"

They scrambled to the edge of the nest and, bracing themselves against a limb, aimed at the next oak. Gleefully, John pretended that Ruth was crouching under the branches.

He was sorry to see her emerge from an elm instead of the inundated oak and rejoin them in the nest.

"I was looking for rushes to keep us warm," she said. "But I didn't find a single one. We'll have to lie close together." She chose the middle of the nest, anticipating, no doubt, a boy to warm her on either side, and Stephen obligingly stretched on her left.

With the speed and deftness of Lucifer disguised as a serpent, John wriggled between them, forcing Ruth to the far side of the nest. Much to his disappointment, she accepted the arrangement without protest and leaned against him with a fragrance of galangal, the aromatic plant imported from Outre-Mer and used as a base for perfume by the ladies of England.

"The stars are bright tonight," she said. "See, John, there's Arcturus peeping through the leaves, and there's Sirius, the North Star. The Vikings called it the Lamp of the Wanderer."

Stephen nudged him as if to say: "You see! Only an angel knows such things."

"Stephen," he whispered.

"Yes?"

"I'm not afraid anymore. Of leaving the castle. Not even of the forest!"

"Aren't you, John?"

"Because I'm not alone."

"I told you we were safe with our angel."

"I don't mean the angel." He made a pillow of Stephen's shoulder, and the scent of dogs and haylofts, effaced Ruth's galangal.

"Go to sleep, little brother. Dream about London— and the Holy Land."

But fear returned to John before he could dream. At an hour with the feel of midnight, chill and misty and hushed of owls, he was roused by the blast of a horn and a simultaneous shriek like that of a hundred otters caught in a millwheel. The sounds seemed to come from a distance and yet were harsh enough to make him throw up his hands to his ears.

"Hunters have found a Mandrake!" cried Stephen, sitting up in the nest. "It's a moonless night, and it must be just after twelve. That's when they hunt, you know. They blow on a horn to muffle the shriek. Let's see what they've caught."

But John was not eager to leave the tree. "If they've killed a Mandrake, they won't want to share it. Besides, they might be brigands."

Ruth had also been roused by the shriek. "John is right," she said. "You shouldn't want to see such a horrible sight. A baby torn from the earth!"

"I'll stay and keep Ruth company," said John, but Stephen hauled him out of the nest and sent him slipping and scraping down the trunk.

"But we can't leave Ruth alone!" he groaned, picking himself up from a bed of acorns.

"Angels don't need protection. Hurry now, or we'll miss the hunters."

They found the Mandrake hunters across the road and deep among the trees, a pair of rough woodsmen, father and son to judge from their height, build, and flaxen hair, though the elder was as bent and brown as a much-used sickle, and his son wore a patch over one of his eyes. The woodsmen were contemplating a dead Mandrake the size and shape of a new-born baby, except for the dirt-trailing tendrils, the outsized genitals, and the greenish tangle of hair which had grown above ground with purple, bell-shaped flowers. The pathetic body twitched like a hatcheted chicken. Dead at its side and bound to it by a rope lay a dog with bloody ears.

Though the night was moonless and the great stars,

Arcturus and Sirius, were veiled by the mist of the forest, one of the hunters carried a lantern, and John saw the Mandrake, the dog, the blood in an eerie, flickering light which made him remember Lucifer's fall to Hell and wonder if he and Stephen had fallen after him.

One of the woodsmen saw them. "Might have gotten yourselves killed, both of you," he scolded, digging bees-wax out of his ears with his little finger. "Laid out like that old hound with busted eardrums." He removed a long-bladed knife from his tunic and under his father's direction—"no, no, clean and quick . . . cut it, don't bruise it"—sliced the Mandrake into little rootlike por-tions, resinous rather than bloody, which he wrapped in strips of muslin and placed carefully in a sharkskin pouch.

"One less of the devils," muttered the father, unbend-ing himself to a rake instead of a sickle. "Another week and it'd have climbed right out of the ground. Joined its folk in the warrens."

"A Richard's ransom in aphroaphro*disiacs*!" stuttered the son, completing the word with a flourish of triumph. The market for Mandrake roots was lucrative and inex-haustible: aging barons deserted by sexual powers; lovers whose love was unrequited. From Biblical times, the times of Jacob and Leah, the root had been recognized as the one infallible aphrodisiac. Yes, a Richard's ransom was hardly an overstatement. A man would pay gold and silver, land and livestock, to win his love or resurrect his lust.

When the woodsmen had finished their grisly disec-tion, the son smiled at the boys and offered them a frag-ment the size of a small pea. "You fellows put this in a girl's gruel, and she'll climb all over you."

"He doesn't need it," said John, intercepting the gift. "Girls climb over him as it is. Like ants on a crock of sugar!"

"But you need it, eh?" laughed the son, winking his single eye at John. One-eyed serfs were common in France and England, and most of them had lost their eyes to angry masters and not in fights. Perhaps the young woodsman had not been prompt to deliver firewood for the hearth in a great hall. "Now you'll be the crock. But where's the sugar?"

"He'll have it," said Stephen, noticing John's embarrassment. "Sugar enough for a nest! Give him a year or two. He's only twelve." Then he pointed to the carcass of the dog. "Did you have to use a greyhound? Couldn't you have done it yourselves? After all, you had the wax in your ears."

"Everyone knows a dog gives a sharper jerk. Gets the whole Mandrake at once. Like pulling a tooth, root and all. Besides, he was an old dog. Not many more years in his bones. We can buy a whole kennel with what we make from the root."

When the men had departed, talking volubly about the sale of their treasure at the next fair, and how they would spend their money in secret and keep their lord from his customary third, the boys buried the dog.

"I wish they had put beeswax in his ears too," said Stephen bitterly. "And see where they whipped him to make him jump!"

"Beeswax doesn't help a dog," said John. "At least I read that in a bestiary. His ears are so keen that the shriek penetrates the wax and kills him anyway."

"It's no wonder the Mandrakes eat us. The way we drag their babies from the ground and cut them up! If it weren't for my parents, I could pity the poor little brutes. Now, a lot of dirty old men will strut like coxcombs and chase after kitchen wenches."

"I suppose," said John, who had furtively buried the fragment of Mandrake with the dog, "the question is, who started eating whom first." Then he clutched Stephen's hand and said: "I think I'm going to be sick."

"No, you're not," said Stephen, steadying John with his arm, "We're going back to the tree and get some sleep."

But Stephen was trembling too; John could feel the tremors in his arm. He's sad for the dog, he thought. I *won't* be sick. It would only make him sadder.

Ruth was waiting for them with a look which they could not read in the misted light of the stars.

"We're sorry we left you so long," said Stephen, "but the hunters had just killed a Mandrake, and . . ."

"I don't want to hear about it."

"Mandrakes can't climb trees, can they?" asked John. "The parents might be about, you know."

"Of course they can climb trees," said Stephen, who was very knowledgeable about the woods and improvised what he did not know. "They *are* trees, in a way. Roots at least."

"Do you think they suspect we're up here? They can't see us, but can they sniff us out?"

"I wish you two would stop talking about Mandrakes," snapped Ruth. "You would think they surrounded us, when everyone knows the poor creatures are almost extinct."

"Stephen's parents were killed by Mandrakes," said John sharply. He would have liked to slap the girl. She had a genius for interruptions or improprieties. It was proper and generous for Stephen to express compassion for a Mandrake baby, but unforgivable for this ignorant girl to sympathize with the whole murderous race. Her ethereal origins now seemed about as likely to him as an angel dancing on the head of a pin, a possibility which, to John's secret amusement, his Abbot had often debated with utmost seriousness.

Ruth gave a cry. "I didn't know."

"How could you?" said Stephen. "At least the ones who killed my parents fought like men. They didn't sneak up in the dark. They stormed out of the forest before dusk, waving their filthy arms and swinging clubs. We had a chance against them—except my mother, who was bringing us beer in the fields. We were haying at the time and we had our scythes for weapons. They only got one of us besides my parents, and we got four of them. It's the females who're really dangerous—the young ones who pass for human and come to live in the towns. The males can't do it; they're much too hairy right from the start, and—well, *you* know. Too well endowed. But the little girls look human, at least on the outside. Inside, it's a different matter—resin instead of blood; brown skeletons which're—what would you call them, John?"

"Fibrous."

Ruth listened in silence and shrank herself into a little ball. Like a diadem spider, thought John, with brilliant gold patterns. Drawing in her legs and looking half her size.

"Tell her about them, John," said Stephen, who was getting breathless from such a long speech. "You know the whole story." And then to Ruth: "He knows everything. French, English, Latin. All our kings and queens from Arthur down to bad old King John. Even those naughty pagan goddesses who went about naked and married their brothers."

John was delighted to continue the history. He liked to deliver lectures, but nobody except Stephen ever listened to him.

"In the old days, before the Crusades," said John, who warmed to his tale like a traveling story teller, "in the old days the Mandrakes lived in the forest, and they were so dirty and hairy that you could never mistake them for human. They weren't particular about their diet. They liked any meat—animal or human—and they trapped hunters in nets and roasted them over hot coals and then strewed their bones on the ground as we do with drumsticks at Michaelmas." Here, like a skilled jongleur, he paused and looked at Ruth to gauge the effect of his tale. The sight of her reassured him. If she pressed any harder against the edge of the nest, she would roll from the tree. "But one day a little Mandrake girl wandered out of the forest, and a simple blacksmith took her for a lost human child, naked and dirty from the woods, and took her into his family. The child grew plump and beautiful, the man and his wife grew peaked, and everyone said how generous it was for a poor blacksmith to give his choicest food—and there wasn't much food that winter for anyone—to a foundling. But in the summer the girl was run down and killed by a wagon loaded with hay. The townspeople were all ready to garrot the driver—until they noticed that the girl's blood was a mixture of normal red fluid and thick, viscous resin."

"What does 'viscous' mean?" interrupted Stephen.

"Gluey. Like that stuff that comes out of a spider when she's spinning her web. Thus, it was learned that Mandrakes are vampires as well as cannibals, and that the more they feed on humans, the less resinous their blood becomes, until the resin is almost replaced, though their bones never do turn white. But they have to keep on feeding or else their blood will revert.

"Well, the Mandrakes heard about the girl—from a runaway thief, no doubt, before they ate him—and how she had 'passed' until the accident. They decided to send some more of their girls into the villages, where life was easier than in the forest. Some of the Mandrakes slipped into houses at night and left their babies, well-scrubbed of course, in exchange for humans, which they carried off into the woods for you can imagine what foul purposes. The next morning the family would think that the fairies had brought them a changeling, and everyone knows that if you disown a fairy's child, you'll have bad luck for the rest of your life. It was a long time before the plan of the Mandrakes became generally known around the forest. Now, whenever a mother finds a strange baby in her crib, or a new child wanders into town, it's usually stuck with a knife. If resin flows out, the child is suffocated and burned. Still, an occasional Mandrake does manage to pass.

"You see, they aren't at all like the Crusaders in the last century who became vampires when they marched through Hungary—the Hungarian campfollowers, remember, gave them the sickness, and then the Crusaders brought it back to England. They had to break the skin to get at your blood, and they had a cadaverous look about them before they fed, and then they grew pink and bloated. It was no problem to recognize and burn them. But the Mandrake girls, by pressing their lips against your skin, can draw blood right through the pores, and the horrible thing is that they don't look like vampires and sometimes they don't even know what they are or how they were born from a seed in the ground. They feed in a kind of dream and forget everything the next morning."

"I think it's monstrous," said Ruth.

"They are, aren't they?" agreed John happily, satisfied that his story had been a success.

"Not *them*. I mean sticking babies with knives."

"But how else can you tell them from roots? It's because a few people are sentimental like you that Mandrakes still manage to pass."

"Frankly," said Ruth, "I don't think Mandrakes pass at all. I think they keep to themselves in the forest and eat venison and berries and *not* hunters. Now go to sleep. From what you've told me, it's a long way to London. We all need some rest."

"Good night," said Stephen.

"Sweet dreams," said Ruth.

III

The next morning, the sun was a Saracen shield in the sky—Saladin's Shield, a Crusader would have said—and the forest twinkled with paths of sunlight and small white birds which spun in the air or perched on limbs and constantly flickered their tails. Ruth and Stephen stood in the crook of the tree and smiled down at John as he opened his eyes.

"We decided to let you sleep," said Stephen. "You grunted like a boar when I first shook you. So we followed a wagtail to find some breakfast."

"And found you some wild strawberries," said Ruth, her lips becomingly red from the fruit. She gave him a deep, brimming bowl. "I wove it from sedges." For one who professed an ignorance of the forest, she possessed some remarkable skills.

Once on the ground, they finished their breakfast with three-cornered, burry beechnuts, which required some skillful pounding and deft fingers to extract the kernels; and Ruth, appropriating Stephen's beer, took such a generous swallow that she drained the flask.

"To wash down the beechnuts," she explained.

"I don't know why the pigs like them so much," said Stephen. "They're not worth the trouble of shelling."

"The pigs don't shell them," reminded the practical John.

"Anyway," continued Stephen, "we hadn't much choice in this part of the forest. We found a stream though." Hoisting the pouch which held their remnants of food and their few extra garments, he said: "Ruth, get your bundle and let's take a swim."

"I hid it," she reminded him, almost snappishly. "There may be thieves about. I'll get it after we swim."

All that mystery about a crucifix, thought John. As if she suspected Stephen and me of being brigands. And after she drank our beer!

The stream idled instead of gushed, and pepperwort, shaped like four-leafed clovers, grew in the quiet waters along the banks. Stephen, who took a monthly bath in a tub with the stable hands while the daughters of villeins doused him with water, hurried to pull his tunic over his head. He was justly proud of his body and had once remarked to John, "The less I wear, the better I look. In a gentleman's clothes like yours, I'd still be a yokel. But naked—! Even gentlewomen seem to stare."

But John was quick to restore the proprieties. In the presence of Ruth, he had no intention of showing his thin, white body, or allowing Stephen to show his radiant nakedness.

"You can swim first," he said to her. "Stephen and I will wait in the woods."

"No," she laughed. "You go first. Stephen is already down to his breechclout, and *that* is about to fall. But I won't be far away."

"You won't peep, will you?" John called after her, but Ruth, striding into the forest as if she had a destination, did not answer him.

The stream was chilly in spite of the Saracen sun. John huddled among the pepperwort, the water as high as his knees, till Stephen drenched him with a monumental splash, and then they frolicked among the plants and into the current and scraped each other's backs with sand scooped from the bottom and, as far as John was concerned, Ruth and the road to London could wait till the Second Coming!

When they climbed at last on the bank, they rolled in the grass to dry their bodies. Stephen, an expert wrestler, surprised John with what he called his amphisbaena grip; his arms snaked around John's body like the ends of the two-headed serpent and flattened him on the ground.

"I'm holding you for ransom," he cried, perched on John's chest like the seasprite Dylan astride a dolphin. "Six flagons of beer with roasted malt!"

"I promise—" John began, and freed himself with such a burst of strength that Stephen sprawled in the grass beneath the lesser but hardly less insistent weight of John. "I promise you sixteen licks with an abbot's rod!"

Stephen was not disgruntled. "By Robin's bow," he cried, "you've learned all my tricks!"

"I guess we had better dress," said John, releasing his friend to avoid another reversal. "Ruth will want to swim too. I hope she didn't peep," he added, looking askance at some furiously agitated ferns beyond the grassy bank. To his great relief, they disgorged a white wagtail and not a girl. Still, something had frightened the bird.

"What do you think she would see?" laughed Stephen.

"You," said John, eyeing his friend with an admiration which was more wistful than envious. Stephen was a boy with a man's body, "roseate-brown from toe to crown," to quote a popular song, and comely enough to tempt an angel. When he shook his wet hair, a great armful of daffodils seemed to bestrew his head. A marriage of beauty and strength, thought John. For the hundredth time he marveled that such a boy could have chosen him for a brother; actually chosen, when they had no bond of blood, nor even of race. He peered down at himself and wished for his clothes. At the castle he never bathed in the tub with his father's friends: only with Stephen, sometimes, in the stream of the old millwheel, or alone in the heath from his own little bucket (even in the castle, he had no private room, but slept with the rancid sons of his father's knights).

But Stephen said: "You know, John, you're not so skinny now. You've started to fill out. The bones are there. The strength too, as you just proved. All you need is a little more meat. You'll be a man before you know it."

"Next year?" asked John, though such a prospect seemed as far from his grasp as a fiery-plummaged phoenix. "You were a man at thirteen."

"Eleven. But I'm different. I'm a villein. We grow fast. With you, I'd say two or possibly three more years. Then we can wench together for sure."

"Who would want me when she could have you?"

Stephen led him to the bank of the stream. "Look," he said, and pointed to their reflections in a space of clear water between the pepperworts: the bright and the dark, side by side; the two faces of the moon. "I have muscles, yes. But you have brains. They show in your face."

"I don't like my face. I won't even look in those glass mirrors they bring back from the Holy Land. I always look startled."

"Not as much as you did. Why, just since we left the castle, I've seen a change. Yesterday, when you faced down the Knight Templar, I was ready to wet my breechclout! But you never batted an eye. And you looked so wise. One day you'll have my muscles, but you can bet a brace of pheasants I'll never have your brains. Come on now, let's give Ruth a chance."

At Stephen's insistence—and he had to insist vigorously—they bundled their tunics and wore only their breechclouts, the shapeless strips of cloth which every man, whether priest, baron, or peasant, twisted around his loins. Now they would look like field hands stripped for a hot day's work, and John's fine tunic would not arouse suspicion or tempt thieves.

"But my shoulders," John began, "they're so white."

"They'll brown in the sun on the way to London," he said, and then: "*Ruth*, you can take your swim!"

He had to repeat her name before she answered in a thin, distant voice: "Yes, Stephen?"

"You can swim now. You'll have the stream to yourself." To John he smiled, "She took you seriously about not peeping. But you know, John, *we* didn't promise."

"You'd spy on an angel?"

Stephen slapped his back. "Now who's calling her an angel. No, I wouldn't spy. I'd just *think* about it. I've always wondered if angels are built like girls. Let's do a bit of exploring while she bathes. I could eat another breakfast after that swim. But we mustn't stray too far from the stream."

Beyond a coppice of young beeches, Stephen discovered a cluster of slender stalks with fragrant, wispy leaves. "Fennels. Good for the fever you catch in London. We might pick a few, roots and all."

But John, thinking of Mandrakes, had no use for roots and followed his nose to a bed of mint. "This is what your mother used to sweeten her gowns, isn't it?"

"Yes, and it's also good to eat." They knelt in the moist soil to pluck and chew the leaves, whose sweetly burning juices left them hoarse and breathless, as if they had gulped a heady muscatel.

But where was the stream, the road, the oak in which they had slept?

"The trees all look the same," said Stephen, "but there, that old beech. Haven't we seen it before? And there, the torn ground—"

They had wandered, it seemed, to the place of the Mandrake hunt. The hole remained in the earth, disturbingly human-shaped, with branching clefts from which the limbs had been wrenched by the hapless dog.

"Let's get away from here," said John, as nausea slapped him like the foul air of a *garderobe*.

"Wait," said Stephen. "There's a second hole. It's— it's where we buried the dog. *God's bowels!*" It was his crudest oath. "The dirty Infidels have dug him up and—"

Around the hole they saw a litter of bones . . . skull . . . femur . . . pelvis . . . stripped of their meat and scattered carelessly through the grass.

"Stephen," said John, seizing his friend's hand. "I know how you feel. It was cruel of them to eat the dog. But we've got to get away from here. They'll take us for the hunter!"

Something had waited for them.

At first it looked like a tree. No, a corpse exhumed from a grave with roots entwining its limbs. It wheezed; lurched; moved, swaying, toward them. It was bleached to the color of a beechnut trunk—at least, those parts of the skin (or was it bark?) which showed through the greenish forest of hair (or rootlets?). Red eyes burned in black hollows (tiny fire-dragons peering from caves, thought John). The mouth seemed a single hairlip until it split into a grin which revealed triangular teeth like those of a shark: to crush, tear, shred.

"Run!" screamed John, tugging at his friend, but proud Stephen had chosen to fight.

"Dog-eater!" He charged the Mandrake and used his head for a ram.

The creature buckled like a rotten door but flung out

its limbs and enveloped Stephen into its fall; fallen, it seemed a vegetable octopus, lashing viny tentacles around its prey.

Unlike Stephen, John grew cold with anger instead of hot; blue instead of flushed; as if he had plunged in a river through broken ice. First he was stunned. Then the frost-caves of his brain functioned with crystalline clarity. He knew that he was young and relatively weak; against that bark-tough skin, his naked fists would beat in vain. A blind, weaponless charge would not avail his friend. He fell to his knees and mole-like clawed the ground. Pebbles. Pine cones. Beechnuts. Pretty, petty, useless. Then, a stone, large and jagged. With raw, bleeding hands, he wrestled the earth for his desperately needed weapon and, without regaining his feet, lunged at the fallen Mandrake. The fibrous skull cracked and splintered sickeningly beneath the stone and spewed him with resin and green vegetable matter like a cabbage crushed by a millstone.

"Stephen!" he cried, but the answer hissed above him, shrill with loathing:

"Human!"

Multitudinous fingers caught and bound him with coils of wild grapevine and dragged him, together with Stephen, over the bruising earth.

The Mandrake warrens were not so much habitations as lightless catacombs for avoiding men and animals. No one knew if the creatures had built them or found, enlarged, and connected natural caves and covered the floors with straw. John was painfully conscious as his thin body, little protected by the shreds of his breechclout, lurched and scraped down a tortuous passage like the throat of a dragon. His captors, he guessed, could see in the dark, but only the scraping of Stephen's body told him that he had not been separated from his friend.

"Mother of God," he breathed, "let him stay unconscious!"

For a long time he had to judge their passage from room to room by the sudden absence of straw which marked a doorway. Finally, a dim, capricious light announced their approach to a fire; a council chamber perhaps; the end of the brutal journey.

The room of the fire was a round, spacious chamber where Mandrake females were silently engaged in piling chunks of peat on a bed of coals. Neither roots nor branches were used as fuel, John saw, since that which began as a root did not use wood for any purpose. Wryly he wondered how the Mandrakes would feel if they knew that the fuel they burned had once been vegetation.

Their captors dumped them as men might deposit logs beside a hearth, and joined the women in feeding the fire. John was tightly trussed, his feet crossed, his hands behind his back, but he rolled his body to lie on his side and look at Stephen's face. His friend's cheeks were scratched; his forehead was blue with a large bruise; and the daffodils of his hair were wilted with blood and cobwebs.

"Stephen, Stephen, what have they done to you?" he whispered, biting his lip to stifle the threat of tears. His hero, fallen, moved him to tenderness transcending worship. For once he had to be strong for Stephen. He had to think of escape.

He examined the room. There were neither beds nor pallets. Apparently the Mandrakes slept in the smaller rooms and used their council chamber as a baron used his hall. It was here that they met to talk and feast. The earthen walls were blackened from many fires. Bones littered the straw, together with teeth, fur, and hair; inedible items. The stench of the refuse was overpowering and, coupled with that of excrement and urine, almost turned John's stomach. He fought nausea by wondering how his fastidious Abbot would have faced the situation: identified himself, no doubt, with Hercules in the Aegean stables or Christ amid the corruptions of the Temple.

Then, across the room, he saw the crucifix. Yes, it was unmistakable, a huge stone cross. Latin, with arms of unequal length, and set in an alcove shaped like an apse. Turtle-backed stones served as seats. Between the seats the ground had been packed and brushed by the knees of suppliants. The place was clearly a chapel, and John remembered the tale—a myth, he had always supposed— that after the Christians had come to England with Augustine, a priest had visited the Mandrakes in their warrens. Once they had eaten him, they had reconsidered his words and adopted Christianity.

"Bantling-killer!"

A Mandrake slouched above him, exuding a smell of tarns stagnant with scum. His voice was gutteral and at first unintelligible. Bantling-killer. Of course. *Baby*-killer. The creature was speaking an early form of English. He went on to curse all athelings in their byrnies—knights in their mail—and to wish that the whale-road would swallow that last of them as they sailed to their wars in ring-prowed ships of wood. Then, having blasted John's people, he became specific and accused John and Stephen of having killed the bantling with their dog. *His* bantling, he growled, grown from his own seed. Though the Mandrakes copulated like men and animals, John gathered that their females gave birth to objects resembling acorns which they planted in the ground and nurtured into roots. If allowed by hunters to reach maturity, the roots burst from the ground like a turtle out of an egg, and their mothers bundled them into the warrens to join the tribe—hence, the word "bantling" from "bantle" or "bundle."

"No," John shook his head. "No. We did not kill your baby. Your bantling. It was hunters who killed him!"

The creature grinned. A grin, it seemed, was a Mandrake's one expression; anger or pleasure provoked the same bared teeth. Otherwise, he looked as vacant as a cabbage.

"Hunters," he said. "You."

The crowded room had grown as hot as the kitchen before a feast in a castle, but the figures tending the fire, hunched as if with the weight of dirt, toil, and time, seemed impervious to the heat. They had obviously built the fire to cook their dinner, and now they began to sharpen stakes on weathered stones. Even the stakes were tin instead of wood.

The whir of the flames must have alerted the young Mandrakes in the adjacent chambers. They trooped into the room and gathered, gesticulating, around the two captives. They had not yet lapsed into the tired shuffle of their elders; they looked both energetic and intelligent. Life in the forest, it seemed, slowly stultified quick

minds and supple bodies. It was not surprising that the
weary elders, however they hated men, should try to pass
their daughters into the villages.

The girls John saw, except for one, appeared to be
adolescents, but hair had already forested their arms and
thickened their lips. The one exception, a child of perhaps four, twinkled a wistful prettiness through her
grime. Her eyes had not yet reddened and sunken into
their sockets; her mouth was the color of wild raspber-
ries. She could still have passed.

The children seemed to have come from the midst of
a game. Dice, it appeared, from the small white objects
they rattled, a little like the whale-bone cubes which
delighted the knights in John's castle. But the dice of the
Mandrake children were not so much cubes as irregular,
bony lumps scratched with figures. The Greeks, John
recalled from the Abbot's lectures, had used the knuckle-
bones of sheep and other animals in place of cubes.

But the Mandrake children had found a livelier game.
They stripped John and Stephen of their breechclouts
and began to prod their flesh with fingers like sharp car-
rots and taunt them for the inadequacy of human loins.
The Mandrake boys, naked like their parents, possessed
enormous genitals; hence, the potency of the murdered,
fragmented roots as aphrodisiacs. Stephen stirred fitfully
but to John's relief did not awake to find himself the
object of ridicule. With excellent reason, he had always
taken pride in the badge of his manhood, and to find
himself surpassed and taunted by boys of eight and nine
would have hurt him more than blows. Only the girl of
four, staring reproachfully at her friends, took no part in
the game.

A church bell chimed, eerily, impossibly it seemed to
John in such a place, and a hush enthralled the room.
An aged Mandrake, rather like a tree smothered by
moss, hobbled among the silenced children and paused
between John and Stephen. Examining. Deliberating.
Choosing. He chose Stephen. When he tried to stoop,
however, his back creaked like a rusty drawbridge. He
will break, thought John. He will never reach the ground.
But he reached the ground and gathered Stephen in his
mossy arms.

"Bloody Saracen!" shouted John. "Take your hands off my friend!" Stretching prodigiously, he managed to burst the bonds which held his ankles and drive his knee into the Mandrake's groin. The creature gave such a yelp that red-hot pokers seemed to have gouged John's ears. He writhed on the ground and raised his hands to shut out the shriek and pain. Shadows cobwebbed his brain. When he struggled back to clarity, Stephen lay in the chapel before the crucifix. Looming above him, the aged Mandrake stood like Abraham above Isaac. The other adults, perhaps twenty of them, sat on the turtle-shaped stones, while the children sat near the fire to watch the proceedings from which their elders had barred them. The impression John caught of their faces—brief, fleeting, hazy with smoke and the dim light of the room— was not one of malice or even curiosity, but respect and fear, and the pretty child who had turned her back and buried her face in the arms of an older girl.

The officiating Mandrake intoned what seemed to be a prayer and a dedication. John caught words resembling "Father" and "Son" and realized with horror if not surprise that just as the Christian humans burned a Yule log and decked their castles with hawthorn, holly, and mistletoe in honor of Christ, so the Christian Mandrakes were dedicating Stephen to a different conception of the same Christ. First, the offering, then the feast. The same victim would serve both purposes.

He had already burst the grapevines which held his ankles. In spite of his bound hands, he struggled to his feet and reeled toward the chapel. Once, he had killed a Mandrake with cold implacability. Now he had turned to fire: the Greek fire of the East, hurled at ships and flung from walls; asphalt and crude petroleum, sulphur and lime, leaping and licking to the incandescence of Hell. He felt as if stones and Mandrakes must yield before his advance; as if Mary, the Mother of Christ, must descend from the castles of heaven or climb from the sanctuary of his heart and help him deliver his friend.

But the Mandrakes rose in a solid palisade; and, shrunk to a boy of twelve, he hammered his impotent fists against their wood.

"No," he sobbed, falling to his knees. "Me. Not Stephen."

"*John.*"

His name tolled through the room like the clash of a mace against an iron helmet. "John, he will be all right." Her flaxen hair, coarsened with dirt and leaves, rioted over her shoulders like tarnished gold coins. She wore her linen robe, but the white cloth had lost its purity to stains and tears. She might have been a fallen angel, and her eyes seemed to smoulder with memories of heaven or visions of Hell.

She had entered the room accompanied, not compelled. She was not their captive. She has gained their favor, he thought, by yielding to their lust. But God will forgive her if she saves my friend, and I, John, will serve her until I die. If she saves my friend—

He saw that she held her crucifix; gripped it as if you would have to sever the hand before you could pry her fingers from its gold arms.

One of her companions called to the priest, who stood impassively between his cross of stone and his congregation, and above Stephen. He neither spoke nor gestured, but disapproval boomed in his silence.

Ruth advanced to the fire and held her crucifix in the glow of the flames, which ignited the golden arms to a sun-washed sea, milkily glinting with pearls like Saracen ships, and the Mandrakes gazed on such a rarity as they had never seen with their poor sunken eyes or fancied in their dim vegetable brains. In some pathetic, childlike way, they must have resembled the men of the First Crusade who took Jerusalem from the Seljuk Turks and gazed, for the time, at the Holy Sepulchre; whatever ignoble motives had led them to Outre-Mer, they were purged for that one transcendent moment of pride and avarice and poised between reverence and exaltation. It was the same with the Mandrakes.

The priest nodded in grudging acquiescence. Ruth approached him through the ranks of the Mandrakes, which parted murmurously like rushes before the advancing slippers of the wind, and placed the crucifix in his hands. His fingers stroked the gold with slow, loving caresses and paused delicately on the little mounds of the pearls. She did not wait to receive his dismissal. Without hesitation and without visible fear, she walked to John and unbound his hands.

"Help me with Stephen," she said. "I have traded the cross for your lives."

Once they had stooped from the shadows of the last cave and risen to face the late morning sun, the Mandrake left them without a look or a gesture, avid, it seemed, to return to the council chamber and the bartered crucifix. In the dark corridors, Stephen had regained consciousness but leaned on Ruth and John and allowed them to guide his steps, their own steps guided by the slow, creaking shuffle of the Mandrake.

"Stephen, are you all right?" John asked.

"Tired," he gasped, stretching his battered limbs in the grass and closing his eyes.

"And you, Ruth?" John looked at her with awe and wonderment and not a little fear. He had witnessed a miracle.

She did not look miraculous as she lay beside Stephen. Once she had seemed to shrink into a spider; now she reminded him of a wet linen tunic, flung to the ground, torn, trampled, forsaken.

"What happened, Ruth?"

"They found me by the bank after my swim. I reached for a stocking and looked up to see—them."

"And—?"

"They laid hands on me. Dragged me toward their warrens. I fought them, but the one who held me was very strong."

"And you thought of the crucifix? How they were Christians and might value it?"

"Yes. You remember, I had hidden it in our tree. I tried to make them understand that I would give them a treasure if they let me go. You know how they talk. Like little children just learning to speak. Words and phrases all run together. But strange, old-fashioned words. I kept shouting, 'Treasure, treasure!' But they didn't understand. Finally, I remembered an old word used by our ancestors. 'Folk-hoarding,' I cried, and 'Crucifix!' and they understood. They're very devout in their way. They grinned, argued, waved their snaky arms. Then they let me go. I led them to the tree. We passed the place where you and Stephen had fought. I saw bits of your breechclouts and knew their friends had captured you. I stopped in my tracks and said I wanted your freedom as well as mine. Otherwise, no exchange. One of them said, 'If crucifix ring-bright. If time—'

"They climbed right after me up the trunk of the tree. The sight of the crucifix as I unwrapped it made them hold their breath. I held it out to them, but they shook their heads. No, they wouldn't touch it. It was for their priest. They seemed to feel their own filth and ugliness might tarnish the gold or lessen the magic. They didn't grin or look vacant anymore. They looked as if they wanted to cry. They turned their backs and let me dress in the robe—and brought me here."

"And they kept their promise."

"Of course. They're Christians, aren't they?"

Her story troubled him. He had heard of many Christians who failed to keep promises; Crusaders, for example, with Greeks or Saracens. "But why—" he began, meaning to ask why the Mandrakes would feel bound by a promise to a hated human girl.

"We can't sit here all day," she interrupted. "They might change their minds, Christian or not. Where is the road?"

Shakily they climbed to their feet, Stephen without help at his own request ("I must get my balance back."), and saw the trees which encircled and encaged them, great sycamores and greater oaks, looking as if they were sentient old kings in an old country, Celt, Roman, and Saxon, watchfully standing guard until the usurping Normans had felt the slow fingers of the land shape them to the lineaments of Britannia, Britain, England, as the paws and tongue of a bear sculpture her cub into her own small likeness.

"I think," said Stephen, "that the road lies *that* way."

But Stephen was still befuddled by the blows to his head. They walked for a long time and did not come to the road . . . but came to the Manor of Roses.

IV

I watched them as they struggled out of the forest, the stalwart boy supported by his friends, the slighter, dark-haired boy and the girl with angel hair. On a sunny morning, you see, I leave the Manor with the first twittering of sparrows and gather the white roses from the hedge which surrounds my estate, or visit the windmill, the first, I believe, in southern England, and watch the millstones, powered no longer by water, grinding grain for the bread of my kitchen. Now, it was afternoon. I had lunched in the shade of a mulberry tree (apricots, bread, and mead), returned to the hedge of roses, and seen the children. I must have gasped at the sight. They stopped and stared at me over the hedge. The girl stiffened and whispered to the boys. It was not a time when children called at strange manor houses. Startled sparrows, they seemed. Not in littleness of frailty, you understand. The girl and the older boy were more than children. It was rather their vulnerability. Something had almost broken them, and they did not know if I were hunter or friend. I had to prove my friendliness as if I were coaxing sparrows to eat from my hand.

"Follow the hedge to the right," I smiled. "You will see the gate. If you've come from the forest, you must be tired and hungry. I can give you food and a place to sleep." I had made a basket of roses out of my arms. I had no fear of thorns, with my gloves of antelope leather; my long, tight sleeves buttoned at the wrist; my wimple and cap; and my blue, ankle-length skirt, brocaded with star-colored fleurs-de-lis and hanging in folds from my low-belted waist. I watched the boys, clad in breechclouts clumsily fashioned from leaves, and envied them a man's freedom to dress and ride where he will (unless he dresses in armor and rides to war).

The youngest, the dark-haired boy, still supporting his friend, addressed me with the courteous French of a gentleman:

"We are not attired for the company of a lady. You see, we have come from the forest." His face confirmed the impression of his speech. It is said that Saladin, England's noblest enemy, had such a face as a boy:

ascetic, scholar, poet. But first and last, I saw his need and that of his friend, the Saxon lad with the build of wandering Aengus, the Great Youth, whose kisses were called his birds. Even the breechclout seemed an affront to his body. Still, he needed me. His mouth, though forced to a smile, was tight with fatigue and hunger, and a wound had raked his forehead. Both were spider-webbed with scratches.

The girl, though her white gown was stained and torn, resembled an angel sculptured from ivory and set in the tympanum of a London cathedral: beautiful, aloof, expressionless. She is tired, I thought. Weariness has drained her face. Later I will read her heart.

I met them at the wicket in the hedge, a gate so small and low that my son had jumped it in a single bound when he rode for the Stane and London.

I held out my arms to greet them; my armful of roses.

They kept their ground, the dark boy straining toward me, the Saxon drawn between them.

"I can offer you more than flowers," I said, spilling the roses.

The Norman said, "My Lady, whom have we the honor of addressing?"

"I am called the Lady Mary. You have come to the Manor of Roses."

"I thought," he said, "you might be another Mary. Will you help my friend? He has suffered a blow to his head." But it was the Norman and not his friend I helped. He swayed on his feet, leaned to my strength, and caught my out-stretched hand.

"I will soil your gown."

"With the good brown earth? It is the purest of all substances. The mother of roses."

"But you scattered your flowers on the ground."

"I have others." Supporting him with my arm and followed by his friends, I drew him toward the house.

Once, a moat had surrounded the Manor, but after my husband's death I had filled the water with earth and planted mulberry trees, aflutter now with linnets and silvery filamented with the webs of silkworms; the trees formed a smaller ring within the ring of the rose hedge to island but not to isolate my house, which was built of bricks instead of the cold grey stones preferred by the neighboring barons. My husband had offered to build me a manor for my wedding gift.

"Build it of bricks," I had said. "The color of your hair."

"And stoutly," he said. But the high curtain wall with its oaken door, its rows of weathered bricks from a ruined Roman villa, and its narrow embrasures for bow-men to fire their arrows, had somehow a look of having lost its threat, like armor hung on the wall. Gabriel knows, I could not stand a siege with my poor, bedraggled retainers: gardeners, gatemen, cooks, seneschal, stable-boy—thirty in all, without a knight among them. The wasting fever had not been kind to the Manor of Roses.

The gatekeeper moved to help me with the boy. "He will tire you, my Lady."

I shook my head. No burden can equal the ache of emptiness.

Once we had entered the bailey, Sarah the cook, who had slipped out of the kitchen and thrown back her hood to catch some sun, tossed up her ponderous hands—I suspect it required some effort—and squealed, "My Lady, what have you found?"

"Children, what else? Sarah, hurry to the kitchen and prepare a meal such as young boys—young men—like. Pheasant and—"

"I know, I know," she said. "You forget I've sons of my own, who serve you every night!" Sarah, her three sons and her two daughters, were new to the Manor, but she acted as if she had been my nurse since childhood. "I know what young boys like. The beast of the chase and the fowl of the warren. All that flies and all that goes on hooves, and two of everything unless it's as big as a boar!" She waddled ahead of us up the stairs to the door and, laboriously genuflecting, vanished under the lintel with its wooden Madonna cradling the Holy Infant.

"It's a lovely house," said the Saxon boy in English. "It looks like an abbot's grange."

"A very rich abbot," explained the Norman, fearful no doubt that I had misunderstood his friend's compliment, since poor abbots lived in squalid cottages.

"I meant," stammered the Saxon, "it looks so bright

and peaceful, with its Mother and Child, and its—" He waited for his friend to complete his sentence.

"Its two pointed roofs instead of battlements, and real windows instead of slits for archers, with *glass* in the windows! And Stephen, see the herb garden. Parsley, thyme, bay leaf, marjoram, mace, tarragon—"

"You know a lot about herbs," I said.

"I've read an herbal."

Once in the Manor, I took them to the bath. In all the Weald, I think, in all of England, no other house can claim a fountain for bathing enclosed under the roof. The mouth of a dolphin, hammered from bronze by the artisans of Constantinople, spewed a vigorous streamlet into a basin where Tritons gamboled on vari-colored tiles. For baths in the cold of winter, I stuffed the dolphin's mouth and filled the basin with kettles hot from the kitchen.

"Your friend shall bathe first," I said to the boys. All of us now were speaking English. And to her: "Your name is—?"

When the girl was slow to answer, the Saxon said: "Ruth. She is our guardian angel. She rescued us."

"From wild beasts?"

"From Mandrakes."

I shuddered. "They are much in the woods, poor misshapen brutes. They have never harmed me, though. You must tell me later about your escape. Now then, Ruth. You shall have the bath to yourself. After you have bathed, I shall send you clothes, and a perfume made from musk, and. . ."

She looked at me with cool, veiled eyes. "You are very kind." I wanted to say to her: I am more than twice your age, and far less beautiful. Trust me, my dear. Trust me!

I turned to the boys. The Norman, I learned, was John; the Saxon, Stephen. "When Ruth has finished, it will be your turn."

"Thank you, my lady," said John. "We would like to bathe with a dolphin. But—"

"You would rather eat! What about bread and cheese and pennyroyal tea to hold you till time for supper? Or," I added quickly, "beer instead of tea." Pennyroyal! I had been too much with women.

"Beer," they said in one breath. "But," said John, "my brother has a wound."

"Brother?" I asked, surprised. A Norman gentleman and a Saxon peasant!

"We adopted each other. Have you something for his head?"

"For my stomach," grinned Stephen. "That's where I hurt the most."

"For both," I said.

The hall of my manor house is hot and damp in the summer, and cold in the winter even with pine logs, as big around as a keg of beer, crackling on the hearth. It has always been a room for men: shouting, roistering, warming themselves with mead. For myself, I prefer the solar, the room of many purposes in which I sleep and dine and weave, and entertain the friends who come infrequently now to visit me. I left the boys in the solar with three loaves of bread, two enormous cheeses, and a flagon of beer, and told them to eat and afterwards to bathe themselves with cloths dipped in camphor and wrap fresh linen around their waists.

"Call me after you've finished."

I had scarcely had time to find a gown for Ruth when I heard John's voice: "Lady Mary, we've finished."

I found them so fragrant with camphor that I overlooked the patches of dirt they had left on their knees and elbows. The bread, cheese, and beer had vanished as if there had been a raid by kitchen elves, denied their nightly tribute of crumbs. I tended the boys' wounds with a paste of fennel and dittany and they yielded themselves to my fingers without embarrassment, sons to a mother, and made me feel as if my hands had rediscovered their purpose.

"It doesn't burn at all," said Stephen. "My father used a poultice of adder's flesh pounded with wood-lice and spiders. But it burned like the devil, and stank."

"Lady Mary's hands are like silk," said John. "That's why it doesn't burn."

The boys began to dress in tunics which had belonged to my son: John in green, with a fawn-colored cape drawn through a ring-brooch and knotted at his shoulder, and *chausses* or stockings to match the cape, and black leather shoes with straps; Stephen in blue, with a pale rose cape and silver *chausses*, but looking with each additional garment as if another chain had shackled him to the wall.

"I wouldn't show myself in the forest like this," he muttered. "I'd be taken for a pheasant and shot on sight."

"It's only for tonight," I said. "Don't you want to look the gallant for Ruth?"

"She's used to me naked. She'll take me for a jester."

"My lady."

Ruth had entered the room. She was dressed in a crimson gown or *cotte*, caught at the waist by a belt of gilded doeskin but falling around her feet in billows through which the toes of her slippers peeped like small green lizards. She had bound her hair in a moss-green net, and her yellow tresses twinkled like caged fireflies. (Strange, I always thought of her in terms of forest creatures: wild, unknowable, untamable.)

"My lady, the boys may have their bath. I thank you for sending me so lovely a gown."

"We've had our bath," said Stephen with indignation. "Can't you see we're dressed as gallants?"

"Lady Mary put fennel and dittany on our wounds," said John, "and now they don't hurt any more."

"And we're going to eat," said Stephen.

"Again," said John.

Ruth examined the solar and almost relaxed from her self-containment. "Why, it's lovely," she said, extending her arm to include the whole of the room. "It's all made of sunlight."

"Not entirely," I smiled, pointing to the high, raftered ceiling with its tie-beam and king-post. "Cobwebs collect unless I keep after Sarah's sons. They have to bring a ladder, you see, and they don't like dusting among the dark crevices. They're afraid of elves."

"But the rest," Ruth said. "There's no darkness anywhere."

The room was kindled with afternoon light from the windows: the fireplace, heaped with logs; a tall-backed chair with square sides and embroidered cushions or bankers; a huge recessed window shaped like an arch and filled with roseate panes of glass from Constantinople; and, hiding the wooden timbers of the floor, a Saracen carpet of polygons, red, yellow, and white, with a border of stylized Persian letters. My wainscotted walls, however, were purely English, their oaken panels painted the green of leaves and bordered with roses to match the carpet.

Ruth explored the room with the air of a girl familiar with beauty, its shapes and its colors, but not without wonder. She touched my loom with loving recognition and paused at my canopied bed to exclaim: "It's like a silken tent!

"But the linnets," she said, pointing to the wicker cage which hung beside the bed. "Don't they miss the forest?"

"They are quite content. I feed them sunflower seeds and protect them from stoats and weasels. In return, they sing for me."

"Is it true that a caged linnet changes his song?"

"Yes. His voice softens."

"That's what I mean. The wildness goes."

"Shouldn't it, my dear?"

"I don't know, Lady Mary."

We sat on benches drawn to a wooden table with trestles, John and I across from Ruth and Stephen. My husband and I had been served in the great hall by nimble, soft-toed squires who received the dishes from kitchen menials. After his death, however, I began to dine in the solar instead of the hall. For the last year I had been served by Shadrach, Meshach, and Abednego, the three illegitimate sons of my cook, Sarah. As a rule, I liked to dine without ceremony, chatting with the sons—identical triplets with fiery red hair on their heads and arms, and thus their name: they seemed to have stepped out of a furnace. But tonight, for the sake of my guests, I had ordered Sarah and her two illegitimate daughters, Rahab and Magdalena, to prepare, and her sons to serve, a banquet instead of a supper. The daughters had laid the table with a rich brocade of Saracen knights astride their swift little ponies, and they had placed among the knights, as if it were under seige, a molded castle of sugar, rice-flour, and almond-paste.

After I had said the grace, the sons appeared with

lavers, ewers, and napkins and passed them among my guests. Stephen lifted a laver to his mouth and started to drink, but John whispered frantically:

"It isn't soup, it's to wash your hands."

"There'll be other things to drink," I promised.

"I haven't felt this clean since I was baptized!" Stephen laughed, splattering the table with water from his laver.

Both Ruth and John, though neither had eaten from dishes of beaten silver, were fully at ease with knives and spoons; they cut the pheasant and duck before they used their fingers and scooped the fish-and-crab-apple pie with the spoons. But Stephen watched his friends with wry perplexity.

"I never used a knife except to hunt or fish," he sighed. "I'll probably cut off a finger. Then you can see if I'm a Mandrake!"

"We'd know that already," said John. "You'd look like a hedgehog and somebody would have chopped you up a long time ago for aphrodisiacs. You'd have brought a fortune." His gruesome remarks, I gathered, were meant to divert me from the fact that he had furtively dropped his knife, seized a pheasant, and wrestled off a wing. His motive was as obvious as it was generous. He did not wish to shame his friend by his own polished manners.

I laughed heartily for the first time since the death of my son. "Knives were always a nuisance. Spoons too. What are fingers for if not to eat with? So long as you don't bite yourself!" I wrenched a drumstick and thigh from the parent bird and felt the grease, warm and mouthwatering, ooze between my fingers. "Here," I said to Stephen. "Take hold of the thigh and we'll divide the piece." The bone parted, the meat split into decidedly unequal portions. Half of my drumstick accompanied John's thigh.

"It means you're destined for love," I said.

"He's already had it," said John. "Hay-lofts full of it."

"She doesn't mean that kind," said Stephen, suddenly serious. "She means caring—taking care of—don't you, Lady Mary? I've had that too, of course." He looked at John.

"Then it means you'll always have it."

"I know," he said.

John smiled at Stephen and then at me, happy because the three of us were friends, but silent Ruth continued to cut her meat into snail-sized portions and lift them to her mouth with the fastidiousness of a nun (her fingers, however, made frequent trips).

Shadrach, Meshach, and Abednego scurried between the solar and the kitchen, removing and replenishing, but it looked as if John and Stephen would never satisfy their hunger. With discreet if considerable assistance from Ruth, they downed three pheasants, two ducks, two fish-and-crab-apple pies, and four tumblers of mead.

"Leave some for us," hissed Shadrach in Stephen's ear. "This is the *last* bird." Stephen looked surprised, then penitent, and announced himself as full as a tick on the ear of a hound. Shadrach hurried the last bird back to the kitchen.

After the feast the boys told me about their adventures, encouraging rather than interrupting each other with such comments as, "You tell her about the stream with the pepperwort, John," or "Stephen you're better about the fighting." John talked more because he was more at ease with words; Stephen gestured as much as he talked and sometimes asked John to finish a sentence for him; and Ruth said nothing until the end of the story, when she recounted, quietly, without once meeting my gaze, the episode of her capture and bargain with the Mandrakes. I studied her while she spoke. Shy? Aloof, I would say. Mistrustful. Of me, at least. Simple jealousy was not the explanation. I was hardly a rival for the kind of love she seemed to want from Stephen. No, it was not my beauty which troubled her, but the wisdom which youth supposes to come with age; in a word, my mature perceptions. There was something about her which she did not wish perceived.

"And now for the gifts," I said.

"Gifts?" cried John.

"Yes. The dessert of a feast is the gifts and not the pies."

"But we have nothing to give you."

"You have told me a wondrous and frightening story.

No jongleur could have kept me more enthralled. And for you, I have—" I clapped my hands and Shadrach, Meshach, and Abednego appeared with my gifts, some musical instruments which had once belonged to my son. For Ruth, a rebec, a pear-shaped instrument from the East, three-stringed and played with a bow; for the boys, twin nakers or kettledrums which Stephen strapped to his back and John began to pound with soft-headed wooden drumsticks.

Ruth hesitated with her rebec till Stephen turned and said, "Play for us, Ruth! What are you waiting for, a harp?"

Then Ruth joined them, the boys marching round and round the solar, Stephen first, John behind him pounding on the drums and thumping the carpet with his feet, and finally Ruth, playing with evident skill and forgetting to look remote and enigmatic. Shadrach, Meshach, and Abednego had lingered in the doorway, and behind them Sarah appeared with her plump, swarthy daughters. I was not surprised when they started to sing; I was only surprised to find myself joining them in the latest popular song:

Summer is a-comin' in,
Loud sing cuckoo.
Groweth seed and bloweth mead,
And springs the wood anew.
  Sing, cuckoo!

In an hour the three musicians, their audience departed to the kitchen, had exhausted the energies which the meal had revived. Ruth sank in the chair beside the hearth. The boys, thanking me profusely for their gifts, climbed into the window seats. Stephen yawned and began to nod his head. John, in the opposite seat, gave him a warning kick.

"Come," I said to them, "there's a little room over the kitchen which used to belong to my son. The hall was too big, the solar too warm, he felt. I'll show you his room while Ruth prepares for bed. Ruth, we'll fix you a place in the window. You see how the boys are sitting opposite each other. I've only to join the seats with a wooden stool and add a few cushions to make a couch. Or"—and I made the offer, I fear, with visible reluctance—"you may share my own bed under the canopy."

"The window seats will be fine."

I pointed to the Aumbry, a wooden cupboard aswirl with wrought-iron scroll work, almost like the illuminated page of a psalter. "There's no lock. Open the doors and find yourself a night-dress while I show the boys their room."

My son's room was as small as a chapel in a keep, with one little square of a window, but the bed was wide as well as canopied, and irresistible to the tired boys.

"It's just like yours!" John cried.

"Smaller. But just as soft."

"At home I slept on a bench against the wall, in a room with eight other boys—sons of my father's knights. I got the wall bench because my father owned the castle."

"I slept on straw," said Stephen, touching the mattress, sitting, stretching himself at length, and uttering a huge, grateful sigh. "It's like a nest of puppies. What makes it so soft?"

"Goose-feathers."

"The geese we ate tonight—*their* feathers will stuff a mattress, won't they?"

"Two, I suspect." I fetched them a silk-covered bearskin from a small, crooked cupboard which my son had built at the age of thirteen. "And now I must see to Ruth."

I am not a reticent person, but the sight of the boys— Stephen in bed and sleepily smiling goodnight, John respectfully standing but sneaking an envious glance at his less respectful friend—wrenched me almost to tears. I did not trust myself to say that I was very glad to offer them my son's bed for as long as they chose to stay in the Manor of Roses.

I could only say: "Sleep as late as you like. Sarah can fix you breakfast at any hour."

"You're very kind," said Stephen. "But tomorrow, I think, we must get an early start for London."

"London!" I cried. "But your wounds haven't healed!"

"They were just scratches really, and now you've cured them with your medicine. If we stayed, we might *never* want to go."

"I might never want you to go."

"But don't you see, Lady Mary, we have to fight for Jerusalem."

"You expect to succeed where kings have failed? Frederick Barbarossa? Richard-the-Lion-Hearted? Two little boys without a weapon between them!"

"We're not little boys," he protested. "I'm a young swain—*fifteen winters old*—and John here is a—stripling who will grow like a bindweed. Aren't you, John?"

"Grow, anyway," said John without enthusiasm. "But I don't see why we have to leave in the morning."

"Because of Ruth."

"And Ruth is your guardian angel?" I asked with an irony lost on the boy.

"Yes. Already she's saved our lives."

"Has she, Stephen? Has she? Sleep now. We'll talk tomorrow. I want to tell you about my own son."

I returned to the solar heavy of foot. It was well for Ruth that she had changed to a nightdress, joined the window seats with the necessary stool, and retired to bed in a tumble of cushions. Now she was feigning sleep but forgetting to mimic the slow, deep breaths of the true sleeper. Well, I could question her tomorrow. One thing I knew. She would lead my boys on no unholy Crusade.

A chill in the air awakened me. It was not unusual for a hot summer day to grow wintry at night. I rose, lit a candle, and found additional coverlets for myself and Ruth. Her face seemed afloat in her golden hair; decapitated, somehow; or drowned.

I thought of the boys, shivering in the draft of their glassless window. I had not remembered to draw the canopy of their bed. In my linen nightdress and my pointed satin slippers which, like all the footwear expected of English ladies, cruelly pinched my toes, I passed through the hall and then the kitchen, tiptoed among the pallets of Sarah and her children stretched near the oven, and climbed a staircase whose steepness resembled a ladder.

Lifting aside a coarse leather curtain, I stood in the doorway of my son's room and looked at the boys. They had fallen asleep without extinguishing the pewter lamp which hung from a rod beside their bed. The bearskin covered their chins, and their bodies had met for warmth in the middle of the bed. I leaned above them and started to spread my coverlet. John, who was closer to me, opened his eyes and smiled.

"Mother," he said.

"Mary," I said, sitting on the edge of the bed.

"That's what I meant."

"I'm sorry I woke you."

"I'm glad. You came to bring us a coverlet, didn't you?"

"Yes. Won't we wake your brother?"

His smile broadened; he liked my acceptance of Stephen as his brother and equal. "Not our voices. Only if I got out of bed. Then he would feel me gone. But once he's asleep, he never hears anything, unless it's one of his hounds."

"You're really going tomorrow?"

"I don't want to go. I don't think Stephen does either. It's Ruth's idea. She whispered to him in the solar, when you and I were talking. But I heard her just the same. She said they must get to London. She said it was why she had come, and why she had saved us from the Mandrakes."

"Why won't she trust me, John?"

"I think she's afraid of you. Of what you might guess."

"What is there to guess?"

There was fear in his eyes. He looked at Stephen, asleep, and then at me. "I think that Ruth is a Mandrake. One who has passed."

I flinched. I had thought: thief, adventuress, harlot, carrier of the plague, but nothing so terrible as Mandrake. Though fear was a brand in my chest, I spoke quietly. I did not want to judge her until he had made his case. He might be a too imaginative child, frightened by the forest and now bewildered with sleep. He was only twelve. And yet, from what I had seen, I had thought him singularly rational for his years. Stephen, one might have said, would wake in the night and babble of Mandrake girls. Never John. Not without reason, at least.

"Why do you think that, John?"

His words cascaded like farthings from a purse cut by a pickpocket: swift, confused at times, and yet a thread of logic which made me share his suspicions. Ruth's mysterious arrival in the Mithraeum. Her vague answers and her claim to forgetfulness. Her lore of the forest. Her shock and disgust when he and Stephen had told her about the Mandrake hunters. Her strangely successful bargain with the crucifix.

"And they kept their word," he said. "Even when they thought Stephen and I had killed one of their babies. It was as if they let us go so that she could *use* us."

"It's true they're Christians," I said. "I've found their stone crosses in the woods around my Manor. They might have felt bound by their word. An oath to a savage, especially a Christian savage, can be a sacred thing. Far more sacred than to some of our own Crusaders, who have sacked the towns of their sworn friends. Ruth may have told you the truth about the crucifix."

"I know," he said. "I know. It's wicked of me to suspect her. She's always been kind to me. She brought me strawberries in the forest once! And Stephen worships her. But I had to tell you, didn't I? She might have passed when she was a small child. Grown up in a village. But someone became suspicious. She fled to the forest. Took shelter in the Mithraeum where Stephen and I found her. You see, if I'm right—"

"We're all in danger. You and Stephen most of all. You have been exposed to her visitations. We shall have to learn the truth before you leave this house."

"You mean we must wound her? But if she passed a long time ago, we would have to cut to the bone."

"We wouldn't so much as scratch her. We would simply confront her with an accusation. Suppose she is a Mandrake. Either she knew already when she first met you or else her people told her in the forest. Told her with pride: 'See, we have let you grow soft and beautiful in the town.' Tomorrow we shall demand proof of her innocence. Innocent, she will offer herself to the knife. The offer alone will suffice. But a true Mandrake will surely refuse such a test, and then we will know her guilt."

"It's rather like trial by combat, isn't it?" he said at last. "God condemns the guilty. Pricks him with conscience until he loses the fight. But this way, there won't be a combat, just a trial. God will make Ruth reveal her guilt or innocence."

"And you and I will be His instruments. Nothing more."

"And if she's guilty?"

"We'll send her into the forest and let her rejoin her people."

"It will break Stephen's heart."

"It will save his life. Save him from Ruth—and from going to London. Without his angel, do you think he'll still persist in his foolish crusade? He will stay here with you and me. The Manor of Roses has need of two fine youths."

"You won't make him a servant because he's a villein? His ancestors were Saxon earls when mine were pirates."

"Mine were pirates too. Blood-thirsty ones, at that. No, you and Stephen shall both be my sons. You adopted him. Why shouldn't I?"

"You know," he said, "when you first spoke to us at the hedge—after we had come from the forest—you said we'd come to the Manor of Roses. At first I thought you meant the *manner* of roses. Without the capitals."

"Did you, John?"

"Yes. And it's quite true. Of the house, I mean, and you. The manner of roses."

"But I have thorns to protect the ones I love. Ruth will feel them tomorrow." I knelt beside him and touched my lips to his cheek. It was not as if I were kissing him for the first time, but had kissed him every night for—how many years?—the years of my son when he rode to London.

"You're crying," he said.

"It's the smoke from the lamp. It has stung my eyes."

He clung to my neck, no longer a boy; a small child I could almost feed at my breast.

"I like your hair when it's loose," he said. "It's like a halo that comes all the way to your shoulders."

He fell asleep in my arms.

V

I woke to the strident twittering of sparrows. Their little shapes flickered against the window panes, and for once I regretted the glass. I would have liked them to flood the room with their unmelodious chirpings and share in my four-walled, raftered safety. Minikin beings, they reveled in the sun, noisily, valiantly, yet prey to eagle and hawk from the wilderness of sky, and the more they piped defiance, the more they invited death.

But other sparrows were not beyond my help.

I rose and dressed without assistance. I did not call Sarah's daughters to comb my hair and exclaim, "But it's like black samite!" and fasten the sleeves above my wrists and burden my fingers with jade and tourmaline. I did not wish to awaken Ruth. I dreaded the confrontation.

Encased from the tip of my toes to the crest of my hair, amber and green in wimple, robe, gloves, stockings, and slippers, I walked into the courtyard and sat on a bench among my herbs, lulled by the soft scent of lavender, but not from my hesitations; piqued by the sharp pungency of tarragon, but not to pride in what I must ask of Ruth.

The sun was as high as a bell-tower before the sounds from the solar told me that the children had waked and met. Ruth and Stephen were belaboring John when I entered the room. Stephen looked liberated in his breechclout, and Ruth disported herself in his blue tunic, the one he had worn reluctantly to my feast, but without the *chausses* or the cape. They were telling John that he ought to follow their example and dress for the woods.

"You're white as a sheep this morning," chided Stephen. "Your shoulders need the sun."

John, engulfed by his cape and tunic, might have been ten instead of twelve. I pitied the child. He would have to side with me against his friends. He returned my smile with a slight nod of his head, as if to say, "It must be now."

Stephen's voice was husky with gratitude: "Lady Mary, we must leave you and make our way to London. You've fed us and given us a roof, and we won't forget you. In a dark forest, you have been our candle. Your gifts—the drums and rebec—will help us to earn our passage to the Holy Land."

"Knights and abbots will throw you pennies," I said. "Robbers will steal them. It will take you a long time to earn your passage."

"But that's why we have to go! To start earning. And when we come back this way, we'll bring you a Saracen shield to hang above your hearth." He kissed my hand with a rough, impulsive tenderness. An aura of camphor wreathed him from yesterday's bath. He had combed his hair in a fringe across his forehead, like jonquils above his bluer-than-larkspur eyes. I thought how the work of the comb would soon be spoiled; the petals wilted by the great forest, tangled with cobwebs, matted perhaps with blood.

"I think you should know the nature of your company."

His eyes widened into a question. The innocence of them almost shook my resolve. "John? But he's my friend! If you mean he's very young, you ought to have seen him fight the Mandrakes."

"Ruth."

"Ruth is an angel." He made the statement as one might say, "I believe in God."

"You want her to be an angel. But is she, Stephen? Ask her."

He turned to Ruth for confirmation. "You said you came from the sky, didn't you?"

"I said I didn't remember." She stared at the Persian carpet and seemed to be counting the polygons or reading the cryptic letters woven into the border.

"But you said you remembered falling a great distance."

"There are other places to fall than out of the sky."

John spoke at last. "But you remembered things." His voice seemed disembodied. It might have come from the vault of a deep Mithraeum. "About the forest. Where to find wild strawberries. How to weave a cup out of rushes. How to escape from the Mandrakes."

"Ruth," I said. "Tell them who you are. Tell me. We want to know."

She began to tremble. "I don't know. I don't know."
I was ready to pity her when she told the truth.

I walked to the Aumbry with slow, deliberate steps.
In spite of my silken slippers, I placed each foot as if I
were crushing a mite which threatened my roses. I
opened the doors, knelt, and reached to the lowest shelf
for a Saracen poniard, its ivory hilt emblazoned with sap-
phires in the shape of a running gazelle. The damascene
blade was very sharp: steel inlaid with threads of silver.

There was steel in my voice as I said, "You are not to
leave my house till I know who you are. I accepted you
as a guest and friend. Now I have reason to believe that
you are dangerous. To the boys, if not to me."

"You would harm me, Lady Mary?" She shrank from
the light of the window and joined the shadows near the
hearth. I half expected her to dwindle into a spider and
scuttle to safety among the dark rafters.

"I would ask you to undergo a test."

She said: "You think I am a Mandrake."

"I think you must show us that you are not a Mandrake." I walked toward her with the poniard. "My husband killed the Saracen who owned this blade. Wrestled
him for it. Drove it into his heart. You see, the point is
familiar with blood. It will know what to do."

"Lady Mary!" It was Stephen who stepped between
us; charged, I should say, like an angry stag, and almost
took the blade in his chest. "What are you saying, Lady
Mary?"

"Ask her," I cried. "Ask her! Why does she fear the
knife? Because it will prove her guilt!"

He struck my hand and the poniard fell to the floor.
He gripped my shoulders.

"Witch! You have blasphemed an angel!"

Anger had drained me; indignation; doubts. I dropped
in his punishing hands. I wanted to sleep.

John awoke from his torpor and beat on his friend
with desperate fists. "It's true, it's true! You must let her
go!"

Stephen unleashed a kick like a javelin hurled from an
arblast. I forgot the poniard; forgot to watch the girl. All
I could see was John as he struck the doors of the
Aumbry and sank, winded and groaning to the floor.

Twisting from Stephen's fingers, I knelt to the wounded boy and took him in my arms.

"I'm not hurt," he gasped. "But Ruth . . . the poniard . . ."

I saw the flash of light on the blade in Ruth's hand. Stephen swayed on his feet, a stag no longer: a bear chained in a pit, baited by some, fed by others—how can he tell his tormentors from his friends? Wildly he stared from the boy he had hurt to the girl he had championed. Ruth walked toward me with soundless feet and eyes as cold as hornstones under a stream. She might have been dead.

The poniard flashed between us. I threw up my hands for defense: of myself and John. She brought the blade down sharply against her own hand, the mount of the palm below her thumb. I heard—I actually heard—the splitting of flesh, the rasp of metal on bone. The blade must have cut through half of her hand before it lodged in the bone, and then she withdrew it without a cry, with a sharp, quick jerk, like a fisherman removing a hook, and stretched her fingers to display her wound. The flesh parted to reveal white bone, and crimson blood, not in the least resinous, swelled to fill the part. She smiled at me with triumph but without malice, a young girl who had vindicated herself before an accuser more than twice her years.

"Did you think I mean to hurt you?" she said almost playfully and then, seeing her blood as it reddened the carpet, winced and dropped the poniard.

Stephen steadied her into the chair by the hearth and pressed her palm to staunch the flow.

"You are an evil woman," he glared at me. "Your beauty is a lie. It hides an old heart."

"Both of your friends are in pain," I said. "It isn't a time for curses."

He looked at John in my arms and stiffened as if he would drop Ruth's hand and come to his friend.

"No. Stay with Ruth." I helped John across the room to a seat in the window; the tinted panes ruddied his pale cheeks. "He will be all right. Ruth is in greater need. Let me tend her, Stephen."

"You shan't touch her."

Ruth spoke for herself. "The pain is very sharp. Can you ease it, Lady Mary?"

I treated the wound with a tincture of opium and powdered rose petals and swaddled her hand with linen. John rose from the window and stood behind me, in silent attendance on Ruth—and in atonement. Stephen, an active boy denied a chance to act, stammered to his friends:

"Forgive me, both of you. It was my Crusade, wasn't it? I brought you to this."

Ruth's face was as white as chalk-rubbed parchment awaiting the quill of a monk. Her smile was illumination. "But you see, Stephen, Lady Mary was right to a point. I am no more an angel than you are. Less, in fact. You're a dreamer. I'm a liar. I've lied to you from the start, as Lady Mary guessed. That's why I couldn't trust her— because I saw that she couldn't trust me. My name isn't Ruth, it's Madeleine. I didn't come from heaven but the Castle of the Boar, three miles from your own kennels. My father was noble of birth, brother to the Boar. But he hated the life of a knight—the hunts, the feasts, the joustings—and most of all, the Crusades without God's blessing. He left his brother's castle to live as a scholar in Chichester, above a butcher's shop. He earned his bread by copying manuscripts or reading the stars. It was he who taught me my languages—English and Norman French and Latin—and just as if I were a boy, the lore of the stars, the sea, and the forest. He also taught me to play the rebec and curtsey and use a spoon at the table. 'Someday,' he said, 'you will marry a knight, a gentle one, I hope, if such still exist, and you have to be able to talk to him about a man's interests, and also delight him with the ways of woman. Then he won't ride off to fight in a foolish Crusade, as most men do because of ignorant wives.' He taught me well and grew as poor as a Welshman. When he died of the plague last year, he left me pennies instead of pounds, and no relatives except my uncle, the Boar, who despised my father and took me into his castle only because I was brought to him by an abbot from Chichester.

"But the Boar was recently widowed, and he had a taste for women. Soon I began to please him. I think I must have grown—how shall I say it?—riper, more womanly. He took me hawking and praised my lore of the forest. I sat beside him at banquets, drank his beer, laughed at his bawdy tales, and almost forgot my Latin. But after a feast one night he followed me to the chapel and said unspeakable things. My own uncle! I hit him with a crucifix from the altar. No one stopped me when I left the castle. No one knew the master was not at his prayers! But where could I go? Where but Chichester. Perhaps the Abbot would give me shelter.

"But John, as I passed near your father's castle I heard a rider behind me. I ducked in a thicket of gorse and tumbled down some stairs into a dark vault. You see, I did have a kind of fall, though not from heaven. I was stiff and tired and scared, and I fell asleep and woke up to hear Stephen proclaiming me an angel and talking about London and the Holy Land. London! Wasn't that better than Chichester? Further away from my uncle? Stephen, I let you think me an angel because I was tired of men and their lust. I had heard stories about you even at the castle—your way with a wench. After I knew you, though, I *wanted* your way. You weren't at all the boy in the stories, but kind and trusting. But I couldn't admit my lie and lose your respect.

"As for the crucifix you found in my hands, I had stolen it from my uncle. He owed me *something*, I felt. I had heard him say it was worth a knight's ransom. I hoped to sell it and buy a seamstress' shop and marry a fine gentleman who brought me stockings to mend. When I traded it to the Mandrakes, it was just as I said. They kept their promise for the sake of their faith. You see, they were much more honest than I have been."

Stephen was very quiet. I had seen him pressed for words but never for gestures, the outstretched hand, the nod, the smile. I wanted to ease the silence with reassurances and apologies. But Ruth was looking to Stephen; it was he who must speak.

"Now I'm just another wench to you," she said with infinite wistfulness. "I should have told you the truth. Let you have your way. This way, I've nothing at all."

He thought for a long time before he spoke, and the words he found were not an accusation. "I think a part of me never really took you for an angel. At least, not after the first. I'm not good enough to deserve a guardian from heaven. Besides, you stirred me like a girl of flesh and blood. But I wanted a reason for running away. An excuse and a hope. I lacked courage, you see. It's a fearful thing for a villein to leave his master. John's father could have me killed, or cut off my hands and feet. So I lied to myself: An angel had come to guide me! We were both dishonest, Ruth—Madeleine."

"Ruth. That's the name you gave me."

"Ruth, we can still go to London. Without any lies between us." Gestures returned to him; he clasped her shoulders with the deference of a brother (and looked to John: "My arms are not yet filled"). "But Lady Mary, it was cruel of you to find the truth in such a way."

"She never meant to touch Ruth," said John. "Only to test her. It was things I told Lady Mary that made her suspicious."

"John, John," said Ruth, walking to him and placing her swaddled hand on his arm. "I know you've never liked me. You saw through my tale from the first. You thought I wanted your friend. You were right, of course. I wouldn't trade him for Robin Hood, if Robin were young again and Lord of the forest! But I never wished you ill. You were his chosen brother. How could I love him without loving you? I wanted to say: 'Don't be afraid of losing Stephen to me. It was you he loved first. If I take a part of his heart, it won't be a part that belongs to you. Can't you see, John, that the heart is like the catacombs of the old Christians? You can open a second chamber without closing the first. Trust your friend to have chambers for both of us.' But I said nothing. It would have shown me to be a girl instead of an angel."

"You're coming with us, John?" asked Stephen doubtfully. "I didn't mean to hurt you. It was like the time you stepped on my dog. But you forgave me then."

"There's no reason for us to stay."

"You'll go on a Crusade without a guardian angel?"

"We'll walk to London and then—who knows? Venice, Baghdad. Cathay! Maybe it was just to run away I wanted, and not to save Jerusalem." He pressed John between his big hands. "You *are* coming, aren't you, brother?"

"No," said John. "No, Stephen. Lady Mary needs me."

"So does Stephen," said Ruth.

"Stephen is strong. I was never any use to him. Just the one he protected."

"Someday," said Ruth, "you'll realize that needing a person is the greatest gift you can give him."

"I need all of you," I said. "Stay here. Help me. Let me help you. London killed my son. It's a city forsaken by God."

Stephen shook his head. "We have to go, Ruth and I. The Boar might follow her here. She hurt his pride as well as his skill and stole his crucifix."

John said: "I'm going to stay."

I packed them provisions of bread, beer, and salted bacon; gave them the Saracen poniard to use against thieves or sell in London; and strapped the rebec and kettledrums on their backs.

"You must have a livelihood in London," I said, when Stephen wanted to leave the instruments with John.

I walked with Stephen and Ruth to the wicket and gave them directions for finding the road: Walk a mile to the east . . . look for the chestnut tree with a hole like a door in the trunk.

But Stephen was looking over his shoulder for John.

"He stayed in the solar," I said. "He loves you too much to say good-bye."

"Or too little. Why else is he staying with you?"

"The world is a harsh place, Stephen. Harsher than the forest, and without any islands like the Manor of Roses." How could I make him understand that God had given me John in return for the son I had lost to the devil?

"I would be his island," said Stephen, his big frame shaken with sobs.

"Never mind," said Ruth. "Never mind. We'll come back for him, Stephen." And then to me: "My lady, we thank you for your hospitality." She curtsied and kissed my hand with surprising warmth.

I said: "May an angel truly watch over you."

They marched toward the forest as proud and straight as Vikings, in spite of their wounds and their burdens. No more tears for Stephen. Not a backward look. London. Baghdad. Cathay!

It was then that I saw the face in the dense foliage, a bleached moon in a dusk of tangled ivy.

"Ruth, Stephen," I started to call. "You are being watched!"

But she had no eye for the children. She was watching me. I had seen her several times in the forest. Something of curiosity—no, of awe—distinguished her from the gray, anonymous tribe. Perhaps it was she who had left the crosses around my estate, like charms to affright the devil. She had never threatened me. Once I had run from her. Like a wraith of mist before the onslaught of sunlight, she had wasted into the trees. I had paused and watched her with shame and pity.

Now, I walked toward her, compelled by a need which surpassed my fear. "I won't hurt you," I said. I was deathly afraid. Her friends could ooze from the trees and envelop me before I could cry for help. "I won't hurt you," I repeated. "I only want to talk."

The rank vegetable scent of her clogged my nostrils. I had always felt that the rose and the Mandrake represented the antitheses of the forest: grace and crookedness. Strange, though, now that I looked at her closely for the first time, she was like a crooked tree mistreated by many weathers; a natural object unanswerable to human concepts of beauty and ugliness.

Dredging archaic words from memories of old books, I spoke with soft emphasis. "Tell me," I said. "Why do you watch my house—my mead-hall? Is it treasure-rich to you? Broad-gabled?"

She caught my meaning at once. "Not mead-hall."

"What then? The roses perhaps? You may pick some if you like."

"Bantling,"

"Bantling? *In my house?*"

She knelt and seized my hand and pressed her hairy lips against my knuckles.

"Here," she said.

I flung my hands to my ears as if I had heard a Man-

drakc shriek in the night. It was I who had shrieked. I
fled . . . I fled . . .

His eyes were closed, he rested against a cushion
embroidered with children playing Hoodman Blind.
He rose from his seat when he heard me enter the
room.

"They're gone?"

"What? What did you say, John?"

"Stephen and Ruth are gone?"

"Yes."

He came toward me. "You're pale, Lady Mary. Don't
be sad for me. I wanted to stay."

I said quietly: "I think you should go with your friends.
They asked me to send you after them."

He blinked his eyes. The lids looked heavy and gray.
"But I am staying to protect you. To be your son. You
said—"

"It was really Stephen I wanted. You're only a little
boy. Stephen is a young man. I would have taught him
to be a gentleman and a knight. But now that he's gone,
what do I need with a skinny child of twelve?"

"But I don't ask to be loved likc Stephen!"

I caught him between my hands, and his lean, hard-
muscled shoulders, the manhood stirring within him,
belied my taunts.

"Go to him," I cried. "Now, John. You'll lose him if
you wait!"

Pallor drained from his face, like pain routed by
opium. "Lady Mary," he whispered. "I think I understand. You *do* love me, don't you? Enough to let me go.
So much—"

I dropped my hands from his shoulders. I must not touch
him. I must not kiss him. "So much. So much . . ."

Beyond the hedge, he turned and waved to me, laughing, and ran to catch his friends. Before he could reach
the woods, Stephen blazed from the trees.

"I waited," he cried. "I knew you would come!"

The boys embraced in such a swirl of color, of whirling
bodies and clattering kettle drums, that the fair might
have come to London Town! Then, arm in arm with
Ruth, they entered the woods:

Summer is a-comin' in,
Loud sing cuckoo . . .

I, also, entered the woods. For a long time I knelt
before one of the stone crosses left by the Mandrakes—
set like a bulwark between enormous oaks to thwart
whatever of evil, griffins, wolves, men, might threaten
my house. My knees sank through the moss to ache
against stone; my lips were dry of prayer. I knelt,
waiting.

I did not turn when the vegetable scent of her was a
palpable touch. I said: "Would you like to live with me
in the mead-hall?"

Her cry was human; anguish born of ecstasy. I might
have said: "Would you like to see the Holy Grail?"

"Serve you?"

"Help me. You and your friends. Share with me."

I leaned to the shy, tentative fingers which loosened
my hair and spread my tresses, as one spreads a fine
brocade to admire its weave and the delicacy of its
figures.

"Bantling," she said. "Madonna-beautiful." What had
John said? "I love your hair when it's loose. It's like a
halo . . ." Roses and I have this in common: we have
been judged too kindly by the softness of our petals.

"I must go now. Those in the mead-hall would not
welcome you. I shall have to send them away. For your
sake—and theirs. Tomorrow I will meet you here and
take you back with me."

Earth, the mother of roses, has many children.

THE FAIRY PRINCE

By H. C. Bailey

The town was a mess of crowded houses and huts, without form, like a heap of stones. It had been that, indeed, only a little while before. There were many Welshmen who boasted and prayed that it should be so again. But already there lay about it a low girdle of white, and the din and dust of King Edward's Flemish masons arose from sundown to sunset every day. Carnarvon would have its walls before winter drove the English soldiers back across the marches, before the hundred ships that furrowed the straits and lay, a dark forest, in the silver river mouth, fled from the equinox.

It was six hundred years ago, but if you know where to look you may still find the fairy ring on the side of Cefn-du, and the cave from which the little man came. His body was covered with a grey wolf's skin that left arms and legs bare. His head was all black beard and hair. On his left arm he wore a bracelet of wolf's teeth and yellow stones. Beside and behind him stood a woman, who wore a sheepskin dyed with madder. They were both very small and frail, but with the quick life of a wild animal in eye and poise. He spoke to her in a guttural droning language, and turned and went down the mountain side light and very swift of foot. They were of the race who held Wales before the Welshmen came; who wrought their axes and arrow-heads of stone; who were so strange of life that the Welsh accounted them not human nor mortal. They were of the little people whom we call fairies.

It was an evening in early spring, and after a day of showers the sky spread all lucid in pale blue and violet

79

and lavender grey, and the vast jagged mountain peaks seemed close upon the green and silver of the sea. Some way down the slope the little man checked and stood at gaze. He looked across stony, barren land to the rich, dark vale of the Seiont. In among its blue-green tilth were patches of black desolation. He croned some melancholy song, and went on more slowly, swaying as he went. The little people loathed war and its havoc as things unclean.

The hand of the English conqueror lay heavy upon Wales. Llewelyn, her last prince, had been slain, and all his fastnesses were fallen, and the English king held his court in Carnarvon. Still the stubborn mountaineers of Gwynedd would not own him master. The English soldiery might march up and down their valleys and burn every homestead that offered defiance, but till the mountains were laid low there was refuge for every man who dared starvation, and, if they were but a remnant, the rest could go sullenly about their business, yielding no more than they must, and making the English infinite toil and hardship, and promising themselves rebellion at the first chance. Wales was conquered, but no man supposed that it was won, and, least of all men, the king in Carnarvon.

The little man, whom his wife called Corb, went down the valley while twilight fell, and slowly and more slowly, for he would not come near the houses of men who used iron and ate baked bread till nightfall. The stars stood in a dark sky before he came to the gate of Geulan for the "good piece," the sodden goat's meat and the bowl of milk which the womenfolk of David, the maer of the cymwd, ever put outside for the fairies. But on this night "good piece" there was none, and lights were burning in the house, and a roaring din came from it. Corb shrank away, vanishing like a shadow behind the byres. He smelt the loathsome breath of war, and trembled like a wild animal aware of peril.

The house was built of stakes and wattle, roofed with branches and a thatch of furze. Within, two tree trunks, stripped of their bark and polished, supported the centre of the roof. Between them it was open to the sky, and smoke and sparks of a blazing fire shot upwards. The house was round and its earthen floor strewn with rushes. A table stood at one side laden with steaming dishes and horns of mead. At the head of it a rawboned, black-browed fellow lolled in the only chair. He wore a long surcoat, much stained and faded, but gaudy still with a hundred embroideries. By the benches on either hand were a dozen fellows like him, but something less richly put on. They ate ravenously, and shouted at each other over their meat, and loudly and violently when they turned to ask more.

Two women waited on them and a lad, with hate and fear in their eyes. An old man crouched over the fire hugging to his bosom a thing like a rude violin, and crooning to himself. The elder woman whispered something to the younger, a slight, pretty thing, all grace in her close white tunic, and she fled out into the night. The man at the head of the table turned with an oath:

"How now, you witch?" He caught the woman's wrist. "Bring your poppet back. I want her for my sport."

The woman answered nothing, but her eyes told that she understood and defied him. He haled her close and tore off the white veil that she wore folded over her grey hair, and was saying something foul when the lad sprang in and tore her away. The soldier heaved himself up with a laugh: "Here's a snarling puppy!" quoth he, and struck the lad down into the fire. Then he stood holding his sides and chuckling while the woman dragged the senseless body from the flames. "What, you would deny the King's men would you, you Welsh vermin?" he said. "Out into the night with you and cool your blood. Mark you, bring me that girl back, or when we ride in the morning I will leave your homestead ashes." He reached for the old man and dragged him up. "Tell her that in her own whining tongue, you croaking minstrel," he roared, and shook him and hurled him upon the woman who was still kneeling by her son. Then he fell upon them and flung them out, and kicked the stunned boy after them. The others cheered him with laughing oaths, but as he came grinning back with an "I would teach Edward Longshanks a way to ha' done with these Welsh *pardi!*" there was one who twisted a lip and said, "He, too, hath a fancy for teaching at whiles."

They drank up all the mead in the house, and then this captain of theirs, who was called Eustace o' Dover, rolled to the door and howled for the Welsh women. But they were fled away up the valley, and out of the darkness he heard no answer save a strange moaning song that rose and fell like a stormy wind, inhuman. Corb was singing a charm against him and all horsemen, after the manner of the little people when they were troubled by ill passion and violence. Eustace o' Dover fell silent and listened, and felt a chilled sobriety and fear steal over him, and cried a querulous question. But only the moaning of the song answered him, and he barred the door in a hurry and went back to the fire. Certainly the mountains were full of devils.

But in the morning, when sunlight flooded the valley and there was no sound but bird song and the music of the river, he was mighty bold again, and swore the Welsh girl should not escape him. Then said one who had marked his fears, Grey Roger: "Ay, and you swore we should burn the house. But a man grows wise o' nights."

"I'll leave the nest to lure the birds back," quoth Eustace. "By sundown we will have them again." So they rode away.

On that morning the King rode out from Carnarvon with his wolfhounds and his foresters. You see a tower of a man on the great black charger, lean, but huge of bone. His green surcoat is weatherbeaten and worn. The hat slung behind him leaves his close dark curls bare to the wind. It is a square-wrought head borne boldly, and never still, as his eyes look all ways. For all the dark curls, beard and moustache are red gold.

They were to rouse a wolf in the glens beneath Tryfan, but the din of war had driven the beasts from their haunts, and vainly the hounds ranged round Tryfan and across the valley to the glens beneath Moel Eilio. There they found, and to wild music thundered on up and down the glens towards Cefn-du.

So the little people saw them from their cave, and Corb stole out to join the sport. Never a fairy but counted it good work done to spoil a hunt that came nigh his dwelling, and these huntsmen were of the hated folk who had brought war to the mountains. So Corb laughed as he flitted on. Over the brow of a hill he caught the wolf's foam flecks from the furze and laid them on another line, and broke puff balls, and flung himself down in a tarn. Off on the false scent the hounds sped, and from above, from a cave, another of the little people echoed a wolf's yelp, and the hounds answered madly. But when the King crested the hill he marked the quarry against the skyline beyond the glen and checked a moment, and shouted to his foresters to whip the hounds back from the false scent, and dashed right on. The foresters rode off with blowing of horn and hallooing, but the din of wolves from the caves had made the hounds mad, and they would not be turned. So the foresters thundered after them, falling further and still further behind, while the King rode alone after his quarry.

Once and again he saw the wolf, and then in the combes to northward lost him altogether, and drew rein swearing, and turned to search for the hounds; but they were far away on the slopes above Llyn Padarn. He heard a shout, and rode to it. But that shout came from Corb, who lurked on the hillside above a bog. Again came the shout, and the King put spurs to his weary horse. The next moment green sward yielded beneath them with a hollow sucking sound, and the horse neighed in wild terror and plunged, and black slime rose like spray. The King hurled himself from the saddle, and, wriggling on the mire that sucked at him, reached a tussock of rushes, and another and another, and haled himself panting on to solid earth.

He had his reins still, and braced himself and flung back his shoulders and hauled at them, shouting jollily. Madly the horse struggled, ruthlessly the King hauled at the reins, and as though he were swimming in mud the horse plunged on, slowly, slowly, till his hoofs found something firm beneath the mire, and, with an ugly gulp of the sucking bog, he came out and stood streaming slime and shivering. And the King, who had no breath left to speak, whose sides were heaving as his, caressed him and leaned upon his neck.

Slowly down the hillside came Corb, sobbing fear. Behold, he had dared a mad deed. He had mocked at a magician. Never since the world began had man or beast fallen into that bog and come out again alive. But this giant had saved his horse and himself. Plainly a giant endued with the mastery of the elements, lord of earth and water and air and fire, a magician to be worshipped like the storm-cloud. Fearing doom for himself and all the little people, came Corb.

And behold the giant began to laugh! Corb was so quaint a thing, like a goblin from some minister's carving, so little and hairy, and bowed and quaking with fear. Corb bowed himself to the very ground, and put dirt upon his head. The giant laughed louder. Corb quaked the more. Such awful mirth must be omen of a grim doom. "Who art thou, o' God's Name?" the King roared. "Nay, nay, if thou art man do not play the worm." For Corb had gone down grovelling. The King heaved him up by his wolfskin, and "Welsh art thou, little man?" he cried. And seeing that Corb understood nothing, he stumbled the question out in Welsh words.

Corb shook his head vehemently. "Of the mountain men," he said, calling his race by the name themselves used. "Of the little people"—that was the Welsh name for them.

"A hobgoblin, *pardi!*" the King cried. "A fairy man!" and laughed again. "Well, Sieur Fairy, hast a house for me or so much as a stable? Our stomachs cry manger." He made some more broken Welsh and signs, and Corb understood him, and, turning, beckoned him on. If this dread magician wanted no more than a meal he could be taken to the homestead of David the maer and left there, while Corb fled away to his cave.

The day was waning now, and the shadows of the mountains lay black across the glens. Before they came to the homestead—the King's horse was lame—the sun was gone, and light and shadow mingled in a cool grey mist.

Eustace and his men had been before them. All day Eustace lurked in a combe above the steading, and when he saw the Welsh women creep back through the shadows of sundown, he broke in for his prey. The boy tried to bar the door against him, and was dashed aside. Eustace snatched the girl with a loud laugh, and crushed her to his breast. She made no sound, only she fought him with every muscle of body and limb, fierce, indomitable. Her mother stood aloof, giving no cry nor aiding her, but staring at the Englishman hate and a cruel defiance. The rest of the soldiery began to jeer and laugh. For all his bulk and strength, Eustace could not master his lithe quarry. He cursed her, and put a hand to his dagger. Then Grey Roger waddled up and gripped his wrist, and chuckled: "Nay, nay, my master. Naked hand to naked hand is vantage enough for any man. And I'll lay a noble on the lass."

The others laughed, but Eustace buffeted him off with an oath. "Out on you, knave. Who leads this troop, thou or I?"

"The lass is the better man," Roger chuckled; and, indeed, the girl tore herself free and darted away and crouched behind her mother, clinging to her. The troop broke out in a great roar of laughter. Eustace strode upon her again cursing, but now Roger stood in his way. "No, by my faith! The lass hath won the bout, and Bully Eustace pays forfeit by all the laws of arms. How say you, lads?"

"Forfeit, forfeit!" they chuckled.

"I will ha' forfeit o' thy bones, Bully Roger," Eustace roared. "Stand off, I say. And you——" he grasped at the girl.

He was suddenly aware of silence. The room was still as death. He turned and looked into the eyes of the King and let the girl go, and shrank back and made a salute and shrank back again.

"Say your say," growled the King.

Eustace looked at him a moment and down again at the ground. "I ha' nought to say," he muttered.

"Till I came you had enough to say, methinks," quoth the King. He looked round the house, at its dishevelled ugliness, the scattered refuse of food, the cowering woman, the mass of ashes on the hearth where the old minstrel crouched and fumbled, seeking among them the seed of fire. For if once the fire was out the life of the house was gone.

"Come hither, woman," he said in his stumbling Welsh. "Fear nothing. I am the King."

"There is no King in Wales," she said fiercely. "Our King Llewelyn is dead and hath left no seed."

He looked down at her haughtily, and for a moment there was silence. On a sudden Grey Roger darted to the door and peered out and thrust it to and barred it, and turning with his back against it hissed out, "Sir, there are Welsh spearmen all about us."

The King sat himself down on a bench. "Who is captain here?" he said, placidly.

Eustace saluted again.

"Methinks you have work to do," the King smiled grim.

"We will bear you safe through them, sir," Eustace muttered.

"They should have our horses by now," said the King.

Roger turned from the lattice window. "The horses are taken," said he. "I reckon the Welshmen a hundred and more."

"A hundred and more," said the King, quietly. "Well, sir, I reckon you no paladin to fight a host. What brought them down on you?"

"It must be the imp of a boy," Eustace muttered; and then the woman laughed loud.

The King turned to her: "What had he done to your boy?"

"What have you done to all Wales?" she cried, fiercely.

The King glanced at her daughter. "What hath he done by you, mistress?"

"Nothing, nothing! I am not hurt"; and she laughed.

The woman came a step nearer, and her eyes flamed at him: "Fool, fool!" she cried. "I made her the bait to tempt your wild beasts to their death, and now you, too, are caught."

With grave eyes the King considered her and turned away. "It seems that you are a very skillful captain, Master Eustace," said he. "Go to, order your battle."

"We can hold the house," said Eustace, sullenly.

"And if they fire it?" quoth Roger.

"They'll not fire it while the women are in."

"I do not like your battle," said the King. "The women shall go out to their kinsfolk, and with them, Master

Eustace, go you and I, for I think it is I and you whom these Welshmen would choose."

Eustace started back. "Not you, my lord!" he cried. "I will go. Yes, *pardi*, I will go yield myself, and the others may hold the house with the women and hold you safe till help comes from Carnarvon. I will go."

There was a scream from the old minstrel: "The seed of fire! The seed lives!" He had found a living ember and blown it red, and was feeding it with dried furze and the flames leapt up. "The soul of the house is not dead!" and he began a wild, hoarse song.

The King stood up and laid his hand on Eustace's shoulder. "We go together," he said. "For the rest— stand to your arms, hold out to the end." He strode to the door and drew the bar and beckoned the women. Slowly, amazed they came, and close behind them Eustace and he marched out on the Welsh spears.

In the misty twilight they saw saffron cloaks clustering and the spearheads glitter. The girl's mother cried out: "Iestyn! Iestyn! we have trapped their King. See, he follows after me to render himself." There was a rustle, like the sound of bees in a grove of limes on a summer's day, and the Welshmen were all round them—a mob of sturdy, small men, for the most part with no armour above their tunics and saffron cloaks, for the most part bare-legged and bare-foot; but some few with little coats of mail and battle-axe, and sword in place of spear. They all chattered together. One who seemed the leader, not much more than a lad, and beardless, thrust through the midst and laid his hand on the King's arm, crying, "Yield thee to me, Iestyn, son of David, son of Owen."

The King laughed, and put on his hand a hand that swallowed it up. "I am your King," he said.

"He is taken. He shall pay the blood debt for David thy father, for Llewelyn our prince," the woman cried, and there were shouts.

"I am your King," he said again. "I come not to yield myself, but to do you justice."

But it was plain that they made nothing of his broken Welsh. They were muttering and pressing closer when the girl cried out: "He is our King. He comes not to yield himself, but to do us justice."

Then the crowd surged one way and another with a roar of talk, and Iestyn, the leader, turned upon his sister as her mother clutched her: "Nest! What sayest thou? They have wronged thee even as——"

"I am not wronged. I am my own," she cried.

Her mother screamed out: "The Englishman there, he laid hands upon her. He beat down Idwal into the fire."

"I am the King," the deep voice thundered. He smiled at the girl. "Speak my words in thy tongue, wench."

So clear tones ringing phrase for phrase with the deep, it came in Welsh and English. "He says: 'I am the King. I come to assure you justice on this man who hath wronged the homestead here, and justice on any man whosoever that wrongs man or maid of you. For I will show favour to none that plunders or does violence, and of me the humblest serf in Wales shall have his equal right. I am your King.' "

Then there was silence awhile and looks of wonder and questioning, and then a wave of chatter, and the woman cried out: "An English king is no king of ours. We will have a Welshman to our prince."

But as she spoke the blast of a horn broke through her words, and they were all hushed and straining to listen. The boom and clang of men-at-arms came near, and a man thrust breathless through the throng, crying: "The English knights!"

Iestyn, the leader, gripped the King's arm harder, and his mother cried out: "The blood debt! The blood debt! Strike while you may!"

But the girl screamed: "They came out to us with naked hands, Iestyn!" And Iestyn wavered, and his spearmen swayed and surged, and some gathered together and ran upon the King. Eustace hurled himself in the way, and their points clashed upon his coat of mail and slipped aside, but he was borne down. Falling, he snatched at Nest and dragged her with him, and shouted: "The girl dies if you strike the King!"

With an oath the King tore her away from him; but she, laughing wildly, cried out: "Let be, let it be so, my lord," and struggled, and falling again into Eustace's arms, shrieked, "I die if you strike the King."

On the tumult the English horsemen broke, and the

Welsh scattered before them. But the King shouted: "Halt! Halt! We be all friends here. Who strikes, strikes the King."

Then their captain rode up and saluted. "Orders, sir?" he asked, gruffly.

"Have this fellow in guard, Bertram," quoth the King, thrusting at Eustace with his foot. He hauled the girl up again, and "Speak for me, mistress," he said. "I charge you all come to me in Carnarvon on St. Mark's Day. Then shall you see this knave who hath wronged you judged before a Welsh prince. For I will give you a prince that was born in Wales, and can speak no word of English, and he shall rule you according to the ancient laws of Wales."

Then the woman muttered: "A fairy prince!"

And the King laughed. "Come and see."

The dawn of St. Mark's Day broke grey and golden over the mountains, and a haze of misty rain fled up the straits before the rising wind. In the huddled streets of Carnarvon garlands and chains of branches tossed and rustled and gleamed. Soon the town was teeming with people, the streets all eddying, crowded life. There were men-at-arms with coifs of mail and steel caps glittering above their blazoned surcoats, and the craftsmen and traders had on their gayest jerkins of russet and sarcitis and even marble cloth, each with a sprig of sweet herbs stuck in his cap. The girls had bound their hair with flowers or fillets of white, and their mothers' gorgets were never so gay, and never had the Welsh town seen such a show of scarlet and purple tyretaine. Among all these you might see the white head cloths, folded like crowns, of Welsh women and Welsh saffron and madder gowns, and Welshmen holding together in little companies, muttering together, and looking askance at the Englishry, bare-legged and bare-footed, unarmed or hiding their arms beneath cloak and tunic. Beyond the half-built walls, where no guards were set, all along the green valleys beyond eyeshot, there were splashes of colour, white and crimson and gold, where from each homestead and hamlet Welsh folk were hurrying to the town.

Close above the quay, where the old tower stood green and yellow with lichen, where the first courses of the walls already marked the plan of the new castle, the yeomen of the King's household kept clear a great space. There flaunted banners, the three lions of England, gold upon red; the red cross of St. George, the three crowns of St. Edmund, gold upon blue; the cross and martlets of St. Edward the Confessor, in blue and gold. In a little while, when the crowd was already a score ranks deep beyond the barriers and the halberds, English nobles and knights came in state to the open space in the midst. "There had they many rich ornaments, broidered on cendals and samites; many a fair pennon fixed on a lance, many a banner displayed," so that the gay spring air was alive with lions and leopards and stags and boars and trees and cinquefoil and roses and stars in all the colours of heraldry.

There was a daïs covered in crimson with gilt chairs upon it, and above a canopy all white and gold. Two hours before noon, marshalled by heralds in their tabards and led by the Justiciar of Wales, came a company of the Uchelwyr, the men of note among the Welsh. They were unarmed like the English knights, and their women walked with them; but against the English they were of a strange simplicity: no long trains nor mantles of velvet on the women, no broidery of gold to their gorgets and wimples; and the men, neither clean-shaven nor bearded like the English, but all with moustaches. The men had only cloaks and tunics that left knee and leg bare to their wadded boots, and there were but the three colours, white and saffron and madder, among them all.

When they were drawn up in ranks before the daïs, the trumpets sounded, and out from the tower came King Edward and his Queen. A gold diadem glittered on his close dark curls; her black hair flowed upon her shoulders from a band of gold. He wore a gown of red and gold, and her mantle was gold and white. Behind them walked the pageant of their lords and ladies. To the daïs they came and saluted the people and sat them down, and Robert Burnell, the Chancellor, a heavy man of heavy head, took stand beside the King; and beside the Queen came the women with the baby son that had been born to her in Carnarvon a little while before. Then the King stood up, a giant of a man, and he smiled down at the Queen, who sat very still and pale, her hands nervous on the white silk of her mantle. The Chancellor turned and made a sign to a black-gowned monk, and he came forward, and as the King spoke, spoke sentence for sentence in Welsh.

"My good folk of Wales," the King cried, "to have your goodwill as I have your obedience I have bidden you here to-day. Ye have told me that ye will be content to take for your Prince any man so he be a Welshman. Say ye so still?"

Then there came from the Welsh folk before him mutterings and cries and shouts, and the monk turned to the King: "They say they will welcome any Prince to Wales that is Welshman born. But none other."

The King laughed. "I will name you a Prince," he cried, "if you will follow and obey him whom I name."

And again there was muttering and shouting, and the monk turned and said: "So they swear to do if the King shall appoint one of their nation."

The King strode forward: "I will name you one that was born in Wales and can speak never a word of English. In whose life and conversation you shall find nought of Englishry."

Whereat the Welsh shouted loud and long, and the monk said: "For such an one they swear to give their lives."

Then the King took from the captain of his yeomen, Sir Bertram Daylesford, his shield, and on it put his baby son that lay there murmuring softly, and he held the shield with its burden aloft and cried: "Behold your Prince! Here in Carnarvon was he born, and of England he knows nought. I give you mine own son to guard you. Hold him dear and cherish him, Prince of Wales."

For a moment there was silence. Then the air was rent with shouts and laughter. After a while, from the midst of the Welsh folk, came out an old man and said: "Him we will hold dear and cherish, and for him we will give our lives," and again the shouts rose loud.

The King called out for silence: "Look you, the first thing that your Prince shall do shall be justice. Stand forth you, Iestyn, and your mother and your sister. Bring me that knave Eustace." Iestyn came from the crowd, flushed and uneasy, leading his mother Etthil, and the girl Nest clung to her. Two yeomen marched Eustace up. Then the King lowered the shield. "Here is one that hath wronged a Welsh homestead," he cried. "Look, child!" and he made the baby look at Eustace, who was indeed no pretty sight, so that the baby cried bitterly. "Thy doom is said," quoth the King, grimly. "Take him away and let him hang," and Eustace bowed his head.

Then the girl Nest cried out: "My lord, my lord!" and flung wide her arms.

And her mother said quickly: "No, no! the babe must not send him to death."

And Iestyn drew himself up: "My lord, let the first thing we have of our Prince be mercy."

The King put the child aside and said: "Hearken, Welsh folk! here be some of you that ask mercy on an Englishman that hath wronged a Welsh home. How say you?"

Loudly, they shouted "Mercy! Mercy!"

"So be it," quoth the King. "Let him go!" and the yeomen left their hold of Eustace, and he slunk away, and the eyes of the girl Nest followed him. "But hereafter, if any man whosoever doth wrong to Welsh folk their Prince will hold him to stern account."

Again the shouts rose wildly, and in eager ranks the Welsh came up to look upon their Prince as he lay in his mother's arms.

That night in the caves of the little people it was told that peace had come again to Wales, and Corb and all the little people knew that it was their work.

THE UGLY UNICORN

Jessica Amanda Salmonson

In a garden in China five hundred years ago, there was a maiden whose eyes were so pretty, it was difficult to believe she was blind.

The blind girl's name was Kwa Wei. She was befriended by the Liu-mu, a homely silver-haired creature like a one-horned jackass. As Kwa Wei was blind, she had no idea the Liu-mu was ugly.

It came the first time in spring. Kwa Wei had been smelling orange blossoms and plums. On hearing the beast's hoofs upon the lawn, she thought it was a pony broken loose from Uncle Lu Wei's stables.

It was friendly, so she petted its head, and felt the single horn, blunt at the end.

At once she thought it had to be a young Poh, the strongest and most beautiful unicorn of the many kinds that live in China. She clapped her hands and giggled. "It's a Poh! Have you come to visit me in my darkness? I'm glad!"

The Liu-mu was too embarrassed and ashamed to say, "I am not the strong, good-looking Poh, but only an unfortunate Liu-mu." He had never been mistaken for anything beautiful until now. So all he said was, "Yes, I have come to visit you."

"Oh! How I wish I could see you with these useless eyes!" said Kwa Wei, and giggled anew.

The Liu-mu lowered his broad head until the blunt horn touched the ground. His eyes were as sad as a deer's.

"Would you like a ride through the garden?" asked the Liu-mu. Kwa Wei clapped her hands delightedly and climbed upon the ugly unicorn. "Hold on to my mane," he said, then trotted off through a maze of hedges.

Such creatures as the Liu-mu are able to run through more than one world. Kwa Wei knew at once that the garden had changed. The air was thicker with perfume. Grander flowers pressed around her as she rode around and about Fairyland.

"Wheee!" exclaimed Kwa Wei, feeling the gentle wind in her hair. "Faster!" she said, laughing. "Faster!"

"Not too fast," said the Liu-mu. "I'll get worn out."

Such was the first meeting of Kwa Wei and the ugly unicorn.

The girl's uncle was a famous general under the rule of Duke Ling. Such important families live sad and violent lives.

On the day of Kwa Wei's birth, it had been arranged that she would marry Hah Ling Me, Duke Ling's grandson. When the girl was two years old, she became ill and lost her sight. She hardly remembered what it was like to see.

It was difficult to dissolve a marriage agreement between important families. Year after year, Duke Ling wished that Kwa Wei would die, so that his favorite grandson needn't be burdened with a blind wife. If the marriage agreement were cancelled, there might be war between Duke Ling and his own general.

As for Uncle Lu Wei, he knew it was a painful situation. Over the years he had sought the aid of famous physicians from all over China.

"Her eyes are so beautiful," he said. "Why can't you make them work?"

The physicians could do nothing.

When his niece approached the year of marriage, Uncle Lu sent in desperation for the wizard-woman of Mount Tzu.

The wizard-woman was thin and tiny and wrinkled. She looked like an old fairy, that's how small she was. She had no teeth and her nose was so small you could hardly see it. She looked into Kwa Wei's face and in her eyes and finally said, "She can be cured."

Lu Wei was delighted. "How can she be cured?" he asked.

"It requires only the rind of an orange and the pit of a plum, ground together with the horn of a Liu-mu."

Uncle Lu's spirits fell. "I have oranges and plums in my garden. They will bear fruit soon. But as to the horn of the Liu-mu, who has ever seen one?"

To Kwa Wei the little old wizard-woman said, "Pretty girl, would you like to be able to see through those eyes?"

"I cannot remember what it was like to see," she said. "The world is very nice even so." Then wistfully she added, "But I would like to see my friend the Poh, the most beautiful unicorn in China."

"Have you the Poh as your friend?"

"Yes I do."

"Well, you may go now. I must speak to your uncle in private."

When the blind girl left the hall, the wizard-woman said to Lu Wei: "There were silver hairs on her dress. They are the hairs of the Liu-mu. It may have represented itself as a glorious Poh, being ashamed of its ugliness."

From her bag of medicine, the wizard-woman retrieved two cubes of sugar. She said, "This is Liu-mu poison. The Liu-mu is intelligent and will not eat from the hand of anyone it doesn't know. Kwa Wei herself must feed the Liu-mu the poison. Then you can tear out the horn from its brow and grind it with the orange peel and plum pit. When Kwa Wei eats biscuits made of this mixture, her eyes will be cured."

When the wizard-woman returned to her mountain retreat, Uncle Lu sat in his high-backed wooden chair and sighed. He said to himself, "I must let Kwa Wei believe the Liu-mu is a Poh. I must trick her into believing these poisonous cubes are sugar for her pet Poh. When the Liu-mu is dead, I will take its horn to make the curative biscuits. But Kwa Wei must never know how it happened, or she will be unhappy. It is a sad thing, but if I do not do it, there will be war with Duke Ling."

Uncle Lu was not a bad man. Nevertheless, he planned to do this bad thing. Kwa Wei would have her sight; she would be able to marry her betrothed; no one would be offended, so there would be no war. What was the life of the Liu-mu, which after all was ugly, compared to all these good outcomes? Even so, Uncle Lu felt terrible.

The following afternoon, Kwa Wei once more rode the Liu-mu in and out of Fairyland. "I smell a flower unlike anything in my uncle's garden!" she said excitedly. "What does it look like, oh most beautiful and strong Poh?"

"It looks like a persimmon tree, but its flowers are lacy hollow balls that glow in the middle."

"Oh! And I smell something like a tulip tree, but it's different!"

"Its leaves are purple and red, but its flowers are emerald green."

"Is it true?" Kwa Wei asked. "Fairyland is a beautiful place for a unicorn as beautiful as you."

The Liu-mu felt guilty not to admit it was not a Poh-unicorn. To make amends for his lie, he said to the rider on his back: "I would like to take you to visit the Vale of the Unicorns."

"Is there such a Vale?" asked Kwa Wei enthusiastically.

"The Vale of the Unicorns is terrifyingly beautiful, so much so that mortals go blind if they see it. As you are already blind, it will be perfectly safe. Even without your sight, you will feel the beauty, and smell the beauty, and hear the beauty of the Vale of the Unicorns."

Therefore the Liu-mu took his rider toward two stone lanterns. The lanterns began to grow until they were as large as temples. Then Kwa Wei and the ugly unicorn were in the Vale of the Unicorns. The first unicorn they met was the fierce Hiai-chi. It was humming to itself a primitive chant in a deep voice. If birds were as big as dragons, they might sound like the humming Hiai-chi.

"What is making such a deep song?" asked Kwa Wei, clinging tightly to the Liu-mu's curly mane.

"It is my friend the Hiai-chi. You can say hello to it."

"Hello, Hiai-chi. I have come to the Vale of the Unicorns riding the beautiful, strong Poh."

The Hiai-chi was a unicorn twice the size of an elephant. Its horn sprouted between the eyes of its dragon head. It had a tail like a hundred brooms and a mane like a lion. When this wonderful animal heard Kwa Wei say she was riding on a Poh, the Hiai-chi began to laugh in its bass voice. It said, "Are you riding on a Poh? Ha ha ha! You're a funny maiden!"

"Yes, I am the Poh-unicorn," said the Liu-mu sternly, and the Hiai-chi stopped laughing.

"You have a marvelous voice to chant with," said Kwa Wei. "Will you chant sutras for my Uncle Lu, who has been unhappy for several days?"

"I will chant sutras for your uncle," said the Hiai-chi. Then Kwa Wei and the ugly unicorn went elsewhere in the Vale. The next beast they encountered was the Kio-toan tiger-unicorn. It had striped fur and three pairs of legs. Its horn was like a licorice-and-orange candy stick. It was purring like a big kitten.

"What a pleasant sound," said Kwa Wei. "What sort of unicorn is it?"

"The tiger-unicorn, Kio-toan," said the Liu-mu. "If you reach over to one side, you can scratch behind one of its ears."

Kwa Wei scratched behind the Kio-toan's ear. The beast purred louder. "Such gentle hands!" said the Kio-toan. "Scratch a little to the left."

"I'm glad to meet you," said Kwa Wei as she continued to scratch behind the ear. "As I am blind, the beauty of the Vale cannot hurt me. Even without sight, I can tell that it is a splendid place. And the tiger-unicorn is almost as lovely as the Poh that I am riding."

The Kio-toan laughed. "So that is a Poh you are riding? Well, thank you for the nice rub behind my ear."

The next unicorn they met was the Pih Sie, a little goat-unicorn with long white fur, golden eyes, and sweet pink lips. It made a sound like a gentle lamb and Kwa Wei guessed at once, "It's the Pih Sie! Oh, sweet little goat-unicorn, am I glad to meet you, riding as I am on China's most beautiful unicorn, the Poh!"

"That is very funny," said the Pih Sie in a musical voice. "That is funny indeed. This is the most beautiful Poh, is it?"

"Yes I am," said the Liu-mu. "Don't pretend you don't know me."

"I know you very well, Master Poh, O Most Beautiful Among Us. But that ugly fellow over there among the peony flowers knows you better."

Among the peony flowers stood the actual Poh, a graceful horned horse with strength to devour lions. Suddenly the Liu-mu began to tremble.

"What's wrong?" asked Kwa Wei, feeling her friend shake.

The Poh spoke with the voice of an angelic being. "The Poh that you are riding is afraid because I am the vicious Kutiao, the leopard-unicorn. I am usually dangerous. But here in the Vale of the Unicorns, I am harmless. Don't worry about me, strong and beautiful Poh-unicorn, Ruler of the Vale of Unicorns. But as you leave, take care not to run into the ugly face of the Liu-mu, or your friend might not think the Vale is excellent after all."

Then the Poh, pretending to be a leopard-unicorn, leapt across the hedge of peonies and was gone.

The Liu-mu, ashamed of itself, took Kwa Wei back toward the temple-sized lanterns. The two stone lanterns began to shrink until they were ordinary garden decorations. Then Kwa Wei recognized the sounds and smells of her uncle's garden.

"I am glad you took me to that place," said Kwa Wei as she climbed down from the back of the ugly unicorn. "The biggest surprise was the Kutiao. I never would have guessed a leopard-unicorn would sound like an angel instead of a grouchy old leopard."

"Kwa Wei," said the Liu-mu. "What if I weren't the most beautiful unicorn in China, but only an unfortunate Liu-mu that looks like a silly old donkey."

"Ha ha!" laughed Kwa Wei. "It could never be true, so why think about it? You are gentle and the best friend anyone could have. What could you be but the strong and gorgeous Poh? Anyway, you are the most beautiful to me."

Then remembering something, Kwa Wei opened the pouch dangling from her belt, and removed two sugar cubes. She said, "Uncle Lu gave me these candies and said they would be a nice treat for my friend the Poh.

Here, this one's your reward for taking me through the Vale of the Unicorns."

"Thank you, I accept," said the Liu-mu as it ate the sugar.

Kwa Wei laughed musically and said, "I'm a selfish girl, so I'll eat the other one myself." She put it right in her mouth. It was tasty but it made her head swim. She said goodbye to the ugly unicorn and started away through the familiar garden.

When it was time for the day's last meal, Kwa Wei did not show up at the table. Servants went to find out what she was doing. They found her on the ground outside the mansion, unable to get up. She was carried to bed and the local physician was sent for. Uncle Lu Wei arrived to see what was wrong. Kwa Wei said, "Oh, Uncle, I don't feel very well. Do I have to eat my dinner?"

"Not if you don't want to," said Uncle Lu.

The doctor said, "It is something in her stomach. What did you eat today, young mistress Kwa Wei?"

The girl replied, "Nothing since lunch, except a piece of candy."

Lu Wei became pale when he heard this. He backed out of the room, stumbling. When the doctor came out, Kwa Wei's uncle said, "She has eaten Liu-mu poison prepared by the wizard-woman of Mount Tzu. What can we do?"

"She must have the antidote in two or three hours or she will die," said the doctor.

Soldiers employed by Uncle Lu Wei, along with everyone else available in and around his mansion, were sent immediately to Mount Tzu to search for the wizard-woman. Lu Wei himself went, it was so important.

Every afternoon, Duke Ling's favorite grandson, young master Hah Ling Me, visited the old ruler for a game of checkers. But today, the old man's favorite grandson hadn't come. When a servant went to check on Hah Ling Me and find out why he was tardy, they discovered, stretched out on the floor in the young man's house, an ugly unicorn too sick to stand up.

Soldiers came and surrounded the sick animal and pointed spears at him. "What have you done with Hah Ling Me!" demanded one of the soldiers.

The sick unicorn said, "I am none other than Hah Ling Me, too sick to return to my human shape."

The soldiers weren't sure they believed it, but took the sick Liu-mu to the palace on the back of a cart. Duke Ling came out into the yard to talk to the Liu-mu. He recognized Hah Ling Me's sorrowful eyes and gentle voice. "Grandfather," said the ugly unicorn, "as I was never allowed to see my betrothed, General Lu Wei's niece, I took this other form to see her in her uncle's garden. Now I am sick and cannot change back."

Duke Ling looked around at the members of his household, who were gathered in the yard to see the ugly unicorn. Then the duke announced the long hidden secret:

"My son Prince Ling, who died in brave battle ten years ago, had three wives. His favorite was Princess Chu, who vanished after the death of my son. It was often rumored that the beautiful woman was a fairy princess, and that she returned to Fairyland after the death of her husband. She left behind their only child, young master Hah Ling Me, a homely boy, but so gentle and kind that everyone loved him. As you can see, he is a fairy-boy after all, and has fallen ill in his other shape as a Liu-mu. There is only one person with the skill to nurse a Liu-mu: the wizard-woman of Mount Tzu. All my soldiers and even the scullery maids and servants must go at once to Mount Tzu to find the wizard-woman in order to save my fairy grandson."

Everyone from Lu Wei's mansion had already rushed into the mountains to seek the wizard-woman. The exception was one nurse who remained at pitiful Kwa Wei's side, mopping her brow with a silk rag. The girl moaned. Suddenly there was a commotion against the outside wall of the bedroom, as though something were trying to knock the mansion over.

The nurse hurried to a place beside the door to the hallway and grabbed a long wooden pole. She stood ready to fight. But when the wall crumbled, the nurse saw a big animal, China's most beautiful unicorn, its one horn as long as a spear, its nostrils flaring, its four hooves like big hammers pounding the floor of the bedroom.

The nurse dropped her fighting-stick and fell down in a swoon.

Kwa Wei sat up slowly and asked, "Is it an earthquake? Why has the wall fallen in?"

Then Kwa Wei heard the huge footsteps and asked, "Who is it?"

"You have met me once before," said the Poh, and Kwa Wei recognized the angelic voice.

"You are the leopard-unicorn! You said you were dangerous outside the Vale of the Unicorns. Will you eat me?"

"I am not the leopard-unicorn, but the ruler of unicorns, the Poh that all call beautiful. I said I was the Kutiao because your friend the Liu-mu pretended to be me."

"My dear friend is not the Poh but the Liu-mu?"

"Now you know the truth. He is the ugliest of unicorns. He is also sick, just like you, because you both ate poison. Come quickly! Ride upon my shoulders! I will take you to the only one that can save your life!"

Kwa Wei struggled from beneath the covers and went to the Poh's side wearing her silk nightgown. The Poh-unicorn knelt so that Kwa Wei could climb wearily onto the strong white shoulders. Then the Poh leapt through the hole in the wall and ran across the tops of trees.

Duke Ling's soldiers and servants and Duke Ling himself were all in the mountains looking for the wizard-woman, leaving behind one elderly gardener to stand over the sick Liu-mu. When the gardener saw the fiercely beautiful Poh running toward the castle, right across the tops of trees, what could the old man do but hide in the bushes?

The Poh and its rider, Lu Wei's blind niece, landed gracefully in the yard. The elderly gardener trembled as he saw the Poh snatch up the Liu-mu in its mouth as a mother cat snatches up a kitten. Then the Poh ran off in the direction of a small stone garden ornament, where the Poh, the Liu-mu, and General Lu Wei's blind niece, disappeared.

Just like Kwa Wei's nurse, Duke Ling's gardener fainted.

Goodness! What a strange story! Does anyone know what is likely to happen next? The most beautiful unicorn in China, with the most ugly unicorn held by the scruff, and the beautiful blind maiden riding on its back, hurried into Fairyland where the Poh deposited its cargo before the throne of the Fairy Queen.

The queen lived in a crystal palace. She was more beautiful than mortal eyes can tell. She kept at the side of her throne a small bag that looked exactly like the bag owned by the wrinkled old wizard-woman of Mount Tzu. Was it possible that the withered up mountain hag and this beautiful queen were the same woman? Who knows! In any case, the Fairy Queen was instantly able to cure Kwa Wei and the Liu-mu of the poison.

When the Liu-mu opened its eyes, it turned into the homely but sweet young master Hah Ling Me, Duke Ling's grandson. He looked up at the Queen of Fairyland and exclaimed, "Mother! I haven't seen you in so long! I thought you must have died. I was sad!"

"You were meant for the mortal world, Hah Ling Me, and you were meant for this mortal girl. But your grandfather Duke Ling didn't want you to marry her because she is blind. Due to my tricks, I have gotten you together. Now you will be married in Fairyland where no one can stop you. You will be sent home with many wedding presents to start your own house and be independent of the families Ling and Wei. You can do what you please from now on."

"And will you cure my bride of blindness?" asked Hah Ling Me.

"Fairies cannot undo what Gods require. The only cure for her blindness involves your death, Hah Ling Me."

"I will gladly die for Kwa Wei!" said Hah Ling Me.

"Wait a minute," said Kwa Wei. "Have I complained because I'm blind? If I had my vision, you could never again take me to the Vale of the Unicorns, because in the first place you'd be dead, and second of all, if I saw the Vale with my eyes, it would blind me! I want to marry you, Hah Ling Me, oh most beautiful boy in China!"

"I am not beautiful, Kwa Wei, but you are very beautiful. Can you really marry such an ugly fellow?"

Kwa Wei laughed as though it were a joke. "Anyway," she said, "let's get married right now."

Up on the side of Mount Tzu, the soldiers and household members of Duke Ling's palace had come to blows with the soldiers and household of Lu Wei's mansion. Scullery maids and stable workers and soldiers used their kung-fu to give each other black eyes and bloody noses. After a while, they were all worn out. Their bones were sore. The fighters were scattered on the ground, sweating and puffing and unable to move. Duke Ling and General Lu Wei shouted for both sides to get up and fight some more. They finally did get up, but not to fight. Instead, a wonderful thing began to happen, and everyone stood to see it.

Coming down from the highest part of the mountain was a wedding-parade of a startling kind. Riding on the back of the Poh were a groom and a bride. Hah Ling Me and Kwa Wei were both dressed in fabulous costumes and wore bright opera paint on their faces. Behind them came a whole train of animals with carts full of useful and valuable objects.

The Pih Sie or goat-unicorn pulled a cart laden with gold coins.

The purring Kio-toan or tiger-unicorn's cart was full of fine lacquered furniture, bolts of cloth that shimmered like precious stones and metals, and swords encrusted with gems.

The Hiai-chi or dragon-unicorn was humming the wedding song. It pulled a gigantic cart on which sat a big house with prettily carved doors and windows and roofs.

Walking alongside this procession was the old wizard-woman of the mountain. She had married them herself. When the procession stopped, the wizard-woman said, "Hah Ling Me and Kwa Wei have been married in Fairyland. These gifts will set them up in their own house. It is for Duke Ling and Lu Wei to decide where the newly-weds' house will be."

"I will give my north acres, closest to Duke Ling's palace," said Uncle Lu Wei happily.

"I will give my south acres, closest to Lu Wei's mansion," said Duke Ling, equally glad.

Then the beat-up and bruised members of the two households began to dance and sing together. They followed the wedding procession down from the mountain.

For five hundred years this story has waited to be told. Now it has been.

THE BROWNIE OF THE BLACK HAGGS

by James Hogg

When the Sprots were Lairds of Wheelhope, which is now a long time ago, there was one of the ladies who was very badly spoken of in the country. People did not just openly assert that Lady Wheelhope (for every landward laird's wife was then styled Lady) was a witch, but every one had an aversion even at hearing her named; and when by chance she happened to be mentioned, old men would shake their heads and say, "Ah! let us alane o' her! The less ye meddle wi' her the better." Old wives would give over spinning, and, as a pretence for hearing what might be said about her, poke in the fire with the tongs, cocking up their ears all the while; and then, after some meaning coughs, hems, and haws, would haply say, "Hech-wow, sirs! An a' be true that's said!" or something equally wise and decisive.

In short, Lady Wheelhope was accounted a very bad woman. She was an inexorable tyrant in her family, quarrelled with her servants, often cursing them, striking them, and turning them away, especially if they were religious, for she could not endure people of that character, but charged them with every thing bad. Whenever she found out that any of the servant men of the Laird's establishment were religious, she gave them up to the military, and got them shot; and several girls that were regular in their devotions, she was supposed to have got rid of by poison. She was certainly a wicked woman, else many good people were mistaken in her character; and the poor persecuted Covenanters were obliged to unite in their prayers against her.

As for the Laird, he was a big, dun-faced, pluffy body,

that cared neither for good nor evil, and did not well know the one from the other. He laughed at his lady's tantrums and barley-hoods; and the greater the rage that she got into, the Laird thought it the better sport. One day, when two maid-servants came running to him, in great agitation, and told him that his lady had felled one of their companions, the Laird laughed heartily, and said he did not doubt it.

"Why, sir, how can you laugh?" said they. "The poor girl is killed."

"Very likely, very likely," said the Laird. "Well, it will teach her to take care who she angers again."

"And, sir, your lady will be hanged."

"Very likely; well, it will teach her not to strike so rashly again—Ha, ha, ha! Will it not, Jessy?"

But when this same Jessy died suddenly one morning, the Laird was greatly confounded, and seemed dimly to comprehend that there had been unfair play going. There was little doubt that she was taken off by poison; but whether the Lady did it through jealousy or not, was never divulged; but it greatly bamboozled and astonished the poor Laird, for his nerves failed him, and his whole frame became paralytic. He seems to have been exactly in the same state of mind with a colley that I once had. He was extremely fond of the gun as long as I did not kill anything with it (there being no game laws in Ettrick Forest in those days), he got a grand chase after the hares when I missed them. But there was one day that I chanced for a marvel to shoot one dead, a few paces before his nose. I'll never forget the astonishment that the poor beast manifested. He stared one while at the gun, and another while at the dead hare, and seemed to be drawing the conclusion, that if the case stood thus, there was no creature sure of its life. Finally, he took his tail between his legs and ran away home, and never would face a gun all his life again.

So was it precisely with Laird Sprot of Wheelhope. As long as his Lady's wrath produced only noise and uproar among the servants, he thought it fine sport; but when he saw what he believed the dreadful effects of it, he became like a barrel organ out of tune, and could only discourse one note, which he did to every one he met.

"I wish she mayna hae gotten something she had been the waur of." This note he repeated early and late, night and day, sleeping and waking, alone and in company, from the moment that Jessy died till she was buried; and on going to the churchyard as chief mourner, he whispered it to her relatives by the way. When they came to the grave, he took his stand at the head, nor would he give place to the girl's father; but there he stood, like a huge post, as though he neither saw nor heard; and when he had lowered her head into the grave and dropped the cord, he slowly lifted his hat with one hand, wiped his dim eyes with the back of the other, and said, in a deep tremulous tone, "Poor lassie! I wish she didna get something she had been the waur of."

This death made a great noise among the common people; but there was little protection for the life of the subject in those days; and provided a man or woman was a real Anti-Covenanter, they might kill a good many without being quarrelled for it. So there was no one to take cognizance of the circumstances relating to the death of poor Jessy.

After this the Lady walked softly for the space of two or three years. She saw that she had rendered herself odious, and had entirely lost her husband's countenance, which she liked worst of all. But the evil propensity could not be overcome; and a poor boy, whom the Laird out of sheer compassion had taken into his service, being found dead one morning, the country people could no longer be restrained; so they went in a body to the Sheriff, and insisted on an investigation. It was proved that she detested the boy, had often threatened him, and had given him brose and butter the afternoon before he died; but notwithstanding of all this, the cause was ultimately dismissed, and the pursuers fined.

No one can tell to what height of wickedness she might now have proceeded, had not a check of a very singular kind been laid upon her. Among the servants that came home at the next term, was one who called himself Merodach; and a strange person he was. He had the form of a boy, but the features of one a hundred years old, save that his eyes had a brilliancy and restlessness, which were very extraordinary, bearing a strong resemblance to the eyes of a well-known species of monkey. He was forward and perverse, and disregarded the pleasure or displeasure of any person; but he performed his work well and with apparent ease. From the moment he entered the house, the Lady conceived a mortal antipathy against him, and besought the Laird to turn him away. But the Laird would not consent; he never turned away any servant, and moreover he had hired this fellow for a trivial wage, and he neither wanted activity nor perseverance. The natural consequence of this refusal was, that the Lady instantly set herself to embitter Merodach's life as much as possible, in order to get early quit of a domestic every way so disagreeable. Her hatred of him was not like a common antipathy entertained by one human being against another—she hated him as one might hate a toad or an adder; and his occupation of jotteryman (as the Laird termed his servant of all work) keeping him always about her hand, it must have proved highly annoying.

She scolded him, she raged at him; but he only mocked her wrath, and giggled and laughed at her, with the most provoking derision. She tried to fell him again and again, but never, with all her address, could she hit him; and never did she make a blow at him, that she did not repent it. She was heavy and unwieldy, and he as quick in his motions as a monkey; besides, he generally contrived that she should be in such an ungovernable rage, that when she flew at him, she hardly knew what she was doing. At one time she guided her blow towards him, and he at the same instant avoided it with such dexterity that she knocked down the chief hind, or foresman; and then Merodach giggled so heartily, that, lifting the kitchen poker, she threw it at him with a full design of knocking out his brains; but the missile only broke every article of crockery on the kitchen dresser.

She then hasted to the Laird, crying bitterly, and telling him she would not suffer that wretch Merodach, as she called him, to stay another night in the family.

"Why, then, put him away, and trouble me no more about him," said the Laird.

"Put him away!" exclaimed she; "I have already ordered him away a hundred times, and charged him never to let me see his horrible face again; but he only grins, and answers with some intolerable piece of impertinence."

The pertinacity of the fellow amused the Laird; his dim eyes turned upwards into his head with delight; he then looked two ways at once, turned round his back, and laughed till the tears ran down his dun cheeks; but he could only articulate, "You're fitted now."

The Lady's agony of rage still increasing from this derision, she upbraided the Laird bitterly, and said he was not worthy the name of man, if he did not turn away that pestilence, after the way he had abused her.

"Why, Shusy, my dear, what has he done to you?"

"What done to me! has he not caused me to knock down John Thomson? and I do not know if ever he will come to life again!"

"Have you felled your favourite John Thomson?" said the Laird, laughing more heartily than before; "you might have done a worse deed than that."

"And has he not broke every plate and dish on the whole dresser?" continued the Lady; "and for all this devastation, he only mocks at my displeasure—absolutely mocks me—and if you do not have him turned away, and hanged or shot for his deeds, you are not worthy the name of man."

"O alack! What a devastation among the cheena metal!" said the Laird; and calling on Merodach, he said, "Tell me, thou evil Merodach of Babylon, how thou daredst knock down thy Lady's favourite servant, John Thomson?"

"Not I, your honour. It was my Lady herself, who got into such a furious rage at me, that she mistook her man, and felled Mr. Thomson; and the good man's skull is fractured."

"That was very odd," said the Laird, chuckling; "I do not comprehend it. But then, what set you on smashing all my Lady's delft and cheena ware?—That was a most infamous and provoking action."

"It was she herself, your honour. Sorry would I be to break one dish belonging to the house. I take all the house servants to witness, that my Lady smashed all the dishes with a poker; and now lays the blame on me!"

The Laird turned his dim eyes on his Lady, who was

crying with vexation and rage, and seemed meditating
another personal attack on the culprit, which he did not
at all appear to shun, but rather to court. She, however,
vented her wrath in threatenings of the most deep and
desperate revenge, the creature all the while assuring her
that she would be foiled, and that in all her encounters
and contests with him, she would uniformly come to the
worst; he was resolved to do his duty, and there before
his master he defied her.

The Laird thought more than he considered it prudent
to reveal; he had little doubt that his wife would find
some means of wreaking her vengeance on the object of
her displeasure; and he shuddered when he recollected
on who had taken "something that she had been the
waur of."

In a word, the Lady of Wheelhope's inveterate malig-
nity against this one object, was like the rod of Moses,
that swallowed up the rest of the serpents. All her wicked
and evil propensities seemed to be superseded if not
utterly absorbed by it. The rest of the family now lived
in comparative peace and quietness; for early and late
her malevolence was venting itself against the jotteryman, and against him alone. It was a delirium of hatred
and vengeance, on which the whole bent and bias of her
inclination was set. She could not stay from the creature's
presence, or, in the intervals when absent from him, she
spent her breath in curses and execrations; and then, not
able to rest, she ran again to seek him, her eyes gleaming
with the anticipated delights of vengeance, while, ever
and anon, all the ridicule and the harm rebounded on
herself.

Was it not strange that she could not get quit of this
sole annoyance of her life? One would have thought she
easily might. But by this time there was nothing farther
from her wishes; she wanted vengeance, full, adequate,
and delicious vengeance, on her audacious opponent. But
he was a strange and terrible creature, and the means of
retaliation constantly came, as it were, to his hand.

Bread and sweet milk was the only fare that Merodach
cared for, and having bargained for that, he would not
want it, though he often got it with a curse and with ill
will. The Lady having, upon one occasion, intentionally

kept back his wonted allowance for some days, on the Sabbath morning following, she set him down a bowl of rich sweet milk, well drugged with a deadly poison; and then she lingered in a little ante-room to watch the success of her grand plot, and prevent any other creature from tasting of the potion. Merodach came in, and the housemaid said to him, "There is your breakfast, creature."

"Oho! my Lady has been liberal this morning," said he; "but I am beforehand with her. Here, little Missie, you seem very hungry today—take you my breakfast." And with that he set the beverage down to the Lady's little favourite spaniel. It so happened that the Lady's only son came at that instant into the ante-room seeking her, and teasing his mamma about something, which withdrew her attention from the hall-table for a space. When she looked again, and saw Missie lapping up the sweet milk, she burst from her hiding-place like a fury, screaming as if her head had been on fire, kicked the remainder of its contents against the wall, and lifting Missie in her bosom, retreated hastily, crying all the way.

"Ha, ha, ha—I have you now!" cried Merodach, as she vanished from the hall.

Poor Missie died immediately, and very privately; indeed, she would have died and been buried, and never one have seen her, save her mistress, had not Merodach, by a luck that never failed him, looked over the wall of the flower garden, just as his lady was laying her favourite in a grave of her own digging. She, not perceiving her tormentor, plied on at her task, apostrophising the insensate little carcass—"Ah! poor dear little creature, thou hast had a hard fortune, and hast drank of the bitter potion that was not intended for thee; but he shall drink it three times double for thy sake!"

"Is that little Missie?" said the eldrich voice of the jotteryman, close at the Lady's ear. She uttered a loud scream, and sank down on the bank. "Alack for poor Missie!" continued the creature in a tone of mockery, "my heart is sorry for Missie. What has befallen her—whose breakfast cup did she drink?"

"Hence with thee, fiend!" cried the Lady; "what right hast thou to intrude on thy mistress's privacy? Thy turn is coming yet; or may the nature of woman change within me!"

"It is changed already," said the creature, grinning with delight; "I have thee now, I have thee now! And were it not to show my superiority over thee, which I do every hour, I should soon see thee strapped like a mad cat, or a worrying bratch. What wilt thou try next?"

"I will cut thy throat, and if I die for it, will rejoice in the deed; a deed of charity to all that dwell on the face of the earth."

"I have warned thee before, dame, and I now warn thee again, that all thy mischief meditated against me will fall double on thine own head."

"I want none of your warning, fiendish cur. Hence with your elvish face, and take care of yourself."

It would be too disgusting and horrible to relate or read all the incidents that fell out between this unaccountable couple. Their enmity against each other had no end, and no mitigation; and scarcely a single day passed over on which the Lady's acts of malevolent ingenuity did not terminate fatally for some favourite thing of her own. Scarcely was there a thing, animate or inanimate, on which she set a value, left to her, that was not destroyed; and yet scarcely one hour or minute could she remain absent from her tormentor, and all the while, it seems, solely for the purpose of tormenting him. While all the rest of the establishment enjoyed peace and quietness from the fury of their termagant dame, matters still grew worse and worse between the fascinated pair. The Lady haunted the menial, in the same manner as the raven haunts the eagle, for a perpetual quarrel, though the former knows that in every encounter she is to come off the loser. Noises were heard on the stairs by night, and it was whispered among the servants, that the Lady had been seeking Merodach's chamber, on some horrible intent. Several of them would have sworn that they had seen her passing and repassing on the stair after midnight, when all was quiet; but then it was likewise well known that Merodach slept with well-fastened doors, and a companion in another bed in the same room, whose bed, too, was nearest the door. Nobody cared much what became of the jotteryman, for he was an unsocial and disagreeable person; but someone told him what they had seen, and hinted a suspicion of the Lady's intent. But the creature only bit his upper lip, winked with his eyes, and said, "She had better let that alone; she will be the first to rue that."

Not long after this, to the horror of the family and the whole countryside, the Laird's only son was found murdered in his bed one morning, under circumstances that manifested the most fiendish cruelty and inveteracy on the part of his destroyer. As soon as the atrocious act was divulged, the Lady fell into convulsions, and lost her reason; and happy had it been for her had she never recovered the use of it, for there was blood upon her hand, which she took no care to conceal, and there was little doubt that it was the blood of her own innocent and beloved boy, the sole heir and hope of the family.

This blow deprived the Laird of all power of action; but the Lady had a brother, a man of the law, who came and instantly proceeded to an investigation of this unaccountable murder. Before the Sheriff arrived, the housekeeper took the Lady's brother aside, and told him he had better not go on with the scrutiny, for she was sure the crime would be brought home to her unfortunate mistress; and after examining into several corroborative circumstances, and viewing the state of the raving maniac, with the blood on her hand and arm, he made the investigation a very short one, declaring the domestics all exculpated.

The Laird attended his boy's funeral, and laid his head in the grave, but appeared exactly like a man walking in a trance, an automaton, without feelings or sensations, oftentimes gazing at the funeral procession, as on something he could not comprehend. And when the deathbell of the parish church fell a-tolling, as the corpse approached the kirk-stile, he cast a dim eye up towards the belfry, and said hastily, "What, what's that? Och ay, we're just in time, just in time." And often was he hammering over the name of "Evil Merodach, King of Babylon," to himself. He seemed to have some farfetched conception that his unaccountable jotteryman was in some way connected with the death of his only son, and other lesser calamities, although the evidence in favour of Merodach's innocence was as usual quite decisive.

This grievous mistake of Lady Wheelhope can only be accounted for, by supposing her in a state of derangement, or rather under some evil influence, over which she had no control; and to a person in such a state, the mistake was not so very unnatural. The mansion-house of Wheelhope was old and irregular. The stair had four acute turns, and four landing-places, all the same. In the uppermost chamber slept the two domestics—Merodach in the bed farthest in, and in the chamber immediately below that, which was exactly similar, slept the Young Laird and his tutor, the former in the bed farthest in; and thus, in the turmoil of her wild and raging passions, her own hand made herself childless.

Merodach was expelled by the family forthwith, but refused to accept his wages, which the man of law pressed upon him, for fear of further mischief; but he went away in apparent sullenness and discontent, no one knowing whither.

When his dismissal was announced to the Lady, who was watched day and night in her chamber, the news had such an effect on her, that her whole frame seemed electrified: the horrors of remorse vanished, and another passion, which I neither can comprehend nor define, took the sole possession of her distempered spirit. "He *must* not go!—He *shall* not go!" she exclaimed. "No, no, no—he shall not—he shall not—he shall not!" and then she instantly set herself about making ready to follow him, uttering all the while the most diabolical expressions, indicative of anticipated vengeance. "Oh, could I but snap his nerves one by one, and birl among his vitals! Could I but slice his heart off piecemeal in small messes, and see his blood lopper, and bubble, and spin away in purple slays: and then to see him grin, and grin, and grin, and grin! Oh—oh—oh—How beautiful and grand a sight it would be to see him grin, and grin, and grin!" And in such a style would she run on for hours together.

She thought of nothing, she spake of nothing, but the discarded jotteryman, whom most people now began to regard as a creature that was "not canny." They had seen him eat and drink, and work, like other people; still he had that about him that was not like other men. He was a boy in form, and an antediluvian in feature. Some thought he was a mongrel, between a man and an ape, some a wizard, some a kelpie, or a fairy, but most of all, that he was really and truly a Brownie. What he was I do not know, and therefore will not pretend to say; but be that as it may, in spite of locks and keys, watching and waking, the Lady of Wheelhope soon made her escape, and eloped after him. The attendants, indeed, would have made oath that she was carried away by some invisible hand, for it was impossible, they said, that she could have escaped on foot like other people; and this edition of the story took in the country; but sensible people viewed the matter in another light.

As for instance, when Wattie Blythe, the Laird's old shepherd, came in from the hill one morning, his wife Bessie thus accosted him. "His presence be about us, Wattie Blythe! Have ye heard what has happened at the ha'? Things are aye turning waur and waur there, and it looks like as if Providence had gi'en up our Laird's house to destruction. This grand estate maun now gang frae the Sprots; for it has finished them."

"Na, na, Bessie, it isna the estate that has finished the Sprots, but the Sprots that hae finished the estate, and themsells into the boot. They hae been a wicked and degenerate race, and aye the langer the waur, till they hae reached the utmost bounds o' earthly wickedness; and it's time the deil were looking after his ain."

"Ah, Wattie Blythe, ye never said a truer say. And that's just the very point where your story ends, and mine begins; for hasna the deil, or the fairies, or the brownies, ta'en away our Leddy bodily! And the hail country is running and riding in search o' her; and there is twenty hunder merks offered to the first that can find her, and bring her safe back. They hae ta'en her away, skin and bane, body and soul, and a', Wattie!"

"Hech-wow! but that is awesome! And where is it thought they have ta'en her to, Bessie?"

"O, they hae some guess at that frae her ain hints afore. It is thought they hae carried her after that satan of a creature, wha wrought sae muckle wae about the house. It is for him they are a' looking, for they ken weel, that where they get the tane they will get the tither."

"Whew! is that the gate o't, Bessie? Why, then, the awfu' story is nouther mair nor less than this, that the Leddy has made a 'lopement, as they ca't, and run away after a blackguard jotteryman. Heck-wow! wae's me for human frailty! But that's just the gate! When aince the deil gets in the point o' his finger, he will soon have in his haill hand. Ay, he wants but a hair to make a tether of, ony day! I hae seen her a braw sonsy lass; but even then I feared she was devoted to destruction, for she aye mockit at religion, Bessie, and that's no a good mark of a young body. And she made a' its servants her enemies; and think you these good men's prayers were a' to blaw away i' the wind, and be nae mair regarded? Na, na, Bessie, my woman, take ye this mark baith o' our bairns and other folk's—If ever ye see a young body that disregards the Sabbath, and makes a mock at the ordinances o' religion, ye will never see that body come to muckle good. A braw hand our Leddy has made o' her gibes and jeers at religion, and her mockeries o' the poor persecuted hill-folk!—sunk down by degrees into the very dregs o' sin and misery! Run away after a scullion!"

"Fy, fy, Wattie, how can ye say sae? It was weel kenn'd that she hatit him wi' a perfect and mortal hatred, and tried to make away wi' him mae ways nor ane."

"Aha, Bessie; but nipping and scarting is Scots folk's wooing; and though it is but right that we suspend our judgments, there will naebody persuade me if she be found alang wi' the creature, but that she has run away after him in the natural way, on her twa shanks, without help either frae fairy or brownie."

"I'll never believe sic a thing of ony woman born, let be a leddy weel up in years."

"Od help ye, Bessie! Ye dinna ken the stretch o' corrupt nature. The best o' us, when left to oursells, are nae better than strayed sheep, that will never find the way back to their ain pastures; and of a' things made o' mortal flesh, a wicked woman is the warst."

"Alack-a-day! we got the blame o' muckle that we little deserve. But, Wattie, keep ye a geyan sharp lookout about the cleuchs and the caves o' our hope; for the

Leddy kens them a' geyan weel; and gin the twenty hunder merks wad come our way, it might gang a waur gate. It wad tocher a' our bonny lasses."

"Ay, weel I wat, Bessie, that's nae lee. And now, when ye bring me amind o't, I'm sair mista'en if I didna hear a creature up in the Brockholes this morning, skirling as if something were cutting its throat. It gars a' the hairs stand on my head when I think it may hae been our Leddy, and the droich of a creature murdering her. I took it for a battle of wulcats, and wished they might pu' out ane anither's thrapples; but when I think on it again, they war unco like some o' our Leddy's unearthly screams."

"His presence be about us, Wattie! Haste ye—pit on your bonnet—tak' your staff in your hand, and gang and see what it is."

"Shame fa' me, if I daur gang, Bessie."

"Hout, Wattie, trust in the Lord."

"Aweel, sae I do. But ane's no to throw himsell ower a linn, and trust that the Lord will kep him in a blanket. And it's nae muckle safer for an auld stiff man like me to gang away out to a wild remote place, where there is ae body murdering another. What is that I hear, Bessie? Haud the lang tongue o' you, and rin to the door, and see what noise that is."

Bessie ran to the door, but soon returned, with her mouth wide open, and her eyes set in her head.

"It is them, Wattie! it is them! His presence be about us! What will we do?"

"Them? whaten them?"

"Why, that blackguard creature, coming here, leading our Leddy by the hair o' the head, and yerking her wi' a stick. I am terrified out o' my wits. What will we do?"

"We'll see what they say," said Wattie, manifestly in as great terror as his wife; and by a natural impulse, or as a last resource, he opened the Bible, not knowing what he did, then hurried on his spectacles; but before he got two leaves turned over, the two entered, a frightful-looking couple indeed. Merodach, with his old withered face, and ferret eyes, leading the Lady of Wheelhope by the long hair, which was mixed with grey, and whose face was all bloated with wounds and bruises, and having stripes of blood on her garments.

"How's this!—How's this, sirs?" said Wattie Blythe.

"Close that book, and I will tell you, goodman," said Merodach.

"I can hear what you hae to say wi' the beuk open, sir," said Wattie, turning over the leaves, pretending to look for some particular passage, but apparently not knowing what he was doing. "It is a shamefu' business this; but some will hae to answer for't. My Leddy, I am unco grieved to see you in sic a plight. Ye hae surely been dooms sair left to yoursell."

The Lady shook her head, uttered a feeble hollow laugh, and fixed her eyes on Merodach. But such a look! It almost frightened the simple aged couple out of their senses. It was not a look of love nor of hatred exclusively; neither was it of desire or disgust, but it was a combination of them all. It was such a look as one fiend would cast on another, in whose everlasting destruction he rejoiced. Wattie was glad to take his eyes from such countenances, and look into the Bible, that firm foundation of all his hopes and all his joy.

"I request that you will shut that book, sir," said the horrible creature; "or if you do not, I will shut it for you with a vengeance"; and with that he seized it, and flung it against the wall. Bessie uttered a scream, and Wattie was quite paralysed; and although he seemed disposed to run after his best friend, as he called it, the hellish looks of the Brownie interposed, and glued him to his seat.

"Hear what I have to say first," said the creature, "and then pore your fill on that precious book of yours. One concern at a time is enough. I came to do you a service. Here, take this cursed, wretched woman, whom you style your Lady, and deliver her up to the lawful authorities, to be restored to her husband and her place in society. She has followed one that hates her, and never said one kind word to her in his life; and though I have beat her like a dog, still she clings to me, and will not depart, so enchanted is she with the laudable purpose of cutting my throat. Tell your master and her brother, that I am not to be burdened with their maniac. I have scourged—I have spurned and kicked her, afflicting her night and day, and yet from my side she will not depart. Take her. Claim the reward in full, and your fortune is made; and so farewell!"

The creature went away, and the moment his back was turned, the Lady fell a-screaming and struggling, like one in an agony, and, in spite of all the couple's exertions, she forced herself out of their hands, and ran after the retreating Merodach. When he saw better would not be, he turned upon her, and, by one blow with his stick, struck her down; and, not content with that, continued to maltreat her in such a manner, as to all appearance would have killed twenty ordinary persons. The poor devoted dame could do nothing, but now and then utter a squeak like a half-worried cat, and writhe and grovel on the sward, till Wattie and his wife came up, and withheld her tormentor from further violence. He then bound her hands behind her back with a strong cord, and delivered her once more to the charge of the old couple, who contrived to hold her by that means, and take her home.

Wattie was ashamed to take her into the hall, but led her into one of the out-houses, whither he brought her brother to receive her. The man of the law was manifestly vexed at her reappearance, and scrupled not to testify his dissatisfaction; for when Wattie told him how the wretch had abused his sister, and that, had it not been for Bessie's interference and his own, the Lady would have been killed outright, he said, "Why, Walter, it is a great pity that he did *not* kill her outright. What good can her life now do to her, or of what value is her life to any creature living? After one has lived to disgrace all connected with them, the sooner they are taken off the better."

The man, however, paid old Walter down his two thousand merks, a great fortune for one like him in those days; and not to dwell longer on this unnatural story, I shall only add, very shortly, that the Lady of Wheelhope soon made her escape once more, and flew, as if drawn by an irresistible charm, to her tormentor. Her friends looked no more after her; and the last time she was seen alive, it was following the uncouth creature up the water of Daur, weary, wounded, and lame, while he was all the way beating her, as a piece of excellent amusement. A few days after that, her body was found among some wild haggs, in a place called Crook-burn, by a party of the persecuted Covenanters that were in hiding there, some of the very men whom she had exerted herself to destroy, and who had been driven, like David of old, to pray for a curse and earthly punishment upon her. They buried her like a dog at the Yetts of Keppel, and rolled three huge stones upon her grave, which are lying there to this day. When they found her corpse, it was mangled and wounded in a most shocking manner, the fiendish creature having manifestly tormented her to death. He was never more seen or heard of in this kingdom, though all that countryside was kept in terror of him for many years afterwards; and to this day, they will tell you of *The Brownie of the Black Haggs*, which title he seems to have acquired after his disappearance.

THE DREAM OF AKINOSUKÉ

Lafcadio Hearn

In the district called Toïchi of Yamato province, there used to live a gōshi named Miyata Akinosuké. . . . [Here I must tell you that in Japanese feudal times there was a privileged class of soldier-farmers,—free-holders,—corresponding to the class of yeomen in England; and these were called gōshi.]

In Akinosuké's garden there was a great and ancient cedar-tree, under which he was wont to rest on sultry days. One very warm afternoon he was sitting under this tree with two of his friends, fellow-gōshi, chatting and drinking wine, when he felt all of a sudden very drowsy,—so drowsy that he begged his friends to excuse him for taking a nap in their presence. Then he lay down at the foot of the tree, and dreamed this dream:—

He thought that as he was lying there in his garden, he saw a procession, like the train of some great daimyō, descending a hill near by, and that he got up to look at it. A very grand procession it proved to be,—more imposing than anything of the kind which he had ever seen before; and it was advancing toward his dwelling. He observed in the van of it a number of young men richly appareled, who were drawing a great lacquered palace-carriage, or *gosho-guruma*, hung with bright blue silk. When the procession arrived within a short distance of the house it halted; and a richly dressed man—evidently a person of rank—advanced from it, approached Akinosuké, bowed to him profoundly, and then said:—

121

"Honored Sir, you see before you a *kérai* [vassal] of the Kokuō of Tokoyo.* My master, the King, commands me to greet you in his august name, and to place myself wholly at your disposal. He also bids me inform you that he augustly desires your presence at the palace. Be therefore pleased immediately to enter this honorable carriage, which he has sent for your conveyance."

Upon hearing these words Akinosuké wanted to make some fitting reply; but he was too much astonished and embarrassed for speech;—and in the same moment his will seemed to melt away from him, so that he could only do as the *kérai* bade him. He entered the carriage; the *kérai* took a place beside him, and made a signal; the drawers, seizing the silken ropes, turned the great vehicle southward;—and the journey began.

In a very short time, to Akinosuké's amazement, the carriage stopped in front of a huge two-storied gateway (*rōmon*), of Chinese style, which he had never before seen. Here the *kérai* dismounted, saying, "I go to announce the honorable arrival,"—and he disappeared. After some little waiting, Akinosuké saw two noble-looking men, wearing robes of purple silk and high caps of the form indicating lofty rank, come from the gateway. These, after having respectfully saluted him, helped him to descend from the carriage, and led him through the great gate and across a vast garden, to the entrance of a palace whose front appeared to extend, west and east, to a distance of miles. Akinosuké was then shown into a reception-room of wonderful size and splendor. His guides conducted him to the place of honor, and respectfully seated themselves apart; while serving-maids, in costume of ceremony, brought refreshments. When Akinosuké had partaken of the refreshments, the two purple-robed attendants bowed low before

*This name "Tokoyo" is indefinite. According to circumstances it may signify any unknown country,—or that undiscovered country from whose bourn no traveler returns,—or that Fairyland of far-eastern fable, the Realm of Hōrai. The term "Kokuō" means the ruler of a country,—therefore a king. The original phrase, *Tokoyo no Kokuō*, might be rendered here as "the Ruler of Hōrai," or "the King of Fairyland."

him, and addressed him in the following words,—each speaking alternately, according to the etiquette of courts:—

"It is now our honorable duty to inform you . . . as to the reason of your having been summoned hither. . . . Our master, the King, augustly desires that you become his son-in-law; . . . and it is his wish and command that you shall wed this very day . . . the August Princess, his maiden-daughter. . . . We shall now conduct you to the presence-chamber . . . where His Augustness even now is waiting to receive you. . . . But it will be necessary that we first invest you . . . with the appropriate garments of ceremony."*

Having thus spoken, the attendants rose together, and proceeded to an alcove containing a great chest of gold lacquer. They opened the chest, and took from it various robes and girdles of rich material, and a *kamuri*, or regal headdress. With these they attired Akinosuké as befitted a princely bridegroom; and he was then conducted to the presence-room, where he saw the Kokuō of Tokoyo seated upon the *daiza*,† wearing the high black cap of state, and robed in robes of yellow silk. Before the *daiza*, to left and right, a multitude of dignitaries sat in rank, motionless and splendid as images in a temple; and Akinosuké, advancing into their midst, saluted the king with the triple prostration of usage. The king greeted him with gracious words, and then said:—

"You have already been informed as to the reason of your having been summoned to Our presence. We have decided that you shall become the adopted husband of Our only daughter;—and the wedding ceremony shall now be performed."

As the king finished speaking, a sound of joyful music was heard; and a long train of beautiful court ladies

*The last phrase, according to old custom, had to be uttered by both attendants at the same time. All these ceremonial observances can still be studied on the Japanese stage.
†This was the name given to the estrade, or dais, upon which a feudal prince or ruler sat in state. The term literally signifies "great seat."

advanced from behind a curtain, to conduct Akinosuké
to the room in which his bride awaited him.

The room was immense; but it could scarcely contain
the multitude of guests assembled to witness the wedding
ceremony. All bowed down before Akinosuké as he took
his place, facing the King's daughter, on the kneeling-
cushion prepared for him. As a maiden of heaven the
bride appeared to be; and her robes were beautiful as a
summer sky. And the marriage was performed amid
great rejoicing.

Afterwards the pair were conducted to a suite of
apartments that had been prepared for them in another
portion of the palace; and there they received the con-
gratulations of many noble persons, and wedding gifts
beyond counting.

Some days later Akinosuké was again summoned to
the throne-room. On this occasion he was received even
more graciously than before; and the King said to him:—

"In the southwestern part of Our dominion there is
an island called Raishū. We have now appointed you
Governor of that island. You will find the people loyal
and docile; but their laws have not yet been brought into
proper accord with the laws of Tokoyo; and their customs
have not been properly regulated. We entrust you with
the duty of improving their social condition as far as may
be possible; and We desire that you shall rule them with
kindness and wisdom. All preparations necessary for
your journey to Raishū have already been made."

So Akinosuké and his bride departed from the palace
of Tokoyo, accompanied to the shore by a great escort
of nobles and officials; and they embarked upon a ship of
state provided by the king. And with favoring winds they
safely sailed to Raishū, and found the good people of
that island assembled upon the beach to welcome them.

Akinosuké entered at once upon his new duties; and
they did not prove to be hard. During the first three
years of his governorship he was occupied chiefly with
the framing and the enactment of laws; but he had wise
counselors to help him, and he never found the work

unpleasant. When it was all finished, he had no active duties to perform, beyond attending the rites and ceremonies ordained by ancient custom. The country was so healthy and so fertile that sickness and want were unknown; and the people were so good that no laws were ever broken. And Akinosuké dwelt and ruled in Raishū for twenty years more,—making in all twenty-three years of sojourn, during which no shadow of sorrow traversed his life.

But in the twenty-fourth year of his governorship, a great misfortune came upon him; for his wife, who had borne him seven children,—five boys and two girls,—fell sick and died. She was buried, with high pomp, on the summit of a beautiful hill in the district of Hanryōkō; and a monument, exceedingly splendid, was placed above her grave. But Akinosuké felt such grief at her death that he no longer cared to live.

Now when the legal period of mourning was over, there came to Raishū, from the Tokoyo palace, a *shisha*, or royal messenger. The *shisha* delivered to Akinosuké a message of condolence, and then said to him:—

"These are the words which our august master, the King of Tokoyo, commands that I repeat to you: 'We will now send you back to your own people and country. As for the seven children, they are the grandsons and the granddaughters of the King, and shall be fitly cared for. Do not, therefore, allow your mind to be troubled concerning them.' "

On receiving this mandate, Akinosuké submissively prepared for his departure. When all his affairs had been settled, and the ceremony of bidding farewell to his counselors and trusted officials had been concluded, he was escorted with much honor to the port. There he embarked upon the ship sent for him; and the ship sailed out into the blue sea, under the blue sky; and the shape of the island of Raishū itself turned blue, and then turned gray, and then vanished forever. . . . And Akinosuké suddenly awoke—under the cedar-tree in his own garden! . . .

For the moment he was stupefied and dazed. But he perceived his two friends still seated near him,—drinking and chatting merrily. He stared at them in a bewildered way, and cried aloud,—

"How strange!"

"Akinosuké must have been dreaming," one of them exclaimed, with a laugh. "What did you see, Akinosuké, that was strange?"

Then Akinosuké told his dream,—that dream of three-and-twenty years' sojourn in the realm of Tokoyo, in the island of Raishū;—and they were astonished, because he had really slept for no more than a few minutes.

One gōshi said:—

"Indeed, you saw strange things. We also saw something strange while you were napping. A little yellow butterfly was fluttering over your face for a moment or two; and we watched it. Then it alighted on the ground beside you, close to the tree; and almost as soon as it alighted there, a big, big ant came out of a hole, and seized it and pulled it down into the hole. Just before you woke up, we saw that very butterfly come out of the hole again, and flutter over your face as before. And then it suddenly disappeared: we do not know where it went."

"Perhaps it was Akinosuké's soul," the other gōshi said;— "certainly I thought I saw it fly into his mouth. . . . But, even if that butterfly *was* Akinosuké's soul, the fact would not explain his dream."

"The ants might explain it," returned the first speaker. "Ants are queer beings—possibly goblins. . . . Anyhow, there is a big ant's nest under that cedar-tree." . . .

"Let us look!" cried Akinosuké, greatly moved by this suggestion. And he went for a spade.

The ground about and beneath the cedar-tree proved to have been excavated, in a most surprising way, by a prodigious colony of ants. The ants had furthermore built inside their excavations; and their tiny constructions of straw, clay, and stems bore an odd resemblance to miniature towns. In the middle of a structure considerably larger than the rest there was a marvelous swarming of small ants around the body of one very big ant, which had yellowish wings and a long black head.

"Why, there is the King of my dream!" cried Akino-

suké; "and there is the palace of Tokoyo! . . . How
extraordinary! . . . Raishū ought to lie somewhere south-
west of it—to the left of that big root. . . . Yes!—here
it is! . . . How very strange! Now I am sure that I can
find the mountain of Hanryōkō, and the grave of the
princess." . . .

In the wreck of the nest he searched and searched,
and at last discovered a tiny mound, on the top of which
was fixed a water-worn pebble, in shape resembling a
Buddhist monument. Underneath it he found—embedded in clay—the dead body of a female ant.

ELFINLAND

Johann Ludwig Tieck
(TRANSLATED BY THOMAS CARLYLE)

"Where is our little Mary?" said the father.

"She is playing out upon the green there with our neighbour's boy," replied the mother.

"I wish they may not run away and lose themselves," said he; "they are so thoughtless."

The mother looked for the little ones, and brought them their evening luncheon. "It is warm," said the boy; "and Mary had a longing for the red cherries."

"Have a care, children," said the mother, "and do not run too far from home, and not into the wood; Father and I are going to the fields."

Little Andres answered: "Never fear, the wood frightens us; we shall sit here by the house, where there are people near us."

The mother went in, and soon came out again with her husband. They locked the door, and turned towards the fields to look after their labourers, and see their hay harvest in the meadow. Their house lay upon a little green height, encircled by a pretty ring of paling, which likewise enclosed their fruit and flower garden. The hamlet stretched somewhat deeper down, and on the other side lay the castle of the Count. Martin rented the large farm from this nobleman; and was living in contentment with his wife and only child; for he yearly saved some money, and had the prospect of becoming a man of substance by his industry, for the ground was productive, and the Count not illiberal.

As he walked with his wife to the fields, he gazed cheerfully round and said: "What a different look this quarter has, Brigitta, from the place we lived in formerly!

128

Here it is all so green; the whole village is bedecked with thick-spreading fruit-trees; the ground is full of beautiful herbs and flowers; all the houses are cheerful and cleanly, the inhabitants are at their ease: nay, I could almost fancy that the woods are greener here than elsewhere, and the sky bluer; and, so far as the eye can reach, you have pleasure and delight in beholding the bountiful Earth."

"And whenever you cross the stream," said Brigitta, "you are, as it were, in another world, all is so dreary and withered; but every traveller declares that our village is the fairest in the country far and near."

"All but that fir-ground," said her husband; "do but look back to it, how dark and dismal that solitary spot is lying in the gay scene: the dingy fir-trees with the smoky huts behind them, the ruined stalls, the brook flowing past with a sluggish melancholy."

"It is true," replied Brigitta; "if you but approach that spot, you grow disconsolate and sad, you know not why. What sort of people can they be that live there, and keep themselves so separate from the rest of us, as if they had an evil conscience?"

"A miserable crew," replied the young Farmer: "gipsies, seemingly, that steal and cheat in other quarters, and have their hoard and hiding place here. I wonder only that his Lordship suffers them."

"Who knows," said the wife, with an accent of pity, "but perhaps they may be poor people, wishing, out of shame, to conceal their poverty; for, after all, no one can say aught ill of them; the only thing is, that they do not go to church, and none knows how they live; for the little garden, which indeed seems altogether waste, cannot possibly support them; and fields they have none."

"God knows," said Martin, as they went along, "what trade they follow; no mortal comes to them; for the place they live in is as if bewitched and excommunicated, so that even our wildest fellows will not venture into it."

Such conversation they pursued, while walking to the fields. That gloomy spot they spoke of lay aside from the hamlet. In a dell, begirt with firs, you might behold a hut, and various ruined office-houses; rarely was smoke seen to mount from it, still more rarely did men appear

there; though at times curious people, venturing somewhat nearer, had perceived upon the bench before the
hut, some hideous women, in ragged clothes, dandling in
their arms some children equally dirty and ill-favoured;
black dogs were running up and down upon the bound-
ary; and, of an evening, a man of monstrous size was
seen to cross the footbridge of the brook, and disappear
in the hut; and, in the darkness, various shapes were
observed, moving like shadows round a fire in the open
air. This piece of ground, the firs and the ruined huts,
formed in truth a strange contrast with the bright green
landscape, the white houses of the hamlet, and the stately
new-built castle.

The two little ones had now eaten their fruit; it came
into their heads to run races; and the little nimble Mary
always got the start of the less active Andres. "It is not
fair," cried Andres at last: "let us try it for some length,
then we shall see who wins."

"As thou wilt," said Mary; "only to the brook we must
not run."

"No," said Andres; "but there, on the hill, stands the
large pear-tree, a quarter of a mile from this. I shall run
by the left, round past the fir-ground; thou canst try it
by the right over the fields; so we do not meet till we
get up, and then we shall see which of us is swifter."

"Done," cried Mary, and began to run: "for we shall
not mar one another by the way, and my father says it
is as far to the hill by that side of the Gipsies' house as
by this."

Andres had already started, and Mary, turning to the
right, could no longer see him. "It is very silly," said she
to herself: "I have only to take heart, and run along the
bridge, past the hut, and through the yard, and I shall
certainly be first." She was already standing by the brook
and the clump of firs. "Shall I? No; it is too frightful,"
said she. A little white dog was standing on the farther
side, and barking with might and main. In her terror,
Mary thought the dog some monster, and sprang back.
"Fy! Fy!" said she: "the dolt is gone half way by this
time, while I stand here considering." The little dog kept
barking, and, as she looked at it more narrowly, it
seemed no longer frightful, but, on the contrary, quite

pretty; it had a red collar round its neck, with a glittering bell; and as it raised its head, and shook itself in barking, the little bell sounded with the finest tinkle. "Well, I must risk it!" cried she, "I will run for life; quick, quick, I am through; certainly to Heaven, they cannot eat me up alive in half a minute!" And with this, the gay, courageous little Mary sprang along the footbridge; passed the dog, which ceased its barking and began to fawn on her; and in a moment she was standing on the other bank, and the black firs all round concealed from view her father's house, and the rest of the landscape.

But what was her astonishment when here! The loveliest, most variegated flower-garden, lay round her; tulips, roses, and lilies were glittering in the fairest colours; blue and gold-red butterflies were wavering in the blossoms; cages of shining wire were hung on the espaliers, with many-coloured birds in them, singing beautiful songs; and children, in short white frocks with flowing yellow hair and brilliant eyes, were frolicking about, some playing with lambkins, some feeding the birds, or gathering flowers, and giving them to one another; some, again, were eating cherries, grapes, and ruddy apricots. No hut was to be seen; but instead of it, a large fair house, with a brazen door and lofty statues, stood glancing in the middle of the space. Mary was confounded with surprise, and knew not what to think; but, not being bashful, she went right up to the first of the children, held out her hand, and wished the little creature good-even.

"Art thou come to visit us, then?" said the glittering child; "I saw thee running, playing on the other side, but thou wert frightened at our little dog."

"So you are not gipsies and rogues," said Mary, "as Andres always told me? He is a stupid thing, and talks of much he does not understand."

"Stay with us," said the strange little girl; "thou wilt like it well."

"But we are running a race."

"Thou wilt find thy comrade soon enough. There, take and eat."

Mary ate, and found the fruit more sweet than any she had ever tasted in her life before; and Andres, and the race, and the prohibition of her parents, were entirely forgotten.

A stately woman, in a shining robe, came towards them, and asked about the stranger child. "Fairest lady," said Mary, "I came running hither by chance, and now they wish to keep me."

"Thou art aware, Zerina," said the lady, "that she can be here but for a little while; besides, thou shouldst have asked my leave."

"I thought," said Zerina, "when I saw her admitted across the bridge, that I might do it; we have often seen her running in the fields, and thou thyself hast taken pleasure in her lively temper. She will have to leave us soon enough."

"No, I will stay here," said the little stranger; "for here it is so beautiful, and here I shall find the prettiest playthings, and store of berries and cherries to boot. On the other side it is not half so grand."

The gold-robed lady went away with a smile; and many of the children now came bounding round the happy Mary in their mirth, and twitched her, and incited her to dance; others brought her lambs, or curious playthings; others made music on instruments, and sang to it.

She kept, however, by the playmate who had first met her; for Zerina was the kindest and loveliest of them all. Little Mary cried and cried again: "I will stay with you forever; I will stay with you, and you shall be my sisters"; at which the children all laughed, and embraced her. "Now we shall have a royal sport," said Zerina. She ran into the palace, and returned with a little golden box, in which lay a quantity of seeds, like glittering dust. She lifted of it with her little hand, and scattered some grains on the green earth. Instantly the grass began to move, as in waves; and, after a few moments, bright rosebushes started from the ground, shot rapidly up, and budded all at once, while the sweetest perfume filled the place. Mary also took a little of the dust, and, having scattered it, she saw white lilies, and the most variegated pinks, pushing up. At a signal from Zerina, the flowers disappeared, and others rose in their room. "Now," said Zerina, "look for something greater." She laid two pine seeds in the ground, and stamped them in sharply with her foot. Two green bushes stood before them. "Grasp me fast," said she; and Mary threw her arms about the slender form. She felt herself borne upwards; for the trees were springing under them with the greatest speed; the tall pines waved to and fro, and the two children held each other fast embraced, swinging this way and that in the red clouds of the twilight, and kissed each other; while the rest were climbing up and down the trunks with quick dexterity, pushing and teasing one another with loud laughter when they met; if any one fell down in the press, it flew through the air, and sank slowly and surely to the ground. At length Mary was beginning to be frightened; and the other little child sang a few loud tones, and the trees again sank down and set them on the ground as gradually as they had lifted them before to the clouds.

They next went through the brazen door of the palace. Here many fair women, elderly and young, were sitting in the round hall, partaking of the fairest fruits, and listening to glorious invisible music. In the vaulting of the ceiling, palms, flowers, and groves stood painted, among which little figures of children were sporting and winding in every graceful posture; and with the tones of the music, the images altered and glowed with the most burning colours; now the blue and green were sparkling like radiant light, now these tints faded back in paleness, the purple flamed up, and the gold took fire; and then the naked children seemed to be alive among the flower-garlands and to draw breath, and emit it through their ruby-coloured lips; so that by fits you could see the glance of their little white teeth, and the lighting up of their azure eyes.

From the hall, a stair of brass led down to a subterranean chamber. Here lay much gold and silver, and precious stones of every hue shone out between them. Strange vessels stood along the walls, and all seemed filled with costly things. The gold was worked into many forms, and glittered with the friendliest red. Many little dwarfs were busied sorting the pieces from the heap, and putting them in the vessels; others, hunch-backed and bandy-legged, with long red noses, were tottering slowly along, half-bent to the ground, under full sacks, which they bore as millers do their grain; and, with much panting, shaking out the gold-dust on the ground. Then they darted awkwardly to the right and left, and caught the rolling balls that were like to run away; and it happened now and then that one in his eagerness overset the other, so that both fell heavily and clumsily to the ground. They made angry faces, and looked askance, as Mary laughed at their gestures and their ugliness. Behind them sat an old crumpled little man, whom Zerina reverently greeted; he thanked her with a grave inclination of his head. He held a sceptre in his hand, and wore a crown upon his brow, and all the other dwarfs appeared to regard him as their master, and obey his nod.

"What more wanted?" asked he, with a surly voice, as the children came a little nearer. Mary was afraid, and did not speak; but her companion answered, they were only come to look about them in the chambers. "Still your old child's tricks!" replied the dwarf: "Will there never be an end to idleness?" With this, he turned again to his employment, kept his people weighing and sorting the ingots; some he sent away on errands, some he chid with angry tones.

"Who is the gentleman?" said Mary.

"Our Metal-Prince," replied Zerina, as they walked along.

They seemed once more to reach the open air, for they were standing by a lake, yet no sun appeared, and they saw no sky above their heads. A little boat received them, and Zerina steered it diligently forwards. It shot rapidly along. On gaining the middle of the lake, the stranger saw that multitudes of pipes, channels, and brooks, were spreading from the little sea in every direction. "These waters to the right," said Zerina, "flow beneath your garden, and this is why it blooms so freshly; by the other side we get down into the great stream." On a sudden, out of all the channels, and from every quarter of the lake, came a crowd of little children swimming up; some wore garlands of sedge and water-lily; some had red stems of coral, others were blowing on crooked shells; a tumultuous noise echoed merrily from the dark shores; among the children might be seen the fairest women sporting in the waters, and often several of the children sprang about some one of them, and with

kisses hung upon her neck and shoulders. All saluted the
strangers; and these steered onwards through the revelry
out of the lake, into a little river, which grew narrower
and narrower. At last the boat came aground. The
strangers took their leave, and Zerina knocked against
the cliff. This opened like a door, and a female form, all
red, assisted them to mount. "Are you all brisk here?"
inquired Zerina. "They are just at work," replied the
other, "and happy as they could wish; indeed, the heat
is very pleasant."

They went up a winding stair, and on a sudden Mary
found herself in a most resplendent hall, so that as she
entered, her eyes were dazzled by the radiance. Flame-
coloured tapestry covered the walls with a purple glow;
and when her eye had grown a little used to it, the
stranger saw, to her astonishment, that, in the tapestry,
there were figures moving up and down in dancing joy-
fulness; in form so beautiful, and of so fair proportions,
that nothing could be seen more graceful; their bodies
were as of red crystal, so that it appeared as if the blood
were visible within them, flowing and playing in its
courses. They smiled on the stranger, and saluted her
with various bows; but as Mary was about approaching
nearer them, Zerina plucked her sharply back, crying:
"Thou wilt burn thyself, my little Mary, for the whole of
it is fire."

Mary felt the heat. "Why do the pretty creatures not
come out," said she, "and play with us?"

"As thou livest in the Air," replied the other, "so are
they obliged to stay continually in Fire, and would faint
and languish if they left it. Look now, how glad they are,
how they laugh and shout; those down below spread out
the fire-floods everywhere beneath the earth, and
thereby the flowers, and fruits, and wine, are made to
flourish; these red streams again, are to run beside the
brooks of water; and thus the fiery creatures are kept
ever busy and glad. But for thee it is too hot here; let
us return to the garden."

In the garden, the scene had changed since they left
it. The moonshine was lying on every flower; the birds
were silent, and the children were asleep in complicated
groups, among the green groves. Mary and her friend,

however, did not feel fatigue, but walked about in the warm summer night, in abundant talk, till morning.

When the day dawned, they refreshed themselves on fruit and milk, and Mary said: "Suppose we go, by way of change, to the firs, and see how things look there?"

"With all my heart," replied Zerina; "thou wilt see our watchmen too, and they will surely please thee; they are standing up among the trees on the mound." The two proceeded through the flower-garden by pleasant groves, full of nightingales; then they ascended a vine-hill; and at last, after long following the windings of a clear brook, arrived at the firs, and the height which bounded the domain. "How does it come," said Mary, "that we have to walk so far here, when without, the circuit is so narrow?"

"I know not," said her friend; "but so it is."

They mounted to the dark firs, and a chill wind blew from without in their faces; a haze seemed lying far and wide over the landscape. On the top were many strange forms standing: with mealy, dusty faces; their misshapen heads not unlike those of white owls; they were clad in folded cloaks of shaggy wool; they held umbrellas of curious skins stretched out above them; and they waved and fanned themselves incessantly with large bat's wings, which flared out curiously beside the woollen roquelaures. "I could laugh, yet I am frightened," cried Mary.

"These are our good trusty watchmen," said her playmate; "they stand here and wave their fans, that cold anxiety and inexplicable fear may fall on every one that attempts to approach us. They are covered so, because without it is now cold and rainy, which they cannot bear. But snow, or wind, or cold air, never reaches down to us; here is an everlasting spring and summer: yet if these poor people on the top were not frequently relieved, they would certainly perish."

"But who are you, then?" said Mary, while again descending to the flowery fragrance; "or have you no name at all?"

"We are called the Elves," replied the friendly child; "people talk about us in the Earth, as I have heard."

They now perceived a mighty bustle on the green. "The fair Bird is come!" cried the children to them: all

hastened to the hall. Here, as they approached, young
and old were crowding over the threshold, all shouting
for joy; and from within resounded a triumphant peal of
music. Having entered, they perceived the vast circuit
filled with the most varied forms, and all were looking
upwards to a large Bird with glancing plumage, that was
sweeping slowly round in the dome, and in its stately
flight describing many a circle. The music sounded more
gaily than before; the colours and lights alternated more
rapidly. At last the music ceased; and the Bird, with a
rustling noise, floated down upon a glittering crown that
hung hovering in air under the high window, by which
the hall was lighted from above. His plumage was purple
and green, and shining golden streaks played through it;
on his head there waved a diadem of feathers, so resplendent that they glanced like jewels. His bill was red, and
his legs of a glancing blue. As he moved, the tints
gleamed through each other, and the eye was charmed
with their radiance. His size was as that of an eagle. But
now he opened his glittering beak; and sweetest melodies
came pouring from his moved breast, in finer tones than
the lovesick nightingale gives forth; still stronger rose the
song, and streamed like floods of Light, so that all, the
very children themselves, were moved by it to tears of
joy and rapture. When he ceased, all bowed before him;
he again flew round the dome in circles, then darted
through the door, and soared into the light heaven,
where he shone far up like a red point, and then soon
vanished from their eyes.

"Why are ye all so glad?" inquired Mary, bending to
her fair playmate, who seemed smaller than yesterday.

"The King is coming!" said the little one; "many of us
have never seen him, and whithersoever he turns his
face, there is happiness and mirth; we have long looked
for him, more anxiously than you look for spring when
winter lingers with you; and now he has announced, by
his fair herald, that he is at hand. This wise and glorious
Bird, that has been sent to us by the King, is called
Phoenix; he dwells far off in Arabia, on a tree, which
there is no other that resembles it on Earth, as in like
manner there is no second Phoenix. When he feels himself grown old, he builds a pile of balm and incense,

kindles it, and dies singing; and then from the fragrant ashes, soars up the renewed Phoenix with unlessened beauty. It is seldom he so wings his course that men behold him; and when once in centuries this does occur, they note it in their annals, and expect remarkable events. But now, my friend, thou and I must part; for the sight of the King is not permitted thee."

Then the lady with the golden robe came through the throng, and beckoning Mary to her, led her into a sequestered walk. "Thou must leave us, my dear child," said she; "the King is to hold his court here for twenty years, perhaps longer; and fruitfulness and blessings will spread far over the land, but chiefly here beside us; all the brooks and rivulets will become more bountiful, all the fields and gardens richer, the wine more generous, the meadows more fertile, and the woods more fresh and green; a milder air will blow, no hail shall hurt, no flood shall threaten. Take this ring, and think of us: but beware of telling anyone of our existence; or we must fly this land, and thou and all around will lose the happiness and blessing of our neighbourhood. Once more, kiss thy playmate, and farewell." They issued from the walk; Zerina wept, Mary stooped to embrace her, and they parted. Already she was on the narrow bridge; the cold air was blowing on her back from the firs; the little dog barked with all its might, and rang its little bell: she looked around, then hastened over, for the darkness of the firs, the bleakness of the ruined huts, the shadows of the twilight, were filling her with terror.

"What a night my parents must have had on my account!" said she within herself, as she stept on the green; "and I dare not tell them where I have been, or what wonders I have witnessed, nor indeed would they believe me." Two men passing by saluted her; and as they went along, she heard them say: "What a pretty girl! Where can she come from?" With quickened steps she approached the house: but the trees which were hanging last night loaded with fruit were now standing dry and leafless; the house was differently painted, and a new barn had been built beside it. Mary was amazed, and thought she must be dreaming. In this perplexity she opened the door; and behind the table sat her father, between an unknown woman and a stranger youth. "Good God! Father," cried she, "where is my mother?"

"Thy mother!" said the woman, with a forecasting tone, and sprang towards her: "Ha, thou surely canst not—Yes, indeed, indeed thou art my lost, long-lost dear, only Mary!" She had recognised her by a little brown mole beneath the chin, as well as by her eyes and shape. All embraced her, all were moved with joy, and the parents wept. Mary was astonished that she almost reached to her father's stature; and she could not understand how her mother had become so changed and faded; she asked the name of the stranger youth. "It is our neighbour's Andres," said Martin. "How comest thou to us again, so unexpectedly, after seven long years? Where hast thou been? Why didst thou never send us tidings of thee?"

"Seven years!" said Mary, and could not order her ideas and recollections. "Seven whole years?"

"Yes, yes," said Andres, laughing, and shaking her trustfully by the hand; "I have won the race, good Mary; I was at the pear-tree and back again seven years ago, and thou, sluggish creature, art but just returned!"

They again asked, they pressed her; but remembering her instruction, she could answer nothing. It was they themselves chiefly that, by degrees, shaped a story for her: How, having lost her way, she had been taken up by a coach, and carried to a strange remote part, where she could not give the people any notion of her parents' residence; how she was conducted to a distant town, where certain worthy persons brought her up and loved her; how they had lately died, and at length she had recollected her birthplace, and so returned. "No matter how it is!" exclaimed her mother; "enough, that we have thee again, my little daughter, my own, my all!"

Andres waited supper, and Mary could not be at home in anything she saw. The house seemed small and dark; she felt astonished at her dress, which was clean and simple, but appeared quite foreign; she looked at the ring on her finger, and the gold of it glittered strangely, enclosing a stone of burning red. To her father's question, she replied that the ring also was a present from her benefactors.

She was glad when the hour of sleep arrived, and she hastened to her bed. Next morning she felt much more collected; she had now arranged her thoughts a little, and could better stand the questions of the people in the village, all of whom came in to bid her welcome. Andres was there too with the earliest, active, glad, and serviceable beyond all others. The blooming maiden of fifteen had made a deep impression on him; he had passed a sleepless night. The people of the castle likewise sent for Mary, and she had once more to tell her story to them, which was now grown quite familiar to her. The old Count and his Lady were surprised at her good-breeding; she was modest, but not embarrassed; she made answer courteously in good phrases to all their questions; all fear of noble persons and their equipage had passed away from her; for when she measured these halls and forms by the wonders and the high beauty she had seen with the Elves in their hidden abode, this earthly splendour seemed but dim to her, the presence of men was almost mean. The young lords were charmed with her beauty.

It was now February. The trees were budding earlier than usual; the nightingale had never come so soon; the spring rose fairer in the land than the oldest men could recollect it. In every quarter, little brooks gushed out to irrigate the pastures and meadows; the hills seemed heaving, the vines rose higher and higher, the fruit-trees blossomed as they had never done; and a swelling fragrant blessedness hung suspended heavily in rosy clouds over the scene. All prospered beyond expectation; no rude day, no tempest injured the fruits, the wine flowed blushing in immense grapes; and the inhabitants of the place felt astonished, and were captivated as in a sweet dream. The next year was like its forerunner; but men had now become accustomed to the marvellous. In autumn Mary yielded to the pressing entreaties of Andres and her parents; she was betrothed to him, and in winter they were married.

She often thought with inward longing of her residence behind the fir-trees; she continued serious and still. Beautiful as all that lay around her was, she knew of something yet more beautiful; and from the remembrance of this, a faint regret attuned her nature to soft melancholy. It smote her painfully when her father and mother talked about the gipsies and vagabonds, that dwelt in the dark spot of ground. Often she was on the point of speaking out in defence of those good beings, whom she knew to be the benefactors of the land; especially to Andres, who appeared to take delight in zealously abusing them. Yet still she repressed the word that was struggling to escape her bosom. So passed this year; in the next, she was solaced by a little daughter, whom she named Elfrida, thinking of the designation of her friendly Elves.

The young people lived with Martin and Brigitta, the house being large enough for all; and helped their parents in conducting their now extended husbandry. The little Elfrida soon displayed peculiar faculties and gifts; for she could walk at a very early age, and could speak perfectly before she was a twelvemonth old; and after some few years, she had become so wise and clever, and of such wondrous beauty, that all people regarded her with astonishment; and her mother could not keep away the thought that her child resembled one of those shining little ones in the space behind the Firs. Elfrida cared not to be with other children; but seemed to avoid, with a sort of horror, their tumultuous amusements; and liked best to be alone. She would then retire into a corner of the garden, and read, or work diligently with her needle; often also you might see her sitting, as if deep sunk in thought; or violently walking up and down the alleys, speaking to herself. Her parents readily allowed her to have her will in these things, for she was healthy, and waxed apace; only her strange sagacious answers and observations often made them anxious. "Such wise children do not grow to age," her grandmother, Brigitta, many times observed; "they are too good for this world; the child, besides, is beautiful beyond nature, and will never find its proper place on Earth."

The little girl had this peculiarity, that she was very loath to let herself be served by any one, but endeavoured to do everything herself. She was almost the earliest riser in the house; she washed herself carefully, and dressed without assistance: at night she was equally careful; she took special heed to pack up her clothes and washed them with her own hands, allowing no one, not even her mother, to meddle with her articles. The mother humoured her in this caprice, not thinking it of any consequence. But what was her astonishment, when, happening one holiday to insist, regardless of Elfrida's tears and screams, on dressing her out for a visit to the castle, she found upon her breast, suspended by a string, a piece of gold of a strange form, which she directly recognised as one of that sort she had seen in such abundance in the subterranean vault! The little thing was greatly frightened; and at last confessed that she had found it in the garden, and as she liked it much, had kept it carefully: she at the same time prayed so earnestly and pressingly to have it back, that Mary fastened it again on its former place, and, full of thoughts, went out with her in silence to the castle.

Sidewards from the farmhouse lay some offices for the storing of produce and implements; and behind these there was a little green, with an old grove, now visited by no one as, from the new arrangement of the buildings, it lay too far from the garden. In this solitude Elfrida delighted most; and it occurred to nobody to interrupt her here, so that frequently her parents did not see her for half a day. One afternoon her mother chanced to be in these buildings, seeking for some lost article among the lumber; and she noticed that a beam of light was coming in, through a chink in the wall. She took a thought of looking through this aperture, and seeing what her child was busied with; and it happened that a stone was lying loose, and could be pushed aside, so that she obtained a view right into the grove. Elfrida was sitting there on a little bench, and beside her the well-known Zerina; and the children were playing, and amusing one another, in the kindliest unity. The Elf embraced her beautiful companion, and said mournfully: "Ah! dear little creature, as I sport with thee, so have I sported with thy mother, when she was a child; but you mortals so soon grow tall and thoughtful! It is very hard: wert thou but to be a child as long as I!"

"Willingly would I do it," said Elfrida; "but they all say, I shall come to sense, and give over playing altogether; for I have great gifts, as they think, for growing wise. Ah! and then I shall see thee no more, thou dear Zerina! Yet it is with us as with the fruit-tree flowers: how glorious the blossoming apple-tree, with its red bursting buds! It looks so stately and broad; and every one, that passes under it, thinks surely something great will come of it; then the sun grows hot, and the buds come joyfully forth; but the wicked kernel is already there, which pushes off and casts away the fair flower's dress; and now, in pain and waxing, it can do nothing more, but must grow to fruit in harvest. An apple, to be sure, is pretty and refreshing; yet nothing to the blossom of spring. So it is also with us mortals: I am not glad in the least at growing to be a tall girl. Ah! Could I but once visit you!"

"Since the King is with us," said Zerina, "it is quite impossible; but I will come to thee, my darling, often, often; and none shall see me either here or there. I will pass invisible through the air, or fly over to thee like a bird. O! we will be much, much together, while thou art still little. What can I do to please thee?"

"Thou must like me very dearly," said Elfrida, "as I like thee in my heart. But come, let us make another rose."

Zerina took the well-known box from her bosom, threw two grains from it on the ground; and instantly a green bush stood before them, with two deep-red roses, bending their heads, as if to kiss each other. The children plucked them smiling, and the bush disappeared. "O that it would not die so soon!" said Elfrida; "this red child, this wonder of the Earth!"

"Give it me here," said the little Elf; then breathed thrice upon the budding rose, and kissed it thrice. "Now," said she, giving back the rose, "it will continue fresh and blooming till winter."

"I will keep it," said Elfrida, "as an image of thee; I will guard it in my little room, and kiss it night and morning, as if it were thyself."

"The sun is setting," said the other; "I must go home." They embraced again, and Zerina vanished.

In the evening, Mary clasped her child to her breast, with a feeling of alarm and veneration. She henceforth allowed the good little girl more liberty than formerly;

and often calmed her husband when he came to search for the child; which for some time he was wont to do, as her retiredness did not please him; and he feared that, in the end, it might make her silly, or even pervert her understanding. The mother often glided to the chink; and almost always found the bright Elf beside her child, employed in sport, or in earnest conversation.

"Wouldst thou like to fly?" inquired Zerina once.

"O well! How well!" replied Elfrida; and the fairy clasped her mortal playmate in her arms, and mounted with her from the ground, till they hovered above the grove. The mother, in alarm, forgot herself, and pushed out her head in terror to look after them; when Zerina, from the air, held up her finger, and threatened yet smiled; then descended with the child, embraced her, and disappeared. After this, it happened more than once that Mary was observed by her; and every time, the shining little creature shook her head, or threatened, yet with friendly looks.

Often, in disputing with her husband, Mary had said in her zeal: "Thou dost injustice to the poor people in the hut!" But when Andres pressed her to explain why she differed in opinion from the whole village, nay, from his Lordship himself; and how she could understand it better than the whole of them, she still broke off embarrassed, and became silent. One day, after dinner, Andres grew more violent than ever; and maintained that, by one means or another, the crew must be packed away, as a nuisance to the country; when his wife, in anger, said to him: "Hush! for they are benefactors to thee and to every one of us."

"Benefactors!" cried the other, in astonishment: "These rogues and vagabonds?"

In her indignation, she was now at last tempted to relate to him, under promise of the strictest secrecy, the history of her youth: and as Andres at every word grew more incredulous, and shook his head in mockery, she took him by the hand, and led him to the chink; where, to his amazement, he beheld the glittering Elf sporting with his child, and caressing her in the grove. He knew not what to say; an exclamation of astonishment escaped him, and Zerina raised her eyes. On the instant she grew pale, and trembled violently; not with friendly, but with indignant looks, she made the sign of threatening, and then said to Elfrida: "Thou canst not help it, dearest heart; but they will never learn sense, wise as they believe themselves." She embraced the little one with stormy haste; and then, in the shape of a raven, flew with hoarse cries over the garden, toward the Firs.

In the evening, the little one was very still; she kissed her rose with tears; Mary felt depressed and frightened, Andres scarcely spoke. It grew dark. Suddenly there went a rustling through the trees; birds flew to and fro with wild screaming, thunder was heard to roll, the Earth shook, and tones of lamentation moaned in the air. Andres and his wife had not courage to rise; they shrouded themselves within the curtains, and with fear and trembling awaited the day. Towards morning, it grew calmer; and all was silent when the Sun, with his cheerful light, rose over the wood.

Andres dressed himself; and Mary now observed that the stone of the ring upon her finger had become quite pale. On opening the door, the sun shone clear on their faces, but the scene around them they could scarcely recognise. The freshness of the wood was gone; the hills were shrunk, the brooks were flowing languidly with scanty streams, the sky seemed grey; and when you turned to the Firs, they were standing there no darker or more dreary than the other trees. The huts behind them were no longer frightful; and several inhabitants of the village came and told about the fearful night, and how they had been across the spot where the gipsies had lived; how these people must have left the place at last, for their huts were standing empty, and within had quite a common look, just like the dwellings of other poor people: some of their household gear was left behind.

Elfrida in secret said to her mother: "I could not sleep last night; and in my fright at the noise, I was praying from the bottom of my heart, when the door suddenly opened, and my playmate entered to take leave of me. She had a travelling pouch slung round her, a hat on her head, and a large staff in her hand. She was very angry at thee; since on thy account she had now to suffer the severest and most painful punishments, as she had always been so fond of thee; for all of them, she said, were very loath to leave this quarter."

Mary forbade her to speak of this; and now the ferryman came across the river, and told them new wonders. As it was growing dark, a stranger man of large size had come to him, and hired his boat till sunrise; and with this condition, that the boatman should remain quiet in his house, at least should not cross the threshold of his door. "I was frightened," continued the old man, "and the strange bargain would not let me sleep. I slipped softly to the window, and looked towards the river. Great clouds were driving restlessly through the sky, and the distant woods were rustling fearfully; it was as if my cottage shook, and moans and lamentations glided round it. On a sudden, I perceived a white streaming light, that grew broader and broader, like many thousands of falling stars; sparkling and waving, it proceeded forward from the dark Fir-ground, moved over the fields, and spread itself along towards the river. Then I heard a trampling, a jingling, a bustling, and rushing, nearer and nearer; it went forwards to my boat, and all stept into it, men and women, as it seemed, and children; and the tall stranger ferried them over. In the river were by the boat swimming many thousands of glittering forms; in the air white clouds and lights were wavering; and all lamented and bewailed that they must travel forth so far, far away, and leave their beloved dwelling. The noise of the rudder and the water creaked and gurgled betweenwhiles, and then suddenly there would be silence. Many a time the boat landed, and went back, and was again laden; many heavy casks, too, they took along with them, which multitudes of horrid-looking little fellows carried and rolled; whether they were devils or goblins, Heaven only knows. Then came, in waving brightness, a stately freight; it seemed an old man, mounted on a small white horse, and all were crowding round him. I saw nothing of the horse but its head; for the rest of it was covered with costly glittering cloths and trappings: on his brow the old man had a crown, so bright that, as he came across, I thought the sun was rising there, and the redness of the dawn glimmering in my eyes. Thus it went on all night; I at last fell asleep in the tumult, half in joy, half in terror. In the morning all was still; but the river is, as it were, run off, and I know not how I am to steer my boat in it now."

The same year there came a blight; the woods died away, the springs ran dry; and the scene, which had once been the joy of every traveller, was in autumn standing waste, naked and bald; scarcely showing here and there, in the sea of sand, a spot or two where grass, with a dingy greenness, still grew up. The fruit-trees all withered, the vines faded away, and the aspect of the place became so melancholy, that the Count, with his people, next year left the castle, which in time decayed and fell to ruins.

Elfrida gazed on her rose day and night with deep longing, and thought of her kind playmate; and as it drooped and withered, so did she also hang her head; and before the spring the little maiden had herself faded away. Mary often stood upon the spot before the hut, and wept for the happiness that had departed. She wasted herself away like her child, and in a few years she too was gone. Old Martin, with his son-in-law, returned to the quarter where he had lived before.

DARBY O'GILL AND THE GOOD PEOPLE

Herminie Templeton

On the road between Kilcuny and Balinderg, Jerry Murtaugh, the car-driver, told me his story:

Although only one living man of his own free will ever went among them there, still, any well-learned person in Ireland can tell you that the abode of the Good People is in the hollow heart of the great mountain Sleive-na-mon. That same one man was Darby O'Gill, a cousin of my own mother.

One night the Good People took the eldest of Darby's three fine pigs. The next week a second pig went the same way. The third week not a thing had Darby left for the Balinrobe fair. You may aisily think how sore and sorry the poor man was, an' how Bridget his wife an' the childher carried on. The rent was due, and all left was to sell his cow Rosie to pay it. Rosie was the apple of his eye; he admired and rayspected the pigs, but he loved Rosie.

Worst luck of all was yet to come. On the morning when Darby went for the cow to bring her into market, bad scrans to the hoof was there; but in her place only a wisp of dirty straw to mock him. Millia murther! What a howlin' and screechin' and cursin' did Darby bring back to the house!

Now Darby was a bould man, and a desperate man in his anger, as you soon will see. He shoved his feet into a pair of brogues, clapped his hat on his head, gripped his stick in his hand.

"Fairy or no fairy, ghost or goblin, livin' or dead, who took Rosie'll rue this day," he says.

With those wild words he bolted in the direction of Sleive-na-mon.

All day long he climbed like an ant over the hill, looking for a hole or cave through which he could get at the prison of Rosie. At times he struck the rocks with his black-thorn, cryin' out challenge.

"Come out, you that took her," he called. "If ye have the courage of a mouse, ye murtherin' thieves, come out!"

No one made answer—at laste, not just then. But at night, as he turned, hungry and footsore, toward home, who should he meet up with on the crossroads but the ould fairy doctor, Sheela Maguire. Well known she was as a spy for the Good People. She spoke up:

"Oh, then, you're the foolish, blundherin'-headed man to be saying what you've said, and doing what you've done this day, Darby O'Gill," says she.

"What do I care!" says he fiercely. "I'd fight the divil to-night for my beautiful cow."

"Then go into Mrs. Hagan's meadow beyant," says Sheela, "and wait till the moon is up. By-an'-by ye'll see a herd of cows come down from the mountain, and yer own'll be among them."

"What'll I do then?" asked Darby, his voice thrembling with excitement.

"Sorra a hair I care what ye do! But there'll be lads there, and hundreds you won't see, that'll stand no ill words, Darby O'Gill."

"I thank you kindly," says Darby, "and I bid you good-evening, ma'am." He turned away, leaving her standing there alone, looking after him; but he was sure he heard voices talkin' to her, and laughin' and tittherin' behind him.

It was dark night when Darby stretched himself on the ground in Hagan's meadow; the yellow rim of the moon just tipped the edge of the hills. The time passed mortal slow; and it was an hour later when a hundred slow shadows, stirring up the mists, crept from the mountain way toward him. First he must find was Rosie among the herd. To creep quiet as a cat through the hedge and reach the first cow was only a minute's work. Then his plan—to wait till cock-crow—with all other sober, sensible thoughts, went clean out of the lad's head before his rage; for, cropping eagerly the long sweet grass, the first baste he met was Rosie.

With a leap Darby was behind her, his stick falling sharply on her flanks. The ingratitude of that cow almost broke Darby's heart. Rosie turned fiercely on him, with a vicious lunge, her two horns aimed at his breast. There was no suppler boy in the parish than Darby, and well for him it was so, for the mad rush the cow gave would have caught any man the laste thrifle heavy on his legs, and ended his days right there.

As it was, our hayro sprang to one side. As Rosie passed, his left hand gripped her tail. When one of the O'Gills takes hould of a thing, he hangs on like a bull terrier. Away he went, rushing with her.

Now began a race the like of which was never heard of before or since. Ten jumps to the second, and a hundred feet to the jump. Rosie's tail standing straight up in the air, firm as an iron bar, and Darby floating straight out behind; a thousand furious fairies flying a short distance after, filling the air with wild commands and threatenings.

Suddenly the sky opened for a crash of lightning that shivered the hills, and a roar of thunder that turned out of their beds every man, woman, and child in four counties. Flash after flash came the lightning, hitting on every side of Darby. If it wasn't for fear of hurting Rosie, the fairies would sartenly have killed Darby. As it was, he was stiff with fear, afraid to hould on and afraid to lave go, but flew, waving in the air at Rosie's tail like a flag.

As the cow turned into the long, narrow valley which cuts into the east side of the mountain, the Good People caught up with the pair, and what they didn't do to Darby, in the line of sticking pins, pulling whiskers, and pinching wouldn't take long to tell. In troth, he was just about to let go his hould, and take the chances of a fall, when the hillside opened and—whisk! the cow turned into the mountain. Darby found himself flying down a wide, high passage which grew lighter as he went along. He heard the opening behind shut like a trap, and his heart almost stopped beating, for this was the fairies' home in the heart of Sleive-na-mon. He was captured by them!

When Rosie stopped, so stiff were all Darby's joints, that he had great trouble loosening himself to come down. He landed among a lot of angry-faced little people, each no higher than your hand, every one wearing a green velvet cloak and a red cap.

"We'll take him to the king," says a red-whiskered wee chap. "What he'll do to the murtherin' spalpeen 'll be good and plenty!"

With that they marched our bould Darby, a prisoner, down the long passage, which every second grew wider and lighter, and fuller of little people.

Sometimes, though, he met with human beings like himself, only the black charm was on them, they having been stolen at some time by the Good People. He saw Lost People there from every parish in Ireland, both commoners and gentry. Each was laughing, talking, and divarting himself with another. Off to the sides he could see small cobblers making brogues, tinkers mending pans, tailors sewing cloth, smiths hammering horseshoes, every one merrily to his trade, making a divarsion out of work.

Down near the center of the mountain was a room twenty times higher and broader than the biggest church in the world. As they drew near this room, there arose the sound of a reel played on bagpipes. The music was so bewitching that Darby, who was the gracefullest reel dancer in all Ireland, could hardly make his feet behave.

At the room's edge Darby stopped short and caught his breath, the sight was so entrancing. Set over the broad floor were thousands and thousands of the Good People, facing this way and that, and dancing to a reel; while on a throne in the middle of the room sat ould Brian Conners, King of the Fairies, blowing on the bagpipes. The little king, with a goold crown on his head, wearing a beautiful green velvet coat and red knee breeches, sat with his legs crossed, beating time with his foot to the music.

There were many from Darby's own parish; and what was his surprise to see there Maureen McGibney, his own wife's sister, whom he had supposed resting dacintly in her grave in holy ground these three years.

There she was, gliding back and forth, ferninst a little gray-whiskered, round-stomached fairy man, as though there was never a care nor a sorrow in the world.

As I told you before, I tell you again, Darby was the finest reel dancer in all Ireland; and he came from a family of dancers, though I say it who shouldn't, as he was my mother's own cousin. Three things in the world banish sorrow—love and whisky and music. So, when the surprise of it all melted a little, Darby's feet led him in to the thick of the throng, right under the throne of the king, where he flung care to the winds, and put his heart and mind into his two nimble feet. Darby's dancing was such that purty soon those around stood still to admire.

Backward and forward, sidestep and turn; cross over, then forward; a hand on his hip and his stick twirling free; sidestep and forward; cross over again; bow to his partner, and hammer the floor.

It wasn't long till half the dancers crowded around admiring, clapping their hands, and shouting encouragement. The ould king grew so excited that he laid down the pipes, took up his fiddle, came down from the throne, and standing ferninst Darby began a finer tune than the first.

The dancing lasted a whole hour, no one speaking a word except to cry out, "Foot it, ye divil!" "Aisy now, he's threading on flowers!" "More power to you!" "Play faster, king!" "Hooroo! hooroo! hooray!"

Then the king stopped and said:

"Well, that bates Banagher, and Banagher bates the world! Who are you, and how came you here?"

Then Darby up and tould the whole story.

When he had finished, the king looked sayrious. "I'm glad you came, an' I'm sorry you came," he says. "If we had put our charm on you outside to bring you in, you'd never die till the end of the world, when we here must all go to hell. But," he added quickly, "there's no use in worrying about that now. That's nayther here nor there! Those willing to come with us can't come at all, at all; and here you are of your own free act and will. Howsom-ever, you're here, and we daren't let you go outside to tell others of what you have seen, and so give us a bad name about—about taking things, you know. We'll make you as comfortable as we can; and so you won't worry about Bridget and the childher, I'll have a goold sovereign left with them every day of their lives. But I wish we had the comeither on you," he says, with a sigh, "for it's aisy to see you're great company. Now come up to my place an' have a noggin of punch for friendship's sake," says he.

That's how Darby O'Gill began his six months' stay with the Good People. Not a thing was left undone to make Darby contented and happy. A civiler people than the Good People he never met. At first he couldn't get over saying, "God keep all here," and "God save you kindly," and things like that, which was like burning them with a hot iron.

If it weren't for Maureen McGibney, Darby would be in Sleive-na-mon at this hour. Sure she was always the wise girl, ready with her crafty plans and warnings. On a day when they two were sitting alone together, she says to him:

"Darby, dear," says she, "it isn't right for a dacint man of family to be spending his days cavortin', and idlin', and fillin' the hours with sport and nonsense. We must get you out of here; for what is a sovereign a day to compare with the care and protection of a father?" she says.

"Thrue for ye!" moaned Darby, "and my heart is just splittin' for a sight of Bridget an' the childher. Bad luck to the day I set so much store on a dirty, ongrateful, threacherous cow!"

"I know well how you feel," says Maureen, "for I'd give the whole world to say three words to Bob Broderick, that ye tell me that out of grief for me has never kept company with any other girl till this day. But that'll never be," she says, "because I must stop here till the Day of Judgment, and then I must go to——" says she, beginning to cry, "but if you get out, you'll bear a message to Bob for me, maybe?" she says.

"It's aisy to talk about going out, but how can it be done?" asked Darby.

"There's a way," says Maureen, wiping her big gray

eyes, "but it may take years. First, you must know that the Good People can never put their charm on any one who is willing to come with them. That's why you came safe. Then, again, they can't work harm in the daylight, and after cockcrow any mortal eye can see them plain; nor can they harm any one who has a sprig of holly, nor pass over a leaf or twig of holly, because that's Christmas bloom. Well, there's a certain evil word for a charm that opens the side of the mountain, and I will try to find it out for you. Without that word all the armies of the world couldn't get out or in. But you must be patient and wise, and wait."

"I will so, with the help of God," says Darby.

At these words, Maureen gave a terrible screech.

"Cruel man!" she cried, "don't you know that to say pious words to one of the Good People, or to one under their black charm, is like cutting him with a knife?"

The next night she came to Darby again.

"Watch yerself now," she says, "for to-night they're goin' to lave the door of the mountain open, to thry you; and if you stir two steps outside they'll put the comeither on you," she says.

Sure enough, when Darby took his walk down the passage, after supper, as he did every night, there the side of the mountain lay wide open and no one in sight. The temptation to make one rush was great; but he only looked out a minute, and went whistling back down the passage, knowing well that a hundred hidden eyes were on him the while. For a dozen nights after it was the same.

At another time Maureen said:

"The king himself is going to thry you hard the day, so beware!" She had no sooner said the words than Darby was called for, and went up to the king.

"Darby, my sowl," says the king, in a sootherin' way, "have this noggin of punch. A betther never was brewed; it's the last we'll have for many a day. I'm going to set you free, Darby O'Gill, that's what I am."

"Why, king," says Darby, putting on a mournful face, "how have I offended ye?"

"No offense at all," says the king, "only we're depriving you."

"No depravity in life!" says Darby. "I have lashins and lavings to ate and to drink, and nothing but fun an' divarsion all day long. Out in the world it was nothing but work and throuble and sickness, disappointment and care."

"But Bridget and the childher?" says the king, giving him a sharp look out of half-shut eyes.

"Oh, as for that, king," says Darby, "it's aisier for a widow to get a husband, or for orphans to find a father, than it is for them to pick up a sovereign a day."

The king looked mighty satisfied and smoked for a while without a word.

"Would you mind going out an evenin' now and then, helpin' the boys to mind the cows?" he asked at last.

Darby feared to thrust himself outside in their company.

"Well, I'll tell ye how it is," replied my brave Darby. "Some of the neighbors might see me, and spread the report on me that I'm with the fairies, and that'd disgrace Bridget and the childher," he says.

The king knocked the ashes from his pipe. "You're a wise man besides being the hoight of good company," says he, "and it's sorry I am you didn't take me at my word; for then we would have you always, at laste till the Day of Judgment, when—but that's nayther here nor there! Howsomever, we'll bother you about it no more."

From that day they thrated him as one of their own.

It was one day five months after that Maureen plucked Darby by the coat and led him off to a lonely spot.

"I've got the word," she says.

"Have you, faith! What is it?" says Darby, all of a thremble.

Then she whispered a word so blasphemous, so irreligious, that Darby blessed himself. When Maureen saw him making the sign, she fell down in a fit, the holy emblem hurt her so, poor child.

Three hours after this me bould Darby was sitting at his own fireside talking to Bridget and the childher. The neighbors were hurrying to him, down every road and through every field, carrying armfuls of holly bushes, as he had sent word for them to do. He knew well he'd have fierce and savage visitors before morning.

After they had come with the holly, he had them make a circle of it so thick around the house that a fly couldn't walk through without touching a twig or a leaf. But that was not all.

You'll know what a wise girl and what a crafty girl that Maureen was when you hear what the neighbors did next. They made a second ring of holly outside the first, so that the house sat in two great wreaths, one wreath around the other. The outside ring was much the bigger, and left a good space between it and the first, with room for ever so many people to stand there. It was like the inner ring, except for a little gate, left open as though by accident, where the fairies could walk in.

But it wasn't an accident at all, only the wise plan of Maureen's; for nearby this little gap, in the outside wreath, lay a sprig of holly with a bit of twine tied to it. Then the twine ran along up to Darby's house, and in through the window, where its end lay convaynient to his hand. A little pull on the twine would drag the stray piece of holly into the gap, and close tight the outside ring.

It was a trap, you see. When the fairies walked in through the gap, the twine was to be pulled, and so they were to be made prisoners between the two rings of holly. They couldn't get into Darby's house, because the circle of holly nearest the house was so tight that a fly couldn't get through without touching the blessed tree or its wood. Likewise, when the gap in the outer wreath was closed, they couldn't get out again. Well, anyway, these things were hardly finished and fixed, when the dusky brown of the hills warned the neighbors of twilight, and they scurried like frightened rabbits to their homes.

Only one amongst them all had courage to sit inside Darby's house waiting the dreadful visitors, and that one was Bob Broderick. What vengeance was in store couldn't be guessed at all, at all, only it was sure that it was to be more terrible than any yet wreaked on mortal man.

Not in Darby's house alone was the terror, for in their anger the Good People might lay waste the whole parish. The roads and fields were empty and silent in the darkness. Not a window glimmered with light for miles around. Many a blaggard who hadn't said a prayer for years was now down on his marrow bones among the dacint members of his family, thumping his craw, and roaring his Pather and Aves.

In Darby's quiet house, against which the cunning, the power, and the fury of the Good People would first break, you can't think of half the suffering of Bridget and the childher, as they lay huddled together on the settle bed; nor of the sthrain on Bob and Darby, who sat smoking their dudeens and whispering anxiously together.

For some rayson or other the Good People were long in coming. Ten o'clock struck, then eleven, afther that twelve, and not a sound from the outside. The silence and the no sign of any kind had them all just about crazy, when suddenly there fell a sharp rap on the door.

"Millia murther," whispered Darby, "we're in for it. They've crossed the two rings of holly, and are at the door itself."

The childher begun to cry and Bridget said her prayers out loud; but no one answered the knock.

"Rap, rap, rap," on the door, then a pause.

"God save all here!" cried a queer voice from the outside.

Now no fairy would say, "God save all here," so Darby took heart and opened the door. Who should be standing there but Sheelah Maguire, a spy for the Good People. So angry were Darby and Bob that they snatched her within the threshold, and before she knew it they had her tied hand and foot, wound a cloth around her mouth, and rouled her under the bed. Within the minute a thousand rustling voices sprung from outside. Through the window, in the clear moonlight, Darby marked weeds and grass being trampled by invisible feet, beyond the farthest ring of holly.

Suddenly broke a great cry. The gap in the first ring was found. Signs were plainly seen of uncountable feet rushing through, and spreading about the nearer wreath. Afther that a howl of madness from the little men and women. Darby had pulled his twine and the trap was closed, with five thousand of the Good People entirely at his mercy.

Princes, princesses, dukes, dukesses, earls, earlesses, and all the quality of Sleive-na-mon were prisoners. Not more than a dozen of the last to come escaped, and they flew back to tell the king.

For an hour they raged. All the bad names ever called to mortal man were given free, but Darby said never a word. "Pick-pocket," "sheep stayler," "murtherin' thafe of a blaggard," were the softest words trun at him.

By an' by, howsomever, as it begun to grow near to cock-crow, their talk grew a great dale civiler. Then came beggin', pladin', promisin', and enthratin', but the doors of the house still stayed shut an' its windows down.

Purty soon Darby's old rooster, Terry, came down from his perch, yawned, an' flapped his wings a few times. At that the terror and the screechin' of the Good People would have melted the heart of a stone.

All of a sudden a fine, clear voice rose from beyant the crowd. The king had come. The other fairies grew still, listening.

"Ye murtherin' thafe of the world," says the king grandly, "what are ye doin' wid my people?"

"Keep a civil tongue in yer head, Brian Connor," says Darby, sticking his head out the window, "for I'm as good a man as you, any day," says Darby.

At that minute Terry, the cock, flapped his wings and crowed. In a flash there sprang into full view the crowd of Good People—dukes, earls, princes, quality, and commoners, with their ladies, jammed thick together about the house; every one of them with his head thrown back bawling and crying, and tears as big as pigeons' eggs rouling down his cheeks.

A few feet away, on a straw pile in the barnyard, stood the king, his goold crown tilted on the side of his head, his long green cloak about him, and his rod in his hand, but thremblin' all over.

In the middle of the crowd, but towering high above them all, stood Maureen McGibney in her cloak of green an' goold, her purty brown hair fallin' down on her shoulders, an' she—the crafty villain—cryin' an' bawlin', an' abusin' Darby, with the best of them.

"What'll you have an' let them go?" says the king.

"First an' foremost," says Darby, "take yer spell off that slip of a girl there, an' send her into the house."

In a second Maureen was standing inside the door, her both arms about Bob's neck, and her head on his collarbone.

What they said to aich other, and what they done in the way of embracin' an' kissin' an' cryin' I won't take time in telling you.

"Next," says Darby, "send back Rosie and the pigs."

"I expected that," says the king. And at those words they saw a black bunch coming through the air; in a few seconds Rosie and the three pigs walked into the stable.

"Now," says Darby, "promise in the name of Ould Nick" ('tis by him the Good People swear) "never to moil nor meddle again with any one or anything from this parish."

The king was fair put out by this. Howsomever, he said at last, "You ongrateful scoundhrel, in the name of Ould Nick, I promise."

"So far, so good," says Darby; "but the worst is yet to come. Now you must ralayse from your spell every soul you've stole from this parish; and besides, you must send me ten thousand pounds in goold."

Well, the king gave a roar of anger that was heard in the next barony.

"Ye high-handed, hard-hearted robber," he says, "I'll never consent!" he says.

"Plase yerself," says Darby. "I see Father Cassidy comin' down the hedge," he says, "an' he has a prayer for ye all in his book that'll burn ye up like wisps of sthraw ef he ever catches ye here," says Darby.

With that the roaring and bawling was pitiful to hear, and in a few minutes a bag with ten thousand goold sovereigns in it was trun at Darby's threshold; and fifty people, young an' some of them ould, flew over an' stood beside the king. Some of them had spent years with the fairies. Their relatives thought them dead an' buried. They were the Lost Ones from that parish.

With that Darby pulled the bit of twine again, opening the trap, and it wasn't long until every fairy was gone.

The green coat of the last one was hardly out of sight when, sure enough, who should come up but Father Cassidy, his book in his hand. He looked at the fifty people who had been with the fairies standin' there—the poor crathures—thremblin' an' wondherin', an' afeared to go to their homes.

Darby tould him what had happened.

"Ye foolish man," says the priest, "you could have got out every poor prisoner that's locked in Sleive-na-mon, let alone those from this parish."

"Would yer Reverence have me let out the Corko-niens, the Connaught men, and the Fardowns, I ask ye?" he says hotly. "When Mrs. Malowney there goes home and finds that Tim has married the Widow Hogan, ye'll say I let out too many, even of this parish, I'm thinkin'."

"But," says the priest, "ye might have got ten thousand pounds for aich of us."

"If aich had ten thousand pounds, what comfort would I have in being rich?" asked Darby again. "To enjoy well being rich, there should be plenty of poor," says Darby.

"God forgive ye, ye selfish man!" says Father Cassidy.

"There's another rayson besides," says Darby. "I never got betther nor friendlier thratement than I had from the Good People. An' the divil a hair of their heads I'd hurt more than need be," he says.

Some way or other the king heard of this saying, an' was so mightily pleased that next night a jug of the finest poteen was left at Darby's door.

After that, indade, many's the winter night, when the snow lay so heavy that no neighbor was stirrin', and when Bridget and the childher were in bed, Darby sat by the fire, a noggin of hot punch in his hand, argyin an' getting news of the whole world. A little man, with a goold crown on his head, a green cloak on his back, and one foot thrown over the other, sat ferninst him by the hearth.

NO MAN'S LAND

John Buchan

CHAPTER I. THE SHIELING OF FARAWA

It was with a light heart and a pleasing consciousness of holiday that I set out from the inn at Allermuir to tramp my fifteen miles into the unknown. I walked slowly, for I carried my equipment on my back—my basket, fly-books and rods, my plaid of Grant tartan (for I boast myself a distant kinsman of that house), and my great staff, which had tried ere then the front of the steeper Alps. A small valise with books and some changes of linen clothing had been sent on ahead in the shepherd's own hands. It was yet early April, and before me lay four weeks of freedom—twenty-eight blessed days in which to take fish and smoke the pipe of idleness. The Lent term had pulled me down, a week of modest enjoyment there after in town had finished the work; and I drank in the sharp moorish air like a thirsty man who has been forwandered among deserts.

I am a man of varied tastes and a score of interests. As an undergraduate I had been filled with the old mania for the complete life. I distinguished myself in the Schools, rowed in my college eight, and reached the distinction of practising for three weeks in the Trials. I had dabbled in a score of learned activities, and when the time came that I won the inevitable St Chad's fellowship on my chaotic acquirements, and I found myself compelled to select if I would pursue a scholar's life, I had some toil in finding my vocation. In the end I resolved that the ancient life of the North, of the Celts and the Northmen and the unknown Pictish tribes, held for me

the chief fascination. I had acquired a smattering of
Gaelic, having been brought up as a boy in Lochaber,
and now I set myself to increase my store of languages.
I mastered Erse and Icelandic, and my first book—a
monograph on the probable Celtic elements in the Eddic
songs—brought me the praise of scholars and the deputy-
professor's chair of Northern Antiquities. So much for
Oxford. My vacations had been spent mainly in the
North—in Ireland, Scotland, and the Isles, in Scandina-
via and Iceland, once even in the far limits of Finland. I
was a keen sportsman of a sort, an old-experienced
fisher, a fair shot with gun and rifle, and in my hillcraft
I might well stand comparison with most men. April has
ever seemed to me the finest season of the year even in
our cold northern altitudes, and the memory of many
bright Aprils had brought me up from the South on the
night before to Allerfoot, whence a dogcart had taken
me up Glen Aller to the inn at Allermuir; and now the
same desire had set me on the heather with my face to
the cold brown hills.

You are to picture a sort of plateau, benty and rock-
strewn, running ridge-wise above a chain of little peaty
lochs and a vast tract of inexorable bog. In a mile the
ridge ceased in a shoulder of hill, and over this lay the
head of another glen, with the same doleful accompani-
ment of sunless lochs, mosses, and a shining and resolute
water. East and west and north, in every direction save
the south, rose walls of gashed and serrated hills. It was
a grey day with blinks of sun, and when a ray chanced
to fall on one of the great dark faces, lines of light and
colour sprang into being which told of mica and granite.
I was in high spirits, as on the eve of holiday; I had
breakfasted excellently on eggs and salmon-steaks; I had
no cares to speak of, and my prospects were not uninvit-
ing. But in spite of myself the landscape began to take
me in thrall and crush me. The silent vanished peoples
of the hills seemed to be stirring; dark primeval faces
seemed to stare at me from behind boulders and jags of
rock. The place was so still, so free from the cheerful
clamour of nesting birds, that it seemed a *temenos* sacred
to some old-world god. At my feet the lochs lapped
ceaselessly; but the waters were so dark that one could

not see bottom a foot from the edge. On my right the
links of green told of snake-like mires waiting to crush
the unwary wanderer. It seemed to me for the moment
a land of death, where the tongues of the dead cried
aloud for recognition.

My whole morning's walk was full of such fancies. I lit
a pipe to cheer me, but the things would not be got rid
of. I thought of the Gaels who had held those fastnesses;
I thought of the Britons before them, who yielded to
their advent. They were all strong peoples in their day,
and now they had gone the way of the earth. They had
left their mark on the levels of the glens and on the more
habitable uplands, both in names and in actual forts, and
graves where men might still dig curios. But the hills—
that black stony amphitheatre before me—it seemed
strange that the hills bore no traces of them. And then
with some uneasiness I reflected on that older and
stranger race who were said to have held the hill-tops.
The Picts, the Picti—what in the name of goodness were
they? They had troubled me in all my studies, a sort of
blank wall to put an end to speculation. We knew nothing of them save certain strange names which men called
Pictish, the names of those hills in front of me—the Muneraw, the Yirnie, the Calmarton. They were the *corpus
vile* for learned experiment; but Heaven alone knew what
dark abyss of savagery once yawned in the midst of the
desert.

And then I remembered the crazy theories of a pupil
of mine at St Chad's, the son of a small landowner on
the Aller, a young gentleman who had spent his substance too freely at Oxford, and was now dreeing his
weird in the Backwoods. He had been no scholar; but a
certain imagination marked all his doings, and of a Sunday night he would come and talk to me of the North.
The Picts were his special subject, and his ideas were
mad. "Listen to me," he would say, when I had mixed
him toddy and given him one of my cigars; "I believe
there are traces—ay, and more than traces—of an old
culture lurking in those hills and waiting to be discovered. We never hear of the Picts being driven from the
hills. The Britons drove them from the lowlands, the
Gaels from Ireland did the same for the Britons; but the

hills were left unmolested. We hear of no one going near them except outlaws and tinklers. And in that very place you have the strangest mythology. Take the story of the Brownie. What is that but the story of a little swart man of uncommon strength and cleverness, who does good and ill indiscriminately, and then disappears. There are many scholars, as you yourself confess, who think that the origin of the Brownie was in some mad belief in the old race of the Picts, which still survived somewhere in the hills. And do we not hear of the Brownie in authentic records right down to the year 1756? After that, when people grew more incredulous, it is natural that the belief should have begun to die out; but I do not see why stray traces should not have survived till late."

"Do you not see what that means?" I had said in mock gravity. "Those same hills are, if anything, less known now than they were a hundred years ago. Why should not your Picts or Brownies be living to this day?"

"Why not, indeed?" he had rejoined, in all seriousness.

I laughed, and he went to his rooms and returned with a large leather-bound book. It was lettered, in the rococo style of a young man's taste, "Glimpses of the Unknown," and some of the said glimpses he proceeded to impart to me. It was not pleasant reading; indeed, I had rarely heard anything so well fitted to shatter sensitive nerves. The early part consisted of folk-tales and folk-sayings, some of them wholly obscure, some of them with a glint of meaning, but all of them with some hint of a mystery in the hills. I heard the Brownie story in countless versions. Now the thing was a friendly little man, who wore grey breeches and lived on brose; now he was a twisted being, the sight of which made the ewes miscarry in the lambing-time. But the second part was the stranger, for it was made up of actual tales, most of them with date and place appended. It was a most Bedlamite catalogue of horrors, which, if true, made the wholesome moors a place instinct with tragedy. Some told of children carried away from villages, even from towns, on the verge of the uplands. In almost every case they were girls, and the strange fact was their utter disappearance. Two little girls would be coming home from school, would be seen last by a neighbour just where the road crossed a patch of heath or entered a wood, and then—no human eye ever saw them again. Children's cries had startled outlying shepherds in the night, and when they had rushed to the door they could hear nothing but the night wind. The instances of such disappearances were not very common—perhaps once in twenty years—but they were confined to this one tract of country, and came in a sort of fixed progression from the middle of last century, when the record began. But this was only one side of the history. The latter part was all devoted to a chronicle of crimes which had gone unpunished, seeing that no hand had ever been traced. The list was fuller in last century; in the earlier years of the present it had dwindled; then came a revival about the 'fifties; and now again in our own time it had sunk low. At the little cottage of Auchterbrean, on the roadside in Glen Aller, a labourer's wife had been found pierced to the heart. It was thought to be a case of a woman's jealousy, and her neighbour was accused, convicted, and hanged. The woman, to be sure, denied the charge with her last breath; but circumstantial evidence seemed sufficiently strong against her. Yet some people in the glen believed her guiltless. In particular, the carrier who had found the dead woman declared that the way in which her neighbour received the news was a sufficient proof of innocence; and the doctor who was first summoned professed himself unable to tell with what instrument the wound had been given. But this was all before the days of expert evidence, so the woman had been hanged without scruple. Then there had been another story of peculiar horror, telling of the death of an old man at some little lonely shieling called Carrickfey. But at this point I had risen in protest, and made to drive the young idiot from my room.

"It was my grandfather who collected most of them," he said. "He had theories,* but people called him mad,

---

*In the light of subsequent events I have jotted down the materials to which I refer. The last authentic record of the Brownie is in the narrative of the shepherd of Clachlands, taken down towards the close of last century by the Reverend Mr. Gillespie, minister of Allerkirk, and included by him in his "Songs and Legends of Glen Aller." The authorities on the strange carrying-away of children are

so he was wise enough to hold his tongue. My father declares the whole thing mania; but I rescued the book, had it bound, and added to the collection. It is a queer hobby; but, as I say, I have theories, and there are more things in heaven and earth——"

But at this he heard a friend's voice in the Quad., and dived out, leaving the *banal* quotation unfinished.

Strange though it may seem, this madness kept coming back to me as I crossed the last few miles of moor. I was now on a rough tableland, the watershed between two lochs, and beyond and above me rose the stony backs of the hills. The burns fell down in a chaos of granite boulders, and huge slabs of grey stone lay flat and tumbled in the heather. The full waters looked prosperously for my fishing, and I began to forget all fancies in anticipation of sport.

Then suddenly in a hollow of land I came on a ruined cottage. It had been a very small place, but the walls were still half-erect, and the little moorland garden was outlined on the turf. A lonely apple-tree, twisted and gnarled with winds, stood in the midst.

From higher up on the hill I heard a loud roar, and I knew my excellent friend the shepherd of Farawa, who had come thus far to meet me. He greeted me with the boisterous embarrassment which was his way of prefacing hospitality. A grave reserved man at other times, on such occasions he thought it proper to relapse into hilarity. I fell into step with him, and we set off for his dwelling. But first I had the curiosity to look back to the tumbledown cottage and ask him its name.

A queer look came into his eyes. "They ca' the place

---

to be found in a series of articles in a local paper, the "Allerfoot Advertiser," September and October 1878, and a curious book published anonymously at Edinburgh in 1848, entitled "The Weathergaw." The records of the unexplained murders in the same neighbourhood are all contained in Mr. Fordoun's "Theory of Expert Evidence," and an attack on the book in the "Law Review" for June 1881. The Carrickfey case has a pamphlet to itself—now extremely rare—a copy of which was recently obtained in a bookseller's shop in Dumfries by a well-known antiquary, and presented to the library of the Supréme Court in Edinburgh.

Carrickfey," he said. "Naebody has daured to bide there this twenty year sin'—but I see ye ken the story." And, as if glad to leave the subject, he hastened to discourse on fishing.

CHAPTER II. TELLS OF AN EVENING'S TALK.

The shepherd was a masterful man; tall, save for the stoop which belongs to all moorland folk, and active as a wild goat. He was not a new importation, nor did he belong to the place; for his people had lived in the remote Borders, and he had come as a boy to this shieling of Farawa. He was unmarried, but an elderly sister lived with him and cooked his meals. He was reputed to be extraordinarily skilful in his trade; I know for a fact that he was in his way a keen sportsman; and his few neighbours gave him credit for a sincere piety. Doubtless this last report was due in part to his silence, for after his first greeting he was wont to relapse into a singular taciturnity. As we strode across the heather he gave me a short outline of his year's lambing. "Five pair o' twins yestreen, twae this morn; that makes thirty-five yowes that hae lambed since the Sabbath. I'll dae weel if God's willin'." Then, as I looked towards the hill-tops whence the thin mist of morn was trailing, he followed my gaze. "See," he said with uplifted crook—"see that sicht. Is that no what is written of in the Bible when it says, 'The mountains do smoke.' " And with this piece of apologetics he finished his talk, and in a little we were at the cottage.

It was a small enough dwelling in truth, and yet large for a moorland house, for it had a garret below the thatch, which was given up to my sole enjoyment. Below was the wide kitchen with box-beds, and next to it the inevitable second room, also with its cupboard sleeping-places. The interior was very clean, and yet I remember to have been struck with the faint musty smell which is inseparable from moorland dwellings. The kitchen pleased me best, for there the great rafters were black with peat-reek, and the uncovered stone floor, on which the fire gleamed dully, gave an air of primeval simplicity. But the walls spoiled all, for tawdry things of to-day had penetrated even there. Some grocers' almanacs—years old—hung in places of honour, and an extraordinary lithograph of the Royal Family in its youth. And this, mind you, between crooks and fishing-rods and old guns, and horns of sheep and deer.

The life for the first day or two was regular and placid. I was up early, breakfasted on porridge (a dish which I detest), and then off to the lochs and streams. At first my sport prospered mightily. With a drake-wing I killed a salmon of seventeen pounds, and the next day had a fine basket of trout from a hill-burn. Then for no earthly reason the weather changed. A bitter wind came out of the north-east, bringing showers of snow and stinging hail, and lashing the waters into storm. It was now farewell to fly-fishing. For a day or two I tried trolling with the minnow on the lochs, but it was poor sport, for I had no boat, and the edges were soft and mossy. Then in disgust I gave up the attempt, went back to the cottage, lit my biggest pipe, and sat down with a book to await the turn of the weather.

The shepherd was out from morning till night at his work, and when he came in at last, dog-tired, his face would be set and hard, and his eyes heavy with sleep. The strangeness of the man grew upon me. He had a shrewd brain beneath his thatch of hair, for I had tried him once or twice, and found him abundantly intelligent. He had some smattering of an education, like all Scottish peasants, and, as I have said, he was deeply religious. I set him down as a fine type of his class, sober, serious, keenly critical, free from the bondage of superstition. But I rarely saw him, and our talk was chiefly in monosyllables—short interjected accounts of the number of lambs dead or alive on the hill. Then he would produce a pencil and notebook, and be immersed in some calculation; and finally he would be revealed sleeping heavily in his chair, till his sister wakened him, and he stumbled off to bed.

So much for the ordinary course of life; but one day— the second I think of the bad weather—the extraordinary happened. The storm had passed in the afternoon into a resolute and blinding snow, and the shepherd, finding it hopeless on the hill, came home about three o'clock. I could make out from his way of entering that he was in a great temper. He kicked his feet savagely against the door-post. Then he swore at his dogs, a thing I had never heard him do before. "Hell!" he cried, "can ye no keep out o' my road, ye britts?" Then he came sullenly into the kitchen, thawed his numbed hands at the fire, and sat down to his meal.

I made some aimless remark about the weather.

"Death to man and beast," he grunted. "I hae got the sheep doun frae the hill, but the lambs will never thole this. We maun pray that it will no last."

His sister came in with some dish. "Margit," he cried, "three lambs away this morning, and three deid wi' the hole in the throat."

The woman's face visibly paled. "Guid help us, Adam; that hasna happened this three year."

"It has happened noo," he said, surlily. "But, by God! if it happens again I'll gang mysel' to the Scarts o' the Muneraw."

"O Adam!" the woman cried shrilly, "haud your tongue. Ye kenna wha hears ye." And with a frightened glance at me she left the room.

I asked no questions, but waited till the shepherd's anger should cool. But the cloud did not pass so lightly. When he had finished his dinner he pulled his chair to the fire and sat staring moodily. He made some sort of apology to me for his conduct. "I'm sore troubled sir; but I'm vexed ye should see me like this. Maybe things will be better the morn." And then, lighting his short black pipe, he resigned himself to his meditations.

But he could not keep quiet. Some nervous unrest seemed to have possessed the man. He got up with a start and went to the window, where the snow was drifting unsteadily past. As he stared out into the storm I heard him mutter to himself, "Three away, God help me, and three wi' the hole in the throat."

Then he turned round to me abruptly. I was jotting down notes for an article I contemplated in the "Revue Celtique," so my thoughts were far away from the present. The man recalled me by demanding fiercely, "Do ye believe in God?"

I gave him some sort of answer in the affirmative.

"Then do ye believe in the Devil?" he asked.

The reply must have been less satisfactory, for he came forward and flung himself violently into the chair before me.

"What do ye ken about it?" he cried. "You that bides in a southern toun, what can ye ken o' the God that works in thae hills and the Devil—ay, the manifold devils—that He suffers to bide here? I tell ye, man, that if ye had seen what I have seen ye wad be on your knees at this moment praying to God to pardon your unbelief. There are devils at the back o' every stane and hidin' in every cleuch, and it's by the grace o' God alone that a man is alive upon the earth." His voice had risen high and shrill, and then suddenly he cast a frightened glance towards the window and was silent.

I began to think that the man's wits were unhinged, and the thought did not give me satisfaction. I had no relish for the prospect of being left alone in this moorland dwelling with the cheerful company of a maniac. But his next movements reassured me. He was clearly only dead-tired, for he fell sound asleep in his chair, and by the time his sister brought tea and wakened him, he seemed to have got the better of his excitement.

When the window was shuttered and the lamp lit, I set myself again to the completion of my notes. The shepherd had got out his Bible, and was solemnly reading with one great finger travelling down the lines. He was smoking, and whenever some text came home to him with power he would make pretence to underline it with the end of the stem. Soon I had finished the work I desired, and, my mind being full of my pet hobby, I fell into an inquisitive frame of mind, and began to question the solemn man opposite on the antiquities of the place.

He stared stupidly at me when I asked him concerning monuments or ancient weapons.

"I kenna," said he. "There's a heap o' queer things in the hills."

"This place should be a centre for such relics. You know that the name of the hill behind the house, as far as I can make it out, means the 'Place of the Little Men.' It is a good Gaelic word, though there is some doubt about its exact interpretation. But clearly the Gaelic peoples did not speak of themselves when they gave the name; they must have referred to some older and stranger population."

The shepherd looked at me dully, as not understanding.

"It is partly this fact—besides the fishing, of course—which interests me in this countryside," said I, gaily.

Again he cast the same queer frightened glance towards the window. "If ye'll tak the advice of an aulder man," he said, slowly, "ye'll let well alane and no meddle wi' uncanny things."

I laughed pleasantly, for at last I had found out my hardheaded host in a piece of childishness. "Why, I thought that you of all men would be free from superstition."

"What do ye call supersteetion?" he asked.

"A belief in old wives' tales," said I, "a trust in the crude supernatural and the patently impossible."

He looked at me beneath his shaggy brows. "How do ye ken what is impossible? Mind ye, sir, ye're no in the toun just now, but in the thick of the wild hills."

"But, hang it all, man," I cried, "you don't mean to say that you believe in that sort of thing? I am prepared for many things up here, but not for the Brownie,—though, to be sure, if one could meet him in the flesh, it would be rather pleasant than otherwise, for he was a companionable sort of fellow."

"When a thing pits the fear o' death on a man he aye speaks well of it."

It was true—the Eumenides and the Good Folk over again; and I awoke with interest to the fact that the conversation was getting into strange channels.

The shepherd moved uneasily in his chair. "I am a man that fears God, and has nae time for daft stories; but I havena traivelled the hills for twenty years wi' my een shut. If I say that I could tell ye stories o' faces seen in the mist, and queer things that have knocked against me in the snaw, wad ye believe me? I wager ye wadna. Ye wad say I had been drunk, and yet I am a God-fearing temperate man."

He rose and went to a cupboard, unlocked it, and brought out something in his hand, which he held out to me. I took it with some curiosity, and found that it was a flint arrow-head.

Clearly a flint arrow-head, and yet like none that I had ever seen in any collection. For one thing it was larger, and the barb less clumsily thick. More, the chipping was new, or comparatively so; this thing had not stood the wear of fifteen hundred years among the stones of the hillside. Now there are, I regret to say, institutions which manufacture primitive relics; but it is not hard for a practised eye to see the difference. The chipping has either a regularity and a balance which is unknown in the real thing, or the rudeness has been overdone, and the result is an implement incapable of harming a mortal creature. But this was the real thing if it ever existed; and yet—I was prepared to swear on my reputation that it was not half a century old.

"Where did you get this?" I asked with some nervousness.

"I hae a story about that," said the shepherd. "Outside the door there ye can see a muckle flat stane aside the buchts. One simmer nicht I was sitting there smoking till the dark, and I wager there was naething on the stane then. But that same nicht I awoke wi' a queer thocht, as if there were folk moving around the hoose—folk that didna mak' muckle noise. I mind o' lookin' out o' the windy, and I could hae sworn I saw something black movin' amang the heather and intil the buchts. Now I had maybe threescore o' lambs there that nicht, for I had to tak' them many miles off in the early morning. Weel, when I gets up about four o'clock and gangs out, as I am passing the muckle stane I finds this bit errow. 'That's come here in the nicht,' says I, and I wunnered a wee and put it in my pouch. But when I came to my faulds what did I see? Five o' my best hoggs were away, and three mair were lying deid wi' a hole in their throat."

"Who in the world——?" I began.

"Dinna ask," said he. "If I aince sterted to speir about thae maitters, I wadna keep my reason."

"Then that was what happened on the hill this morning?"

"Even sae, and it has happened mair than aince sin' that time. It's the most uncanny slaughter, for sheep-stealing I can understand, but no this pricking o' the puir beasts' wizands. I kenna how they dae't either, for it's no wi' a knife or ony common tool."

"Have you never tried to follow the thieves?"

"Have I no?" he asked, grimly. "If it had been common sheep-stealers I wad hae had them by the heels, though I had followed them a hundred miles. But this is no common. I've tracked them, and it's ill they are to track; but I never got beyond ae place, and that was the Scarts o' the Muneraw that ye've heard me speak o'."

"But who in Heaven's name are the people? Tinklers or poachers or what?"

"Ay," said he, drily. "Even so. Tinklers and poachers whae wark wi' stane errows and kill sheep by a hole in their throat. Lord, I kenna what they are, unless the Muckle Deil himsel'."

The conversation had passed beyond my comprehension. In this prosaic hard-headed man I had come on the dead-rock of superstition and blind fear.

"That is only the story of the Brownie over again, and he is an exploded myth," I said, laughing.

"Are ye the man that exploded it?" said the shepherd, rudely. "I trow no, neither you nor ony ither. My bonny man, if ye lived a twalmonth in thae hills, ye wad sing safter about exploded myths, as ye call them."

"I tell you what I would do," said I. "If I lost sheep as you lose them, I would go up the Scarts of the Muneraw and never rest till I had settled the question once and for all." I spoke hotly, for I was vexed by the man's childish fear.

"I daresay ye wad," he said, slowly. "But then I am no you, and maybe I ken mair o' what is in the Scarts o' the Muneraw. Maybe I ken that whilk, if ye kenned it, wad send ye back to the South Country wi' your hert in your mouth. But, as I say, I am no sae brave as you, for I saw something in the first year o' my herding here which put the terror o' God on me, and makes me a fearfu' man to this day. Ye ken the story o' the gudeman o' Carrickfey?"

I nodded.

"Weel, I was the man that fand him. I had seen the deid afore and I've seen them since. But never have I

seen aucht like the look in that man's een. What he saw
at his death I may see the morn, so I walk before the
Lord in fear."

Then he rose and stretched himself. "It's bedding-
time, for I maun be up at three," and with a short good
night he left the room.

CHAPTER III. THE SCARTS OF THE MUNERAW

The next morning was fine, for the snow had been inter-
mittent, and had soon melted except in the high corries.
True, it was deceptive weather, for the wind had gone
to the rainy south-west, and the masses of cloud on that
horizon boded ill for the afternoon. But some days' inaction had made me keen for a chance of sport, so I rose
with the shepherd and set out for the day.

He asked me where I proposed to begin.

I told him the tarn called the Loch o' the Threshes,
which lies over the back of the Muneraw on another
watershed. It is on the ground of the Rhynns Forest, and
I had fished it of old from the Forest House. I knew the
merits of the trout, and I knew its virtues in a south-west
wind, so I had resolved to go thus far afield.

The shepherd heard the name in silence. "Your best
road will be ower that rig, and syne on to the water o'
Caulds. Keep abune the moss till ye come to the place
they ca' the Nick o' the Threshes. That will take ye to
the very lochside, but it's a lang road and a sair."

The morning was breaking over the bleak hills. Little
clouds drifted athwart the corries, and wisps of haze fluttered from the peaks. A great rosy flush lay over one
side of the glen, which caught the edge of the sluggish
bog-pools and turned them to fire. Never before had I
seen the mountain-land so clear, for far back into the
east and west I saw mountain-tops set as close as flowers
in a border, black crags seamed with silver lines which I
knew for mighty waterfalls, and below at my feet the
lower slopes fresh with the dewy green of spring. A name
stuck in my memory from the last night's talk.

"Where are the Scarts of the Muneraw?" I asked.

The shepherd pointed to the great hill which bears the
name, and which lies, a huge mass, above the watershed.

"D'ye see yon corrie at the east that runs straucht up the side? It looks a bit scart, but it's sae deep that it's aye derk at the bottom o't. Weel, at the tap o' the rig it meets anither corrie that runs doun the ither side, and that one they ca' the Scarts. There is a sort o' burn in it that flows intil the Dule and sae intil the Aller, and, indeed, if ye were gaun there it wad be from Aller Glen that your best road wad lie. But it's an ill bit, and ye'll be sair guidit if ye try't."

There he left me and went across the glen, while I struck upwards over the ridge. At the top I halted and looked down on the wide glen of the Caulds, which there is little better than a bog, but lower down grows into a green pastoral valley. The great Muneraw still dominated the landscape, and the black scaur on its side seemed blacker than before. The place fascinated me, for in that fresh morning air the shepherd's fears seemed monstrous. "Some day," said I to myself, "I will go and explore the whole of that mighty hill." Then I descended and struggled over the moss, found the Nick, and in two hours' time was on the loch's edge.

I have little in the way of good to report of the fishing. For perhaps one hour the trout took well; after that they sulked steadily for the day. The promise, too, of fine weather had been deceptive. By midday the rain was falling in that soft soaking fashion which gives no hope of clearing. The mist was down to the edge of the water, and I cast my flies into a blind sea of white. It was hopeless work, and yet from a sort of ill-temper I stuck to it long after my better judgment had warned me of its folly. At last, about three in the afternoon, I struck my camp, and prepared myself for a long and toilsome retreat.

And long and toilsome it was beyond anything I had ever encountered. Had I had a vestige of sense I would have followed the burn from the loch down to the Forest House. The place was shut up, but the keeper would gladly have given me shelter for the night. But foolish pride was too strong in me. I had found my road in mist before, and could do it again.

Before I got to the top of the hill I had repented my decision; when I got there I repented it more. For below me was a dizzy chaos of grey; there was no landmark visible; and before me I knew was the bog through which the Caulds Water twined. I had crossed it with some trouble in the morning, but then I had light to pick my steps. Now I could only stumble on, and in five minutes I might be in a bog-hole, and in five more in a better world.

But there was no help to be got from hesitation, so with a rueful courage I set off. The place was if possible worse than I had feared. Wading up to the knees with nothing before you but a blank wall of mist and the cheerful consciousness that your next step may be your last—such was my state for one weary mile. The stream itself was high, and rose to my armpits, and once and again I only saved myself by a violent leap backwards from a pitiless green slough. But at last it was past, and I was once more on the solid ground of the hillside.

Now, in the thick weather I had crossed the glen much lower down than in the morning, and the result was that the hill on which I stood was one of the giants which, with the Muneraw for centre, guard the watershed. Had I taken the proper way, the Nick o' the Threshes would have led me to the Caulds, and then once over the bog a little ridge was all that stood between me and the glen of Farawa. But instead I had come a wild cross-country road, and was now, though I did not know it, nearly as far from my destination as at the start.

Well for me that I did not know, for I was wet and dispirited, and had I not fancied myself all but home, I should scarcely have had the energy to make this last ascent. But soon I found it was not the little ridge I had expected. I looked at my watch and saw that it was five o'clock. When, after the weariest climb, I lay on a piece of level ground which seemed the top, I was not surprised to find that it was now seven. The darkening must be at hand, and sure enough the mist seemed to be deepening into a greyish black. I began to grow desperate. Here was I on the summit of some infernal mountain, without any certainty where my road lay. I was lost with a vengeance, and at the thought I began to be acutely afraid.

I took what seemed to me the way I had come, and began to descend steeply. Then something made me halt, and the next instant I was lying on my face trying painfully to retrace my steps. For I had found myself slipping, and before I could stop, my feet were dangling over a precipice with Heaven alone knows how many yards of sheer mist between me and the bottom. Then I tried keeping the ridge, and took that to the right, which I thought would bring me nearer home. It was no good trying to think out a direction, for in the fog my brain was running round, and I seemed to stand on a pin-point of space where the laws of the compass had ceased to hold.

It was the roughest sort of walking, now stepping warily over acres of loose stones, now crawling down the face of some battered rock, and now wading in the long dripping heather. The soft rain had begun to fall again, which completed my discomfort. I was now seriously tired, and, like all men who in their day have bent too much over books, I began to feel it in my back. My spine ached, and my breath came in short broken pants. It was a pitiable state of affairs for an honest man who had never encountered much grave discomfort. To ease myself I was compelled to leave my basket behind me, trusting to return and find it, if I should ever reach safety and discover on what pathless hill I had been strayed. My rod I used as a staff, but it was of little use, for my fingers were getting too numb to hold it.

Suddenly from the blankness I heard a sound as of human speech. At first I thought it mere craziness—the cry of a weasel or a hill-bird distorted by my ears. But again it came, thick and faint, as through acres of mist, and yet clearly the sound of "articulate-speaking men." In a moment I lost my despair and cried out in answer. This was some forwandered traveller like myself, and between us we could surely find some road to safety. So I yelled back at the pitch of my voice and waited intently.

But the sound ceased, and there was utter silence again. Still I waited, and then from some place much nearer came the same soft mumbling speech. I could make nothing of it. Heard in that drear place it made the nerves tense and the heart timorous. It was the strangest jumble of vowels and consonants I had ever met.

A dozen solutions flashed through my brain. It was some maniac talking Jabberwock to himself. It was some belated traveller whose wits had given out in fear. Perhaps it was only some shepherd who was amusing himself thus, and whiling the way with nonsense. Once again I cried out and waited.

Then suddenly in the hollow trough of mist before me, where things could still be half discerned, there appeared a figure. It was little and squat and dark; naked, apparently, but so rough with hair that it wore the appearance of a skin-covered being. It crossed my line of vision, not staying for a moment, but in its face and eyes there seemed to lurk an elder world of mystery and barbarism, a troll-like life which was too horrible for words.

The shepherd's fear came back on me like a thunderclap. For one awful instant my legs failed me, and I had almost fallen. The next I had turned and ran shrieking up the hill.

If he who may read this narrative has never felt the force of an overmastering terror, then let him thank his Maker and pray that he never may. I am no weak child, but a strong grown man, accredited in general with sound sense and little suspected of hysterics. And yet I went up that brae-face with my heart fluttering like a bird and my throat aching with fear. I screamed in short dry gasps; involuntarily, for my mind was beyond any purpose. I felt that beast-like clutch at my throat; those red eyes seemed to be staring at me from the mist; I heard ever behind and before and on all sides the patter of those inhuman feet.

Before I knew I was down, slipping over a rock and falling some dozen feet into a soft marshy hollow. I was conscious of lying still for a second and whimpering like a child. But as I lay there I awoke to the silence of the place. There was no sound of pursuit; perhaps they had lost my track and given up. My courage began to return, and from this it was an easy step to hope. Perhaps after all it had been merely an illusion, for folk do not see clearly in the mist, and I was already done with weariness.

But even as I lay in the green moss and began to hope, the faces of my pursuers grew up through the mist. I stumbled madly to my feet; but I was hemmed in, the rock behind and my enemies before. With a cry I rushed

forward, and struck wildly with my rod at the first dark
body. It was as if I had struck an animal, and the next
second the thing was wrenched from my grasp. But still
they came no nearer. I stood trembling there in the centre of those malignant devils, my brain a mere weather-
cock, and my heart crushed shapeless with horror. At
last the end came, for with the vigour of madness I flung
myself on the nearest, and we rolled on the ground. Then
the monstrous things seemed to close over me, and with
a choking cry I passed into unconsciousness.

CHAPTER IV. THE DARKNESS THAT IS UNDER THE EARTH

There is an unconsciousness that is not wholly dead,
where a man feels numbly and the body lives without the
brain. I was beyond speech or thought, and yet I felt the
upward or downward motion as the way lay in hill or
glen, and I most assuredly knew when the open air was
changed for the close underground. I could feel dimly
that lights were flared in my face, and that I was laid in
some bed on the earth. Then with the stopping of movement the real sleep of weakness seized me, and for long
I knew nothing of this mad world.

Morning came over the moors with bird-song and the
glory of fine weather. The streams were still rolling in
spate, but the hill-pastures were alight with dawn, and
the little seams of snow glistened like white fire. A ray
from the sunrise cleft its path somehow into the abyss,
and danced on the wall above my couch. It caught my
eye as I wakened, and for long I lay crazily wondering
what it meant. My head was splitting with pain, and in
my heart was the same fluttering nameless fear. I did not
wake to full consciousness; not till the twinkle of sun
from the clean bright out-of-doors caught my senses did
I realise that I lay in a great dark place with a glow of
dull firelight in the middle.
    In time things rose and moved around me, a few rag-
ged shapes of men, without clothing, shambling with
their huge feet and looking towards me with curved
beast-like glances. I tried to marshal my thoughts, and
slowly, bit by bit, I built up the present. There was no

question to my mind of dreaming; the past hours had scored reality upon my brain. Yet I cannot say that fear was my chief feeling. The first crazy terror had subsided, and now I felt mainly a sickened disgust with just a tinge of curiosity. I found that my knife, watch, flask, and money had gone, but they had left me a map of the countryside. It seemed strange to look at the calico, with the name of a London printer stamped on the back, and lines of railway and highroad running through every shire. Decent and comfortable civilisation! And here was I a prisoner in this den of nameless folk, and in the midst of a life which history knew not.

Courage is a virtue which grows with reflection and the absence of the immediate peril. I thought myself into some sort of resolution, and lo! when the Folk approached me and bound my feet I was back at once in the most miserable terror. They tied me all but my hands with some strong cord, and carried me to the centre, where the fire was glowing. Their soft touch was the acutest torture to my nerves, but I stifled my cries lest some one should lay his hand on my mouth. Had that happened, I am convinced my reason would have failed me.

So there I lay in the shine of the fire, with the circle of unknown things around me. There seemed but three or four, but I took no note of number. They talked huskily among themselves in a tongue which sounded all gutturals. Slowly my fear became less an emotion than a habit, and I had room for the smallest shade of curiosity. I strained my ear to catch a word, but it was a mere chaos of sound. The thing ran and thundered in my brain as I stared dumbly into the vacant air. Then I thought that unless I spoke I should certainly go crazy, for my head was beginning to swim at the strange cooing noise.

I spoke a word or two in my best Gaelic, and they closed round me inquiringly. Then I was sorry I had spoken, for my words had brought them nearer, and I shrank at the thought. But as the faint echoes of my speech hummed in the rock-chamber, I was struck by a curious kinship of sound. Minè was sharper, more distinct, and staccato; theirs was blurred, formless, but still with a certain root-resemblance.

Then from the back there came an older being, who seemed to have heard my words. He was like some foul grey badger, his red eyes sightless, and his hands trembling on a stump of bog-oak. The others made way for him with such deference as they were capable of, and the thing squatted down by me and spoke.

To my amazement his words were familiar. It was some manner of speech akin to the Gaelic, but broadened, lengthened, coarsened. I remembered an old booktongue, commonly supposed to be an impure dialect once used in Brittany, which I had met in the course of my researches. The words recalled it, and as far as I could remember the thing, I asked him who he was and where the place might be.

He answered me in the same speech—still more broadened, lengthened, coarsened. I lay back with sheer amazement. I had found the key to this unearthly life.

For a little an insatiable curiosity, the ardour of the scholar, prevailed. I forgot the horror of the place, and thought only of the fact that here before me was the greatest find that scholarship had ever made. I was precipitated into the heart of the past. Here must be the fountainhead of all legends, the chrysalis of all beliefs. I actually grew light-hearted. This strange folk around me were now no more shapeless things of terror, but objects of research and experiment. I almost came to think them not unfriendly.

For an hour I enjoyed the highest of earthly pleasures. In that strange conversation I heard—in fragments and suggestions—the history of the craziest survival the world has ever seen. I heard of the struggles with invaders, preserved as it were in a sort of shapeless poetry. There were bitter words against the Gaelic oppressor, bitterer words against the Saxon stranger, and for a moment ancient hatreds flared into life. Then there came the tale of the hill-refuge, the morbid hideous existence preserved for centuries amid a changing world. I heard fragments of old religions, primeval names of god and goddess, half-understood by the Folk, but to me the key to a hundred puzzles. Tales which survive to us in broken disjointed riddles were intact here in living form. I lay on my elbow and questioned feverishly. At any moment they might become morose and refuse to speak. Clearly it was my duty to make the most of a brief good fortune.

And then the tale they told me grew more hideous. I heard of the circumstances of the life itself and their daily shifts for existence. It was a murderous chronicle—a history of lust and rapine and unmentionable deeds in the darkness. One thing they had early recognised—that the race could not be maintained within itself; so that ghoulish carrying away of little girls from the lowlands began, which I had heard of but never credited. Shut up in those dismal holes, the girls soon died, and when the new race had grown up the plunder had been repeated. Then there were bestial murders in lonely cottages, done for God knows what purpose. Sometimes the occupant had seen more than was safe, sometimes the deed was the mere exuberance of a lust of slaying. As they gabbled their tales my heart's blood froze, and I lay back in the agonies of fear. If they had used the others thus, what way of escape was open for myself? I had been brought to this place, and not murdered on the spot. Clearly there was torture before death in store for me, and I confess I quailed at the thought.

But none molested me. The elders continued to jabber out their stories, while I lay tense and deaf. Then to my amazement food was brought and placed beside me—almost with respect. Clearly my murder was not a thing of the immediate future. The meal was some form of mutton—perhaps the shepherd's lost ewes—and a little smoking was all the cooking it had got. I strove to eat, but the tasteless morsels choked me. Then they set drink before me in a curious cup, which I seized on eagerly, for my mouth was dry with thirst. The vessel was of gold, rudely formed, but of the pure metal, and a coarse design in circles ran round the middle. This surprised me enough, but a greater wonder awaited me. The liquor was not water, as I had guessed, but a sort of sweet ale, a miracle of flavour. The taste was curious, but somehow familiar; it was like no wine I had ever drunk, and yet I had known that flavour all my life. I sniffed at the brim, and there rose a faint fragrance of thyme and heather honey and the sweet things of the moorland. I almost dropped the thing in my surprise; for here in this rude place I had stumbled upon that lost delicacy of the North, the heather ale.

For a second I was entranced with my discovery, and then the wonder of the cup claimed my attention. Was it a mere relic of pillage, or had this folk some hidden mine of the precious metal? Gold had once been common in these hills. There were the traces of mines on Cairnsmore; shepherds had found it in the gravel of the Gled Water; and the name of a house at the head of the Clachlands meant the "Home of Gold."

Once more I began my questions, and they answered them willingly. There and then I heard that secret for which many had died in old time, the secret of the heather ale. They told of the gold in the hills, of corries where the sand gleamed and abysses where the rocks were veined. All this they told me, freely, without a scruple. And then, like a clap, came the awful thought that this, too, spelled death. These were secrets which this race aforetime had guarded with their lives; they told them generously to me because there was no fear of betrayal. I should go no more out from this place.

The thought put me into a new sweat of terror—not at death, mind you, but at the unknown horrors which might precede the final suffering. I lay silent, and after binding my hands they began to leave me and go off to other parts of the cave. I dozed in the horrible half-swoon of fear, conscious only of my shaking limbs, and the great dull glow of the fire in the centre. Then I became calmer. After all, they had treated me with tolerable kindness: I had spoken their language, which few of their victims could have done for many a century; it might be that I had found favour in their eyes. For a little I comforted myself with this delusion, till I caught sight of a wooden box in a corner. It was of modern make, one such as grocers use to pack provisions in. It had some address nailed on it, and an aimless curiosity compelled me to creep thither and read it. A torn and weather-stained scrap of paper, with the nails at the corner rusty with age; but something of the address might still be made out. Amid the stains my feverish eyes read, "To Mr M——, Carrickfey, by Allerfoot Station."

The ruined cottage in the hollow of the waste with the

single gnarled apple-tree was before me in a twinkling. I remembered the shepherd's shrinking from the place and the name, and his wild eyes when he told me of the thing that had happened there. I seemed to see the old man in his moorland cottage, thinking no evil; the sudden entry of the nameless things; and then the eyes glazed in unspeakable terror. I felt my lips dry and burning. Above me was the vault of rock; in the distance I saw the fire-glow and the shadows of shapes moving around it. My fright was too great for inaction, so I crept from the couch, and silently, stealthily, with tottering steps and bursting heart, I began to reconnoitre.

But I was still bound, my arms tightly, my legs more loosely, but yet firm enough to hinder flight. I could not get my hands at my leg-straps, still less could I undo the manacles. I rolled on the floor, seeking some sharp edge of rock, but all had been worn smooth by the use of centuries. Then suddenly an idea came upon me like an inspiration. The sounds from the fire seemed to have ceased, and I could hear them repeated from another and more distant part of the cave. The Folk had left their orgy round the blaze, and at the end of the long tunnel I saw its glow fall unimpeded upon the floor. Once there, I might burn off my fetters and be free to turn my thoughts to escape.

I crawled a little way with much labour. Then suddenly I came abreast an opening in the wall, through which a path went. It was a long straight rock-cutting, and at the end I saw a gleam of pale light. It must be the open air; the way of escape was prepared for me; and with a prayer I made what speed I could towards the fire.

I rolled on the verge, but the fuel was peat, and the warm ashes would not burn the cords. In desperation I went farther, and my clothes began to singe, while my face ached beyond endurance. But yet I got no nearer my object. The strips of hide warped and cracked, but did not burn. Then in a last effort I thrust my wrists bodily into the glow and held them there. In an instant I drew them out with a groan of pain, scarred and sore, but to my joy with the band snapped in one place. Weak as I was, it was now easy to free myself, and then came the untying of my legs. My hands trembled, my eyes

were dazed with hurry, and I was longer over the job
than need have been. But at length I had loosed my
cramped knees and stood on my feet, a free man once
more.

I kicked off my boots, and fled noiselessly down the
passage to the tunnel mouth. Apparently it was close on
evening, for the white light had faded to a pale yellow.
But it was daylight, and that was all I sought, and I ran
for it as eagerly as ever runner ran to a goal. I came out
on a rock-shelf, beneath which a moraine of boulders fell
away in a chasm to a dark loch. It was all but night, but
I could see the gnarled and fortressed rocks rise in ram-
parts above, and below the unknown screes and cliffs
which make the side of the Muneraw a place only for
foxes and the fowls of the air.

The first taste of liberty is an intoxication, and
assuredly I was mad when I leaped down among the
boulders. Happily at the top of the gully the stones were
large and stable, else the noise would certainly have discovered me. Down I went, slipping, praying, my charred
wrists aching, and my stockinged feet wet with blood.
Soon I was in the jaws of the cleft, and a pale star rose
before me. I have always been timid in the face of great
rocks, and now, had not an awful terror been dogging
my footsteps, no power on earth could have driven me
to that descent. Soon I left the boulders behind, and
came to long spouts of little stones, which moved with
me till the hillside seemed sinking under my feet. Sometimes I was face downwards, once and again I must have
fallen for yards. Had there been a cliff at the foot, I
should have gone over it without resistance; but by the
providence of God the spout ended in a long curve into
the heather of the bog.

When I found my feet once more on soft boggy earth,
my strength was renewed within me. A great hope of
escape sprang up in my heart. For a second I looked
back. There was a great line of shingle with the cliffs
beyond, and above all the unknown blackness of the
cleft. There lay my terror, and I set off running across
the bog for dear life. My mind was clear enough to know
my road. If I held round the loch in front I should come
to a burn which fed the Farawa stream, on whose banks

stood the shepherd's cottage. The loch could not be far; once at the Farawa I would have the light of the shieling clear before me.

Suddenly I heard behind me, as if coming from the hillside, the patter of feet. It was the sound which white hares make in the winter-time on a noiseless frosty day as they patter over the snow. I have heard the same soft noise from a herd of deer when they changed their pastures. Strange that so kindly a sound should put the very fear of death in my heart. I ran madly, blindly, yet thinking shrewdly. The loch was before me. Somewhere I had read or heard, I do not know where, that the brutish aboriginal races of the North could not swim. I myself swam powerfully; could I but cross the loch I should save two miles of a desperate country.

There was no time to lose, for the patter was coming nearer, and I was almost at the loch's edge. I tore off my coat and rushed in. The bottom was mossy, and I had to struggle far before I found any depth. Something plashed in the water before me, and then something else a little behind. The thought that I was a mark for unknown missiles made me crazy with fright, and I struck fiercely out for the other shore. A gleam of moonlight was on the water at the burn's exit, and thither I guided myself. I found the thing difficult enough in itself, for my hands ached, and I was numb with my bonds. But my fancy raised a thousand phantoms to vex me. Swimming in that black bog water, pursued by those nameless things, I seemed to be in a world of horror far removed from the kindly world of men. My strength seemed inexhaustible from my terror. Monsters at the bottom of the water seemed to bite at my feet, and the pain of my wrists made me believe that the loch was boiling hot, and that I was in some hellish place of torment.

I came out on a spit of gravel above the burn mouth, and set off down the ravine of the burn. It was a strait place, strewn with rocks; but now and then the hill turf came in stretches, and eased my wounded feet. Soon the fall became more abrupt, and I was slipping down a hillside, with the water on my left making great cascades in the granite. And then I was out in the wider vale where the Farawa water flowed among links of moss.

Far in front, a speck in the blue darkness, shone the light of the cottage. I panted forward, my breath coming in gasps and my back shot with fiery pains. Happily the land was easier for the feet as long as I kept on the skirts of the bog. My ears were sharp as a wild beast's with fear, as I listened for the noise of pursuit. Nothing came but the rustle of the gentlest hill-wind and the chatter of the falling streams.

Then suddenly the light began to waver and move athwart the window. I knew what it meant. In a minute or two the household at the cottage would retire to rest, and the lamp would be put out. True, I might find the place in the dark, for there was a moon of sorts and the road was not desperate. But somehow in that hour the lamplight gave a promise of safety which I clung to despairingly.

And then the last straw was added to my misery. Behind me came the pad of feet, the pat-patter, soft, eerie, incredibly swift. I choked with fear, and flung myself forward in a last effort. I give my word it was sheer mechanical shrinking that drove me on. God knows I would have lain down to die in the heather, had the things behind me been a common terror of life.

I ran as man never ran before, leaping hags, scrambling through green well-heads, straining towards the fast-dying light. A quarter of a mile and the patter sounded nearer. Soon I was not two hundred yards off, and the noise seemed almost at my elbow. The light went out, and the black mass of the cottage loomed in the dark.

Then, before I knew, I was at the door, battering it wearily and yelling for help. I heard steps within and a hand on the bolt. Then something shot past me with lightning force and buried itself in the wood. The dreadful hands were almost at my throat, when the door was opened and I stumbled in, hearing with a gulp of joy the key turn and the bar fall behind me.

CHAPTER V. THE TROUBLES OF A CONSCIENCE

My body and senses slept, for I was utterly tired, but my brain all the night was on fire with horrid fancies. Again

I was in that accursed cave; I was torturing my hands in the fire; I was slipping barefoot among jagged boulders; and then with bursting heart I was toiling the last mile with the cottage light—now grown to a great fire in the heavens—blazing before me.

It was broad daylight when I awoke, and I thanked God for the comfortable rays of the sun. I had been laid in a box-bed off the inner room, and my first sight was the shepherd sitting with folded arms in a chair regarding me solemnly. I rose and began to dress, feeling my legs and arms still tremble with weariness. The shepherd's sister bound up my scarred wrists and put an ointment on my burns; and, limping like an old man, I went into the kitchen.

I could eat little breakfast, for my throat seemed dry and narrow; but they gave me some brandy-and-milk, which put strength into my body. All the time the brother and sister sat in silence, regarding me with covert glances.

"Ye have been delivered from the jaws o' the Pit," said the man at length. "See that," and he held out to me a thin shaft of flint. "I fand that in the door this morning."

I took it, let it drop, and stared vacantly at the window. My nerves had been too much tried to be roused by any new terror. Out of doors it was fair weather, flying gleams of April sunlight and the soft colours of spring. I felt dazed, isolated, cut off from my easy past and pleasing future, a companion of horrors and the sport of nameless things. Then suddenly my eye fell on my books heaped on a table, and the old distant civilisation seemed for the moment inexpressibly dear.

"I must go—at once. And you must come too. You cannot stay here. I tell you it is death. If you knew what I know you would be crying out with fear. How far is it to Allermuir? Eight, fifteen miles; and then ten down Glen Aller to Allerfoot, and then the railway. We must go together while it is daylight, and perhaps we may be untouched. But quick, there is not a moment to lose." And I was on my shaky feet, and bustling among my possessions.

"I'll gang wi' ye to the station," said the shepherd,

"for ye're clearly no fit to look after yourself. My sister will bide and keep the house. If naething has touched us this ten year, naething will touch us the day."

"But you cannot stay. You are mad," I began; but he cut me short with the words, "I trust in God."

"In any case let your sister come with us. I dare not think of a woman alone in this place."

"I'll bide," said she. "I'm no feared as lang as I'm indoors and there's steeks on the windies."

So I packed my few belongings as best I could, tumbled my books into a haversack, and, gripping the shepherd's arm nervously, crossed the threshold. The glen was full of sunlight. There lay the long shining links of the Farawa burn, the rough hills tumbled beyond, and far over all the scarred and distant forehead of the Muneraw. I had always looked on moorland country as the freshest on earth—clean, wholesome, and homely. But now the fresh uplands seemed like a horrible pit. When I looked to the hills my breath choked in my throat, and the feel of soft heather below my feet set my heart trembling.

It was a slow journey to the inn at Allermuir. For one thing, no power on earth would draw me within sight of the shieling of Carrickfey, so we had to cross a shoulder of hill and make our way down a difficult glen, and then over a treacherous moss. The lochs were now gleaming like fretted silver; but to me, in my dreadful knowledge, they seemed more eerie than on that grey day when I came. At last my eyes were cheered by the sight of a meadow and a fence; then we were on a little byroad; and soon the fir-woods and corn-lands of Allercleuch were plain before us.

The shepherd came no farther, but with brief good-bye turned his solemn face hillwards. I hired a trap and a man to drive, and down the ten miles of Glen Aller I struggled to keep my thoughts from the past. I thought of the kindly South Country, of Oxford, of anything comfortable and civilised. My driver pointed out the objects of interest as in duty bound, but his words fell on unheeding ears. At last he said something which roused me indeed to interest—the interest of the man who hears the word he fears most in the world. On the left side of the river there suddenly sprang into view a long gloomy cleft in the hills, with a vista of dark mountains behind, down which a stream of considerable size poured its waters.

"That is the Water o' Dule," said the man in a reverent voice. "A graund water to fish, but dangerous to life, for it's a' linns. Awa' at the heid they say there's a terrible wild place called the Scarts o' Muneraw,—that's a shouther o' the muckle hill itsel' that ye see,—but I've never been there, and I never kent ony man that had either."

At the station, which is a mile from the village of Allerfoot, I found I had some hours to wait on my train for the south. I dared not trust myself for one moment alone, so I hung about the goods-shed, talked vacantly to the porters, and when one went to the village for tea I accompanied him, and to his wonder entertained him at the inn. When I returned I found on the platform a stray bagman who was that evening going to London. If there is one class of men in the world which I heartily detest it is this; but such was my state that I hailed him as a brother, and besought his company. I paid the difference for a first-class fare, and had him in the carriage with me. He must have thought me an amiable maniac, for I talked in fits and starts, and when he fell asleep I would wake him up and beseech him to speak to me. At wayside stations I would pull down the blinds in case of recognition, for to my unquiet mind the world seemed full of spies sent by that terrible Folk of the Hills. When the train crossed a stretch of moor I would lie down on the seat in case of shafts fired from the heather. And then at last with utter weariness I fell asleep, and woke screaming about midnight to find myself well down in the cheerful English midlands, and red blast-furnaces blinking by the railway-side.

In the morning I breakfasted in my rooms at St Chad's with a dawning sense of safety. I was in a different and calmer world. The lawn-like quadrangles, the great trees, the cawing of rooks, and the homely twitter of sparrows—all seemed decent and settled and pleasing. Indoors the oak-panelled walls, the shelves of books, the pictures, the faint fragrance of tobacco, were very differ-

ent from the grimcrack adornments and the accursed
smell of peat and heather in that deplorable cottage. It
was still vacation-time, so most of my friends were down;
but I spent the day hunting out the few cheerful pedants
to whom term and vacation were the same. It delighted
me to hear again their precise talk, to hear them make
a boast of their work, and narrate the childish little acci-
dents of their life. I yearned for the childish once more;
I craved for women's drawing-rooms, and women's chatter, and everything which makes life an elegant game.
God knows I had had enough of the other thing for a
lifetime!

That night I shut myself in my rooms, barred my windows, drew my curtains, and made a great destruction.
All books or pictures which recalled to me the moorlands
were ruthlessly doomed. Novels, poems, treatises I flung
into an old box, for sale to the second-hand bookseller.
Some prints and water-colour sketches I tore to pieces
with my own hands. I ransacked my fishing-book, and
condemned all tackle for moorland waters to the flames.
I wrote a letter to my solicitors, bidding them go no
further in the purchase of a place in Lorne I had long
been thinking of. Then, and not till then, did I feel the
bondage of the past a little loosed from my shoulders. I
made myself a night-cap of rum-punch instead of my
usual whisky-toddy, that all associations with that dismal
land might be forgotten, and to complete the renuncia-
tion I returned to cigars and flung my pipe into a drawer.

But when I woke in the morning I found that it is
hard to get rid of memories. My feet were still sore and
wounded, and when I felt my arms cramped and reflected
on the causes, there was that black memory always near
to vex me.

In a little term began, and my duties—as deputy-pro-
fessor of Northern Antiquities—were once more clamor-
ous. I can well believe that my hearers found my lectures
strange, for instead of dealing with my favourite subjects
and matters, which I might modestly say I had made my
own, I confined myself to recondite and distant themes,
treating even these cursorily and dully. For the truth is,
my heart was no more in my subject. I hated—or I
thought that I hated—all things Northern with the viru-

lence of utter fear. My reading was confined to science of the most recent kind, to abstruse philosophy, and to foreign classics. Anything which savoured of romance or mystery was abhorrent; I pined for sharp outlines and the tangibility of a high civilisation.

All the term I threw myself into the most frivolous life of the place. My Harrow school-days seemed to have come back to me. I had once been a fair cricketer, so I played again for my college, and made decent scores. I coached an indifferent crew on the river. I fell into the slang of the place, which I had hitherto detested. My former friends looked on me askance, as if some freakish changeling had possessed me. Formerly I had been ready for pedantic discussion, I had been absorbed in my work, men had spoken of me as a rising scholar. Now I fled the very mention of things I had once delighted in. The Professor of Northern Antiquities, a scholar of European reputation, meeting me once in the parks, embarked on an account of certain novel rings recently found in Scotland, and to his horror found that, when he had got well under weigh, I had slipped off unnoticed. I heard afterwards that the good old man was found by a friend walking disconsolately with bowed head in the middle of the High Street. Being rescued from among the horses' feet, he could only murmur, "I am thinking of Graves, poor man! And a year ago he was as sane as I am!"

But a man may not long deceive himself. I kept up the illusion valiantly for the term; but I felt instinctively that the fresh schoolboy life, which seemed to me the extreme opposite to the ghoulish North, and as such the most desirable of things, was eternally cut off from me. No cunning affectation could ever dispel my real nature or efface the memory of a week. I realised miserably that sooner or later I must fight it out with my conscience. I began to call myself a coward. The chief thoughts of my mind began to centre themselves more and more round that unknown life waiting to be explored among the unfathomable wilds.

One day I met a friend—an official in the British Museum—who was full of some new theory about primitive habitations. To me it seemed inconceivably absurd;

but he was strong in his confidence, and without flaw in his evidence. The man irritated me, and I burned to prove him wrong, but I could think of no argument which was final against his. Then it flashed upon me that my own experience held the disproof; and without more words I left him, hot, angry with myself, and tantalised by the unattainable.

I might relate my *bona-fide* experience, but would men believe me? I must bring proofs, I must complete my researches, so as to make them incapable of disbelief. And there in those deserts was waiting the key. There lay the greatest discovery of the century—nay, of the millennium. There, too, lay the road to wealth such as I had never dreamed of. Could I succeed, I should be famous for ever. I would revolutionise history and anthropology; I would systematise folk-lore; I would show the world of men the pit whence they were digged and the rock whence they were hewn.

And then began a game of battledore between myself and my conscience.

"You are a coward," said my conscience.

"I am sufficiently brave," I would answer. "I have seen things and yet lived. The terror is more than mortal, and I cannot face it."

"You are a coward," said my conscience.

"I am not bound to go there again. It would be purely for my own aggrandisement if I went, and not for any matter of duty."

"Nevertheless you are a coward," said my conscience.

"In any case the matter can wait."

"You are a coward."

Then came one awful midsummer night, when I lay sleepless and fought the thing out with myself. I knew that the strife was hopeless, that I should have no peace in this world again unless I made the attempt. The dawn was breaking when I came to the final resolution; and when I rose and looked at my face in a mirror, lo! it was white and lined and drawn like a man of sixty.

CHAPTER VI. SUMMER ON THE MOORS

The next morning I packed a bag with some changes of clothing and a collection of notebooks, and went up to town. The first thing I did was to pay a visit to my solicitors. "I am about to travel," said I, "and I wish to have all things settled in case any accident should happen to me." So I arranged for the disposal of my property in case of death, and added a codicil which puzzled the lawyers. If I did not return within six months, communications were to be entered into with the shepherd at the shieling of Farawa—post-town Allerfoot. If he could produce any papers, they were to be put into the hands of certain friends, published, and the cost charged to my estate. From my solicitors I went to a gun-maker's in Regent Street and bought an ordinary six-chambered revolver, feeling much as a man must feel who proposed to cross the Atlantic in a skiff and purchased a small life-belt as a precaution.

I took the night express to the North, and, for a marvel, I slept. When I woke about four we were on the verge of Westmoreland, and stony hills blocked the horizon. At first I hailed the mountain-land gladly; sleep for the moment had caused forgetfulness of my terrors. But soon a turn of the line brought me in full view of a heathery moor, running far to a confusion of distant peaks. I remembered my mission and my fate, and if ever condemned criminal felt a more bitter regret I pity his case. Why should I alone among the millions of this happy isle be singled out as the repository of a ghastly secret, and be cursed by a conscience which would not let it rest?

I came to Allerfoot early in the forenoon, and got a trap to drive me up the valley. It was a lowering grey day, hot and yet sunless. A sort of heat-haze cloaked the hills, and every now and then a smurr of rain would meet us on the road, and in a minute be over. I felt wretchedly dispirited; and when at last the white-washed kirk of Allermuir came into sight and the broken-backed bridge of Aller, man's eyes seemed to have looked on no drearier scene since time began.

I ate what meal I could get, for, fears or no, I was

voraciously hungry. Then I asked the landlord to find me some man who would show me the road to Farawa. I demanded company, not for protection—for what could two men do against such brutish strength?—but to keep my mind from its own thoughts.

The man looked at me anxiously.

"Are ye acquaint wi' the folks, then?" he asked.

I said I was, that I had often stayed in the cottage.

"Ye ken that they've a name for being queer. The man never comes here forbye once or twice a-year, and he has few dealings wi' other herds. He's got an ill name, too, for losing sheep. I dinna like the country ava. Up by yon Muneraw—no that I've ever been there, but I've seen it afar off—is enough to put a man daft for the rest o' his days. What's taking ye thereaways? It's no the time for the fishing?"

I told him that I was a botanist going to explore certain hill-crevices for rare ferns. He shook his head, and then after some delay found me an ostler who would accompany me to the cottage.

The man was a shock-headed, long-limbed fellow, with fierce red hair and a humorous eye. He talked sociably about his life, answered my hasty questions with deftness, and beguiled me for the moment out of myself. I passed the melancholy lochs, and came in sight of the great stony hills without the trepidation I had expected. Here at my side was one who found some humour even in those uplands. But one thing I noted which brought back the old uneasiness. He took the road which led us farthest from Carrickfey, and when to try him I proposed the other, he vetoed it with emphasis.

After this his good spirits departed, and he grew distrustful.

"What mak's ye a freend o' the herd at Farawa?" he demanded a dozen times.

Finally, I asked him if he knew the man, and had seen him lately.

"I dinna ken him, and I hadna seen him for years till a fortnicht syne, when a' Allermuir saw him. He cam doun one afternoon to the public-hoose, and begood to drink. He had aye been kenned for a terrible godly kind o' a man, so ye may believe folk wondered at this. But when he had stuck to the drink for twae days, and filled himsel' blind-fou half-a-dozen o' times, he took a fit o' repentance, and raved and blethered about siccan a life as he led in the muirs. There was some said he was speakin' serious, but maist thocht it was juist daftness."

"And what did he speak about?" I asked sharply.

"I canna verra weel tell ye. It was about some kind o' bogle that lived in the Muneraw—that's the shouthers o't ye see yonder—and it seems that the bogle killed his sheep and frichted himsel'. He was aye bletherin', too, about something or somebody ca'd Grave; but oh! the man wasna wise." And my companion shook a contemptuous head.

And then below us in the valley we saw the shieling, with a thin shaft of smoke rising into the rainy grey weather. The man left me, sturdily refusing any fee. "I wantit my legs stretched as weel as you. A walk in the hills is neither here nor there to a stoot man. When will ye be back, sir?"

The question was well-timed. "To-morrow fortnight," I said, "and I want somebody from Allermuir to come out here in the morning and carry some baggage. Will you see to that?"

He said "Ay," and went off, while I scrambled down the hill to the cottage. Nervousness possessed me, and though it was broad daylight and the whole place lay plain before me, I ran pell-mell, and did not stop till I reached the door.

The place was utterly empty. Unmade beds, unwashed dishes, a hearth strewn with the ashes of peat, and dust thick on everything, proclaimed the absence of inmates. I began to be horribly frightened. Had the shepherd and his sister, also, disappeared? Was I left alone in the bleak place, with a dozen lonely miles between me and human dwellings? I could not return alone; better this horrible place than the unknown perils of the out-of-doors. Hastily I barricaded the door, and to the best of my power shuttered the windows; and then with dreary forebodings I sat down to wait on fortune.

In a little I heard a long swinging step outside and the sound of dogs. Joyfully I opened the latch, and there was the shepherd's grim face waiting stolidly on what might appear.

At the sight of me he stepped back. "What in the Lord's name are ye daein' here?" he asked. "Didna ye get enough afore?"

"Come in," I said, sharply. "I want to talk."

In he came with those blessed dogs,—what a comfort it was to look on their great honest faces! He sat down on the untidy bed and waited.

"I came because I could not stay away. I saw too much to give me any peace elsewhere. I must go back, even though I risk my life for it. The cause of scholarship demands it as well as the cause of humanity."

"Is that a' the news ye hae?" he said. "Weel, I've mair to tell ye. Three weeks syne my sister Margit was lost, and I've never seen her mair."

My jaw fell, and I could only stare at him.

"I cam hame from the hill at nightfa' and she was gone. I lookit for her up hill and doun, but I couldna find her. Syne I think I went daft. I went to the Scarts and huntit them up and doun, but no sign could I see. The folk can bide quiet enough when they want. Syne I went to Allermuir and drank mysel' blind,—me, that's a God-fearing man and a saved soul; but the Lord help me, I didna ken what I was at. That's my news, and day and nicht I wander thae hills, seekin' for what I canna find."

"But, man, are you mad?" I cried. "Surely there are neighbours to help you. There is a law in the land, and you had only to find the nearest police-office and compel them to assist you."

"What guid can man dae?" he asked. "An army o' sodgers couldna find that hidy-hole. Forby, when I went into Allermuir wi' my story the folk thocht me daft. It was that set me drinking, for—the Lord forgive me!—I wasna my ain maister. I threepit till I was hairse, but the bodies just lauch'd." And he lay back on the bed like a man mortally tired.

Grim though the tidings were, I can only say that my chief feeling was of comfort. Pity for the new tragedy had swallowed up my fear. I had now a purpose, and a purpose, too, not of curiosity but of mercy.

"I go to-morrow morning to the Muneraw. But first I want to give you something to do." And I drew roughly a chart of the place on the back of a letter. "Go into Allermuir to-morrow, and give this paper to the landlord at the inn. The letter will tell him what to do. He is to raise at once all the men he can get, and come to the place on the chart marked with a cross. Tell him life depends on his hurry."

The shepherd nodded. "D'ye ken the Folk are watching for you? They let me pass without trouble, for they've nae use for me, but I see fine they're seeking you. Ye'll no gang half a mile the morn afore they grip ye."

"So much the better," I said. "That will take me quicker to the place I want to be at."

"And I'm to gang to Allermuir the morn," he repeated, with the air of a child conning a lesson. "But what if they'll no believe me?"

"They'll believe the letter."

"Maybe," he said, and relapsed into a doze.

I set myself to put that house in order, to rouse the fire, and prepare some food. It was dismal work; and meantime outside the night darkened, and a great wind rose, which howled round the walls and lashed the rain on the windows.

CHAPTER VII. *IN TUAS MANUS, DOMINE!*

I had not gone twenty yards from the cottage door ere I knew I was watched. I had left the shepherd still dozing, in the half-conscious state of a dazed and broken man. All night the wind had wakened me at intervals, and now in the half-light of morn the weather seemed more vicious than ever. The wind cut my ears, the whole firmament was full of the rendings and thunders of the storm. Rain fell in blinding sheets, the heath was a marsh, and it was the most I could do to struggle against the hurricane which stopped my breath. And all the while I knew I was not alone in the desert.

All men know—in imagination or in experience—the sensation of being spied on. The nerves tingle, the skin grows hot and prickly, and there is a queer sinking of the heart. Intensify this common feeling a hundredfold, and you get a tenth part of what I suffered. I am telling a plain tale, and record bare physical facts. My lips stood out from my teeth as I heard, or felt, a rustle in the heather, a scraping among stones. Some subtle magnetic link seemed established between my body and the mysterious world around. I became sick—acutely sick—with the ceaseless apprehension.

My fright became so complete that when I turned a corner of rock, or stepped in deep heather, I seemed to feel a body rub against me. This continued all the way up the Farawa water, and then up its feeder to the little lonely loch. It kept me from looking forward; but it likewise kept me in such a sweat of fright that I was ready to faint. Then the notion came upon me to test this fancy of mine. If I was tracked thus closely, clearly the trackers would bar my way if I turned back. So I wheeled round and walked a dozen paces down the glen.

Nothing stopped me. I was about to turn again, when something made me take six more paces. At the fourth something rustled in the heather, and my neck was gripped as in a vice. I had already made up my mind on what I would do. I would be perfectly still, I would conquer my fear, and let them do as they pleased with me so long as they took me to their dwelling. But at the touch of the hands my resolutions fled. I struggled and screamed. Then something was clapped on my mouth, speech and strength went from me, and once more I was back in the maudlin childhood of terror.

In the cave it was always a dusky twilight. I seemed to be lying in the same place, with the same dull glare of firelight far off, and the same close stupefying smell. One of the creatures was standing silently at my side, and I asked him some trivial question. He turned and shambled down the passage, leaving me alone.

Then he returned with another, and they talked their guttural talk to me. I scarcely listened till I remembered that in a sense I was here of my own accord, and on a definite mission. The purport of their speech seemed to be that, now I had returned, I must beware of a second flight. Once I had been spared; a second time I should be killed without mercy.

I assented gladly. The Folk, then, had some use for me. I felt my errand prospering.

Then the old creature which I had seen before crept out of some corner and squatted beside me. He put a claw on my shoulder, a horrible, corrugated, skeleton thing, hairy to the finger-tips and nailless. He grinned, too, with toothless gums, and his hideous old voice was like a file on sandstone.

I asked questions, but he would only grin and jabber, looking now and then furtively over his shoulder towards the fire.

I coaxed and humoured him, till he launched into a narrative of which I could make nothing. It seemed a mere string of names, with certain words repeated at fixed intervals. Then it flashed on me that this might be a religious incantation. I had discovered remnants of a ritual and a mythology among them. It was possible that these were sacred days, and that I had stumbled upon some rude celebration.

I caught a word or two and repeated them. He looked at me curiously. Then I asked him some leading question, and he replied with clearness. My guess was right. The midsummer week was the holy season of the year, when sacrifices were offered to the gods.

The notion of sacrifices disquieted me, and I would fain have asked further. But the creature would speak no more. He hobbled off, and left me alone in the rock-chamber to listen to a strange sound which hung ceaselessly about me. It must be the storm without, like a pack of artillery rattling among the crags. A storm of storms surely, for the place echoed and hummed, and to my unquiet eye the very rock of the roof seemed to shake!

Apparently my existence was forgotten, for I lay long before any one returned. Then it was merely one who brought food, the same strange meal as before, and left hastily. When I had eaten I rose and stretched myself. My hands and knees still quivered nervously; but I was strong and perfectly well in body. The empty, desolate, tomb-like place was eerie enough to scare any one; but its emptiness was comfort when I thought of its inmates. Then I wandered down the passage towards the fire which was burning in loneliness. Where had the Folk gone? I puzzled over their disappearance.

Suddenly sounds began to break on my ear, coming from some inner chamber at the end of that in which the fire burned. I could scarcely see for the smoke; but I began to make my way towards the noise, feeling along the sides of rock. Then a second gleam of light seemed to rise before me, and I came to an aperture in the wall which gave entrance to another room.

This in turn was full of smoke and glow—a murky orange glow, as if from some strange flame of roots. There were the squat moving figures, running in wild antics round the fire. I crouched in the entrance, terrified and yet curious, till I saw something beyond the blaze which held me dumb. Apart from the others and tied to some stake in the wall was a woman's figure, and the face was the face of the shepherd's sister.

My first impulse was flight. I must get away and think,—plan, achieve some desperate way of escape. I sped back to the silent chamber as if the gang were at my heels. It was still empty, and I stood helplessly in the centre, looking at the impassable walls of rock as a wearied beast may look at the walls of its cage. I bethought me of the way I had escaped before and rushed thither, only to find it blocked by a huge contrivance of stone. Yards and yards of solid rock were between me and the upper air, and yet through it all came the crash and whistle of the storm. If I were at my wits' end in this inner darkness, there was also high commotion among the powers of the air in that upper world.

As I stood I heard the soft steps of my tormentors. They seemed to think I was meditating escape, for they flung themselves on me and bore me to the ground. I did not struggle, and when they saw me quiet, they squatted round and began to speak. They told me of the holy season and its sacrifices. At first I could not follow them; then when I caught familiar words I found some clue, and they became intelligible. They spoke of a woman, and I asked, "What woman?" With all frankness they told me of the custom which prevailed—how every twentieth summer a woman was sacrificed to some devilish god, and by the hand of one of the stranger race. I said nothing, but my whitening face must have told them a tale, though I strove hard to keep my composure. I asked if they had found the victims. "She is in this place," they said; "and as for the man, thou art he." And with this they left me.

I had still some hours; so much I gathered from their talk, for the sacrifice was at sunset. Escape was cut off for ever. I have always been something of a fatalist, and at the prospect of the irrevocable end my cheerfulness returned. I had my pistol, for they had taken nothing from me. I took out the little weapon and fingered it lovingly. Hope of the lost, refuge of the vanquished, ease to the coward,—blessed be he who first conceived it!

The time dragged on, the minutes grew to hours, and still I was left solitary. Only the mad violence of the storm broke the quiet. It had increased in violence, for the stones at the mouth of the exit by which I had formerly escaped seemed to rock with some external pressure, and cutting shafts of wind slipped past and cleft the heat of the passage. What a sight the ravine outside must be, I thought, set in the forehead of a great hill, and swept clean by every breeze! Then came a crashing, and the long hollow echo of a fall. The rocks are splitting, said I; the road down the corrie will be impassable now and for evermore.

I began to grow weak with the nervousness of the waiting, and by-and-by I lay down and fell into a sort of doze. When I next knew consciousness I was being roused by two of the Folk, and bidden get ready. I stumbled to my feet, felt for the pistol in the hollow of my sleeve, and prepared to follow.

When we came out into the wider chamber the noise of the storm was deafening. The roof rang like a shield which has been struck. I noticed, perturbed as I was, that my guards cast anxious eyes around them, alarmed, like myself, at the murderous din. Nor was the world quieter when we entered the last chamber, where the fire burned and the remnant of the Folk waited. Wind had found an entrance from somewhere or other, and the flames blew here and there, and the smoke gyrated in odd circles. At the back, and apart from the rest, I saw the dazed eyes and the white old drawn face of the woman.

They led me up beside her to a place where there was a rude flat stone, hollowed in the centre, and on it a rusty iron knife, which seemed once to have formed part of a scythe-blade. Then I saw the ceremonial which was marked out for me. It was the very rite which I had dimly figured as current among a rude people, and even in that moment I had something of the scholar's satisfaction.

The oldest of the Folk, who seemed to be a sort of priest, came to my side and mumbled a form of words. His fetid breath sickened me; his dull eyes, glassy like a brute's with age, brought my knees together. He put the knife in my hands, dragged the terror-stricken woman forward to the altar, and bade me begin.

I began by sawing her bonds through. When she felt herself free she would have fled back, but stopped when I bade her. At that moment there came a noise of rending and crashing as if the hills were falling, and for one second the eyes of the Folk were averted from the frustrated sacrifice.

Only for a moment. The next they saw what I had done, and with one impulse rushed towards me. Then began the last scene in the play. I sent a bullet through the right eye of the first thing that came on. The second shot went wide; but the third shattered the hand of an elderly ruffian with a cruel club. Never for an instant did they stop, and now they were clutching at me. I pushed the woman behind, and fired three rapid shots in blind panic, and then, clutching the scythe, I struck right and left like a madman.

Suddenly I saw the foreground sink before my eyes. The roof sloped down, and with a sickening hiss a mountain of rock and earth seemed to precipitate itself on my assailants. One, nipped in the middle by a rock, caught my eye by his hideous writhings. Two only remained in what was now a little suffocating chamber, with embers from the fire still smoking on the floor.

The woman caught me by the hand and drew me with her, while the two seemed mute with fear. "There's a

road at the back," she screamed. "I ken it. I fand it
out." And she pulled me up a narrow hole in the rock.

How long we climbed I do not know. We were both
fighting for air, with the tightness of throat and chest,
and the craziness of limb which mean suffocation. I cannot tell when we first came to the surface, but I remember the woman, who seemed to have the strength of
extreme terror, pulling me from the edge of a crevasse
and laying me on a flat rock. It seemed to be the depth
of winter, with sheer-falling rain and a wind that shook
the hills.

Then I was once more myself and could look about
me. From my feet yawned a sheer abyss, where once had
been a hill-shoulder. Some great mass of rock on the
brow of the mountain had been loosened by the storm,
and in its fall had caught the lips of the ravine and swept
the nest of dwellings into a yawning pit. Beneath a mountain of rubble lay buried that life on which I had thought
to build my fame.

My feeling—Heaven help me!—was not thankfulness
for God's mercy and my escape, but a bitter mad regret.
I rushed frantically to the edge, and when I saw only the
blackness of darkness I wept weak tears. All the time
the storm was tearing at my body, and I had to grip hard
by hand and foot to keep my place.

Suddenly on the brink of the ravine I saw a third figure. We two were not the only fugitives. One of the Folk
had escaped.

The thought put new life into me, for I had lost the
first fresh consciousness of terror. There still remained a
relic of the vanished life. Could I but make the thing my
prisoner, there would be proof in my hands to overcome
a sceptical world.

I ran to it, and to my surprise the thing as soon as it
saw me rushed to meet me. At first I thought it was with
some instinct of self-preservation, but when I saw its eyes
I knew the purpose of fight. Clearly one or other should
go no more from the place.

We were some ten yards from the brink when I grap-
pled with it. Dimly I heard the woman scream with
fright, and saw her scramble across the hillside. Then we

were tugging in a death-throe, the hideous smell of the thing in my face, its red eyes burning into mine, and its hoarse voice muttering. Its strength seemed incredible; but I, too, am no weakling. We tugged and strained, its nails biting into my flesh, while I choked its throat unsparingly. Every second I dreaded lest we should plunge together over the ledge, for it was thither my adversary tried to draw me. I caught my heel in a nick of rock, and pulled madly against it.

And then, while I was beginning to glory with the pride of conquest, my hope was dashed in pieces. The thing seemed to break from my arms, and, as if in despair, cast itself headlong into the impenetrable darkness. I stumbled blindly after it, saved myself on the brink, and fell back, sick and ill, into a merciful swoon.

CHAPTER VIII. NOTE IN CONCLUSION BY THE EDITOR

At this point the narrative of my unfortunate friend, Mr. Graves of St Chad's, breaks off abruptly. He wrote it shortly before his death, and was prevented from completing it by the shock of apoplexy which carried him off. In accordance with the instructions in his will, I have prepared it for publication, and now in much fear and hesitation give it to the world. First, however, I must supplement it by such facts as fall within my knowledge.

The shepherd seems to have gone to Allermuir and by the help of the letter convinced the inhabitants. A body of men was collected under the landlord, and during the afternoon set out for the hills. But unfortunately the great midsummer storm—the most terrible of recent climatic disturbances—had filled the mosses and streams, and they found themselves unable to proceed by any direct road. Ultimately late in the evening they arrived at the cottage of Farawa, only to find there a raving woman, the shepherd's sister, who seemed crazy with brain-fever. She told some rambling story about her escape, but her narrative said nothing of Mr. Graves. So they treated her with what skill they possessed, and sheltered for the night in and around the cottage. Next morning the storm had abated a little, and the woman had recovered something of her wits. From her they

learned that Mr. Graves was lying in a ravine on the side
of the Muneraw in imminent danger of his life. A body
set out to find him; but so immense was the landslip,
and so dangerous the whole mountain, that it was nearly
evening when they recovered him from the ledge of rock.
He was alive, but unconscious, and on bringing him back
to the cottage it was clear that he was, indeed, very ill.
There he lay for three months, while the best skill that
could be got was procured for him. By dint of an uncommon toughness of constitution he survived; but it was an
old and feeble man who returned to Oxford in the early
winter.

The shepherd and his sister immediately left the countryside, and were never more heard of, unless they are
the pair of unfortunates who are at present in a Scottish
pauper asylum, incapable of remembering even their
names. The people who last spoke with them declared
that their minds seemed weakened by a great shock, and
that it was hopeless to try to get any connected or rational statement.

The career of my poor friend from that hour was little
short of a tragedy. He awoke from his illness to find the
world incredulous; even the country-folk of Allermuir set
down the story to the shepherd's craziness and my
friend's credulity. In Oxford his argument was received
with polite scorn. An account of his experiences which
he drew up for the "Times" was refused by the editor;
and an article on "Primitive Peoples of the North,"
embodying what he believed to be the result of his discoveries, was unanimously rejected by every responsible
journal in Europe. Whether he was soured by such treatment, or whether his brain had already been weakened,
he became a morose silent man, and for the two years
before his death had few friends and no society. From
the obituary notice in the "Times" I take the following
paragraph, which shows in what light the world had come
to look upon him:—

"At the outset of his career he was regarded as a rising
scholar in one department of archæology, and his Taffert
lectures were a real contribution to an obscure subject.
But in after-life he was led into fantastic speculations;
and when he found himself unable to convince his col-

leagues, he gradually retired into himself, and lived practically a hermit's life till his death. His career, thus broken short, is a sad instance of the fascination which the recondite and the quack can exercise even on men of approved ability."

And now his own narrative is published, and the world can judge as it pleases about the amazing romance. The view which will doubtless find general acceptance is that the whole is a figment of the brain, begotten of some harmless moorland adventure and the company of such religious maniacs as the shepherd and his sister. But some who knew the former sobriety and calmness of my friend's mind may be disposed timorously and with deep hesitation to another verdict. They may accept the narrative, and believe that somewhere in those moorlands he met with a horrible primitive survival, passed through the strangest adventure, and had his finger on an epoch-making discovery. In this case they will be inclined to sympathise with the loneliness and misunderstanding of his latter days. It is not for me to decide the question. That which alone could bring proof is buried beneath a thousand tons of rock in the midst of an untrodden desert.

JOHN BUCHAN.

THE PRISM

By Mary E. Wilkins

There had been much rain that season, and the vegetation was almost tropical. The wayside growths were jungles to birds and insects, and very near them to humans. All through the long afternoon of the hot August day, Diantha Fielding lay flat on her back under the lee of the stone wall which bordered her stepfather's, Zenas May's, south mowing-lot. It was pretty warm there, although she lay in a little strip of shade of the tangle of blackberry-vines, poison-ivy, and the gray pile of stones; but the girl loved the heat. She experienced the gentle languor which is its best effect, instead of the fierce unrest and irritation which is its worst. She left that to rattlesnakes and nervous women. As for her, in times of extreme heat, she hung over life with tremulous flutters, like a butterfly over a rose, moving only enough to preserve her poise in the scheme of things, and realizing to the full the sweetness of all about her.

She heard, as she lay there, the voice of a pine-tree not far away—a solitary pine which was full of gusty sweetness; she smelled the wild grapes, which were reluctantly ripening across the field over the wall that edged the lane; she smelled the blackberry-vines; she looked with indolent fascination at the virile sprays of poison-ivy. It was like innocence surveying sin, and wondering what it was like. Once her stepmother, Mrs. Zenas May, had been poisoned with ivy, and both eyes had been closed thereby. Diantha did not believe that the ivy would so serve her. She dared herself to touch it, then she looked away again.

She heard a far-carrying voice from the farm-house at

208

the left calling her name. "Diantha! Diantha!" She lay so still that she scarcely breathed. The voice came again. She smiled triumphantly. She knew perfectly well what was wanted: that she should assist in preparing supper. Her stepmother's married daughter and her two children were visiting at the house. She preferred remaining where she was. Her sole fear of disturbance was from the children. They were like little ferrets. Diantha did not like them. She did not like children very well under any circumstances. To her they seemed always out of tune; the jar of heredity was in them, and she felt it, although she did not know enough to realize what she felt. She was only twelve years old, a child still, though tall for her age.

The voice came again. Diantha shifted her position a little; she stretched her slender length luxuriously; she felt for something which hung suspended around her neck under her gingham waist, but she did not then remove it. "Diantha! Diantha!" came the insistent voice.

Diantha lay as irresponsive as the blackberry-vine which trailed beside her like a snake. Then she heard the house door close with a bang; her ears were acute. She felt again of that which was suspended from her neck. A curious expression of daring, of exultation, of fear, was in her face. Presently she heard the shrill voices of children; then she lay so still that she seemed fairly to obliterate herself by silence and motionlessness.

Two little girls in pink frocks came racing past; their flying heels almost touched her, but they never saw her.

When they were well past, she drew a cautious breath, and felt again of the treasure around her neck.

After a while she heard the soft padding of many hoofs in the heavy dust of the road, a dog's shrill bark, the tinkle of a bell, the absent-minded shout of a weary man. The hired man was driving the cows home. The fragrance of milk-dripping udders, of breaths sweetened with clover and meadow-grass, came to her. Suddenly a cold nose rubbed against her face; the dog had found her out. But she was a friend of his. She patted him, then pushed him away gently, and he understood that she wished to remain concealed. He went barking back to the man. The cows broke into a clumsy gallop; the man shouted.

Diantha smelled the dust of the road which flew over the field like smoke. She heard the children returning down the road behind the cows. When the cows galloped, they screamed with half-fearful delight. Then it all passed by, and she heard the loud clang of a bell from the farm-house.

Then Diantha pulled out the treasure which was suspended from her neck by an old blue ribbon, and she held it up to the low western sun, and wonderful lights of red and blue and violet and green and orange danced over the shaven stubble of the field before her delighted eyes. It was a prism which she had stolen from the best-parlor lamp—from the lamp which had been her own mother's, bought by her with her school-teaching money before her marriage, and brought by her to grace her new home.

Diantha Fielding, as far as relatives went, was in a curious position. First her mother died when she was very young, only a few months old; then her father had married again, giving her a stepmother; then her father had died two years later, and her stepmother had married again, giving her a stepfather. Since then the stepmother had died, and the stepfather had married a widow with a married daughter, whose two children had raced down the road behind the cows. Diantha often felt in a sore bewilderment of relationships. She had not even a cousin of her own; the dearest relative she had was the daughter of a widow whom a cousin of her mother's had married for a second wife. The cousin was long since dead. The wife was living, and Diantha's little step second cousin, as she reckoned it, lived in the old homestead which had belonged to Diantha's grandfather, across the way from the May farm-house. It was a gambrel-roof, half-ruinous structure, well banked in front with a monstrous growth of lilacs, and overhung by a great butternut-tree.

Diantha knew well that she was heaping up vials of cold wrath upon her head by not obeying the supper-bell, but she lay still. Then Libby came—Libby, the little cousin, stepping very cautiously and daintily; for she wore slippers of her mother's, which hung from her small heels, and she had lost them twice already.

She stopped before Diantha. Her slender arms, terminating in hands too large for them, hung straight at her sides in the folds of her faded blue-flowered muslin. Her pretty little heat-flushed face had in it no more speculation than a flower, and no more changing. She was like a flower, which would blossom the same next year, and the next year after that, and the same until it died. There was no speculation in her face as she looked at Diantha dangling the prism in the sunlight, merely unimaginative wonder and admiration.

"It's a drop off your best-parlor lamp," said she, in her thin, sweet voice.

"Look over the field, Libby!" cried Diantha, excitedly. Libby looked.

"Tell me what you see, quick!"

"What I see? Why, grass and things."

"No, I don't mean them; what you see from this." Diantha shook the prism violently.

"I see a lot of different colors dancing," replied Libby, "same as you always see. Addie Green had an ear-drop that was broken off their best-parlor lamp. Her mother gave it to her."

"Don't you see anything but different lights?"

"Of course I don't. That's all there is to see." Diantha sighed.

"That drop ain't broken," said the other little girl. "How did she happen to let you have it?" By "she" Libby meant Diantha's stepmother.

"I took it," replied Diantha. She was fastening the prism around her neck again.

Libby gasped and stared at her. "Didn't you ask her?"

"If I'd asked her, she'd said no, and it was my own mother's lamp. I had a right to it."

"What'll she do to you?"

"I don't know, if she finds out. I sha'n't tell her, if I can help it without lying."

Diantha fastened her gingham frock securely over the prism. Then she rose, and the two little girls went home across the dry stubble of the field.

"I didn't go when she called me, and I didn't go when the supper-bell rang," said Diantha.

Libby stared at her wonderingly. She had never felt an impulse to disobedience in her life; she could not understand this other child, who was a law unto herself. She walked very carefully in her large slippers.

"What'll she do to you?" she inquired.

Diantha tossed her head like a colt.

"She won't do anything, I guess, except make me go without my supper. If she does, I ain't afraid; but I guess she won't, and I'd a heap rather go without my supper than go to it when I don't want to."

Libby looked at her with admiring wonder. Diantha was neatly and rigorously, rather than tastefully, dressed. Her dark blue-and-white gingham frock was starched stiffly; it hung exactly at the proper height from her slender ankles; she wore a clean white collar; and her yellow hair was braided very tightly and smoothly, and tied with a punctilious blue bow. In strange contrast with the almost martial preciseness of her attire was the expression of her little face, flushed, eager to enthusiasm, almost wild, with a light in her blue eyes which did not belong there, according to the traditions concerning little New England maidens, with a feverish rose on her cheeks, which should have been cool and pale. However, that had all come since she had dangled the prism in the rays of the setting sun.

"What did you think you saw when you shook that ear-drop off the lamp?" asked Libby; but she asked without much curiosity.

"Red and green and yellow colors, of course," replied Diantha, shortly.

When they reached Diantha's door, Libby bade her good night, and sped across the road to her own house. She stood a little in fear of Diantha's stepmother, if Diantha did not. She knew just the sort of look which would be directed toward the other little girl, and she knew from experience that it might include her. From her Puritan ancestry she had a certain stubbornness when brought to bay, but no courage of aggression; so she ran.

Diantha marched in. She was utterly devoid of fear. Her stepmother, Mrs. Zenas May, was washing the supper dishes at the kitchen sink. All through the house sounded a high sweet voice which was constantly off the key, singing a lullaby to the two little girls, who had to go to bed directly after they had finished their evening meal.

Mrs. Zenas May turned around and surveyed Diantha as she entered. There was nothing in the least unkind in her look; it was simply the gaze of one on a firm standpoint of existence upon another swaying on a precarious balance—the sort of look a woman seated in a car gives to one standing. It was irresponsible, while cognizant of the discomfort of the other person.

"Where were you when the supper-bell rang?" asked Mrs. Zenas May. She was rather a pretty woman, with an exquisitely cut profile. Her voice was very even, almost as devoid of inflections as a deaf-and-dumb person's. Her gingham gown was also rigorously starched. Her fair hair showed high lights of gloss from careful brushing; it was strained back from her blue-veined temples.

"Out in the field," replied Diantha.

"Then you heard it?"

"Yes, ma'am."

"The supper-table is cleared away," said Mrs. May. That was all she said. She went on polishing the tumblers, which she was rinsing in ammonia water.

Diantha glanced through the open door and saw the dining-room table with its chenille after-supper cloth on. She made no reply, but went up-stairs to her own chamber. That was very comfortable—the large south one back of her step-parents'. Not a speck of dust was to be seen in it; the feather-bed was an even mound of snow. Diantha sat down by the window, and gazed out at the deepening dusk. She felt at the prism around her neck, but she did not draw it out, for it was of no use in that low light. She could not invoke the colors which it held. Her chamber door was open. Presently she heard the best-parlor door open, and heard quite distinctly her stepmother's voice. She was speaking to her stepfather.

"There's a drop broken off the parlor lamp," said she.

There was an unintelligible masculine grunt of response.

"I wish you'd look while I hold the lamp, and see if you can find it on the floor anywhere," said her stepmother. Her voice was still even. The loss of a prism

from the best-parlor lamp was not enough to ruffle her
outward composure.

"Don't you see it?" she asked, after a little.

Again came the unintelligible masculine grunt.

"It is very strange," said Mrs. May. "Don't look any
more."

She never inquired of Diantha concerning the prism.
In truth, she believed one of her grandchildren, whom
she adored, to be responsible for the loss of the glittering
ornament, and was mindful of the fact that Diantha's
mother had originally owned that lamp. So she said nothing, but as soon as might be purchased another, and
Diantha kept her treasure quite unsuspected.

She did not, however, tremble in the least while the
search was going on down-stairs. She had her defense
quite ready. To her sense of justice it was unquestion-
able. She would simply say that the lamp had belonged
to her own mother, consequently to her; that she had a
right to do as she chose with it. She had not the slightest
fear of any reproaches which Mrs. May would bring to
bear upon her. She knew she would not use bodily punishment, as she never had; but she would have stood in
no fear of that.

Diantha did not go to bed for a long time. There was
a full moon, and she sat by the window, leaning her two
elbows on the sill, making a cup of her hands, in which
she rested her peaked chin, and peered out.

It was nearly nine o'clock when some one entered the
room with heavy, soft movements, like a great tame dog.
It was her stepfather, and he had in his hand a large
wedge of apple-pie.

"Diantha," he said, in a loud whisper, "you gone to
bed?"

"No, sir," replied Diantha. She liked her stepfather.
She was always aware of a clumsy, covert partizanship
from him.

"Well," said he, "here's a piece of pie. You hadn't
ought to go to bed without any supper. You'd ought to
come in when the bell rings another time, Diantha."

"Thank you, father," said Diantha, reaching out her
hand for the pie.

Zenas May, who was large and shaggily blond, with a

face like a great blank of good nature, placed a heavy hand on her little, tightly braided head, and patted it.

"Better eat your pie and go to bed," he said. Then he shambled down-stairs very softly, lest his wife hear him.

Diantha ate her pie obediently, and went to bed, and with the first morning sunlight she removed her prism from her neck, and flashed it across the room, and saw what she saw, or what she thought she saw.

Diantha kept the prism, and nobody except Libby knew it, and she was quite safe with a secret. While she did not in the least comprehend, she was stanch. Even when she grew older and had a lover, she did not tell him; she did not even tell him when she was married to him that Diantha Fielding always carried a drop off the best-parlor lamp, which belonged to her own mother, and when she flashed it in the sunlight she thought she saw things. She kept it all to herself. Libby married before Diantha, before Diantha had a lover even. Young men, for some reason, were rather shy of Diantha, although she had a little property in her own right, inherited from her own father and mother, and was, moreover, extremely pretty. However, her prettiness was not of a type to attract the village men as quickly as Libby's more material charms. Diantha was very thin and small, and her color was as clear as porcelain, and she gave a curious impression of mystery, although there was apparently nothing whatever mysterious about her.

But her turn came. A graduate of a country college, a farmer's son, who had worked his own way through college, had now obtained the high school. He saw Diantha, and fell in love with her, although he struggled against it. He said to himself that she was too delicate, that he was a poor man, that he ought to have a more robust wife, who would stand a better chance of discharging her domestic and maternal duties without a breakdown. Reason and judgment were strongly developed in him. His passion for Diantha was entirely opposed to both, but it got the better of him. One afternoon in August when Diantha was almost twenty, he, passing by her house, saw her sitting on her front doorstep, stopped, and proposed a little stroll in the woods, and asked her to marry him.

"I never thought much about getting married," said Diantha. Then she leaned toward him as if impelled by some newly developed instinct. She spoke so low that he could not hear her, and he asked her over.

"I never thought much about getting married," repeated Diantha, and she leaned nearer him.

He laughed a great triumphant laugh, and caught her in his arms.

"Then it is high time you did, you darling," he said.

Diantha was very happy.

They lingered in the woods a long time, and when they went home, the young man, whose name was Robert Black, went in with her, and told her stepmother what had happened.

"I have asked your daughter to marry me, Mrs. May," he said, "and she has consented, and I hope you are willing."

Mrs. May replied that she had no objections, stiffly, without a smile. She never smiled. Instead of smiling, she always looked questioningly even at her beloved grandchildren. They had lived with her since their mother's death, two pretty, boisterous girls, pupils of Robert Black, who had had their own inevitable little dreams regarding him, as they had had regarding every man who came in their way.

When their grandmother told them that Diantha was to marry the hero who had dwelt in their own innocently bold air-castles of girlish dreams, they started at first as from a shock of falling imaginations; then they began to think of their attire as bridesmaids.

Mrs. Zenas May was firmly resolved that Diantha should have as grand a wedding as if she had been her own daughter.

"Folks sha'n't say that she didn't have as good an outfit and wedding as if her own mother had been alive to see to it," she said.

As for Diantha, she thought very little about her outfit or the wedding, but about Robert. All at once she was possessed by a strong angel of primal conditions of whose existence she had never dreamed. She poured out her very soul; she made revelations of the inmost innocences of her nature to this ambitious, faithful, unimaginative young man. She had been some two weeks betrothed, and they were walking together one afternoon, when she showed him her prism.

She no longer wore it about her neck as formerly. A dawning unbelief in it had seized her, and yet there were times when to doubt seemed to doubt the evidence of her own senses.

That afternoon, as they were walking together in the lonely country road, she stopped him in a sunny interval between the bordering woods, where the road stretched for some distance between fields foaming with wild carrot and mustard, and swarmed over with butterflies, and she took her prism out of her pocket and flashed it full before her wondering lover's eyes.

He looked astonished, even annoyed; then he laughed aloud with a sort of tender scorn.

"What a child you are, dear!" he said. "What are you doing with that thing?"

"What do you see, Robert?" the girl cried eagerly, and there was in her eyes a light not of her day and generation, maybe inherited from some far-off Celtic ancestor—a strain of imagination which had survived the glaring light of latter days of commonness.

He eyed her with amazement; then he looked at the gorgeous blots and banners of color over the fields.

"See? Why, I see the prismatic colors, of course. What else should I see?" he asked.

"Nothing else?"

"No. Why, what else should I see? I see the prismatic colors from the refraction of the sunlight."

Diantha looked at the dancing tints, then at her lover, and spoke with a solemn candor, as if she were making confession of an alien faith. "Ever since I was a child, I have seen, or thought so—" she began.

"What, for heaven's sake?" he cried impatiently.

"You have read about—fairies and—such things?"

"Of course. What do you mean, Diantha?"

"I have seen, or thought so, beautiful little people moving and dancing in the broken lights across the fields."

"For heaven's sake, put up that thing, and don't talk

such nonsense, Diantha!" cried Robert, almost brutally. He had paled a little.

"I have, Robert."

"Don't talk such nonsense. I thought you were a sensible girl," said the young man.

Diantha put the prism back in her pocket.

All the rest of the way Robert was silent and gloomy. His old doubts had revived. His judgment for the time being got the upper hand of his passion. He began to wonder if he ought to marry a girl with such preposterous fancies as those. He began to wonder if she were just right in her mind.

He parted from her coolly, and came the next evening, but remained only a short time. Then he stayed away several days. He called on Sunday, then did not come again for four days. On Friday Diantha grew desperate. She went by herself out in the sunny field, walking ankle-deep in flowers and weeds, until she reached the margin of a little pond on which the children skated in winter. Then she took her prism from her pocket and flashed it in the sunlight, and for the first time she failed to see what she had either seen, or imagined, for so many years.

She saw only the beautiful prismatic colors flashing across the field in bars and blots and streamers of rose and violet, of orange and green. That was all. She stooped, and dug in the oozy soil beside the pond with her bare white hands, and made, as it were, a little grave, and buried the prism out of sight. Then she washed her hands in the pond, and waved them about until they were dry. Afterward she went swiftly across the field to the road which her lover must pass on his way from school, and, when she saw him coming, met him, blushing and trembling.

"I have put it away, Robert," she said. "I saw nothing; it was only my imagination."

It was a lonely road. He looked at her doubtfully, then he laughed, and put an arm around her.

"It's all right, little girl," he replied; "but don't let such fancies dwell in your brain. This is a plain, common world, and it won't do."

"I saw nothing; it must have been my imagination," she repeated. Then she leaned her head against her lover's shoulder. Whether or not she had sold her birthright, she had got her full measure of the pottage of love which filled to an ecstasy of satisfaction her woman's heart.

She and Robert were married, and lived in a pretty new house, from the western windows of which she could see the pond on whose borders she had buried the prism. She was very happy. For the time being, at least, all the mysticism in her face had given place to an utter revelation of earthly bliss. People said how much Diantha had improved since her marriage, what a fine housekeeper she was, how much common sense she had, how she was such a fitting mate for her husband, whom she adored.

Sometimes Diantha, looking from a western window, used to see the pond across the field, reflecting the light of the setting sun, and looking like an eye of revelation of the earth; and she would remember that key of a lost radiance and a lost belief of her own life, which was buried beside it. Then she would go happily and prepare her husband's supper.

THE KITH OF THE ELF-FOLK

Lord Dunsany

The north wind was blowing, and red and golden the last days of Autumn were streaming hence. Solemn and cold over the marshes arose the evening.

It became very still.

Then the last pigeon went home to the trees on the dry land in the distance, whose shapes already had taken upon themselves a mystery in the haze.

Then all was still again.

As the light faded and the haze deepened, mystery crept nearer from every side.

Then the green plover came in crying, and all alighted.

And again it became still, save when one of the plover arose and flew a little way uttering the cry of the waste. And hushed and silent became the earth, expecting the first star. Then the duck came in, and the widgeon, company by company: and all the light of day faded out of the sky saving one red band of light. Across the light appeared, black and huge, the wings of a flock of geese beating up wind to the marshes. These too went down among the rushes.

Then the stars appeared and shone in the stillness, and there was silence in the great spaces of the night.

Suddenly the bells of the cathedral in the marshes broke out, calling to evensong.

Eight centuries ago on the edge of the marsh men had built the huge cathedral, or it may have been seven centuries ago, or perhaps nine; it was all one to the Wild Things.

So evensong was held, and candles lighted, and the lights through the windows shone red and green in the water, and the sound of the organ went roaring over the marshes. But from the deep and perilous places, edged with bright mosses, the Wild Things came leaping up to dance on the reflection of the stars, and over their heads as they danced the marsh-lights rose and fell.

The Wild Things are somewhat human in appearance, only all brown of skin and barely two feet high. Their ears are pointed like the squirrel's, only far larger, and they leap to prodigious heights. They live all day under deep pools in the loneliest marshes, but at night they come up and dance. Each Wild Thing has over its head a marsh-light, which moves as the Wild Thing moves; they have no souls, and cannot die, and are of the kith of the Elf-folk.

All night they dance over the marshes, treading upon the reflection of the stars (for the bare surface of the water will not hold them by itself); but when the stars begin to pale, they sink down one by one into the pools of their home. Or if they tarry longer, sitting upon the rushes, their bodies fade from view as the marsh-fires pale in the light, and by daylight none may see the Wild Things of the kith of the Elf-folk. Neither may any see them even at night unless they were born, as I was, in the hour of dusk, just at the moment when the first star appears.

Now, on the night that I tell of, a little Wild Thing had gone drifting over the waste, till it came right up to the walls of the cathedral and danced upon the images of the coloured saints as they lay in the water among the reflection of the stars. And as it leaped in its fantastic dance, it saw through the painted windows to where the people prayed, and heard the organ roaring over the marshes. The sound of the organ roared over the marshes, but the song and prayers of the people streamed up from the cathedral's highest tower like thin gold chains, and reached to Paradise, and up and down them went the angels from Paradise to the people, and from the people to Paradise again.

Then something akin to discontent troubled the Wild Thing for the first time since the making of the marshes; and the soft grey ooze and the chill of the deep water seemed to be not enough, nor the first arrival from northwards of the tumultuous geese, nor the wild rejoicing of the wings of the wildfowl when every feather sings, nor the wonder of the calm ice that comes when the snipe depart and beards the rushes with frost and clothes the hushed waste with a mysterious haze where the sun goes red and low, nor even the dance of the Wild Things in the marvellous night; and the little Wild Thing longed to have a soul, and to go and worship God.

And when evensong was over and the lights were out, it went back crying to its kith.

But on the next night, as soon as the images of the stars appeared in the water, it went leaping away from star to star to the farthest edge of the marshlands, where a great wood grew where dwelt the Oldest of Wild Things.

And it found the Oldest of Wild Things sitting under a tree, sheltering itself from the moon.

And the little Wild Thing said: "I want to have a soul to worship God, and to know the meaning of music, and to see the inner beauty of the marshlands and to imagine Paradise."

And the Oldest of the Wild Things said to it: "What have we to do with God? We are only Wild Things, and of the Kith of the Elf-folk."

But it only answered, "I want to have a soul."

Then the Oldest of the Wild Things said: "I have no soul to give you; but if you got a soul, one day you would have to die, and if you knew the meaning of music you would learn the meaning of sorrow, and it is better to be a Wild Thing and not to die."

So it went weeping away.

But they that were kin to the Elf-folk were sorry for the little Wild Thing; and though the Wild Things cannot sorrow long, having no souls to sorrow with, yet they felt for awhile a soreness where their souls should be, when they saw the grief of their comrade.

So the kith of the Elf-folk went abroad by night to make a soul for the little Wild Thing. And they went over the marshes till they came to the high fields among the flowers and grasses. And there they gathered a large piece of gossamer that the spider had laid by twilight; and the dew was on it.

Into this dew had shone all the lights of the long banks of the ribbed sky, as all the colours changed in the restful spaces of evening. And over it the marvellous night had gleamed with all its stars.

Then the Wild Things went with their dew-bespangled gossamer down to the edge of their home. And there they gathered a piece of the grey mist that lies by night over the marshlands. And into it they put the melody of the waste that is borne up and down the marshes in the evening on the wings of the golden plover. And they put into it too the mournful song that the reeds are compelled to sing before the presence of the arrogant North Wind. Then each of the Wild Things gave some treasured memory of the old marshes, "For we can spare it," they said. And to all this they added a few images of the stars that they gathered out of the water. Still the soul that the kith of the Elf-folk were making had no life.

Then they put into it the low voices of two lovers that went walking in the night, wandering late alone. And after that they waited for the dawn. And the queenly dawn appeared, and the marsh-lights of the Wild Things paled in the glare, and their bodies faded from view; and still they waited by the marsh's edge. And to them waiting came over field and marsh, from the ground and out of the sky, the myriad song of the birds.

This too the Wild Things put into the piece of haze that they had gathered in the marshlands, and wrapped it all up in their dew-bespangled gossamer. Then the soul lived.

And there it lay in the hands of the Wild Things no larger than a hedgehog; and wonderful lights were in it, green and blue; and they changed ceaselessly, going round and round, and in the grey midst of it was a purple flare.

And the next night they came to the little Wild Thing and showed her the gleaming soul. And they said to her: "If you must have a soul and go and worship God, and become a mortal and die, place this to your left breast a little above the heart, and it will enter and you will become a human. But if you take it you can never be rid of it to become immortal again unless you pluck it out and give it to another; and *we* will not take it, and most of the humans have a soul already. And if you cannot find a human without a soul you will one day die, and your soul cannot go to Paradise, because it was only made in the marshes."

Far away the little Wild Thing saw the cathedral windows alight for evensong, and the song of the people mounting up to Paradise, and all the angels going up and down. So it bid farewell with tears and thanks to the Wild Things of the kith of Elf-folk, and went leaping away towards the green dry land, holding the soul in its hands.

And the Wild Things were sorry that it had gone, but could not be sorry long, because they had no souls.

At the marsh's edge the little Wild Thing gazed for some moments over the water to where the marsh-fires were leaping up and down, and then pressed the soul against its left breast a little above the heart.

Instantly it became a young and beautiful woman, who was cold and frightened. She clad herself somehow with bundles of reeds, and went towards the lights of a house that stood close by. And she pushed open the door and entered, and found a farmer and a farmer's wife sitting over their supper.

And the farmer's wife took the little Wild Thing with the soul of the marshes up to her room, and clothed her and braided her hair, and brought her down again, and gave her the first food that she had ever eaten. Then the farmer's wife asked many questions.

"Where have you come from?" she said.

"Over the marshes."

"From what direction?" said the farmer's wife.

"South," said the little Wild Thing with the new soul.

"But none can come over the marshes from the south," said the farmer's wife.

"No, they can't do that," said the farmer.

"I lived in the marshes."

"Who are you?" asked the farmer's wife.

"I am a Wild Thing, and have found a soul in the marshes, and we are kin to the Elf-folk."

Talking it over afterwards, the farmer and his wife agreed that she must be a gipsy who had been lost, and that she was queer with hunger and exposure.

So that night the little Wild Thing slept in the farmer's house, but her new soul stayed awake the whole night long dreaming of the beauty of the marshes.

As soon as dawn came over the waste and shone on the farmer's house, she looked from the window towards the glittering waters, and saw the inner beauty of the marsh. For the Wild Things only love the marsh and know its haunts, but now she perceived the mystery of its distances and the glamour of its perilous pools, with their fair and deadly mosses, and felt the marvel of the North Wind who comes dominant out of unknown icy lands, and the wonder of that ebb and flow of life when the wildfowl whirl in at evening to the marshlands and at dawn pass out to sea. And she knew that over her head above the farmer's house stretched wide Paradise, where perhaps God was now imagining a sunrise while angels played low on lutes, and the sun came rising up on the world below to gladden fields and marsh.

And all that heaven thought, the marsh thought too; for the blue of the marsh was as the blue of heaven, and the great cloud shapes in heaven became the shapes in the marsh, and through each ran momentary rivers of purple, errant between banks of gold. And the stalwart army of reeds appeared out of the gloom with all their pennons waving as far as the eye could see. And from another window she saw the vast cathedral gathering its ponderous strength together, and lifting it up in towers out of the marshlands.

She said, "I will never, never leave the marsh."

An hour later she dressed with great difficulty and went down to eat the second meal of her life. The farmer and his wife were kindly folk, and taught her how to eat.

"I suppose the gipsies don't have knives and forks," one said to the other afterwards.

After breakfast the farmer went and saw the Dean, who lived near his cathedral, and presently returned and brought back to the Dean's house the little Wild Thing with the new soul.

"This is the lady," said the farmer. "This is Dean Murnith." Then he went away.

"Ah," said the Dean, "I understand you were lost the

other night in the marshes. It was a terrible night to be lost in the marshes."

"I love the marshes," said the little Wild Thing with the new soul.

"Indeed! How old are you?" said the Dean.

"I don't know," she answered.

"You must know about how old you are," he said.

"Oh, about ninety," she said, "or more."

"Ninety years!" exclaimed the Dean.

"No, ninety centuries," she said; "I am as old as the marshes."

Then she told her story—how she had longed to be a human and go and worship God, and have a soul and see the beauty of the world, and how all the Wild Things had made her a soul of gossamer and mist and music and strange memories.

"But if this is true," said Dean Murnith, "this is very wrong. God cannot have intended you to have a soul.

"What is your name?"

"I have no name," she answered.

"We must find a Christian name and a surname for you. What would you like to be called?"

"Song of the Rushes," she said.

"That won't do at all," said the Dean.

"Then I would like to be called Terrible North Wind, or Star in the Waters," she said.

"No, no, no," said Dean Murnith; "that is quite impossible. We could call you Miss Rush if you like. How would Mary Rush do? Perhaps you had better have another name—say Mary Jane Rush."

So the little Wild Thing with the soul of the marshes took the names that were offered her, and became Mary Jane Rush.

"And we must find something for you to do," said Dean Murnith. "Meanwhile we can give you a room here."

"I don't want to do anything," replied Mary Jane; "I want to worship God in the cathedral and live beside the marshes."

Then Mrs. Murnith came in, and for the rest of that day Mary Jane stayed at the house of the Dean.

And there with her new soul she perceived the beauty

of the world; for it came grey and level out of misty distances, and widened into grassy fields and ploughlands right up to the edge of an old gabled town; and solitary in the fields far off an ancient windmill stood, and his honest handmade sails went round and round in the free East Anglian winds. Close by, the gabled houses leaned out over the streets, planted fair upon sturdy timbers that grew in the olden time, all glorying among themselves upon their beauty. And out of them, buttress by buttress, growing and going upwards, aspiring tower by tower, rose the cathedral.

And she saw the people moving in the streets all leisurely and slow, and unseen among them, whispering to each other, unheard by living men and concerned only with bygone things, drifted the ghosts of very long ago. And wherever the streets ran eastwards, wherever were gaps in the houses, always there broke into view the sight of the great marshes, like to some bar of music weird and strange that haunts a melody, arising again and again, played on the violin by one musician only, who plays no other bar, and he is swart and lank about the hair and bearded about the lips, and his moustache droops long and low, and no one knows the land from which he comes.

All these were good things for a new soul to see.

Then the sun set over green fields and ploughland, and the night came up. One by one the merry lights of cheery lamp-lit windows took their stations in the solemn night.

Then the bells rang, far up in a cathedral tower, and their melody fell on the roofs of the old houses and poured over their eaves until the streets were full, and then flooded away over green fields and plough, till it came to the sturdy mill and brought the miller trudging to evensong, and far away eastwards and seawards the sound rang out over the remoter marshes. And it was all as yesterday to the old ghosts in the streets.

Then the Dean's wife took Mary Jane to evening service, and she saw three hundred candles filling all the aisle with light. But sturdy pillars stood there in unlit vastnesses; great colonnades going away into the gloom, where evening and morning, year in year out, they did their work in the dark, holding the cathedral roof aloft.

And it was stiller than the marshes are still when the ice has come and the wind that brought it has fallen.

Suddenly into this stillness rushed the sound of the organ, roaring, and presently the people prayed and sang.

No longer could Mary Jane see their prayers ascending like thin gold chains, for that was but an elfin fancy, but she imagined clear in her new soul the seraphs passing in the ways of Paradise, and the angels changing guard to watch the World by night.

When the Dean had finished service, a young curate, Mr. Millings, went up into the pulpit.

He spoke of Abana and Pharpar, rivers of Damascus: and Mary Jane was glad that there were rivers having such names, and heard with wonder of Nineveh, that great city, and many things strange and new.

And the light of the candles shone on the curate's fair hair, and his voice went ringing down the aisle, and Mary Jane rejoiced that he was there.

But when his voice stopped she felt a sudden loneliness, such as she had not felt since the making of the marshes; for the Wild Things never are lonely and never unhappy, but dance all night on the reflection of the stars, and, having no souls, desire nothing more.

After the collection was made, before any one moved to go, Mary Jane walked up the aisle to Mr. Millings.

"I love you," she said.

Nobody sympathised with Mary Jane.

"So unfortunate for Mr. Millings," everyone said; "such a promising young man."

Mary Jane was sent away to a great manufacturing city of the Midlands, where work had been found for her in a cloth factory. And there was nothing in that town that was good for a soul to see. For it did not know that beauty was to be desired; so it made many things by machinery, and became hurried in all its ways, and boasted its superiority over other cities and became richer and richer, and there was none to pity it.

In this city Mary Jane had had lodgings found for her near the factory.

At six o'clock on those November mornings, about the

time that, far away from the city, the wildfowl rose up out of the calm marshes and passed to the troubled spaces of the sea, at six o'clock the factory uttered a prolonged howl and gathered the workers together, and there they worked, saving two hours for food, the whole of the daylit hours and into the dark till the bells tolled six again.

There Mary Jane worked with other girls in a long dreary room, where giants sat pounding wool into a long thread-like strip with iron, rasping hands. And all day long they roared as they sat at their soulless work. But the work of Mary Jane was not with these, only their roar was ever in her ears as their clattering iron limbs went to and fro.

Her work was to tend a creature smaller, but infinitely more cunning.

It took the strip of wool that the giants had threshed, and whirled it round and round until it had twisted it into hard thin thread. Then it would make a clutch with fingers of steel at the thread that it had gathered, and waddle away about five yards and come back with more.

It had mastered all the subtlety of skilled workers, and had gradually displaced them; one thing only it could not do, it was unable to pick up the ends if a piece of the thread broke, in order to tie them together again. For this a human soul was required, and it was Mary Jane's business to pick up broken ends; and the moment she placed them together the busy soulless creature tied them for itself.

All here was ugly; even the green wool as it whirled round and round was neither the green of the grass nor yet the green of the rushes, but a sorry muddy green that befitted a sullen city under a murky sky.

When she looked out over the roofs of the town, there too was ugliness; and well the houses knew it, for with hideous stucco they aped in grotesque mimicry the pillars and temples of old Greece, pretending to one another to be that which they were not. And emerging from these houses and going in, and seeing the pretence of paint and stucco year after year until it all peeled away, the souls of the poor owners of those houses sought to be other souls until they grew weary of it.

At evening Mary Jane went back to her lodgings. Only then, after the dark had fallen, could the soul of Mary Jane perceive any beauty in that city, when the lamps were lit and here and there a star shone through the smoke. Then she would have gone abroad and beheld the night, but this the old woman to whom she was confided would not let her do. And the days multiplied themselves by seven and became weeks, and the weeks passed by, and all days were the same. And all the while the soul of Mary Jane was crying for beautiful things, and found not one, saving on Sundays, when she went to church, and left it to find the city greyer than before.

One day she decided that it was better to be a wild thing in the lovely marshes, than to have a soul that cried for beautiful things and found not one. From that day she determined to be rid of her soul, so she told her story to one of the factory girls, and said to her:

"The other girls are poorly clad and they do soulless work; surely some of them have no souls and would take mine."

But the factory girl said to her: "All the poor have souls. It is all they have."

Then Mary Jane watched the rich whenever she saw them, and vainly sought for some one without a soul.

One day at the hour when the machines rested and the human beings that tended them rested too, the wind being at that time from the direction of the marshlands, the soul of Mary Jane lamented bitterly. Then, as she stood outside the factory gates, the soul irresistibly compelled her to sing, and a wild song came from her lips, hymning the marshlands. And into her song came crying her yearning for home and for the sound of the shout of the North Wind, masterful and proud, with his lovely lady the Snow; and she sang of tales that the rushes murmured to one another, tales that the teal knew and the watchful heron. And over the crowded streets her song went crying away, the song of waste places and of wild free lands, full of wonder and magic, for she had in her elf-made soul the song of the birds and the roar of the organ in the marshes.

At this moment Signor Thompsoni, the well-known

English tenor, happened to go by with a friend. They stopped and listened; every one stopped and listened.

"There has been nothing like this in Europe in my time," said Signor Thompsoni.

So a change came into the life of Mary Jane.

People were written to, and finally it was arranged that she should take a leading part in the Covent Garden Opera in a few weeks.

So she went to London to learn.

London and singing lessons were better than the City of the Midlands and those terrible machines. Yet still Mary Jane was not free to go and live as she liked by the edge of the marshlands, and she was still determined to be rid of her soul, but could find no one that had not a soul of their own.

One day she was told that the English people would not listen to her as Miss Rush, and was asked what more suitable name she would like to be called by.

"I would like to be called Terrible North Wind," said Mary Jane, "or Song of the Rushes."

When she was told that this was impossible and Signorina Maria Russiano was suggested, she acquiesced at once, as she had acquiesced when they took her away from her curate; she knew nothing of the ways of humans.

At last the day of the Opera came round, and it was a cold day of the winter.

And Signorina Russiano appeared on the stage before a crowded house.

And Signorina Russiano sang.

And into the song went all the longing of her soul, the soul that could not go to Paradise, but could only worship God and know the meaning of music, and the longing pervaded that Italian song as the infinite mystery of the hills is borne along the sound of distant sheep-bells. Then in the souls that were in that crowded house arose little memories of a great while since that were quite quite dead, and lived awhile again during that marvellous song.

And a strange chill went into the blood of all that listened, as though they stood on the border of bleak marshes and the North Wind blew.

And some it moved to sorrow and some to regret, and

some to an unearthly joy. Then suddenly the song went wailing away, like the winds of the winter from the marshlands when Spring appears from the South.

So it ended. And a great silence fell foglike over all that house, breaking in upon the end of a chatty conversation that a lady was enjoying with a friend.

In the dead hush Signorina Russiano rushed from the stage; she appeared again running among the audience, and dashed up to the lady.

"Take my soul," she said; "it is a beautiful soul. It can worship God, and knows the meaning of music and can imagine Paradise. And if you go to the marshlands with it you will see beautiful things; there is an old town there built of lovely timbers, with ghosts in its streets."

The lady stared. Every one was standing up. "See," said Signorina Russiano, "it is a beautiful soul."

And she clutched at her left breast a little above the heart, and there was the soul shining in her hand, with the green and blue lights going round and round and the purple flare in the midst.

"Take it," she said, "and you will love all that is beautiful, and know the four winds, each one by his name, and the songs of the birds at dawn. I do not want it, because I am not free. Put it to your left breast a little above the heart."

Still everybody was standing up, and the lady felt uncomfortable.

"Please offer it to some one else," she said.

"But they all have souls already," said Signorina Russiano.

And everybody went on standing up. And the lady took the soul in her hand.

"Perhaps it is lucky," she said.

She felt that she wanted to pray.

She half-closed her eyes, and said, "Unberufen." Then she put the soul to her left breast a little above the heart, and hoped that the people would sit down and the singer go away.

Instantly a heap of clothes collapsed before her. For a moment, in the shadow among the seats, those who were born in the dusk hour might have seen a little brown thing leaping free from the clothes; then it sprang into the bright light of the hall, and became invisible to any human eye.

It dashed about for a little, then found the door, and presently was in the lamplit streets.

To those that were born in the dusk hour it might have been seen leaping rapidly wherever the streets ran northwards and eastwards, disappearing from human sight as it passed under the lamps, and appearing again beyond them with a marsh-light over its head.

Once a dog perceived it and gave chase, and was left far behind.

The cats of London, who are all born in the dusk hour, howled fearfully as it went by.

Presently it came to the meaner streets, where the houses are smaller. Then it went due northeastwards, leaping from roof to roof. And so in a few minutes it came to more open spaces, and then to the desolate lands, where market gardens grow, which are neither town nor country. Till at last the good black trees came into view, with their demoniac shapes in the night, and the grass was cold and wet, and the night-mist floated over it. And a great white owl came by, going up and down in the dark. And at all these things the little Wild Thing rejoiced elvishly.

And it left London far behind it, reddening the sky, and could distinguish no longer its unlovely roar, but heard again the noises of the night.

And now it would come through a hamlet glowing and comfortable in the night; and now to the dark, wet, open fields again; and many an owl it overtook as they drifted through the night, a people friendly to the Elf-folk. Sometimes it crossed wide rivers, leaping from star to star; and, choosing its way as it went, to avoid the hard rough roads, came before midnight to the East Anglian lands.

And it heard there the shout of the North Wind, who was dominant and angry, as he drove southwards his adventurous geese; while the rushes bent before him chaunting plaintively and low, like enslaved rowers of some fabulous trireme, bending and swinging under blows of the lash, and singing all the while a doleful song.

And it felt the good dank air that clothes by night the broad East Anglian lands, and came again to some old perilous pool where the soft green mosses grew, and there plunged downward and downward into the near dark water, till it felt the homely ooze once more coming up between its toes. Thence, out of the lovely chill that is in the heart of the ooze, it arose renewed and rejoicing to dance upon the image of the stars.

I chanced to stand that night by the marsh's edge, forgetting in my mind the affairs of men; and I saw the marsh-fires come leaping up from all the perilous places. And they came up by flocks the whole night long to the number of a great multitude, and danced away together over the marshes.

And I believe that there was a great rejoicing all that night among the kith of the Elf-folk.

THE SECRET PLACE

Richard McKenna

This morning my son asked me what I did in the war. He's fifteen and I don't know why he never asked me before. I don't know why I never anticipated the question.

He was just leaving for camp, and I was able to put him off by saying I did government work. He'll be two weeks at camp. As long as the counselors keep pressure on him, he'll do well enough at group activities. The moment they relax it, he'll be off studying an ant colony or reading one of his books. He's on astronomy now. The moment he comes home, he'll ask me again just what I did in the war, and I'll have to tell him.

But I don't understand just what I did in the war. Sometimes I think my group fought a death fight with a local myth and only Colonel Lewis realized it. I don't know who won. All I know is that war demands of some men risks more obscure and ignoble than death in battle. I know it did of me.

It began in 1931, when a local boy was found dead in the desert near Barker, Oregon. He had with him a sack of gold ore and one thumb-sized crystal of uranium oxide. The crystal ended as a curiosity in a Salt Lake City assay office until, in 1942, it became of strangely great importance. Army agents traced its probable origin to a hundred-square-mile area near Barker. Dr. Lewis was called to duty as a reserve colonel and ordered to find the vein. But the whole area was overlain by thousands of feet of Miocene lava flows and of course it was geological insanity to look there for a pegmatite vein. The area had no drainage pattern and had never been glaciated. Dr. Lewis protested that the crystal could have gotten there only by prior human agency.

It did him no good. He was told his was not to reason why. People very high up would not be placated until much money and scientific effort had been spent in a search. The army sent him young geology graduates, including me, and demanded progress reports. For the sake of morale, in a kind of frustrated desperation, Dr. Lewis decided to make the project a model textbook exercise in mapping the number and thickness of the basalt beds over the search area all the way down to the prevolcanic Miocene surface. That would at least be a useful addition to Columbia Plateau lithology. It would also be proof positive that no uranium ore existed there, so it was not really cheating.

That Oregon countryside was a dreary place. The search area was flat, featureless country with black lava outcropping everywhere through scanty gray soil in which sagebrush grew hardly knee high. It was hot and dry in summer and dismal with thin snow in winter. Winds howled across it at all seasons. Barker was about a hundred wooden houses on dusty streets, and some hay farms along a canal. All the young people were away at war or war jobs, and the old people seemed to resent us. There were twenty of us, apart from the contract drill crews who lived in their own trailer camps, and we were gown against town, in a way. We slept and ate at Colthorpe House, a block down the street from our headquarters. We had our own "gown" table there, and we might as well have been men from Mars.

I enjoyed it, just the same. Dr. Lewis treated us like students, with lectures and quizzes and assigned reading. He was a fine teacher and a brilliant scientist, and we loved him. He gave us all a turn at each phase of the work. I started on surface mapping and then worked with the drill crews, who were taking cores through the basalt and into the granite thousands of feet beneath. Then I worked on taking gravimetric and seismic readings. We had fine team spirit and we all knew we were getting priceless training in field geophysics. I decided privately that after the war I would take my doctorate in geophysics. Under Dr. Lewis, of course.

In early summer of 1944 the field phase ended. The contract drillers left. We packed tons of well logs and many boxes of gravimetric data sheets and seismic tapes for a move to Dr. Lewis's Midwestern university. There we would get more months of valuable training while we worked our data into a set of structure contour maps. We were all excited and talked a lot about being with girls again and going to parties. Then the army said part of the staff had to continue the field search. For technical compliance, Dr. Lewis decided to leave one man, and he chose me.

It hit me hard. It was like being flunked out unfairly. I thought he was heartlessly brusque about it.

"Take a jeep run through the area with a Geiger once a day," he said. "Then sit in the office and answer the phone."

"What if the army calls when I'm away?" I asked sullenly.

"Hire a secretary," he said. "You've an allowance for that."

So off they went and left me, with the title of field chief and only myself to boss. I felt betrayed to the hostile town. I decided I hated Colonel Lewis and wished I could get revenge. A few days later old Dave Gentry told me how.

He was a lean, leathery old man with a white mustache and I sat next to him in my new place at the "town" table. Those were grim meals. I heard remarks about healthy young men skulking out of uniform and wasting tax money. One night I slammed my fork into my half-emptied plate and stood up.

"The army sent me here and the army keeps me here," I told the dozen old men and women at the table. "I'd like to go overseas and cut Japanese throats for you kind hearts and gentle people, I really would! Why don't you all write your Congressman?"

I stamped outside and stood at one end of the veranda, boiling. Old Dave followed me out.

"Hold your horses, son," he said. "They hate the government, not you. But government's like the weather, and you're a man they can get aholt of."

"With their teeth," I said bitterly.

"They got reasons," Dave said. "Lost mines ain't supposed to be found the way you people are going at it. Besides that, the Crazy Kid mine belongs to us here in Barker."

He was past seventy and he looked after horses in the local feedyard. He wore a shabby, open vest over faded suspenders and gray flannel shirts and nobody would ever have looked for wisdom in that old man. But it was there.

"This is big, new, lonesome country and it's hard on people," he said. "Every town's got a story about a lost mine or a lost gold cache. Only kids go looking for it. It's enough for most folks just to know it's there. It helps 'em to stand the country."

"I see," I said. Something stirred in the back of my mind.

"Barker never got its lost mine until thirteen years ago," Dave said. "Folks just naturally can't stand to see you people find it this way, by main force and so soon after."

"We know there isn't any mine," I said. "We're just proving it isn't there."

"If you could prove that, it'd be worse yet," he said. "Only you can't. We all saw and handled that ore. It was quartz, just rotten with gold in wires and flakes. The boy went on foot from his house to get it. The lode's got to be right close by out there."

He waved toward our search area. The air above it was luminous with twilight and I felt a curious surge of interest. Colonel Lewis had always discouraged us from speculating on that story. If one of us brought it up, I was usually the one who led the hooting and we all suggested he go over the search area with a dowsing rod. It was an article of faith with us that the vein did not exist. But now I was all alone and my own field boss.

We each put up one foot on the veranda rail and rested our arms on our knees. Dave bit off a chew of tobacco and told me about Owen Price.

"He was always a crazy kid and I guess he read every book in town," Dave said. "He had a curious heart, that boy."

I'm no folklorist, but even I could see how myth elements were already creeping into the story. For one thing, Dave insisted the boy's shirt was torn off and he had lacerations on his back.

"Like a cougar clawed him," Dave said. "Only they ain't never been cougars in that desert. We backtracked that boy till his trail crossed itself so many times it was no use, but we never found one cougar track."

I could discount that stuff, of course, but still the story gripped me. Maybe it was Dave's slow, sure voice; perhaps the queer twilight; possibly my own wounded pride. I thought of how great lava upwellings sometimes tear loose and carry along huge masses of the country rock. Maybe such an erratic mass lay out there, perhaps only a few hundred feet across and so missed by our drill cores, but rotten with uranium. If I could find it, I would make a fool of Colonel Lewis. I would discredit the whole science of geology. I, Duard Campbell, the despised and rejected one, could do that. The front of my mind shouted that it was nonsense, but something far back in my mind began composing a devastating letter to Colonel Lewis and comfort flowed into me.

"There's some say the boy's youngest sister could tell where he found it, if she wanted," Dave said. "She used to go into that desert with him a lot. She took on pretty wild when it happened and then was struck dumb, but I hear she talks again now." He shook his head. "Poor little Helen. She promised to be a pretty girl."

"Where does she live?" I asked.

"With her mother in Salem," Dave said. "She went to business school and I hear she works for a lawyer there."

Mrs. Price was a flinty old woman who seemed to control her daughter absolutely. She agreed Helen would be my secretary as soon as I told her the salary. I got Helen's security clearance with one phone call; she had already been investigated as part of tracing that uranium crystal. Mrs. Price arranged for Helen to stay with a family she knew in Barker, to protect her reputation. It was in no danger. I meant to make love to her, if I had to, to charm her out of her secret, if she had one, but I would not harm her. I knew perfectly well that I was only playing a game called "The Revenge of Duard Campbell." I knew I would not find any uranium.

Helen was a plain little girl and she was made of frightened ice. She wore low-heeled shoes and cotton stockings and plain dresses with white cuffs and collars. Her one good feature was her flawless fair skin against which her peaked, black Welsh eyebrows and smoky blue eyes gave her an elfin look at times. She liked to sit neatly tucked into herself, feet together, elbows in, eyes cast down, voice hardly audible, as smoothly self-contained as an egg. The desk I gave her faced mine and she sat like that across from me and did the busy work I gave her, and I could not get through to her at all.

I tried joking and I tried polite little gifts and attentions, and I tried being sad and needing sympathy. She listened and worked and stayed as far away as the moon. It was only after two weeks and by pure accident that I found the key to her.

I was trying the sympathy gambit. I said it was not so bad, being exiled from friends and family, but what I could not stand was the dreary sameness of that search area. Every spot was like every other spot and there was no single, recognizable *place* in the whole expanse. It sparked something in her and she roused up at me.

"It's full of just wonderful places," she said.

"Come out with me in the jeep and show me one," I challenged.

She was reluctant, but I hustled her along regardless. I guided the jeep between outcrops, jouncing and lurching. I had our map photographed on my mind and I knew where we were every minute, but only by map coordinates. The desert had our marks on it: well sites, seismic blast holes, wooden stakes, cans, bottles and papers blowing in that everlasting wind, and it was all dismally the same anyway.

"Tell me when we pass a 'place' and I'll stop," I said.

"It's all places," she said. "Right here's a place."

I stopped the jeep and looked at her in surprise. Her voice was strong and throaty. She opened her eyes wide and smiled; I had never seen her look like that.

"What's special, that makes it a place?" I asked.

She did not answer. She got out and walked a few

steps. Her whole posture was changed. She almost danced along. I followed and touched her shoulder.

"Tell me what's special," I said.

She faced around and stared right past me. She had a new grace and vitality and she was a very pretty girl.

"It's where all the dogs are," she said.

"Dogs?"

I looked around at the scrubby sagebrush and thin soil and ugly black rock and back at Helen. Something was wrong.

"Big, stupid dogs that go in herds and eat grass," she said. She kept turning and gazing. "Big cats chase the dogs and eat them. The dogs scream and scream. Can't you hear them?"

"That's crazy!" I said. "What's the matter with you?"

I might as well have slugged her. She crumpled instantly back into herself and I could hardly hear her answer.

"I'm sorry. My brother and I used to play out fairy tales here. All this was a kind of fairyland to us." Tears formed in her eyes. "I haven't been here since . . . I forgot myself. I'm sorry."

I had to swear I needed to dictate "field notes" to force Helen into that desert again. She sat stiffly with pad and pencil in the jeep while I put on my act with the Geiger and rattled off jargon. Her lips were pale and compressed and I could see her fighting against the spell the desert had for her, and I could see her slowly losing.

She finally broke down into that strange mood and I took good care not to break it. It was weird but wonderful, and I got a lot of data. I made her go out for "field notes" every morning and each time it was easier to break her down. Back in the office she always froze again and I marveled at how two such different persons could inhabit the same body. I called her two phases "Office Helen" and "Desert Helen."

I often talked with old Dave on the veranda after dinner. One night he cautioned me.

"Folks here think Helen ain't been right in the head since her brother died," he said. "They're worrying about you and her."

"I feel like a big brother to her," I said. "I'd never

hurt her, Dave. If we find the lode, I'll stake the best claim for her."

He shook his head. I wished I could explain to him how it was only a harmless game I was playing and no one would ever find gold out there. Yet, as a game, it fascinated me.

Desert Helen charmed me when, helplessly, she had to uncover her secret life. She was a little girl in a woman's body. Her voice became strong and breathless with excitement and she touched me with the same wonder that turned her own face vivid and elfin. She ran laughing through the black rocks and scrubby sagebrush and momentarily she made them beautiful. She would pull me along by the hand and sometimes we ran as much as a mile away from the jeep. She treated me as if I were a blind or foolish child.

"No, no, Duard, that's a cliff!" she would say, pulling me back.

She would go first, so I could find the stepping stones across streams. I played up. She pointed out woods and streams and cliffs and castles. There were shaggy horses with claws, golden birds, camels, witches, elephants and many other creatures. I pretended to see them all, and it made her trust me. She talked and acted out the fairy tales she had once played with Owen. Sometimes he was enchanted and sometimes she, and the one had to dare the evil magic of a witch or giant to rescue the other. Sometimes I was Duard and other times I almost thought I was Owen.

Helen and I crept into sleeping castles, and we hid with pounding hearts while the giant grumbled in search of us and we fled, hand in hand, before his wrath.

Well, I had her now. I played Helen's game, but I never lost sight of my own. Every night I sketched in on my map whatever I had learned that day of the fairyland topography. Its geomorphology was remarkably consistent.

When we played, I often hinted about the giant's treasure. Helen never denied it existed, but she seemed troubled and evasive about it. She would put her finger to her lips and look at me with solemn, round eyes.

"You only take the things nobody cares about," she

would say. "If you take the gold or jewels, it brings you terrible bad luck."

"I got a charm against bad luck and I'll let you have it too," I said once. "It's the biggest, strongest charm in the whole world."

"No. It all turns into trash. It turns into goat beans and dead snakes and things," she said crossly. "Owen told me. It's a rule, in fairyland."

Another time we talked about it as we sat in a gloomy ravine near a waterfall. We had to keep our voices low or we would wake up the giant. The waterfall was really the giant snoring and it was also the wind that blew forever across that desert.

"Doesn't Owen ever take anything?" I asked.

I had learned by then that I must always speak of Owen in the present tense.

"Sometimes he has to," she said. "Once right here the witch had me enchanted into an ugly toad. Owen put a flower on my head and that made me be Helen again."

"A really truly flower? That you could take home with you?"

"A red-and-yellow flower bigger than my two hands," she said. "I tried to take it home, but all the petals came off."

"Does Owen ever take anything home?"

"Rocks, sometimes," she said. "We keep them in a secret nest in the shed. We think they might be magic eggs."

I stood up. "Come and show me."

She shook her head vigorously and drew back. "I don't want to go home," she said. "Not ever."

She squirmed and pouted, but I pulled her to her feet. "Please, Helen, for me," I said. "Just for one little minute."

I pulled her back to the jeep and we drove to the old Price place. I had never seen her look at it when we passed it and she did not look now. She was freezing fast back into Office Helen. But she led me around the sagging old house with its broken windows and into a tumble-down shed. She scratched away some straw in one corner, and there were the rocks. I did not realize how excited I was until disappointment hit me like a blow in the stomach.

They were worthless waterworn pebbles of quartz and rosy granite. The only thing special about them was that they could never have originated on that basalt desert.

After a few weeks we dropped the pretense of field notes and simply went into the desert to play. I had Helen's fairyland almost completely mapped. It seemed to be a recent fault block mountain with a river parallel to its base and a gently sloping plain across the river. The scarp face was wooded and cut by deep ravines and it had castles perched on its truncated spurs. I kept checking Helen on it and never found her inconsistent. Several times when she was in doubt I was able to tell her where she was, and that let me even more deeply into her secret life. One morning I discovered just how deeply.

She was sitting on a log in the forest and plaiting a little basket out of fern fronds. I stood beside her. She looked up at me and smiled.

"What shall we play today, Owen?" she asked.

I had not expected that, and I was proud of how quickly I rose to it. I capered and bounded away and then back to her and crouched at her feet.

"Little sister, little sister, I'm enchanted," I said. "Only you in all the world can uncharm me."

"I'll uncharm you," she said, in that little girl voice. "What are you, brother?"

"A big, black dog," I said. "A wicked giant named Lewis Rawbones keeps me chained up behind his castle while he takes all the other dogs out hunting."

She smoothed her gray skirt over her knees. Her mouth drooped.

"You're lonesome and you howl all day and you howl all night," she said. "Poor doggie."

I threw back my head and howled.

"He's a terrible, wicked giant and he's got all kinds of terrible magic," I said. "You mustn't be afraid, little sister. As soon as you uncharm me I'll be a handsome prince and I'll cut off his head."

"I'm not afraid." Her eyes sparkled. "I'm not afraid of fire or snakes or pins or needles or anything."

"I'll take you away to my kingdom and we'll live happily ever afterward. You'll be the most beautiful queen in the world and everybody will love you."

I wagged my tail and laid my head on her knees. She stroked my silky head and pulled my long black ears.

"Everybody will love me." She was very serious now. "Will magic water uncharm you, poor old doggie?"

"You have to touch my forehead with a piece of the giant's treasure," I said. "That's the only onliest way to uncharm me."

I felt her shrink away from me. She stood up, her face suddenly crumpled with grief and anger.

"You're not Owen, you're just a man! Owen's enchanted and I'm enchanted too and nobody will ever uncharm us!"

She ran away from me and she was already Office Helen by the time she reached the jeep.

After that day she refused flatly to go into the desert with me. It looked as if my game was played out. But I gambled that Desert Helen could still hear me, underneath somewhere, and I tried a new strategy. The office was an upstairs room over the old dance hall and, I suppose, in frontier days skirmishing had gone on there between men and women. I doubt anything went on as strange as my new game with Helen.

I always had paced and talked while Helen worked. Now I began mixing common-sense talk with fairyland talk and I kept coming back to the wicked giant, Lewis Rawbones. Office Helen tried not to pay attention, but now and then I caught Desert Helen peeping at me out of her eyes. I spoke of my blighted career as a geologist and how it would be restored to me if I found the lode. I mused on how I would live and work in exotic places and how I would need a wife to keep house for me and help with my paper work. It disturbed Office Helen. She made typing mistakes and dropped things. I kept it up for days, trying for just the right mixture of fact and fantasy, and it was hard on Office Helen.

One night old Dave warned me again.

"Helen's looking peaked, and there's talk around. Miz Fowler says Helen don't sleep and she cries at night and she won't tell Miz Fowler what's wrong. You don't happen to know what's bothering her, do you?"

"I only talk business stuff to her," I said. "Maybe she's homesick. I'll ask her if she wants a vacation." I did not like the way Dave looked at me. "I haven't hurt her. I don't mean her any harm, Dave," I said.

"People get killed for what they do, not for what they mean," he said. "Son, there's men in this here town would kill you quick as a coyote, if you hurt Helen Price."

I worked on Helen all the next day and in the afternoon I hit just the right note and I broke her defenses. I was not prepared for the way it worked out. I had just said, "All life is a kind of playing. If you think about it right, everything we do is a game." She poised her pencil and looked straight at me, as she had never done in that office, and I felt my heart speed up.

"You taught me how to play, Helen. I was so serious that I didn't know how to play."

"Owen taught me to play. He had magic. My sisters couldn't play anything but dolls and rich husbands and I hated them."

Her eyes opened wide and her lips trembled and she was almost Desert Helen right there in the office.

"There's magic and enchantment in regular life, if you look at it right," I said. "Don't you think so, Helen?"

"I know it!" she said. She turned pale and dropped her pencil. "Owen was enchanted into having a wife and three daughters and he was just a boy. But he was the only man we had and all of them but me hated him because we were so poor." She began to tremble and her voice went flat. "He couldn't stand it. He took the treasure and it killed him." Tears ran down her cheeks. "I tried to think he was only enchanted into play-dead and if I didn't speak or laugh for seven years, I'd uncharm him."

She dropped her head on her hands. I was alarmed. I came over and put my hand on her shoulder.

"I did speak." Her shoulders heaved with sobs. "They made me speak, and now Owen won't ever come back."

I bent and put my arm across her shoulders.

"Don't cry, Helen. He'll come back," I said. "There are other magics to bring him back."

I hardly knew what I was saying. I was afraid of what I had done, and I wanted to comfort her. She jumped up and threw off my arm.

"I can't stand it! I'm going home!"

She ran out into the hall and down the stairs and from the window I saw her run down the street, still crying. All of a sudden my game seemed cruel and stupid to me and right that moment I stopped it. I tore up my map of fairyland and my letters to Colonel Lewis and I wondered how in the world I could ever have done all that.

After dinner that night old Dave motioned me out to one end of the veranda. His face looked carved out of wood.

"I don't know what happened in your office today, and for your sake I better not find out. But you send Helen back to her mother on the morning stage, you hear me?"

"All right, if she wants to go," I said. "I can't just fire her."

"I'm speaking for the boys. You better put her on that morning stage, or we'll be around to talk to you."

"All right, I will, Dave."

I wanted to tell him how the game was stopped now and how I wanted a chance to make things up with Helen, but I thought I had better not. Dave's voice was flat and savage with contempt and, old as he was, he frightened me.

Helen did not come to work in the morning. At nine o'clock I went out myself for the mail. I brought a large mailing tube and some letters back to the office. The first letter I opened was from Dr. Lewis, and almost like magic it solved all my problems.

On the basis of his preliminary structure contour maps Dr. Lewis had gotten permission to close out the field phase. Copies of the maps were in the mailing tube, for my information. I was to hold an inventory and be ready to turn everything over to an army quartermaster team coming in a few days. There was still a great mass of data to be worked up in refining the maps. I was to join the group again and I would have a chance at the lab work after all.

I felt pretty good. I paced and whistled and snapped my fingers. I wished Helen would come, to help on the inventory. Then I opened the tube and looked idly at the maps. There were a lot of them, featureless bed after bed of basalt, like layers of a cake ten miles across. But when I came to the bottom map, of the prevolcanic Miocene landscape, the hair on my neck stood up.

I had made that map myself. It was Helen's fairyland. The topography was point by point the same.

I clenched my fists and stopped breathing. Then it hit me a second time, and the skin crawled up my back.

The game was real. I couldn't end it. All the time the game had been playing me. It was still playing me.

I ran out and down the street and overtook old Dave hurrying toward the feedyard. He had a holstered gun on each hip.

"Dave, I've got to find Helen," I said.

"Somebody seen her hiking into the desert just at daylight," he said. "I'm on my way for a horse." He did not slow his stride. "You better get out there in your stinkwagon. If you don't find her before we do, you better just keep on going, son."

I ran back and got the jeep and roared it out across the scrubby sagebrush. I hit rocks and I do not know why I did not break something. I knew where to go and feared what I would find there. I knew I loved Helen Price more than my own life and I knew I had driven her to her death.

I saw her far off, running and dodging. I headed the jeep to intercept her and I shouted, but she neither saw me nor heard me. I stopped and jumped out and ran after her and the world darkened. Helen was all I could see, and I could not catch up with her.

"Wait for me, little sister!" I screamed after her. "I love you, Helen! Wait for me!"

She stopped and crouched and I almost ran over her. I knelt and put my arms around her and then it was on us.

They say in an earthquake, when the direction of up and down tilts and wobbles, people feel a fear that drives them mad if they can not forget it afterward. This was worse. Up and down and here and there and now and then all rushed together. The wind roared through the rock beneath us and the air thickened crushingly above our heads. I know we clung to each other, and we were there for each other while nothing else was and that is all I know, until we were in the jeep and I was guiding it back toward town as headlong as I had come.

Then the world had shape again under a bright sun. I saw a knot of horsemen on the horizon. They were heading for where Owen had been found. That boy had run a long way, alone and hurt and burdened.

I got Helen up to the office. She sat at her desk with her head down on her hands and she quivered violently. I kept my arm around her.

"It was only a storm inside our two heads, Helen," I said, over and over. "Something black blew away out of us. The game is finished and we're free and I love you."

Over and over I said that, for my sake as well as hers. I meant and believed it. I said she was my wife and we would marry and go a thousand miles away from that desert to raise our children. She quieted to a trembling, but she would not speak. Then I heard hoofbeats and the creak of leather in the street below and then I heard slow footsteps on the stairs.

Old Dave stood in the doorway. His two guns looked as natural on him as hands and feet. He looked at Helen, bowed over the desk, and then at me, standing beside her.

"Come on down, son. The boys want to talk to you," he said.

I followed him into the hall and stopped.

"She isn't hurt," I said. "The lode is really out there, Dave, but nobody is ever going to find it."

"Tell that to the boys."

"We're closing out the project in a few more days," I

said. "I'm going to marry Helen and take her away with me."

"Come down or we'll drag you down!" he said harshly. "We'll send Helen back to her mother."

I was afraid. I did not know what to do.

"No, you won't send me back to my mother!"

It was Helen beside me in the hall. She was Desert Helen, but grown up and wonderful. She was pale, pretty, aware and sure of herself.

"I'm going with Duard," she said. "Nobody in the world is ever going to send me around like a package again."

Dave rubbed his jaw and squinted his eyes at her.

"I love her, Dave," I said. "I'll take care of her all my life."

I put my left arm around her and she nestled against me. The tautness went out of old Dave and he smiled. He kept his eyes on Helen.

"Little Helen Price," he said, wonderingly. "Who ever would've thought it?" He reached out and shook us both gently. "Bless you youngsters," he said, and blinked his eyes. "I'll tell the boys it's all right."

He turned and went slowly down the stairs. Helen and I looked at each other, and I think she saw a new face too.

That was sixteen years ago. I am a professor myself now, graying a bit at the temples. I am as positivistic a scientist as you will find anywhere in the Mississippi drainage basin. When I tell a seminar student "That assertion is operationally meaningless," I can make it sound downright obscene. The students blush and hate me, but it is for their own good. Science is the only safe game, and it's safe only if it is kept pure. I work hard at that, I have yet to meet the student I cannot handle.

My son is another matter. We named him Owen Lewis, and he has Helen's eyes and hair and complexion. He learned to read on the modern sane and sterile children's books. We haven't a fairy tale in the house—but I have a science library. And Owen makes fairy tales out of science. He is taking the measure of space and time now, with Jeans and Eddington. He cannot possibly understand a tenth of what he reads, in the way I understand it. But he understands all of it in some other way privately his own.

Not long ago he said to me, "You know, Dad, it isn't only space that's expanding. Time's expanding too, and that's what makes us keep getting farther away from when we used to be."

And I have to tell him just what I did in the war. I know I found manhood and a wife. The how and why of it I think and hope I am incapable of fully understanding. But Owen has, through Helen, that strangely curious heart. I'm afraid. I'm afraid he will understand.

THE KING OF THE ELVES

Philip K. Dick

It was raining and getting dark. Sheets of water blew along the row of pumps at the edge of the filling station; the trees across the highway bent against the wind.

Shadrach Jones stood just inside the doorway of the little building, leaning against an oil drum. The door was open and gusts of rain blew in onto the wood floor. It was late; the sun had set, and the air was turning cold. Shadrach reached into his coat and brought out a cigar. He bit the end off it and lit it carefully, turning away from the door. In the gloom, the cigar burst into life, warm and glowing. Shadrach took a deep draw. He buttoned his coat around him and stepped out onto the pavement.

"Darn," he said. "What a night!" Rain buffeted him, wind blew at him. He looked up and down the highway, squinting. There were no cars in sight. He shook his head, locked up the gasoline pumps.

He went back into the building and pulled the door shut behind him. He opened the cash register and counted the money he'd taken in during the day. It was not much.

Not much, but enough for one old man. Enough to buy him tobacco and firewood and magazines, so that he could be comfortable as he waited for the occasional cars to come by. Not very many cars came along the highway any more. The highway had begun to fall into disrepair; there were many cracks in its dry, rough surface, and most cars preferred to take the big state highway that ran beyond the hills. There was nothing in Derryville to attract them, to make them turn toward it. Derryville was a small town, too small to bring in any of the major industries, too small to be very important to anyone. Sometimes hours went by without—

Shadrach tensed. His fingers closed over the money. From outside came a sound, the melodic ring of the signal wire stretched along the pavement.

Dinggg!

Shadrach dropped the money into the till and pushed the drawer closed. He stood up slowly and walked toward the door, listening. At the door, he snapped off the light and waited in the darkness, staring out.

He could see no car there. The rain was pouring down, swirling with the wind; clouds of mist moved along the road. And something was standing beside the pumps.

He opened the door and stepped out. At first, his eyes could make nothing out. Then the old man swallowed uneasily.

Two tiny figures stood in the rain, holding a kind of platform between them. Once, they might have been gaily dressed in bright garments, but now their clothes hung limp and sodden, dripping in the rain. They glanced halfheartedly at Shadrach. Water streaked their tiny faces, great drops of water. Their robes blew about them with the wind, lashing and swirling.

On the platform, something stirred. A small head turned wearily, peering at Shadrach. In the dim light, a rain-streaked helmet glinted dully.

"Who are you?" Shadrach said.

The figure on the platform raised itself up. "I'm the King of the Elves and I'm wet."

Shadrach stared in astonishment.

"That's right," one of the bearers said. "We're all wet."

A small group of elves came straggling up, gathering around their king. They huddled together forlornly, silently.

"The King of the Elves," Shadrach repeated. "Well, I'll be darned."

Could it be true? They were very small, all right, and their dripping clothes were strange and oddly colored.

But *Elves?*

"I'll be darned. Well, whatever you are, you shouldn't be out on a night like this."

"Of course not," the king murmured. "No fault of our own. No fault . . ." His voice trailed off into a choking cough. The Elf soldiers peered anxiously at the platform.

"Maybe you better bring him inside," Shadrach said. "My place is up the road. He shouldn't be out in the rain."

"Do you think we like being out on a night like this?" one of the bearers muttered. "Which way is it? Direct us."

Shadrach pointed up the road. "Over there. Just follow me. I'll get a fire going."

He went down the road, feeling his way onto the first of the flat stone steps that he and Phineas Judd had laid during the summer. At the top of the steps, he looked back. The platform was coming slowly along, swaying a little from side to side. Behind it, the Elf soldiers picked their way, a tiny column of silent dripping creatures, unhappy and cold.

"I'll get the fire started," Shadrach said. He hurried them into the house.

Wearily, the Elf King lay back against the pillow. After sipping hot chocolate, he had relaxed and his heavy breathing sounded suspiciously like a snore.

Shadrach shifted in discomfort.

"I'm sorry," the Elf King said suddenly, opening his eyes. He rubbed his forehead. "I must have drifted off. Where was I?"

"You should retire, Your Majesty," one of the soldiers said sleepily. "It is late and these are hard times."

"True," the Elf King said, nodding. "Very true." He looked up at the towering figure of Shadrach, standing before the fireplace, a glass of beer in his hand. "Mortal, we thank you for your hospitality. Normally, we do not impose on human beings."

"It's those Trolls," another of the soldiers said, curled up on a cushion of the couch.

"Right," another soldier agreed. He sat up, groping for his sword. "Those reeking Trolls, digging and croaking—"

"You see," the Elf King went on, "as our party was crossing from the Great Low Steps toward the Castle, where it lies in the hollow of the Towering Mountains—"

"You mean Sugar Ridge," Shadrach supplied helpfully.

"The Towering Mountains. Slowly we made our way. A rain storm came up. We became confused. All at once a group of Trolls appeared, crashing through the underbrush. We left the woods and sought safety on the Endless Path—"

"The highway. Route Twenty."

"So that is why we're here." The Elf King paused a moment. "Harder and harder it rained. The wind blew around us, cold and bitter. For an endless time we toiled along. We had no idea where we were going or what would become of us."

The Elf King looked up at Shadrach. "We knew only this: Behind us, the Trolls were coming, creeping through the woods, marching through the rain, crushing everything before them."

He put his hand to his mouth and coughed, bending forward. All the Elves waited anxiously until he was done. He straightened up.

"It was kind of you to allow us to come inside. We will not trouble you for long. It is not the custom of the Elves—"

Again he coughed, covering his face with his hand. The Elves drew toward him apprehensively. At last the king stirred. He sighed.

"What's the matter?" Shadrach asked. He went over and took the cup of chocolate from the fragile hand. The Elf King lay back, his eyes shut.

"He has to rest," one of the soldiers said. "Where's your room? The sleeping room."

"Upstairs," Shadrach said. "I'll show you where."

Late that night, Shadrach sat by himself in the dark, deserted living room, deep in meditation. The Elves were asleep above him, upstairs in the bedroom, the Elf King in the bed, the others curled up together on the rug.

The house was silent. Outside, the rain poured down endlessly, blowing against the house. Shadrach could hear the tree branches slapping in the wind. He clasped and unclasped his hands. What a strange business it was—all these Elves, with their old, sick king, their piping voices. How anxious and peevish they were!

But pathetic, too; so small and wet, with water dripping down from them, and all their gay robes limp and soggy.

The Trolls—what were they like? Unpleasant and not very clean. Something about digging, breaking and pushing through the woods . . .

Suddenly, Shadrach laughed in embarrassment. What was the matter with him, believing all this? He put his cigar out angrily, his ears red. What was going on? What kind of joke was this?

Elves? Shadrach grunted in indignation. Elves in Derryville? In the middle of Colorado? Maybe there were Elves in Europe. Maybe in Ireland. He had heard of that. But here? Upstairs in his own house, sleeping in his own bed?

"I've heard just about enough of this," he said. "I'm not an idiot, you know."

He turned toward the stairs, feeling for the banister in the gloom. He began to climb.

Above him, a light went on abruptly. A door opened.

Two Elves came slowly out onto the landing. They looked down at him. Shadrach halted halfway up the stairs. Something on their faces made him stop.

"What's the matter?" he asked hesitantly.

They did not answer. The house was turning cold, cold and dark, with the chill of the rain outside and the chill of the unknown inside.

"What is it?" he said again. "What's the matter?"

"The king is dead," one of the Elves said. "He died a few moments ago."

Shadrach stared up, wide-eyed. "He did? But—"

"He was very old and very tired." The Elves turned away, going back into the room, slowly and quietly shutting the door.

Shadrach stood, his fingers on the banister, hard, lean fingers, strong and thin.

He nodded his head blankly.

"I see," he said to the closed door. "He's dead."

The Elf soldiers stood around him in a solemn circle. The living room was bright with sunlight, the cold white glare of early morning.

"But wait," Shadrach said. He plucked at his necktie. "I have to get to the filling station. Can't you talk to me when I come home?"

The faces of the Elf soldiers were serious and concerned.

"Listen," one of them said. "Please hear us out. It is very important to us."

Shadrach looked past them. Through the window he saw the highway, steaming in the heat of day, and down a little way was the gas station, glittering brightly. And even as he watched, a car came up to it and honked thinly, impatiently. When nobody came out of the station, the car drove off again down the road.

"We beg you," a soldier said.

Shadrach looked down at the ring around him, the anxious faces, scored with concern and trouble. Strangely, he had always thought of Elves as carefree beings, flitting without worry or sense—

"Go ahead," he said. "I'm listening." He went over to the big chair and sat down. The Elves came up around him. They conversed among themselves for a moment, whispering, murmuring distantly. Then they turned toward Shadrach.

The old man waited, his arms folded.

"We cannot be without a king," one of the soldiers said. "We could not survive. Not these days."

"The Trolls," another added. "They multiply very fast. They are terrible beasts. They're heavy and ponderous, crude, bad-smelling—"

"The odor of them is awful. They come up from the dark wet places, under the earth, where the blind, groping plants feed in silence, far below the surface, far from the sun."

"Well, you ought to elect a king, then," Shadrach suggested. "I don't see any problem there."

"We do not elect the King of the Elves," a soldier said. "The old king must name his successor."

"Oh," Shadrach replied. "Well, there's nothing wrong with that method."

"As our old king lay dying, a few distant words came forth from his lips," a soldier said. "We bent closer, frightened and unhappy, listening."

"Important, all right," agreed Shadrach. "Not something you'd want to miss."

"He spoke the name of him who will lead us."

"Good. You caught it, then. Well, where's the difficulty?"

"The name he spoke was—was your name."

Shadrach stared. "*Mine?*"

"The dying king said: 'Make him, the towering mortal, your king. Many things will come if he leads the Elves into battle against the Trolls. I see the rising once again of the Elf Empire, as it was in the old days, as it was before—"

"Me!" Shadrach leaped up. "Me? King of the Elves?"

Shadrach walked about the room, his hands in his pockets. "Me, Shadrach Jones, King of the Elves." He grinned a little. "I sure never thought of it before."

He went to the mirror over the fireplace and studied himself. He saw his thin, graying hair, his bright eyes, dark skin, his big Adam's apple.

"King of the Elves," he said. "King of the Elves. Wait till Phineas Judd hears about this. Wait till I tell him!"

Phineas Judd would certainly be surprised!

Above the filling station, the sun shown, high in the clear blue sky.

Phineas Judd sat playing with the accelerator of his old Ford truck. The motor raced and slowed. Phineas reached over and turned the ignition key off, then rolled the window all the way down.

"What did you say?" he asked. He took off his glasses and began to polish them, steel rims between slender, deft fingers that were patient from years of practice. He restored his glasses to his nose and smoothed what remained of his hair into place.

"What was it, Shadrach?" he said. "Let's hear that again."

"I'm King of the Elves," Shadrach repeated. He changed position, bringing his other foot up on the runningboard. "Who would have thought it? Me, Shadrach Jones, King of the Elves."

Phineas gazed at him. "How long have you been—King of the Elves, Shadrach?"

"Since the night before last."

"I see. The night before last." Phineas nodded. "I see. And what, may I ask, occurred the night before last?"

"The Elves came to my house. When the old Elf king died, he told them that—"

A truck came rumbling up and the driver leaped out. "Water!" he said. "Where the hell is the hose?"

Shadrach turned reluctantly. "I'll get it." He turned back to Phineas. "Maybe I can talk to you tonight when you come back from town. I want to tell you the rest. It's very interesting."

"Sure," Phineas said, starting up his little truck. "Sure, Shadrach. I'm very interested to hear."

He drove off down the road.

Later in the day, Dan Green ran his flivver up to the filling station.

"Hey, Shadrach," he called. "Come over here! I want to ask you something."

Shadrach came out of the little house, holding a waste-rag in his hand.

"What is it?"

"Come here." Dan leaned out the window, a wide grin on his face, splitting his face from ear to ear. "Let me ask you something, will you?"

"Sure."

"Is it true? Are you really the King of the Elves?"

Shadrach flushed a little. "I guess I am," he admitted, looking away. "That's what I am, all right."

Dan's grin faded. "Hey, you trying to kid me? What's the gag?"

Shadrach became angry. "What do you mean? Sure, I'm the King of the Elves. And anyone who says I'm not—"

"All right, Shadrach," Dan said, starting up the flivver quickly. "Don't get mad. I was just wondering."

Shadrach looked very strange.

"All right," Dan said. "You don't hear me arguing, do you?"

By the end of the day, everyone around knew about Shadrach and how he had suddenly become King of the Elves. Pop Richey, who ran the Lucky Store in Derryville, claimed Shadrach was doing it to drum up trade for the filling station.

"He's a smart old fellow," Pop said. "Not very many cars go along there any more. He knows what he's doing."

"I don't know," Dan Green disagreed. "You should hear him. I think he really believes it."

"King of the Elves?" They all began to laugh. "Wonder what he'll say next."

Phineas Judd pondered. "I've known Shadrach for years. I can't figure it out." He frowned, his face wrinkled and disapproving. "I don't like it."

Dan looked at him. "Then you think he believes it?"

"Sure," Phineas said. "Maybe I'm wrong, but I really think he does."

"But how could he believe it?" Pop asked. "Shadrach is no fool. He's been in business for a long time. He must be getting something out of it, the way I see it. But what, if it isn't to build up the filling station?"

"Why, don't you know what he's getting?" Dan said, grinning. His gold tooth shone.

"What?" Pop demanded.

"He's got a whole kingdom to himself, that's what—to do with like he wants. How would you like that, Pop? Wouldn't you like to be King of the Elves and not have to run this old store any more?"

"There isn't anything wrong with my store," Pop said. "I ain't ashamed to run it. Better than being a clothing salesman."

Dan flushed. "Nothing wrong with that, either." He looked at Phineas. "Isn't that right? Nothing wrong with selling clothes, is there, Phineas?"

Phineas was staring down at the floor. He glanced up. "What? What was that?"

"What you thinking about?" Pop wanted to know. "You look worried."

"I'm worried about Shadrach," Phineas said. "He's getting old. Sitting out there by himself all the time, in the cold weather, with the rain water running over the floor—it blows something awful in the winter, along the highway—"

"Then you *do* think he believes it?" Dan persisted. "You *don't* think he's getting something out of it?"

Phineas shook his head absently and did not answer.

The laughter died down. They all looked at one another.

That night, as Shadrach was locking up the filling station, a small figure came toward him from the darkness.

"Hey!" Shadrach called out. "Who are you?"

An Elf soldier came into the light, blinking. He was dressed in a little gray robe, buckled at the waist with a band of silver. On his feet were little leather boots. He carried a short sword at his side.

"I have a serious message for you," the Elf said. "Now, where did I put it?"

He searched his robe while Shadrach waited. The Elf brought out a tiny scroll and unfastened it, breaking the wax expertly. He handed it to Shadrach.

"What's it say?" Shadrach asked. He bent over, his eyes close to the vellum. "I don't have my glasses with me. Can't quite make out these little letters."

"The Trolls are moving. They've heard that the old king is dead, and they're rising, in all the hills and valleys around. They will try to break the Elf Kingdom into fragments, scatter the Elves—"

"I see," Shadrach said. "Before your new king can really get started."

"That's right." The Elf soldier nodded. "This is a crucial moment for the Elves. For centuries, our existence has been precarious. There are so many Trolls, and Elves are very frail and often take sick—"

"Well, what should I do? Are there any suggestions?"

"You're supposed to meet with us under the Great

Oak tonight. We'll take you into the Elf Kingdom, and you and your staff will plan and map the defense of the Kingdom."

"What?" Shadrach looked uncomfortable. "But I haven't eaten dinner. And my gas station—tomorrow is Saturday, and a lot of cars—"

"But you are King of the Elves," the soldier said.

Shadrach put his hand to his chin and rubbed it slowly.

"That's right," he replied. "I am, ain't I?"

The Elf soldier bowed.

"I wish I'd known this sort of thing was going to happen," Shadrach said. "I didn't suppose being King of the Elves—"

He broke off, hoping for an interruption. The Elf soldier watched him calmly, without expression.

"Maybe you ought to have someone else as your king," Shadrach decided. "I don't know very much about war and things like that, fighting and all that sort of business." He paused, shrugged his shoulders. "It's nothing I've ever mixed in. They don't have wars here in Colorado. I mean they don't have wars between human beings."

Still the Elf soldier remained silent.

"Why was I picked?" Shadrach went on helplessly, twisting his hands. "I don't know anything about it. What made him go and pick me? Why didn't he pick somebody else?"

"He trusted you," the Elf said. "You brought him inside your house, out of the rain. He knew that you expected nothing for it, that there was nothing you wanted. He had known few who gave and asked nothing back."

"Oh." Shadrach thought it over. At last he looked up. "But what about my gas station? And my house? And what will they say, Dan Green and Pop down at the store—"

The Elf soldier moved away, out of the light. "I have to go. It's getting late, and at night the Trolls come out. I don't want to be too far away from the others."

"Sure," Shadrach said.

"The Trolls are afraid of nothing, now that the old king is dead. They forage everywhere. No one is safe."

"Where did you say the meeting is to be? And what time?"

"At the Great Oak. When the moon sets tonight, just as it leaves the sky."

"I'll be there, I guess," Shadrach said. "I suppose you're right. The King of the Elves can't afford to let his kingdom down when it needs him most."

He looked around, but the Elf soldier was already gone.

Shadrach walked up the highway, his mind full of doubts and wonderings. When he came to the first of the flat stone steps, he stopped.

"And the old oak tree is on Phineas's farm! What'll Phineas say?"

But he was the Elf King and the Trolls were moving in the hills. Shadrach stood listening to the rustle of the wind as it moved through the trees beyond the highway, and along the far slopes and hills.

Trolls? Were there really Trolls there, rising up, bold and confident in the darkness of the night, afraid of nothing, afraid of no one?

And this business of being Elf King . . .

Shadrach went on up the steps, his lips pressed tight. When he reached the top of the stone steps, the last rays of sunlight had already faded. It was night.

Phineas Judd stared out the window. He swore and shook his head. Then he went quickly to the door and ran out onto the porch. In the cold moonlight a dim figure was walking slowly across the lower field, coming toward the house along the cow trail.

"Shadrach!" Phineas cried. "What's wrong? What are you doing out this time of night?"

Shadrach stopped and put his fists stubbornly on his hips.

"You go back home," Phineas said. "What's got into you?"

"I'm sorry, Phineas," Shadrach answered. "I'm sorry I have to go over your land. But I have to meet somebody at the old oak tree."

"At this time of night?"

Shadrach bowed his head.

"What's the matter with you, Shadrach? Who in the world you going to meet in the middle of the night on my farm?"

"I have to meet with the Elves. We're going to plan out the war with the Trolls."

"Well, I'll be damned," Phineas Judd said. He went back inside the house and slammed the door. For a long time he stood thinking. Then he went back out on the porch again. "What did you say you were doing? You don't have to tell me, of course, but I just—"

"I have to meet the Elves at the old oak tree. We must have a general council of war against the Trolls."

"Yes, indeed. The Trolls. Have to watch for the Trolls all the time."

"Trolls are everywhere," Shadrach stated, nodding his head. "I never realized it before. You can't forget them or ignore them. They never forget you. They're always planning, watching you—"

Phineas gaped at him, speechless.

"Oh, by the way," Shadrach said. "I may be gone for some time. It depends on how long this business is going to take. I haven't had much experience in fighting Trolls, so I'm not sure. But I wonder if you'd mind looking after the gas station for me, about twice a day, maybe once in the morning and once at night, to make sure no one's broken in or anything like that."

"You're going away?" Phineas came quickly down the stairs. "What's all this about Trolls? Why are you going?"

Shadrach patiently repeated what he had said.

"But what for?"

"Because I'm the Elf King. I have to lead them."

There was silence. "I see," Phineas said, at last. "That's right, you *did* mention it before, didn't you? But, Shadrach, why don't you come inside for a while and you can tell me about the Trolls and drink some coffee and—"

"Coffee?" Shadrach looked up at the pale moon above him, the moon and the bleak sky. The world was still and dead and the night was very cold and the moon would not be setting for some time.

Shadrach shivered.

"It's a cold night," Phineas urged. "Too cold to be out. Come on in—"

"I guess I have a little time," Shadrach admitted. "A cup of coffee wouldn't do any harm. But I can't stay very long . . ."

Shadrach stretched his legs out and sighed. "This coffee sure tastes good, Phineas."

Phineas sipped a little and put his cup down. The living room was quiet and warm. It was a very neat little living room with solemn pictures on the walls, gray uninteresting pictures that minded their own business. In the corner was a small reed organ with sheet music carefully arranged on top of it.

Shadrach noticed the organ and smiled. "You still play, Phineas?"

"Not much any more. The bellows don't work right. One of them won't come back up."

"I suppose I could fix it sometime. If I'm around, I mean."

"That would be fine," Phineas said. "I was thinking of asking you."

"Remember how you used to play 'Vilia' and Dan Green came up with that lady who worked for Pop during the summer? The one who wanted to open a pottery shop?"

"I sure do," Phineas said.

Presently, Shadrach set down his coffee cup and shifted in his chair.

"You want more coffee?" Phineas asked quickly. He stood up. "A little more?"

"Maybe a little. But I have to be going pretty soon."

"It's a bad night to be outside."

Shadrach looked through the window. It was darker; the moon had almost gone down. The fields were stark. Shadrach shivered. "I wouldn't disagree with you," he said.

Phineas turned eagerly. "Look, Shadrach. You go on home where it's warm. You can come out and fight Trolls some other night. There'll always be Trolls. You said so yourself. Plenty of time to do that later, when the weather's better. When it's not so cold."

Shadrach rubbed his forehead wearily. "You know, it all seems like some sort of a crazy dream. When did I start talking about Elves and Trolls? When did it all begin?" His voice trailed off. "Thank you for the coffee." He got slowly to his feet. "It warmed me up a lot. And I appreciated the talk. Like old times, you and me sitting here the way we used to."

"Are you going?" Phineas hesitated. "*Home?*"

"I think I better. It's late."

Phineas got quickly to his feet. He led Shadrach to the door, one arm around his shoulder.

"All right, Shadrach, you go on home. Take a good hot bath before you go to bed. It'll fix you up. And maybe just a little snort of brandy to warm the blood."

Phineas opened the front door and they went slowly down the porch steps, onto the cold, dark ground.

"Yes, I guess I'll be going," Shadrach said. "Good night—"

"You go on home." Phineas patted him on the arm. "You run along home and take a good hot bath. And then go straight to bed."

"That's a good idea. Thank you, Phineas. I appreciate your kindness." Shadrach looked down at Phineas's hand on his arm. He had not been that close to Phineas for years.

Shadrach contemplated the hand. He wrinkled his brow, puzzled.

Phineas's hand was huge and rough and his arms were short. His fingers were blunt, his nails broken and cracked. Almost black, or so it seemed in the moonlight.

Shadrach looked up at Phineas. "Strange," he murmured.

"What's strange, Shadrach?"

In the moonlight, Phineas's face seemed oddly heavy and brutal. Shadrach had never noticed before how the jaw bulged, what a great protruding jaw it was. The skin was yellow and coarse, like parchment. Behind the glasses, the eyes were like two stones, cold and lifeless. The ears were immense, the hair stringy and matted.

Odd that he had never noticed before. But he had never seen Phineas in the moonlight.

Shadrach stepped away, studying his old friend. From a few feet off, Phineas Judd seemed unusually short and squat. His legs were slightly bowed. His feet were enormous. And there was something else—

"What is it?" Phineas demanded, beginning to grow suspicious. "Is there something wrong?"

Something was completely wrong. And he had never noticed it, not in all the years they had been friends. All around Phineas Judd was an odor, a faint, pungent stench of rot, of decaying flesh, damp and moldy.

Shadrach glanced slowly about him. "Something wrong?" he echoed. "No, I wouldn't say that."

By the side of the house was an old rain barrel, half fallen apart. Shadrach walked over to it.

"No, Phineas. I wouldn't exactly say there's something wrong."

"What are you doing?"

"Me?" Shadrach took hold of one of the barrel staves and pulled it loose. He walked back to Phineas, carrying the barrel stave carefully. "I'm King of the Elves. Who—or what—are you?"

Phineas roared and attacked with his great murderous shovel hands.

Shadrach smashed him over the head with the barrel stave. Phineas bellowed with rage and pain.

At the shattering sound, there was a clatter and from underneath the house came a furious horde of bounding, leaping creatures, dark bent-over things, their bodies heavy and squat, their feet and heads immense. Shadrach took one look at the flood of dark creatures pouring out from Phineas's basement. He knew what they were.

"Help!" Shadrach shouted. "Trolls! Help!"

The Trolls were all around him, grabbing hold of him, tugging at him, climbing up him, pummeling his face and body.

Shadrach fell to with the barrel stave, swung again and again, kicking Trolls with his feet, whacking them with the barrel stave. There seemed to be hundreds of them.

More and more poured out from under Phineas's house, a surging black tide of pot-shaped creatures, their great eyes and teeth gleaming in the moonlight.

"Help!" Shadrach cried again, more feebly now. He was getting winded. His heart labored painfully. A Troll bit his wrist, clinging to his arm. Shadrach flung it away, pulling loose from the horde clutching his trouser legs, the barrel stave rising and falling.

One of the Trolls caught hold of the stave. A whole group of them helped, wrenching furiously, trying to pull it away. Shadrach hung on desperately. Trolls were all over him, on his shoulders, clinging to his coat, riding his arms, his legs, pulling his hair—

He heard a high-pitched clarion call from a long way off, the sound of some distant golden trumpet, echoing in the hills.

The Trolls suddenly stopped attacking. One of them dropped off Shadrach's neck. Another let go of his arm.

The call came again, this time more loudly.

"Elves!" a Troll rasped. He turned and moved toward the sound, grinding his teeth and spitting with fury.

"Elves!"

The Trolls swarmed forward, a growing wave of gnashing teeth and nails, pushing furiously toward the Elf columns. The Elves broke formation and joined battle, shouting with wild joy in their shrill, piping voices. The tide of Trolls rushed against them, Troll against Elf, shovel nails against golden sword, biting jaw against dagger.

"Kill the Elves!"

"Death to the Trolls!"

"Onward!"

"Forward!"

Shadrach fought desperately with the Trolls that were still clinging to him. He was exhausted, panting and gasping for breath. Blindly, he whacked on and on, kicking and jumping, throwing Trolls away from him, through the air and across the ground.

How long the battle raged, Shadrach never knew. He was lost in a sea of dark bodies, round and evil-smelling, clinging to him, tearing, biting, fastened to his nose and hair and fingers. He fought silently, grimly.

All around him, the Elf legions clashed with the Troll horde, little groups of struggling warriors on all sides.

Suddenly Shadrach stopped fighting. He raised his head, looking uncertainly around him. Nothing moved. Everything was silent. The fighting had ceased.

A few Trolls still clung to his arms and legs. Shadrach whacked one with the barrel stave. It howled and dropped to the ground. He staggered back, struggling with the last troll, who hung tenaciously to his arm.

"Now you!" Shadrach gasped. He pried the Troll loose and flung it into the air. The Troll fell to the ground and scuttled off into the night.

There was nothing more. No Troll moved anywhere. All was silent across the bleak moon-swept fields.

Shadrach sank down on a stone. His chest rose and fell painfully. Red specks swam before his eyes. Weakly, he got out his pocket handkerchief and wiped his neck and face. He closed his eyes, shaking his head from side to side.

When he opened his eyes again, the Elves were coming toward him, gathering their legion together again. The Elves were disheveled and bruised. Their golden armor was gashed and torn. Their helmets were bent or missing. Most of their scarlet plumes were gone. Those that still remained were drooping and broken.

But the battle was over. The war was won. The Troll hordes had been put to flight.

Shadrach got slowly to his feet. The Elf warriors stood around him in a circle, gazing up at him with silent respect. One of them helped steady him as he put his handkerchief away in his pocket.

"Thank you," Shadrach murmured. "Thank you very much."

"The Trolls have been defeated," an Elf stated, still awed by what had happened.

Shadrach gazed around at the Elves. There were many of them, more than he had ever seen before. All the Elves had turned out for the battle. They were grim-faced, stern with the seriousness of the moment, weary from the terrible struggle.

"Yes, they're gone, all right," Shadrach said. He was beginning to get his breath. "That was a close call. I'm glad you fellows came when you did. I was just about finished, fighting them all by myself."

"All alone, the King of the Elves held off the entire Troll army," an Elf announced shrilly.

"Eh?" Shadrach said, taken aback. Then he smiled. "That's true, I *did* fight them alone for a while. I *did* hold off the Trolls all by myself. The whole darn Troll army."

"There is more," an Elf said.

Shadrach blinked. "More?"

"Look over here, O King, mightiest of all the Elves. This way. To the right."

The Elves led Shadrach over.

"What is it?" Shadrach murmured, seeing nothing at first. He gazed down, trying to pierce the darkness. "Could we have a torch over here?"

Some Elves brought little pine torches.

There, on the frozen ground, lay Phineas Judd, on his back. His eyes were blank and staring, his mouth half open. He did not move. His body was cold and stiff.

"He is dead," an Elf said solemnly.

Shadrach gulped in sudden alarm. Cold sweat stood out abruptly on his forehead. "My gosh! My old friend! What have I done?"

"You have slain the Great Troll."

Shadrach paused.

"I *what?*"

"You have slain the Great Troll, leader of all the Trolls."

"This has never happened before," another Elf exclaimed excitedly. "The Great Troll has lived for centuries. Nobody imagined he could die. This is our most historic moment."

All the Elves gazed down at the silent form with awe, awe mixed with more than a little fear.

"Oh, go on!" Shadrach said. "That's just Phineas Judd."

But as he spoke, a chill moved up his spine. He

remembered what he had seen a little while before, as
he stood close by Phineas, as the dying moonlight crossed
his old friend's face.

"Look." One of the Elves bent over and unfastened
Phineas's blue-serge vest. He pushed the coat and vest
aside. "See?"

Shadrach bent down to look.

He gasped.

Underneath Phineas Judd's blue-serge vest was a suit
of mail, an encrusted mesh of ancient, rusting iron, fastened tightly around the squat body. On the mail stood
an engraved insignia, dark and time-worn, embedded
with dirt and rust. A moldering half-obliterated emblem.
The emblem of a crossed owl leg and toadstool.

The emblem of the Great Troll.

"Golly," Shadrach said. "And *I* killed him."

For a long time he gazed silently down. Then, slowly,
realization began to grow in him. He straightened up, a
smile forming on his face.

"What is it, O King?" an Elf piped.

"I just thought of something," Shadrach said. "I just
realized that—that since the Great Troll is dead and the
Troll army has been put to flight—"

He broke off. All the Elves were waiting.

"I thought maybe I—that is, maybe if you don't need
me any more—"

The Elves listened respectfully. "What is it, Mighty
King? Go on."

"I thought maybe now I could go back to the filling
station and not be king any more." Shadrach glanced
hopefully around at them. "Do you think so? With the
war over and all. With him dead. What do you say?"

For a time, the Elves were silent. They gazed unhap-
pily down at the ground. None of them said anything.
At last they began moving away, collecting their banners
and pennants.

"Yes, you may go back," an Elf said quietly. "The
war is over. The Trolls have been defeated. You may
return to your filling station, if that is what you want."

A flood of relief swept over Shadrach. He straightened
up, grinning from ear to ear. "Thanks! That's fine. That's
really fine. That's the best news I've heard in my life."

He moved away from the Elves, rubbing his hands together and blowing on them.

"Thanks an awful lot." He grinned around at the silent Elves. "Well, I guess I'll be running along, then. It's late. Late and cold. It's been a hard night. I'll—I'll see you around."

The Elves nodded silently.

"Fine. Well, good night." Shadrach turned and started along the path. He stopped for a moment, waving back at the Elves. "It was quite a battle, wasn't it? We really licked them." He hurried on along the path. Once again he stopped, looking back and waving. "Sure glad I could help out. Well, good night!"

One or two of the Elves waved, but none of them said anything.

Shadrach Jones walked slowly toward his place. He could see it from the rise, the highway that few cars traveled, the filling station falling to ruin, the house that might not last as long as himself, and not enough money coming in to repair them or buy a better location.

He turned around and went back.

The Elves were still gathered there in the silence of the night. They had not moved away.

"I was hoping you hadn't gone," Shadrach said, relieved.

"And we were hoping you would not leave," said a soldier.

Shadrach kicked a stone. It bounced through the tight silence and stopped. The Elves were still watching him.

"Leave?" Shadrach asked. "And me King of the Elves?"

"Then you will remain our king?" an Elf cried.

"It's a hard thing for a man of my age to change. To stop selling gasoline and suddenly be a king. It scared me for a while. But it doesn't any more."

"You will? You *will?*"

"Sure," said Shadrach Jones.

The little circle of Elf torches closed in joyously. In their light, he saw a platform like the one that had carried the old King of the Elves. But this one was much larger, big enough to hold a man, and dozens of the soldiers waited with proud shoulders under the shafts.

A soldier gave him a happy bow. "For you, Sire."

Shadrach climbed aboard. It was less comfortable than walking, but he knew this was how they wanted to take him to the Kingdom of the Elves.

FLYING PAN

Robert F. Young

Marianne Summers worked in a frying-pan factory. For eight hours every day and for five days every week she stood by a production-line conveyor and every time a frying pan went by she put a handle on it. And all the while she stood by one conveyor she rode along on another—a big conveyor with days and nights over it instead of fluorescent tubes, and months standing along it instead of people. And every time she passed a month it added something to her or took something away, and as time went by she became increasingly aware of the ultimate month—the one standing far down the line, waiting to put a handle on her soul.

Sometimes Marianne sat down and wondered how she could possibly have gotten into such a rut, but all the while she wondered she knew that she was only kidding herself, that she knew perfectly well why. Ruts were made for untalented people, and if you were untalented you ended up in one; moreover if you were untalented and were too stubborn to go home and admit you were untalented, you stayed in one.

There was a great deal of difference between dancing on TV and putting handles on frying pans: the difference between being graceful and gawky, lucky and unlucky, or—to get right back to the basic truth again—the difference between being talented and untalented. No matter how hard you practiced or how hard you tried, if your legs were too fat, no one wanted you and you ended up in a rut or in a frying-pan factory, which was the same thing, and you went to work every morning and performed the same tasks and you came home every night

and thought the same thoughts, and all the while you
rode down the big conveyor between the merciless
months and came closer and closer to the ultimate month
that would put the final touches on you and make you
just like everybody else. . . .

Mornings were getting up and cooking breakfasts in
her small apartment and taking the bus to work. Eve-
nings were going home and cooking lonely suppers and
afterward TV. Weekends were writing letters and walking in the park. Nothing ever changed and Marianne had
begun to think that nothing ever would. . . .

And then one night when she came home, she found
a flying frying pan on her window ledge.

It had been a day like all days, replete with frying
pans, superintendents, boredom and tired feet. Around
ten o'clock the maintenance man stopped by and asked
her to go to the Halloween Dance with him. The Halloween Dance was a yearly event sponsored by the company
and was scheduled for that night. So far, Marianne had
turned down fifteen would-be escorts.

A frying pan went by and she put a handle on it. "No,
I don't think so," she said.

"Why?" the maintenance man asked bluntly.

It was a good question, one that Marianne couldn't
answer honestly because she wasn't being honest with
herself. So she told the same little white lie she had told
all the others: "I—I don't like dances."

"Oh." The maintenance man gave her the same look
his fifteen predecessors had given her, and moved on.
Marianne shrugged her shoulders. I don't care what they
think, she told herself. Another frying pan went by, and
another and another.

After a while, noon came, and Marianne and all the
other employees ate frankfurters and sauerkraut in the
company cafeteria. The parade of frying pans recom-
menced promptly at 12:30.

During the afternoon she was approached twice more
by would-be escorts. You'd have thought she was the
only girl in the factory. Sometimes she hated her blue
eyes and round pink face, and sometimes she even hated
her bright yellow hair, which had some of the properties

of a magnet. But hating the way she looked didn't solve her problems—it only aggravated them—and by the time 4:30 came she had a headache and she heartily despised the whole world.

Diminutive trick-or-treaters were already making the rounds when she got off the bus at the corner. Witches walked and goblins leered, and pumpkin candles sputtered in the dusk. But Marianne hardly noticed.

Halloween was for children, not for an embittered old woman of twenty-two who worked in a frying-pan factory.

She walked down the street to the apartment building and picked up her mail at the desk. There were two letters, one from her mother, one from—

Marianne's heart pounded all the way up in the elevator and all the way down the sixth-floor corridor to her apartment. But she forced herself to open her mother's letter first. It was a typical letter, not essentially different from the last one. The grape crop had been good, but what with the trimming and the tying and the disking and the horse-hoeing, and paying off the pickers, there wasn't going to be much left of the check—if and when it came; the hens were laying better, but then they always did whenever egg prices dropped; Ed Olmstead was putting a new addition on his general store (it was high time!); Doris Hickett had just given birth to a 7 lb. baby boy; Pa sent his love, and please forget your foolish pride and come home. P.S.—Marianne should see the wonderful remodeling job Howard King was doing on his house. It was going to be a regular palace when he got done.

Marianne swallowed the lump in her throat. She opened the other letter with trembling fingers:

DEAR MARIANNE,
I said I wasn't going to write you any more, that I'd already written you too many times asking you to come home and marry me and you never gave me an answer one way or the other. But sometimes a fellow's pride don't amount to much.

I guess you know I'm remodeling the house and I guess you know the reason why. In case you don't it's the same reason I bought the house in the first

*place, because of you. I only got one picture window
and I don't know whether I should put it in the parlor
or in the kitchen. The kitchen would be fine, but all
you can see from there is the barn and you know
how the barn looks, but if I put it in the parlor the
northwest wind would be sure to crack it the first
winter though you'd get a good view of the road and
the willows along the creek. I don't know what to do.*

*The hills behind the south meadow are all red and
gold the way you used to like them. The willows look
like they're on fire. Nights I sit on the steps and picture you coming walking down the road and stopping
by the gate and then I get up and walk down the path
and I say, "I'm glad you've come back, Marianne. I
guess you know I still love you." I guess if anybody
ever heard me they'd think I was crazy because the
road is always empty when I get there, and there's no
one ever standing by the gate.*

HOWARD

There had been that crisp December night with the sound
of song and laughter intermingling with the crackling of
the ice beneath the runners and the chug-chugging of the
tractor as it pulled the hay-filled sleigh, and the stars so
bright and close they touched the topmost branches of
the silhouetted trees, and the snow, pale and clean in the
starlight, stretching away over the hills, up and up, into
the first dark fringe of the forest; and herself, sitting on
the tractor with Howard instead of in the hay with the
rest of the party, and the tractor lurching and bumping,
its headbeams lighting the way over the rutted country
road—

Howard's arm was around her and their frosty breaths
blended as they kissed. "I love you, Marianne," Howard
said, and she could see the words issuing from his lips in
little silvery puffs and drifting away into the darkness,
and suddenly she saw her own words, silver too, hovering
tenuously in the air before her, and presently she heard
them in wondrous astonishment: "I love you, too,
Howie. I love you, too. . . ."

*   *   *

She didn't know how long she'd been sitting there crying before she first became aware of the ticking sound. A long time, she guessed, judging by the stiffness of her limbs. The sound was coming from her bedroom window and what it made her think of most was the common pins she and the other kids used to tie on strings and rig up so they'd keep swinging against the windowpanes of lonely old people sitting alone on Halloween.

She had lit the table lamp when she came in, and its beams splashed reassuringly on the living-room rug. But beyond the aura of the light, shadows lay along the walls, coalesced in the bedroom doorway. Marianne stood up, concentrating on the sound. The more she listened the more she doubted that she was being victimized by the neighborhood small fry: the ticks came too regularly to be ascribed to a pin dangling at the end of a string. First there would be a staccato series of them, then silence, then another series. Moreover, her bedroom window was six stories above the street and nowhere near a fire escape.

But if the small fry weren't responsible for the sound, who was? There was an excellent way to find out. Marianne forced her legs into motion, walked slowly to the bedroom doorway, switched on the ceiling light and entered the room. A few short steps brought her to the window by her bed.

She peered through the glass. Something gleamed on the window ledge but she couldn't make out what it was. The ticking noise had ceased and traffic sounds drifted up from below. Across the way, the warm rectangles of windows made precise patterns in the darkness, and down the street a huge sign said in big blue letters: SPRUCK'S CORN PADS ARE THE BEST.

Some of Marianne's confidence returned. She released the catch and slowly raised the window. At first she didn't recognize the gleaming object as a flying saucer; she took it for an upside-down frying pan without a handle. And so ingrained was the habit by now that she reached for it instinctively, with the unconscious intention of putting a handle on it.

"Don't touch my ship!"

That was when Marianne saw the spaceman. He was standing off to one side, his diminutive helmet glimmering in the radiance of SPRUCK'S CORN PADS. He wore a gray, form-fitting space suit replete with ray guns, shoulder tanks, and boots with turned-up toes, and he was every bit of five inches tall. He had drawn one of the ray guns. (Marianne didn't know for sure they were ray guns, but judging from the rest of his paraphernalia, what else could they be?) and was holding it by the barrel. It was clear to Marianne that he had been tapping on the window with it.

It was also clear to Marianne that she was going, or had gone, out of her mind. She started to close the window—

"Stop, or I'll burn you!"

Her hands fell away from the sash. The voice had seemed real enough, a little on the thin side, perhaps, but certainly audible enough. Was it possible? Could this tiny creature be something more than a figment?

He had changed his gun to his other hand, she noticed, and its minute muzzle pointed directly at her forehead. When she made no further move, he permitted the barrel to drop slightly and said, "That's better. Now if you'll behave yourself and do as I say, maybe I can spare your life."

"Who are you?" Marianne asked.

It was as though he had been awaiting the question. He stepped dramatically into the full radiance of the light streaming through the window and sheathed his gun. He bowed almost imperceptibly, and his helmet flashed like the tinsel on a gum wrapper. "Prince Moy Trehano," he said majestically, though the majesty was marred by the thinness of his voice, "Emperor of 10,000 suns, Commander of the vast space fleet which is at this very moment in orbit around this insignificant planet you call 'Earth'!"

"Wh—why?"

"Because we're going to bomb you, that's why!"

"But why do you want to bomb us?"

"Because you're a menace to galactic civilization! Why else?"

"Oh," Marianne said.

"We're going to blow your cities to smithereens. There'll be so much death and destruction in our wake that you'll never recover from it. . . . Do you have any batteries?"

For a moment Marianne thought she had misunderstood. "Batteries?"

"Flashlight batteries will do." Prince Moy Trehano seemed embarrassed, though it was impossible to tell for sure because his helmet completely hid his face. There was a small horizontal slit where, presumably, his eyes were, but that was the only opening. "My atomic drive's been acting up," he went on. "In fact, this was a forced landing. Fortunately, however, I know a secret formula whereby I can convert the energy in a dry-cell battery into a controlled chain reaction. Do you have any?"

"I'll see," Marianne said.

"Remember now, no tricks. I'll burn you right through the walls with my atomic ray gun if you try to call anyone!"

"I—I think there's a flashlight in my bed-table drawer."

There was. She unscrewed the base, shook out the batteries and set them on the window sill. Prince Moy Trehano went into action. He opened a little door on the side of his ship and rolled the batteries through. Then he turned to Marianne. "Don't you move an inch from where you are!" he said. "I'll be watching you through the viewports." He stepped inside and closed the door.

Marianne held her terror at bay and peered at the spaceship more closely. They aren't really flying *saucers* at all, she thought; they're just like frying pans . . . flying frying pans. It even had a little bracket that could have been the place where the handle was supposed to go. Not only that, its ventral regions strongly suggested a frying-pan cover.

She shook her head, trying to clear it. First thing you knew, everything she saw would look like a frying pan. She remembered the viewports Prince Moy Trehano had mentioned, and presently she made them out—a series of tiny crinkly windows encircling the upper part of the saucer. She leaned closer, trying to see into the interior.

"Stand back!"

Marianne straightened up abruptly, so abruptly that she nearly lost her kneeling position before the window and toppled back into the room. Prince Moy Trehano had reemerged from his vessel and was standing imperiously in the combined radiance of the bedroom light and SPRUCK'S CORN PADS.

"The technical secrets of my stellar empire are not for the likes of you," he said. "But as a recompense for your assistance in the repairing of my atomic drive I am going to divulge my space fleet's target areas.

"We do not contemplate the complete destruction of humanity. We wish merely to destroy the present civilization, and to accomplish this it is our intention to wipe out every city on Earth. Villages will be exempt, as will small towns with populations of less than 20,000 humans. The bombings will begin as soon as I get back to my fleet—a matter of four or five hours—and if I do not return, they will begin in four or five hours anyway. So if you value your life, go ho—I mean, leave the city at once. I, Prince Moy Trehano, have spoken!"

Once again the bow, and the iridescing of the tinselly helmet, and then Prince Moy Trehano stepped into the spaceship and slammed the door. A whirring sound ensued, and the vessel began to shake. Colored lights went on in the viewports—a red one here, a blue one there, then a green one—creating a Christmas-tree effect.

Marianne watched, entranced. Suddenly the door flew open and Prince Moy Trehano's head popped out. "Get back!" he shouted. "Get back! You don't want to get burned by the jets, do you?" His head disappeared and the door slammed again.

Jets? Were flying saucers jet-propelled? Even as she instinctively shrank back into her bedroom, Marianne pondered the question. Then, as the saucer rose from the window ledge and into the night, she saw the little streams of fire issuing from its base. They were far more suggestive of sparks from a Zippo lighter than they were of jets, but if Prince Moy Trehano had said they were jets, then jets they were. Marianne was not inclined to argue the point.

When she thought about the incident afterward she remembered a lot of points that she could have argued— if she'd wanted to. Prince Moy Trehano's knowledge of the English language, for one, and his slip of the tongue

when he started to tell her to go home, for another. And
then there was the matter of his atomic drive. Certainly,
Marianne reflected later, if the bombs his fleet was supposed to have carried were as technically naive as his
atomic drive, the world had never had much to worry
about.

But at the moment she didn't feel like arguing any
points. Anyway, she was too busy to argue. Busy pack-
ing. Under ordinary circumstances Prince Moy Trehano's
threatened destruction of the cities of Earth would never
have been reason enough to send her scurrying to the
sticks. But Lord, when you were so sick of the pinched
little channels of blue that city dwellers called a sky, of
the disciplined little plots of grass that took the place of
fields, of bored agents who sneered at you just because
you had fat legs; when, deep in your heart, you wanted
an excuse to go home—then it was reason enough.

More than enough.

At the terminal she paused long enough to send a
telegram:

DEAR HOWIE: PUT THE PICTURE WINDOW IN THE
KITCHEN, I DON'T MIND THE BARN. WILL BE HOME ON
THE FIRST TRAIN.

MARIANNE

When the lights of the city faded into the dark line of
the horizon, Prince Moy Trehano relaxed at the controls.
His mission, he reflected, had come off reasonably well.

Of course there had been the inevitable unforeseen
complication. But he couldn't blame anyone for it besides
himself. He should have checked the flashlight batteries
before he swiped them. He knew well enough that half
the stock in Olmstead's general store had been gathering
dust for years, that Ed Olmstead would rather die than
throw away anything that some unwary customer might
buy. But he'd been so busy rigging up his ship that he
just hadn't thought.

In a way, though, his having to ask Marianne's help in
the repairing of his improvised motor had lent his story
a conviction it might otherwise have lacked. If he'd said
right out of a clear blue sky that his "fleet" was going

to bomb the cities and spare the villages, it wouldn't have sounded right. Her giving him the batteries had supplied him with a motivation. And his impromptu explanation about converting their energy into a controlled chain reaction had been a perfect cover-up. Marianne, he was sure, didn't know any more about atomic drives than he did.

Prince Moy Trehano shifted to a more comfortable position on his matchbox pilot's seat. He took off his tinfoil helmet and let his beard fall free. He switched off the Christmas-tree lights beneath the Saran Wrap viewports and looked out at the village-bejeweled countryside.

By morning he'd be home, snug and secure in his miniature mansion in the willows. First, though, he'd hide the frying pan in the same rabbit hole where he'd hidden the handle, so no one would ever find it. Then he could sit back and take it easy, comforted by the knowledge of a good deed well done—and by the happy prospect of his household chores being cut in half.

A witch went by on a broom. Prince Moy Trehano shook his head in disgust. Such an outmoded means of locomotion! It was no wonder humans didn't believe in witches any more. You had to keep up with the times if you expected to stay in the race. Why, if he were as old-fashioned and as antiquated as his contemporaries he might have been stuck with a bachelor for the rest of his life, and a shiftless bachelor—when it came to housework, anyway—at that. Not that Howard King wasn't a fine human being; he was as fine as they came. But you never got your dusting and your sweeping done mooning on the front steps like a sick calf, talking to yourself and waiting for your girl to come home from the city.

When you came right down to it, you *had* to be modern. Why, Marianne wouldn't even have *seen* him, to say nothing of hearing what he'd had to say, if he'd worn his traditional clothing, used his own name and employed his normal means of locomotion. Twentieth-century humans were just as imaginative as eighteenth-century and nineteenth-century humans: they believed in creatures from black lagoons and monsters from 20,000 fathoms and flying saucers and beings from outer space—

But they didn't believe in brownies. . . .

MY FATHER, THE CAT

Henry Slesar

My mother was a lovely, delicate woman from the coast of Brittany, who was miserable sleeping on less than three mattresses, and who, it is said, was once injured by a falling leaf in her garden. My grandfather, a descendant of the French nobility whose family had ridden the tumbrils of the Revolution, tended her fragile body and spirit with the same loving care given rare, brief-blooming flowers. You may imagine from this his attitude concerning marriage. He lived in terror of the vulgar, heavy-handed man who would one day win my mother's heart, and at last, this persistent dread killed him. His concern was unnecessary, however, for my mother chose a suitor who was as free of mundane brutality as a husband could be. Her choice was Dauphin, a remarkable white cat which strayed onto the estate shortly after his death.

Dauphin was an unusually large Angora, and his ability to speak in cultured French, English, and Italian was sufficient to cause my mother to adopt him as a household pet. It did not take long for her to realize that Dauphin deserved a higher status, and he became her friend, protector, and confidante. He never spoke of his origin, nor where he had acquired the classical education which made him such an entertaining companion. After two years, it was easy for my mother, an unworldly woman at best, to forget the dissimilarity in their species. In fact, she was convinced that Dauphin was an enchanted prince, and Dauphin, in consideration of her illusions, never dissuaded her. At last, they were married by an understanding clergyman of the locale, who solemnly filled in the marriage application with the name of M. Edwarde Dauphin.

I, Etienne Dauphin, am their son.

To be candid, I am a handsome youth, not unlike my mother in the delicacy of my features. My father's heritage is evident in my large, feline eyes, and in my slight body and quick movements. My mother's death, when I was four, left me in the charge of my father and his coterie of loyal servants, and I could not have wished for a finer upbringing. It is to my father's patient tutoring that I owe whatever graces I now possess. It was my father, the cat, whose gentle paws guided me to the treasure houses of literature, art, and music, whose whiskers bristled with pleasure at a goose well cooked, at a meal well served, at a wine well chosen. How many happy hours we shared! He knew more of life and the humanities, my father, the cat, than any human I have met in all my twenty-three years.

Until the age of eighteen, my education was his personal challenge. Then, it was his desire to send me into the world outside the gates. He chose for me a university in America, for he was deeply fond of what he called "that great raw country," where he believed my feline qualities might be tempered by the aggressiveness of the rough-coated barking dogs I would be sure to meet.

I must confess to a certain amount of unhappiness in my early American years, torn as I was from the comforts of the estate and the wisdom of my father, the cat. But I became adapted, and even upon my graduation from the university, sought and held employment in a metropolitan art museum. It was there I met Joanna, the young woman I intended to make my bride.

Joanna was a product of the great American southwest, the daughter of a cattle-raiser. There was a blooming vitality in her face and her body, a lustiness born of open skies and desert. Her hair was not the gold of antiquity; it was new gold, freshly mined from the black rock. Her eyes were not like old-world diamonds; their sparkle was that of sunlight on a cascading river. Her figure was bold, an open declaration of her sex.

She was, perhaps, an unusual choice for the son of a fairy-like mother and an Angora cat. But from the first

meeting of our eyes, I knew that I would someday bring
Joanna to my father's estate to present her as my fiancee.

I approached that occasion with understandable trepidation. My father had been explicit in his advice before
I departed for America, but on no point had he been
more emphatic than secrecy concerning himself. He
assured me that revelation of my paternity would bring
ridicule and unhappiness upon me. The advice was
sound, of course, and not even Joanna knew that our
journey's end would bring us to the estate of a large,
cultured, and conversing cat. I had deliberately fostered
the impression that I was orphaned, believing that the
proper place for revealing the truth was the atmosphere
of my father's home in France. I was certain that Joanna
would accept her father-in-law without distress. Indeed,
hadn't nearly a score of human servants remained
devoted to their feline master for almost a generation?

We had agreed to be wed on the first of June, and on
May the fourth, emplaned in New York for Paris. We
were met at Orly Field by Francois, my father's solemn
manservant, who had been delegated not so much as
escort as he was chaperone, my father having retained
much of the old world proprieties. It was a long trip by
automobile to our estate in Brittany, and I must admit
to a brooding silence throughout the drive which frankly
puzzled Joanna.

However, when the great stone fortress that was our
home came within view, my fears and doubts were
quickly dispelled. Joanna, like so many Americans, was
thrilled at the aura of venerability and royal custom sur-
rounding the estate. Francois placed her in charge of
Madame Jolinet, who clapped her plump old hands with
delight at the sight of her fresh blonde beauty, and chattered and clucked like a mother hen as she led Joanna
to her room on the second floor. As for myself, I had
one immediate wish: to see my father, the cat.

He greeted me in the library, where he had been anxiously awaiting our arrival, curled up in his favorite chair
by the fireside, a wide-mouthed goblet of cognac by his
side. As I entered the room, he lifted a paw formally,
but then his reserve was dissolved by the emotion of our
reunion, and he licked my face in unashamed joy.

Francois refreshed his glass, and poured another for me, and we toasted each other's well-being.

"To you, *mon purr*," I said, using the affectionate name of my childhood memory.

"To Joanna," my father said. He smacked his lips over the cognac, and wiped his whiskers gravely. "And where is this paragon?"

"With Madame Jolinet. She will be down shortly."

"And you have told her everything?"

I blushed. "No, *mon purr*, I have not. I thought it best to wait until we were home. She is a wonderful woman," I added impulsively. "She will not be—"

"Horrified?" my father said. "What makes you so certain, my son?"

"Because she is a woman of great heart," I said stoutly. "She was educated at a fine college for women in Eastern America. Her ancestors were rugged people, given to legend and folklore. She is a warm, human person—"

"Human," my father sighed, and his tail swished. "You are expecting too much of your beloved, Etienne. Even a woman of the finest character may be dismayed in this situation."

"But my mother—"

"Your mother was an exception, a changeling of the Fairies. You must not look for your mother's soul in Joanna's eyes." He jumped from his chair, and came towards me, resting his paw upon my knee. "I am glad you have not spoken of me, Etienne. Now you must keep your silence forever."

I was shocked. I reached down and touched my father's silky fur, saddened by the look of his age in his gray, gold-flecked eyes, and by the tinge of yellow in his white coat.

"No, *mon purr*," I said. "Joanna must know the truth. Joanna must know how proud I am to be the son of Edwarde Dauphin."

"Then you will lose her."

"Never! That cannot happen!"

My father walked stiffly to the fireplace, staring into the gray ashes. "Ring for Francois," he said. "Let him build the fire. I am cold, Etienne."

I walked to the cord and pulled it. My father turned to me and said: "You must wait, my son. At dinner this evening, perhaps. Do not speak of me until then."

"Very well, father."

When I left the library, I encountered Joanna at the head of the stairway, and she spoke to me excitedly.

"Oh, Etienne! What a *beautiful* old house. I know I will love it! May we see the rest?"

"Of course," I said.

"You look troubled. Is something wrong?"

"No, no. I was thinking how lovely you are."

We embraced, and her warm full body against mine confirmed my conviction that we should never be parted. She put her arm in mine, and we strolled through the great rooms of the house. She was ecstatic at their size and elegance, exclaiming over the carpeting, the gnarled furniture, the ancient silver and pewter, the gallery of family paintings. When she came upon an early portrait of my mother, her eyes misted.

"She was lovely," Joanna said. "Like a princess! And what of your father? Is there no portrait of him?"

"No," I said hurriedly. "No portrait." I had spoken my first lie to Joanna, for there was a painting, half-completed, which my mother had begun in the last year of her life. It was a whispering little watercolor, and Joanna discovered it to my consternation.

"What a magnificent cat!" she said. "Was it a pet?"

"It is Dauphin," I said nervously.

She laughed. "He has your eyes, Etienne."

"Joanna, I must tell you something—"

"And this ferocious gentleman with the moustaches? Who is he?"

"My grandfather. Joanna, you must listen—"

Francois, who had been following our inspection tour at shadow's-length, interrupted. I suspected that his timing was no mere coincidence.

"We will be serving dinner at seven-thirty," he said. "If the lady would care to dress—"

"Of course," Joanna said. "Will you excuse me, Etienne?"

I bowed to her, and she was gone.

At fifteen minutes to the appointed dining time, I was

ready, and hastened below to talk once more with my father. He was in the dining room, instructing the servants as to the placement of the silver and accessories. My father was proud of the excellence of his table, and took all his meals in the splendid manner. His appreciation of food and wine was unsurpassed in my experience, and it had always been the greatest of pleasures for me to watch him at table, stalking across the damask and dipping delicately into the silver dishes prepared for him. He pretended to be too busy with his dinner preparations to engage me in conversation, but I insisted.

"I must talk to you," I said. "We must decide together how to do this."

"It will not be easy," he answered with a twinkle. "Consider Joanna's view. A cat as large and as old as myself is cause enough for comment. A cat that speaks is alarming. A cat that dines at table with the household is shocking. And a cat whom you must introduce as your—"

"Stop it!" I cried. "Joanna must know the truth. You must help me reveal it to her."

"Then you will not heed my advice?"

"In all things but this. Our marriage can never be happy unless she accepts you for what you are."

"And if there is no marriage?"

I would not admit to this possibility. Joanna was mine; nothing could alter that. The look of pain and bewilderment in my eyes must have been evident to my father, for he touched my arm gently with his paw and said:

"I will help you, Etienne. You must give me your trust."

"Always!"

"Then come to dinner with Joanna and explain nothing. Wait for me to appear."

I grasped his paw and raised it to my lips. "Thank you, father!"

He turned to Francois, and snapped: "You have my instructions?"

"Yes, sir," the servant replied.

"Then all is ready. I shall return to my room now, Etienne. You may bring your fiancee to dine."

I hastened up the stairway, and found Joanna ready,

strikingly beautiful in shimmering white satin. Together, we descended the grand staircase and entered the room.

Her eyes shone at the magnificence of the service set upon the table, at the soldiery array of fine wines, some of them already poured into their proper glasses for my father's enjoyment: *Haut Medoc*, from *St. Estephe*, authentic *Chablis*, *Epernay Champagne*, and an American import from the Napa Valley of which he was fond. I waited expectantly for his appearance as we sipped our aperitif, while Joanna chatted about innocuous matters, with no idea of the tormented state I was in.

At eight o'clock, my father had not yet made his appearance, and I grew ever more distraught as Francois signalled for the serving of the *bouillon au madere*. Had he changed his mind? Would I be left to explain my status without his help? I hadn't realized until this moment how difficult a task I had allotted for myself, and the fear of losing Joanna was terrible within me. The soup was flat and tasteless on my tongue, and the misery in my manner was too apparent for Joanna to miss.

"What is it, Etienne?" she said. "You've been so morose all day. Can't you tell me what's wrong?"

"No, it's nothing. It's just—" I let the impulse take possession of my speech. "Joanna, there's something I should tell you. About my mother, and my father—"

"Ahem," Francois said.

He turned to the doorway, and our glances followed his.

"Oh, Etienne!" Joanna cried, in a voice ringing with delight.

It was my father, the cat, watching us with his gray, gold-flecked eyes. He approached the dining table, regarding Joanna with timidity and caution.

"It's the cat in the painting!" Joanna said. "You didn't tell me he was here, Etienne. He's beautiful!"

"Joanna, this is—"

"Dauphin! I would have known him anywhere. Here, Dauphin! Here, kitty, kitty, kitty!"

Slowly, my father approached her outstretched hand, and allowed her to scratch the thick fur on the back of his neck.

"Aren't you the pretty little pussy! Aren't you the sweetest little thing!"

"Joanna!"

She lifted my father by the haunches, and held him in her lap, stroking his fur and cooing the silly little words that women address to their pets. The sight pained and confused me, and I sought to find an opening word that would allow me to explain, yet hoping all the time that my father would himself provide the answer.

Then my father spoke.

"Meow," he said.

"Are you hungry?" Joanna asked solicitously. "Is the little pussy hungry?"

"Meow," my father said, and I believed my heart broke then and there. He leaped from her lap and padded across the room. I watched him through blurred eyes as he followed Francois to the corner, where the servant had placed a shallow bowl of milk. He lapped at it eagerly, until the last white drop was gone. Then he yawned and stretched, and trotted back to the doorway, with one fleeting glance in my direction that spoke articulately of what I must do next.

"What a wonderful animal," Joanna said.

"Yes," I answered. "He was my mother's favorite."

KID STUFF

Isaac Asimov

The first pang of nausea had passed and Jan Prentiss said, "Damn it, you're an insect."

It was a statement of fact, not an insult, and the thing that sat on Prentiss' desk said, "Of course."

It was about a foot long, very thin, and in shape a farfetched and miniature caricature of a human being. Its stalky arms and legs originated in pairs from the upper portion of its body. The legs were longer and thicker than the arms. They extended the length of the body, then bent forward at the knee.

The creature sat upon those knees and, when it did so, the stub of its fuzzy abdomen just cleared Prentiss' desk.

There was plenty of time for Prentiss to absorb these details. The object had no objection to being stared at. It seemed to welcome it, in fact, as though it were used to exciting admiration.

"What are you?" Prentiss did not feel completely rational. Five minutes ago, he had been seated at his typewriter, working leisurely on the story he had promised Horace W. Browne for last month's issue of *Farfetched Fantasy Fiction*. He had been in a perfectly usual frame of mind. He had felt quite fine; quite sane.

And then a block of air immediately to the right of the typewriter had shimmered, clouded over and condensed into the little horror that dangled its black and shiny feet over the edge of the desk.

Prentiss wondered in a detached sort of way that he bothered talking to it. This was the first time his profession had so crudely affected his dreams. It *must* be a dream, he told himself.

"I'm an Avalonian," said the being. "I'm from Avalon, in other words." Its tiny face ended in a mandibular mouth. Two swaying three-inch antennae rose from a spot above either eye, while the eyes themselves gleamed richly in their many-faceted fashion. There was no sign of nostrils.

Naturally not, thought Prentiss wildly. It has to breathe through vents in its abdomen. It must be talking with its abdomen then. Or using telepathy.

"Avalon?" he said stupidly. He thought: Avalon? The land of the fay in King Arthur's time?

"Certainly," said the creature, answering the thought smoothly. "I'm an elf."

"Oh, no!" Prentiss put his hands to his face, took them away and found the elf still there, its feet thumping against the top drawer. Prentiss was not a drinking man, or a nervous one. In fact, he was considered a very prosaic sort of person by his neighbors. He had a comfortable paunch, a reasonable but not excessive amount of hair on his head, an amiable wife and an active ten-year-old son. His neighbors were, of course, kept ignorant of the fact that he paid off the mortgage on his house by writing fantasies of one sort or another.

Till now, however, this secret vice had never affected his psyche. To be sure, his wife had shaken her head over his addiction many times. It was her standard opinion that he was wasting, even perverting, his talents.

"Who on Earth reads these things?" she would say. "All that stuff about demons and gnomes and wishing rings and elves. All that *kid* stuff, if you want my frank opinion."

"You're quite wrong," Prentiss would reply stiffly. "Modern fantasies are very sophisticated and mature treatments of folk motifs. Behind the façade of glib unreality there frequently lie trenchant comments on the world of today. Fantasy in modern style is, above all, adult fare."

Blanche shrugged. She had heard him speak at conventions so these comments weren't new to her.

"Besides," he would add, "fantasies pay the mortgage, don't they?"

"Maybe so," she would reply, "but it would be nice if you'd switch to mysteries. At least you'd get quarter-reprint sales out of those and we could even tell the neighbors what you do for a living."

Prentiss groaned in spirit. Blanche could come in now at any time and find him talking to himself (it was too real for a dream; it might be a hallucination). After that he *would* have to write mysteries for a living—or take to work.

"You're quite wrong," said the elf. "This is neither a dream nor a hallucination."

"Then why don't you go away?" asked Prentiss.

"I intend to. This is scarcely my idea of a place to live. And you're coming with me."

"I am *not*. What the hell do you think you are, telling me what I'm going to do?"

"If you think that's a respectful way to speak to a representative of an older culture, I can't say much for your upbringing."

"You're not an older culture——" He wanted to add: You're just a figment of my imagination; but he had been a writer too long to be able to bring himself to commit the chiché.

"We insects," said the elf freezingly, "existed half a billion years before the first mammal was invented. We watched the dinosaurs come in and we watched them go out. As for you man-things—strictly newcomers."

For the first time, Prentiss noted that, from the spot on the elf's body where its limbs sprouted, a third vestigial pair existed as well. It increased the insecticity of the object and Prentiss' sense of indignation grew.

He said, "You needn't waste your company on social inferiors."

"I wouldn't," said the elf, "believe me. But necessity drives, you know. It's a rather complicated story but when you hear it, you'll *want* to help."

Prentiss said uneasily, "Look, I don't have much time. Blanche—my wife will be in here any time. She'll be upset."

"She won't be here," said the elf. "I've set up a block in her mind."

"What!"

"Quite harmless, I assure you. But, after all, we can't afford to be disturbed, can we?"

Prentiss sat back in his chair, dazed and unhappy.

The elf said, "We elves began our association with you man-things immediately after the last ice age began. It had been a miserable time for us, as you can imagine. We couldn't wear animal carcasses or live in holes as your uncouth ancestors did. It took incredible stores of psychic energy to keep warm."

"Incredible stores of what?"

"Psychic energy. You know nothing at all about it. Your mind is too coarse to grasp the concept. Please don't interrupt."

The elf continued, "Necessity drove us to experiment with your people's brains. They were crude, but large. The cells were inefficient, almost worthless, but there were a vast number of them. We could use those brains as a concentrating device, a type of psychic lens, and increase the available energy which our own minds could tap. We survived the ice age handily and without having to retreat to the tropics as in previous such eras.

"Of course, we were spoiled. When warmth returned, we didn't abandon the man-things. We used them to increase our standard of living generally. We could travel faster, eat better, do more, and we lost our old, simple, virtuous way of life forever. Then, too, there was milk."

"Milk?" said Prentiss. "I don't see the connection."

"A divine liquid. I only tasted it once in my life. But elfin classic poetry speaks of it in superlatives. In the old days, men always supplied us plentifully. Why mammals of all things should be blessed with it and insects not is a complete mystery. . . . How unfortunate it is that the men-things got out of hand."

"They did?"

"Two hundred years ago."

"Good for us."

"Don't be narrow-minded," said the elf stiffly. "It was a useful association for all parties until you man-things learned to handle physical energies in quantity. It was just the sort of gross thing your minds are capable of."

"What was wrong with it?"

"It's hard to explain. It was all very well for us to light up our nightly revels with fireflies brightened by use of two manpower of psychic energy. But then you men-creatures installed electric lights. Our antennal reception is good for miles, but then you invented telegraphs, telephones and radios. Our kobolds mined ore with much greater efficiency than man-things do, until man-things invented dynamite. Do you see?"

"No."

"Surely you don't expect sensitive and superior creatures such as the elves to watch a group of hairy mammals outdo them. It wouldn't be so bad if we could imitate the electronic development ourselves, but our psychic energies were insufficient for the purpose. Well, we retreated from reality. We sulked, pined and drooped. Call it an inferiority complex, if you will, but from two centuries ago onward, we slowly abandoned mankind and retreated to such centers as Avalon."

Prentiss thought furiously. "Let's get this straight. You can handle minds?"

"Certainly."

"You can make me think you're invisible? Hypnotically, I mean?"

"A crude term, but yes."

"And when you appeared just now, you did it by lifting a kind of mental block. Is that it?"

"To answer your thoughts, rather than your words: You are not sleeping; you are not mad; and I am not supernatural."

"I was just making sure. I take it, then, you can read my mind."

"Of course. It is a rather dirty and unrewarding sort of labor, but I can do it when I must. Your name is Prentiss and you write imaginative fiction. You have one larva who is at a place of instruction. I know a great deal about you."

Prentiss winced. "And just where is Avalon?"

"You won't find it." The elf clacked his mandibles together two or three times. "Don't speculate on the possibility of warning the authorities. You'll find yourself in a madhouse. Avalon, in case you think the knowledge will help you, is in the middle of the Atlantic and quite invisible, you know. After the steamboat was invented, you man-things got to moving about so unreasonably that we had to cloak the whole island with a psychic shield.

"Of course, incidents *will* take place. Once a huge, barbaric vessel hit us dead center and it took all the psychic energy of the entire population to give the island the appearance of an iceberg. The *Titanic*, I believe, was the name printed on the vessel. And nowadays there are planes flying overhead all the time and sometimes there are crashes. We picked up cases of canned milk once. That's when I tasted it."

Prentiss said, "Well, then, damn it, why aren't you still on Avalon? Why did you leave?"

"I was ordered to leave," said the elf angrily. "The fools."

"Oh?"

"You know how it is when you're a little different. I'm not like the rest of them and the poor tradition-ridden fools resented it. They were jealous. That's the best explanation. Jealous!"

"How are you different?"

"Hand me that light bulb," said the elf. "Oh, just unscrew it. You don't need a reading lamp in the daytime."

With a quiver of repulsion, Prentiss did as he was told and passed the object into the little hands of the elf. Carefully, the elf, with fingers so thin and wiry that they looked like tendrils, touched the bottom and side of the brass base.

Feebly, the filament in the bulb reddened.

"Good God," said Prentiss.

"That," said the elf proudly, "is my great talent. I told you that we elves couldn't adapt psychic energy to electronics. Well, I can! I'm not just an ordinary elf. I'm a mutant! A super-elf! I'm the next stage in elfin evolution. This light is due just to the activity of my own mind, you know. Now watch when I use yours as a focus."

As he said that, the bulb's filament grew white hot and painful to look at, while a vague and not unpleasant tickling sensation entered Prentiss' skull.

The lamp went out and the elf put the bulb on the desk behind the typewriter.

"I haven't tried," said the elf proudly, "but I suspect I can fission uranium too."

"But look here, lighting a bulb takes energy. You can't just hold it——"

"I've *told* you about psychic energy. Great Oberon, man-thing, try to understand."

Prentiss felt increasingly uneasy; he said cautiously, "What do you intend doing with this gift of yours?"

"Go back to Avalon, of course. I *should* let those fools go to their doom, but an elf does have a certain patriotism, even if he *is* a coleopteron."

"A what?"

"We elves are not all of a species, you know. I'm of beetle descent. See?"

He rose to his feet and, standing on the desk, turned his back to Prentiss. What had seemed merely a shining black cuticle suddenly split and lifted. From underneath, two filmy, veined wings fluttered out.

"Oh, you can fly," said Prentiss.

"You're very foolish," said the elf contemptuously, "not to realize I'm too large for flight. But they *are* attractive, aren't they? How do you like the iridescence? The lepidoptera have disgusting wings in comparison. They're gaudy and indelicate. What's more they're always sticking out."

"The lepidoptera?" Prentiss felt hopelessly confused.

"The butterfly clans. They're the proud ones. They were always letting humans see them so they could be admired. Very petty minds in a way. And that's why your legends always give fairies butterfly wings instead of beetle wings which are *much* more diaphanously beautiful. We'll give the lepidoptera what for when we get back, you and I."

"Now hold on——"

"Just think," said the elf, swaying back and forth in what looked like elfin ecstasy, "our nightly revels on the fairy green will be a blaze of sparkling light from curlicues of neon tubing. We can cut loose the swarms of wasps we've got hitched to our flying wagons and install internal-combustion motors instead. We can stop this business of curling up on leaves when it's time to sleep and build factories to manufacture decent mattresses. I tell you, we'll *live*. . . . And the rest of them will eat dirt for having ordered me out."

"But I can't go with you," bleated Prentiss. "I have responsibilities. I have a wife and kid. You wouldn't take a man away from his—his larva, would you?"

"I'm not cruel," said the elf. He turned his eyes full on Prentiss. "I have an elfin soul. Still, what choice have I? I must have a man-brain for focusing purposes or I will accomplish nothing; and not all man-brains are suitable."

"Why not?"

"Great Oberon, creature. A man-brain isn't a passive thing of wood and stone. It must co-operate in order to be useful. And it can only co-operate by being fully aware of our own elfin ability to manipulate it. I can use your brain, for instance, but your wife's would be useless to me. It would take her years to understand who and what I am."

Prentiss said, "This is a damned insult. Are you telling me I believe in fairies? I'll have you know I'm a complete rationalist."

"Are you? When I first revealed myself to you, you had a few feeble thoughts about dreams and hallucinations but you talked to me, you accepted me. Your wife would have screamed and gone into hysterics."

Prentiss was silent. He could think of no answer.

"That's the trouble," said the elf despondently. "Practically all you humans have forgotten about us since we left you. Your minds have closed; grown useless. To be sure, your larvae believe in your legends about the 'little folk,' but their brains are undeveloped and useful only for simple processes. When they mature, they lose belief. Frankly, I don't know what I would do if it weren't for you fantasy writers."

"What do you mean, we fantasy writers?"

"You are the few remaining adults who believe in the insect folk. You, Prentiss, most of all. You've been a fantasy writer for twenty years."

"You're mad. I don't believe the things I write."

"You have to. You can't help it. I mean, while you're actually writing, you take the subject matter seriously.

After a while your mind is just naturally cultivated into usefulness. . . . But why argue? I *have* used you. You saw the light bulb brighten. So you see you must come with me."

"But I won't." Prentiss set his limbs stubbornly. "Can you make me against my will?"

"I could, but I might damage you, and I wouldn't want that. Suppose we say this. If you don't agree to come, I could focus a current of high-voltage electricity through your wife. It would be a revolting thing to have to do, but I understand your own people execute enemies of the state in that fashion, so that you would probably find the punishment less horrible than I do. I wouldn't want to seem brutal even to a man-thing."

Prentiss grew conscious of the perspiration matting the short hairs on his temple.

"Wait," he said, "don't do anything like that. Let's talk it over."

The elf shot out his filmy wings, fluttered them and returned them to their case. "Talk, talk, talk. It's tiring. Surely you have milk in the house. You're not a very thoughtful host or you would have offered me refreshment before this."

Prentiss tried to bury the thought that came to him, to push it as far below the outer skin of his mind as he could. He said casually, "I have something better than milk. Here, I'll get it for you."

"Stay where you are. Call to your wife. She'll bring it."

"But I don't want her to see you. It would frighten her."

The elf said, "You need feel no concern. I'll handle her so that she won't be the least disturbed."

Prentiss lifted an arm.

The elf said, "Any attack you make on me will be far slower than the bolt of electricity that will strike your wife."

Prentiss' arm dropped. He stepped to the door of his study.

"Blanche!" he called down the stairs.

Blanche was just visible in the living room, sitting

woodenly in the armchair near the bookcase. She seemed to be asleep, open-eyed.

Prentiss turned to the elf. "Something's wrong with her."

"She's just in a state of sedation. She'll hear you. Tell her what to do."

"Blanche!" he called again. "Bring the container of eggnog and a small glass, will you?"

With no sign of animation other than that of bare movement, Blanche rose and disappeared from view.

"What is eggnog?" asked the elf.

Prentiss attempted enthusiasm. "It is a compound of milk, sugar and eggs beaten to a delightful consistency. Milk alone is poor stuff compared to it."

Blanche entered with the eggnog. Her pretty face was expressionless. Her eyes turned toward the elf but lightened with no realization of the significance of the sight.

"Here, Jan," she said, and sat down in the old, leather-covered chair by the window, hands falling loosely to her lap.

Prentiss watched her uneasily for a moment. "Are you going to keep her here?"

"She'll be easier to control. . . . Well, aren't you going to offer me the eggnog?"

"Oh, sure. Here!"

He poured the thick white liquid into the cocktail glass. He had prepared five milk bottles of it two nights before for the boys of the New York Fantasy Association and it had been mixed with a lavish hand, since fantasy writers notoriously like it so.

The elf's antennae trembled violently.

"A heavenly aroma," he muttered.

He wrapped the ends of his thin arms about the stem of the small glass and lifted it to his mouth. The liquid's level sank. When half was gone, he put it down and sighed, "Oh, the loss to my people. What a creation! What a thing to exist! Our histories tell us that in ancient days an occasional lucky sprite managed to take the place of a man-larva at birth so that he might draw off the liquid fresh-made. I wonder if even those ever experienced anything like this."

Prentiss said with a touch of professional interest,

"That's the idea behind this business of changelings, is it?"

"Of course. The female man-creature has a great gift. Why not take advantage of it?" The elf turned his eyes upon the rise and fall of Blanche's bosom and sighed again.

Prentiss said (not too eager, now; don't give it away), "Go ahead. Drink all you want."

He, too, watched Blanche, waiting for signs of restoring animation, waiting for the beginnings of breakdown in the elf's control.

The elf said, "When is your larva returning from its place of instruction? I need him."

"Soon, soon," said Prentiss nervously. He looked at his wristwatch. Actually, Jan, Junior, would be back, yelling for a slab of cake and milk, in something like fifteen minutes.

"Fill 'er up," he said urgently. "Fill 'er up."

The elf sipped gaily. He said, "Once the larva arrives, you can go."

"Go?"

"Only to the library. You'll have to get volumes on electronics. I'll need the details on how to build television, telephones, all that. I'll need to have rules on wiring, instructions for constructing vacuum tubes. Details, Prentiss, details! We have tremendous tasks ahead of us. Oil drilling, gasoline refining, motors, scientific agriculture. We'll build a new Avalon, you and I. A technical one. A scientific fairyland. We will create a new world."

"Great!" said Prentiss. "Here, don't neglect your drink."

"You see. You are catching fire with the idea," said the elf. "And you will be rewarded. You will have a dozen female man-things to yourself."

Prentiss looked at Blanche automatically. No signs of hearing, but who could tell? He said, "I'd have no use for female man-th—for women, I mean."

"Come now," said the elf censoriously, "be truthful. You men-things are well known to our folk as lecherous, bestial creatures. Mothers frightened their young for generations by threatening them with men-things. . . .

Young, ah!" He lifted the glass of eggnog in the air and said, "To my own young," and drained it.

"Fill 'er up," said Prentiss at once. "Fill 'er up."

The elf did so. He said, "I'll have lots of children. I'll pick out the best of the coleoptresses and breed my line. I'll continue the mutation. Right now I'm the only one, but when we have a dozen or fifty, I'll interbreed them and develop the race of the super-elf. A race of electro— ulp—electronic marvels and infinite future. . . . If I could only drink more. Nectar! The original nectar!"

There was the sudden noise of a door being flung open and a young voice calling, "Mom! Hey, Mom!"

The elf, his glossy eyes a little dimmed, said, "Then we'll begin to take over the men-things. A few believe already; the rest we will—urp—teach. It will be the old days, but better; a more efficient elf-hood, a tighter union."

Jan, Junior's, voice was closer and tinged with impatience. "Hey, Mom! Ain't you home?"

Prentiss felt his eyes popping with tension. Blanche sat rigid. The elf's speech was slightly thick, his balance a little unsteady. If Prentiss were going to risk it, now, now was the time.

"Sit back," said the elf peremptorily. "You're being foolish. I knew there was alcohol in the eggnog from the moment you thought your ridiculous scheme. You men-things are very shifty. We elves have many proverbs about you. Fortunately, alcohol has little effect upon us. Now if you had tried catnip with just a touch of honey in it . . . Ah, here is the larva. How are you, little man-thing?"

The elf sat there, the goblet of eggnog halfway to his mandibles, while Jan, Junior, stood in the doorway. Jan, Junior's, ten-year-old face was moderately smeared with dirt, his hair was immoderately matted and there was a look of the utmost surprise in his gray eyes. His battered schoolbooks swayed from the end of the strap he held in his hand.

He said, "Pop! What's the matter with Mom? And— and what's that?"

The elf said to Prentiss, "Hurry to the library. No time must be lost. You know the books I need." All trace of incipient drunkenness had left the creature and Prentiss' morale broke. The creature had been playing with him.

Prentiss got up to go.

The elf said, "And nothing human; nothing sneaky; no tricks. Your wife is still a hostage. I can use the larva's mind to kill her; it's good enough for that. I wouldn't want to do it. I'm a member of the Elfitarian Ethical Society and we advocate considerate treatment of mammals so you may rely on my noble principles *if* you do as I say."

Prentiss felt a strong compulsion to leave flooding him. He stumbled toward the door.

Jan, Junior, cried, "Pop, it can talk! He says he'll kill Mom! Hey, don't go away!"

Prentiss was already out of the room, when he heard the elf say, "Don't stare at me, larva. I will not harm your mother if you do exactly as I say. I am an elf, a fairy. You know what a fairy is, of course."

And Prentiss was at the front door when he heard Jan, Junior's, treble raised in wild shouting, followed by scream after scream in Blanche's shuddering soprano.

The strong, though invisible, elastic that was drawing Prentiss out the house snapped and vanished. He fell backward, righted himself and darted back up the stairs.

Blanche, fairly saturated with quivering life, was backed into a corner, her arms about a weeping Jan, Junior.

On the desk was a collapsed black carapace, covering a nasty smear of pulpiness from which colorless liquid dripped.

Jan, Junior, was sobbing hysterically, "I hit it. I hit it with my schoolbooks. It was hurting Mom."

An hour passed and Prentiss felt the world of normality pouring back into the interstices left behind by the creature from Avalon. The elf itself was already ash in the incinerator behind the house and the only remnant of its existence was the damp stain at the foot of his desk.

Blanche was still sickly pale. They talked in whispers.

Prentiss said, "How's Jan, Junior?"

"He's watching television."

"Is he all right?"

"Oh, *he's* all right, but *I'll* be having nightmares for weeks."

"I know. So will I unless we can get it out of our minds. I don't think there'll ever be another of those—things here."

Blanche said, "I can't explain how awful it was. I kept hearing every word he said, even when I was down in the living room."

"It was telepathy, you see."

"I just couldn't move. Then, after you left, I could begin to stir a bit. I tried to scream but all I could do was moan and whimper. Then Jan, Junior, smashed him and all at once I was free. I don't understand how it happened."

Prentiss felt a certain gloomy satisfaction. "I think I know. I was under his control because I accepted the truth of his existence. He held you in check through me. When I left the room, increasing distance made it harder to use my mind as a psychic lens and you could begin moving. By the time I reached the front door, the elf thought it was time to switch from my mind to Jan, Junior's. That was his mistake."

"In what way?" asked Blanche.

"He assumed that all children believe in fairies, but he was wrong. Here in America today children *don't* believe in fairies. They never hear of them. They believe in Tom Corbett, in Hopalong Cassidy, in Dick Tracy, in Howdy Doody, in Superman and a dozen other things, but not in fairies.

"The elf just never realized the sudden cultural changes brought about by comic books and television, and when he tried to grab Jan, Junior's, mind, he couldn't. Before he could recover his psychic balance, Jan, Junior, was on top of him in a swinging panic because he thought you were being hurt and it was all over.

"It's like I've always said, Blanche. The ancient folk motifs of legend survive only in the modern fantasy magazine, and modern fantasy is purely adult fare. Do you finally see my point?"

Blanche said humbly, "Yes, dear."

Prentiss put his hands in his pockets and grinned slowly. "You know, Blanche, next time I see Walt Rae, I think I'll just drop a hint that I write the stuff. Time the neighbors knew, I think."

Jan, Junior, holding an enormous slice of buttered bread, wandered into his father's study in search of the dimming memory. Pop kept slapping him on the back and Mom kept putting bread and cake in his hands and he was forgetting why. There had been this big old thing on the desk that could talk . . .

It had all happened so quickly that it got mixed up in his mind.

He shrugged his shoulders and, in the late afternoon sunlight, looked at the partly typewritten sheet in his father's typewriter, then at the small pile of paper resting on the desk.

He read a while, curled his lip and muttered, "Gee whiz. Fairies again. Always kid stuff!" and wandered off.

THE LONG NIGHT OF WAITING

Andre Norton

"What—what are we going to do?" Lesley squeezed her hands so tightly together they hurt. She really wanted to run, as far and as fast as she could.

Rick was not running. He stood there, still holding to Alex's belt, just as he had grabbed his brother to keep him from following Matt. Following him where?

"We won't do anything," Rick answered slowly.

"But people'll ask—all kinds of questions. You only have to look at that—" Lesley pointed with her chin to what was now before them.

Alex still struggled for freedom. "Want Matt!" he yelled at the top of his voice. He wriggled around to beat at Rick with his fists.

"Let me go! Let me go—with Matt!"

Rick shook him. "Now listen here, shrimp. Matt's gone. You can't get to him now. Use some sense—look there. Do you see Matt? Well, do you?"

Lesley wondered how Rick could be so calm— accepting all of this just as if it happened every day— like going to school, or watching a tel-cast, or the regular, safe things. How could he just stand there and talk to Alex as if he were grown up and Alex was just being pesty as he was sometimes? She watched Rick wonderingly, and tried not to think of what had just happened.

"Matt?" Alex had stopped fighting. His voice sounded as if he were going to start bawling in a minute or two. And when Alex cried—! He would keep on and on, and they would have questions to answer. If they told the real truth—Lesley drew a deep breath and shivered.

No one, no one in the whole world would ever believe

them! Not even if they saw what was right out here in this field now. No one would believe—they would say that she, Lesley, and Rick, and Alex were all mixed up in their minds. And they might even be sent away to a hospital or something! No, they could never tell the truth! But Alex, he would blurt out the whole thing if anyone asked a question about Matt. What could they do about Alex?

Her eyes questioned Rick over Alex's head. He was still holding their young brother, but Alex had turned, was gripping Rick's waist, looking up at him demandingly, waiting, Lesley knew, for Rick to explain as he had successfully most times in Alex's life. And if Rick couldn't explain this time?

Rick hunkered down on the ground, his hands now on Alex's shoulders.

"Listen, shrimp, Matt's gone. Lesley goes, I go, to school—"

Alex sniffed. "But the bus comes then, and you get on while I watch—then you come home again—" His small face cleared. "Then Matt—he'll come back? He's gone to school? But this is Saturday! You an' Lesley don't go on Saturday. How come Matt does? An' where's the bus? There's nothin' but that mean old dozer that's chewin' up things. An' now all these vines and stuff—and the dozer tipped right over an'—" He screwed around a little in Rick's grip to stare over his brother's hunched shoulder at the disaster area beyond.

"No," Rick was firm. "Matt's not gone to school. He's gone home—to his own place. You remember back at Christmas time, Alex, when Peter came with Aunt Fran and Uncle Porter? He came for a visit. Matt came with Lizzy for a visit—how he's gone back home—just like Peter did."

"But Matt said—he said *this* was his home!" countered Alex. "He didn't live in Cleveland like Peter."

"It was his home once," Rick continued still in that grown-up way. "Just like Jimmy Rice used to live down the street in the red house. When Jimmy's Dad got moved by his company, Jimmy went clear out to St. Louis to live."

"But Matt was sure! He said *this* was his home!" Alex

frowned. "He said it over and over, that he had come home again."

"At first he did," Rick agreed. "But later, you know that Matt was not so sure, was he now? You think about that, shrimp."

Alex was still frowning. At least he was not screaming as Lesley feared he would be. Rick, she was suddenly very proud and a little in awe of Rick. How had he known how to keep Alex from going into one of his tantrums?

"Matt—he did say funny things. An' he was afraid of cars. Why was he afraid of cars, Rick?"

"Because where he lives they don't have cars."

Alex's surprise was open. "Then how do they go to the store? An' to Sunday School, an' school, an' every place?"

"They have other ways, Alex. Yes, Matt was afraid of a lot of things, he knew that this was not his home, that he had to go back."

"But—I want him—he—" Alex began to cry, not with the loud screaming Lesley had feared, but in a way now which made her hurt a little inside as she watched him butt his head against Rick's shoulder, making no effort to smear away the tears as they wet his dirty cheeks.

"Sure you want him," Rick answered. "But Matt—he was afraid, he was not very happy here, now was he, shrimp?"

"With me, he was. We had a lot of fun, we did!"

"But Matt wouldn't go in the house, remember? Remember what happened when the lights went on?"

"Matt ran an' hid. An' Lizzy, she kept telling him an' telling him they had to go back. Maybe if Lizzy hadn't all the time told him that—"

Lesley thought about Lizzy. Matt was little—he was not more than Alex's age—not really, in spite of what the stone said. But Lizzy had been older and quicker to understand. It had been Lizzy who had asked most of the questions and then been sick (truly sick to her stomach) when Lesley and Rick answered them. Lizzy had been sure of what had happened then—just like she was sure about the other—that the stone must never be moved, nor that place covered over to trap anybody else. So that nobody would fall through—

Fall through into what? Lesley tried to remember all the bits and pieces Lizzy and Matt had told about where they had been for a hundred and ten years—a *hundred and ten* just like the stone said.

She and Rick had found the stone when Alex had run away. They had often had to hunt Alex like that. Ever since he learned to open the Safe-tee gate he would go off about once a week or so. It was about two months after they moved here, before all the new houses had been built and the big apartments at the end of the street. This was all more like real country then. Now it was different, spoiled—just this one open place left and that (unless Lizzy was right in thinking she'd stopped it all) would not be open long. The men had started to clear it off with the bulldozer the day before yesterday. All the ground on that side was raw and cut up, the trees and bushes had been smashed and dug out.

There had been part of an old orchard there, and a big old lilac bush. Last spring it had been so pretty. Of course, the apples were all little and hard, and had worms in them. But it had been pretty and a swell place to play. Rick and Jim Bowers had a house up in the biggest tree. Their sign said "No girls allowed," but Lesley had sneaked up once when they were playing Little League ball and had seen it all.

Then there was the stone. That was kind of scarey. Yet they had kept going to look at it every once in a while, just to wonder.

Alex had found it first that day he ran away. There were a lot of bushes hiding it and tall grass. Lesley felt her eyes drawn in that direction now. It *was* still there. Though you have to mostly guess about that, only one teeny bit of it showed through all those leaves and things.

And when they had found Alex he had been working with a piece of stick, scratching at the words carved there which were all filled up with moss and dirt. He had been so busy and excited he had not tried to dodge them as he usually did, instead he wanted to know if those were real words, and then demanded that Rick read them to him.

Now Lesley's lips silently shaped what was carved there.

> *A long night of waiting.*
> *To the Memory of our dear children,*
> *Lizzy and Matthew Mendal,*
> *Who disappeared on this spot*
> *June 23, 1861.*
> *May the Good Lord return them*
> *to their loving parents and this*
> *world in His Own reckoned time.*
> *Erected to mark our years of watching,*
> *June 23, 1900.*

It had sounded so queer. At first Lesley had thought it was a grave and had been a little frightened. But Rick had pointed out that the words did not read like those on the stones in the cemetery where they went on Memorial Day with flowers for Grandma and Grandpa Targ. It was different because it never said "dead" but "disappeared."

Rick had been excited, said it sounded like a mystery. He had begun to ask around, but none of the neighbors knew anything—except this had all once been a farm. Almost all the houses on the street were built on that land. They had the oldest house of all. Dad said it had once been the farm house, only people had changed it and added parts like bathrooms.

Lizzy and Matt—

Rick had gone to the library and asked questions, too. Miss Adams, she got interested when Rick kept on wanting to know what this was like a hundred years ago (though of course he did not mention the stone, that was their own secret, somehow from the first they knew they must keep quiet about that). Miss Adams had shown Rick how they kept the old newspapers on film tapes. And when he did his big project for social studies, he had chosen the farm's history, which gave him a good chance to use those films to look things up.

That was how he learned all there was to know about Lizzy and Matt. There had been a lot in the old paper about them. Lizzy Mendal, Matthew Mendal, aged eleven and five—Lesley could almost repeat it word for word she had read Rick's copied notes so often. They had been walking across this field, carrying lunch to their father who was ploughing. He had been standing by a fence talking to Doctor Levi Morris who was driving by. They had both looked up to see Lizzy and Matthew coming and had waved to them. Lizzy waved back and then— she and Matthew—they were just gone! Right out of the middle of an open field they were gone!

Mr. Mendal and the Doctor, they had been so surprised they couldn't believe their eyes, but they had hunted and hunted. And the men from other farms had come to hunt too. But no one ever saw the children again.

Only about a year later, Mrs. Mendal (she had kept coming to stand here in the field, always hoping, Lesley guessed, they might come back as they had gone) came running home all excited to say she heard Matt's voice, and he had been calling "Ma! Ma!"

She got Mr. Mendal to go back with her. And he heard it, too, when he listened, but it was very faint. Just like someone a long way off calling "Ma!" Then it was gone and they never heard it again.

It was all in the papers Rick found, the story of how they hunted for the children and later on about Mrs. Mendal hearing Matt. But nobody ever was able to explain what had happened.

So all that was left was the stone and a big mystery. Rick started hunting around in the library, even after he finished his report, and found a book with other stories about people who disappeared. It was written by a man named Charles Fort. Some of it had been hard reading, but Rick and Lesley had both found the parts which were like what happened to Lizzy and Matt. And in all those other disappearances there had been no answers to what had happened, and nobody came back.

Until Lizzy and Matt. But suppose she and Rick and Alex told people now, would any believe them? And what good would it do, anyway? Unless Lizzy was right and people should know so they would not be caught. Suppose someone built a house right over where the stone stood, and suppose some day a little boy like Alex, or a girl like Lesley, or even a mom or dad, disappeared? She and Rick, maybe they ought to talk and keep on talking until someone believed them, believed them enough to make sure such a house was never going to be built, and this place was made safe.

"Matt—he kept sayin' he wanted his mom," Alex's voice cut through her thoughts. "Rick, where was his mom that she lost him that way?"

Rick, for the first time, looked helpless. How could you make Alex understand?

Lesley stood up. She still felt quite shaky and a little sick from the left-over part of her fright. But the worst was past now, she had to be as tough as Rick or he'd say that was just like a girl.

"Alex," she was able to say that quite naturally, and her voice did not sound too queer, "Matt, maybe he'll find his mom now, he was just looking in the wrong place. She's not here any more. You remember last Christmas when you went with Mom to see Santy Claus at the store and you got lost? You were hunting mom and she was hunting you, and at first you were looking in the wrong places. But you did find each other. Well, Matt's mom will find him all right."

She thought that Alex wanted to believe her. He had not pushed away from Rick entirely, but he looked as if he were listening carefully to every word she said.

"You're sure?" he asked doubtfully. "Matt—he was scared he'd never find his mom. He said he kept calling an' calling an' she never came."

"She'll come, moms always do." Lesley tried to make that sound true. "And Lizzy will help. Lizzy," Lesley hesitated, trying to choose the right words, "Lizzy's very good at getting things done."

She looked beyond to the evidence of Lizzy's getting things done and her wonder grew. At first, just after it had happened, she had been so shocked and afraid, she had not really understood what Lizzy had done before she and Matt had gone again. What—what *had* Lizzy learned during that time when she had been in the other place? And how had she learned it? She had never answered all their questions as if she was not able to tell them what lay on the other side of that door, or whatever it was which was between *here* and *there*.

Lizzy's work was hard to believe, even when you saw it right before your eyes.

The bulldozer and the other machines which had been parked there to begin work again Monday morning— Well, the bulldozer was lying over on its side, just as if it were a toy Alex had picked up and thrown as he did sometimes when he got over-tired and cross. And the other machines—they were all pushed over, some even broken! Then there were the growing things. Lizzy had rammed her hands into the pockets of her dress-like apron and brought them out with seeds trickling between her fingers. And she had just thrown those seeds here and there, all over the place.

It took a long time for plants to grow—weeks—Lesley knew. But look—these were growing right while you watched. They had already made a thick mat over every piece of the machinery they had reached, like they had to cover it from sight quickly. And there were flowers opening—and butterflies—Lesley had never seen so many butterflies as were gathering about those flowers, arriving right out of nowhere.

"Rick—how—?" She could not put her wonder into a full question, she could only gesture toward what was happening there.

Her brother shrugged. It was as if he did not want to look at what was happening. Instead he spoke to both of them sharply.

"Listen, shrimp, Les, it's getting late. Mom and Dad will be home soon. We'd better get there before they do. Remember, we left all the things Matt and Lizzy used out in the summer house. Dad's going to work on the lawn this afternoon. He'll want to get the mower out of there. If he sees what we left there he'll ask questions for sure and we might have to talk. Not that it would do any good."

Rick was right. Lesley looked around her regretfully now. She was not frightened any more—she, well, she would like to just stay awhile and watch. But she reached for Alex's sticky hand. To her surprise he did not object or jerk away, he was still hiccuping a little as he did after he cried. She was thankful Rick had been able to manage him so well.

They scraped through their own private hole in the fence into the backyard, heading to the summer house which Rick and Dad had fixed up into a rainy day place to play and a storage for the outside tools. The camping bags were there, even the plates and cups. Those were still smeared with jelly and peanut butter. Just think, Matt had never tasted jelly and peanut butter before, he said. But he had liked it a lot. Lesley had better sneak those in and give them a good washing. And the milk— Lizzy could not understand how you got milk from a bottle a man brought to your house and not straight from a cow. She seemed almost afraid to drink it. And she had not liked Coke at all—said it tasted funny.

"I wish Matt was here." Alex stood looking down at the sleeping bag, his face clouding up again. "Matt was fun—"

"Sure he was. Here, shrimp, you catch ahold of that and help me carry this back. We've got to get it into the camper before Dad comes."

"Why?"

Oh, dear, was Alex going to have one of his stubborn question-everything times? Lesley had put the plates and cups back into the big paper bag in which she had smuggled the food from the kitchen this morning, and was folding up the extra cover from Matt's bed.

"You just come along and I'll tell you, shrimp." She heard Rick say. Rick was just *wonderful* today. Though Mom always said that Rick could manage Alex better than anyone else in the whole family when he wanted to make the effort.

There, she gave a searching look around as the boys left (one of the bags between them) this was cleared. They would take the other bag, and she would do the dishes. Then Dad could walk right in and never know that Lizzy and Matt had been here for two nights and a day.

Two nights and a day—Lizzy had kept herself and Matt out of sight yesterday when Lesley and Rick had been at school. She would not go near the house, nor let Matt later when Alex wanted him to go and see the train Dad and Rick had set up in the family room. All she had wanted were newspapers. Lesley had taken those to her and some of the magazines Mom had collected for the Salvation Army. She must have read a lot, because when they met her after school, she had a million questions to ask.

It was then that she said she and Matt had to go away, back to where they had come from, that they could not stay in this mixed up horrible world which was not the right one at all! Rick told her about the words on the stones and how long it had been. First she called him a liar and said that was not true. So after dark he had taken a flashlight and went back to show her the stone and the words.

She had been the one to cry then. But she did not for long. She got to asking what was going to happen in the field, looking at the machines. When Rick told her, Lizzy had said quick and hot, no, they mustn't do that, it was dangerous—a lot of others might go through. And *they*, those in the other world, didn't want people who did bad things to spoil everything.

When Rick brought her back she was mad, not at him, but at everything else. She made him walk her down to the place from which you could see the inter-city thruway, with all the cars going whizz. Rick said he was sure she was scared. She was shaking, and she held onto his hand so hard it hurt. But she made herself watch. Then, when they came back, she said Matt and she—they had to go. And she offered to take Alex, Lesley, and Rick with them. She said they couldn't want to go on living *here*.

That was the only time she talked much of what it was like *there*. Birds and flowers, no noise or cars rushing about, nor bulldozers tearing the ground up, everything pretty. It was Lesley who had asked then:

"If it was all that wonderful, why did you want to come back?"

Then she was sorry she had asked because Lizzy's face looked like she was hurting inside when she answered:

"There was Ma and Pa. Matt, he's little, he misses Ma bad at times. Those *others*, they got their own way of life, and it ain't much like ours. So, we've kept a-tryin' to get back. I brought somethin'—just for Ma." She showed them two bags of big silvery leaves pinned together with long thorns. Inside each were seeds, all mixed up big and little together.

"Things grow *there*," she nodded toward the field, "they grow strange-like. Faster than seeds hereabouts. You put one of these," she ran her finger tip in among the seeds, shifting them back and forth, "in the ground, and you can *see* it grow. Honest-Injun-cross-my-heart-an'-hope-to-die if that ain't so. Ma, she hankers for flowers, loves 'em truly. So I brought her some. Only, Ma, she ain't here. Funny thing—*those* over *there*, they have a feelin' about these here flowers and plants. *They* tell you right out that as long as *they* have these growin' 'round *they*'re safe."

"Safe from what?" Rick wanted to know.

"I dunno—safe from somethin' as *they* think may change 'em. See, we ain't the onlyest ones gittin' through to *there*. There's others, we've met a couple. Susan—she's older 'n me and she dresses funny, like one of the real old time ladies in a book picture. And there's Jim—he spends most of his time off in the woods, don't see him much. Susan's real nice. She took us to stay with her when we got *there*. But she's married to one of *them*, so we didn't feel comfortable most of the time. Anyway *they* had some rules—they asked us right away did we have anything made of iron. Iron is bad for *them*, they can't hold it, it burns *them* bad. And *they* told us right out that if we stayed long we'd change. We ate *their* food and drank *their* drink stuff—that's like cider and it tastes good. That changes people from here. So after awhile anyone who comes through is like *them*. Susan mostly is by now, I guess. When you're changed you don't want to come back."

"But you didn't change," Lesley pointed out. "You came back."

"And how come you didn't change?" Rick wanted to know. "You were there long enough—a hundred and ten years!"

"But," Lizzy had beat with her fists on the floor of the summer house then as if she were pounding a drum. "It weren't that long, it couldn't be! Me, I counted every day! It's only been ten of 'em, with us hunting the place to come through on every one of 'em, calling for Ma and Pa to come and get us. It weren't no hundred and ten years—"

And she had cried again in such a way as to make Lesley's throat ache. A moment later she had been bawling right along with Lizzy. For once Rick did not look at her as if he were disgusted, but instead as if he were sorry, for Lizzy, not Lesley, of course.

"It's got to be that time's different in that place," he said thoughtfully. "A lot different. But, Lizzy, it's true, you know—this is 1971, not 1861. We can prove it."

Lizzy wiped her eyes on the hem of her long apron. "Yes, I got to believe. 'Cause what you showed me ain't my world at all. All those cars shootin' along so fast, lights what go on and off when you press a button on the wall—all these houses built over Pa's good farmin' land—what I read today. Yes, I gotta believe it—but it's hard to do that, right hard!

"And Matt 'n' me, we don't belong here no more, not with all this clatter an' noise an' nasty smelling air like we sniffed down there by that big road. I guess we gotta go back *there*. Leastwise, we know what's there now."

"How can you get back?" Rick wanted to know.

For the first time Lizzy showed a watery smile. "I ain't no dunce, Rick. *They* got rules, like I said. You carry something outta that place and hold on to it, an' it pulls you back, lets you in again. I brought them there seeds for Ma. But I thought maybe Matt an' me—we might want to go visitin' *there*. Susan's been powerful good to us. Well, anyway, I got these too."

She had burrowed deeper in her pocket, under the packets of seeds and brought out two chains of woven grass, tightly braided. Fastened to each was a small arrowhead, a very tiny one, no bigger than Lesley's little fingernail.

Rick held out his hand. "Let's see."

But Lizzy kept them out of his reach.

"Them's no Injun arrowheads, Rick. Them's what *they* use for *their* own doin's. Susan, she calls them 'elf-shots.' Anyway, these here can take us back if we wear 'em. And we will tomorrow, that's when we'll go."

They had tried to find out more about *there*, but Lizzy would not answer most of their questions. Lesley thought she could not for some reason. But she remained firm in her decision that she and Matt would be better off *there* than *here*. Then she had seemed sorry for Lesley and Rick and Alex that they had to stay in such a world, and made the suggestion that they link hands and go through together.

Rick shook his head. "Sorry—no. Mom and Dad—well, we belong here."

Lizzy nodded. "Thought you would say that. But—it's so ugly now, I can't see as how you want to." She cupped the tiny arrowheads in her hand, held them close. "Over *there* it's so pretty. What are you goin' to do here when all the ground is covered up with houses and the air's full of bad smells, an' those cars go rush-rush all day and night too? Looky here—" She reached for one of the magazines. "I'm the best reader in the school house. Miss Jane, she has me up to read out loud when the school board comes visitin'." She did not say that boastfully, but as if it were a truth everyone would know. "An' I've been readin' pieces in here. They've said a lot about how bad things are gittin' for you all—bad air, bad water—too many people—everything like that. Seems like there's no end but bad here. Ain't that so now?"

"We've been studying about it in school," Lesley agreed, "Rick and me, we're on the pick-up can drive next week. Sure we know."

"Well, this ain't happening over *there*, you can bet you! *They* won't let it."

"How do they stop it?" Rick wanted to know.

But once more Lizzy did not answer. She just shook her head and said *they* had their ways. And then she had gone on:

"Me an' Matt, we have to go back. We don't belong here now, and back *there* we do, sorta. At least it's more like what we're used to. We have to go at the same hour as before—noon time—"

"How do you know?" Rick asked.

"There's rules. We were caught at noon then, we go at noon now. Sure you don't want to come with us?"

"Only as far as the field," Rick had answered for

them. "It's Saturday, we can work it easy. Mom has a hair appointment in the morning, Dad is going to drive her 'cause he's seeing Mr. Chambers, and they'll do the shopping before they come home. We're supposed to have a picnic in the field, like we always do. Being Saturday the men won't be working there either."

"If you have to go back at noon," Lesley was trying to work something out, "how come you didn't get here at noon? It must have been close to five when we saw you. The school bus had let us off at the corner and Alex had come to meet us—then we saw you—"

"We hid out," Lizzy had said then. "Took a chance on you 'cause you were like us—"

Lesley thought she would never forget that first meeting, seeing the fair haired girl a little taller than she, her hair in two long braids, but such a queer dress on—like a "granny" one, yet different, and over it a big coarse-looking checked apron. Beside her Matt, in a check shirt and funny looking pants, both of them barefooted. They had looked so unhappy and lost. Alex had broken away from Lesley and Rick and had run right over to them to say "Hi" in the friendly way he always did.

Lizzy had been turning her head from side to side as if hunting for something which should be right there before her. And when they had come up she had spoken almost as if she were angry (but Lesley guessed she was really frightened) asking them where the Mendal house was.

If it had not been for the stone and Rick doing all that hunting down of the story behind it, they would not have known what she meant. But Rick had caught on quickly. He had said that they lived in the old Mendal house now, and they had brought Lizzy and Matt along with them. But before they got there they had guessed who Lizzy and Matt were, impossible as it seemed.

Now they were gone again. But Lizzy, what had she done just after she had looped those grass strings around her neck and Matt's and taken his hand? First she had thrown out all those seeds on the ground. And then she had pointed her finger at the bulldozer, and the other machines which were tearing up the rest of the farm she had known.

Lesley, remembering, blinked and shivered. She had expected Lizzy and Matt to disappear, somehow she had never doubted that they would. But she had not foreseen that the bulldozer would flop over at Lizzy's pointing, the other things fly around as if they were being thrown, some of them breaking apart. Then the seeds sprouting, vines and grass, and flowers, and small trees shooting up—just like the time on TV when they speeded up the camera somehow so you actually saw a flower opening up. What had Lizzy learned *there* that she was able to do all that?

Still trying to remember it all, Lesley wiped the dishes. Rick and Alex came in.

"Everything's put away," Rick reported. "And Alex, he understands about not talking about Matt."

"I sure hope so, Rick. But—how did Lizzy do that— make the machines move by just pointing at them? And how can plants grow so quickly?"

"How do I know?" he demanded impatiently. "I didn't see any more than you did. We've only one thing to remember, we keep our mouths shut tight. And we've got to be just as surprised as anyone else when somebody sees what happened there—"

"Maybe they won't see it—maybe not until the men come on Monday," she said hopefully. Monday was a school day, and the bus would take them early. Then she remembered.

"Rick, Alex won't be going to school with us. He'll be here with Mom. What if somebody says something and he talks?"

Rick was frowning. "Yeah, I see what you mean. So— we'll have to discover it ourselves—tomorrow morning. If we're here when people get all excited we can keep Alex quiet. One of us will have to stay with him all the time."

But in the end Alex made his own plans. The light was only grey in Lesley's window when she awoke to find Rick shaking her shoulder.

"What—what's the matter?"

"Keep it low!" He ordered almost fiercely. "Listen, Alex's gone—"

"Gone where?"

"Where do you think? Get some clothes on and come on!"

Gone to *there*? Lesley was cold with fear as she pulled on jeans and a sweat shirt, thrust her feet into shoes. But how could Alex—? Just as Matt and Lizzy had gone the first time. They should not have been afraid of being disbelieved, they should have told Dad and Mom all about it. Now maybe Alex would be gone for a hundred years. No—not Alex!

She scrambled down stairs. Rick stood at the back door waving her on. Together they raced across the back-yard, struggled through the fence gap and—

The raw scars left by the bulldozer were gone. Rich foliage rustled in the early morning breeze. And the birds—! Lesley had never seen so many different kinds of birds in her whole life. They seemed so tame, too, swinging on branches, hopping along the ground, pecking a fruit. Not the sour old apples but golden fruit. It hung from bushes, squashed on the ground from its own ripeness.

And there were flowers—and—

"Alex!" Rick almost shouted.

There he was. Not gone, sucked into *there* where they could never find him again. No he was sitting under a bush where white flowers bloomed. His face was smeared with juice as he ate one of the fruit. And he was patting a bunny! A real live bunny was in his lap. Now and then he held the fruit for the bunny to take a bite too. His face, under the smear of juice, was one big smile. Alex's happy face which he had not worn since Matt left.

"It's real good," he told them.

Scrambling to his feet he would have made for the fruit bush but Lesley swooped to catch him in a big hug.

"You're safe, Alex!"

"Silly!" He squirmed in her hold. "Silly Les. This is a good place now. See, the bunny came 'cause he knows that. An' all the birds. This is a *good* place. Here—" he struggled out of her arms, went to the bush and pulled off two of the fruit. "You eat—you'll like them."

"He shouldn't be eating those. How do we know it's good for him?" Rick pushed by to take the fruit from his brother.

Alex readily gave him one, thrust the other at Lesley. "Eat it! It's better'n anything!"

As if she had to obey him, Lesley raised the smooth yellow fruit to her mouth. It smelled—it smelled good— like everything she liked. She bit into it.

And the taste—it did not have the sweetness of an orange, nor was it like an apple or a plum. It wasn't like anything she had eaten before. But Alex was right, it was good. And she saw that Rick was eating, too.

When he had finished her elder brother turned to the bush and picked one, two, three, four—

"You *are* hungry," Lesley commented. She herself had taken a second. She broke it in two, dropped half to the ground for two birds. Their being there, right by her feet, did not seem in the least strange. Of course one shared. It did not matter if life wore feathers, fur, or plain skin, one shared.

"For Mom and Dad," Rick said. Then he looked around.

They could not see the whole of the field, the growth was too thick. And it was reaching out to the boundaries. Even as Lesley looked up a vine fell like a hand on their own fence, caught fast, and she was sure that was only the beginning.

"I was thinking Les," Rick said slowly. "Do you remember what Lizzy said about the fruit from *there* changing people. Do you feel any different?"

"Why no." She held out her finger. A bird fluttered up to perch there, watching her with shining beads of eyes. She laughed. "No, I don't feel any different."

Rick looked puzzled. "I never saw a bird that tame before. Well, I wonder—Come on, let's take these to Mom and Dad."

They started for the fence where two green runners now clung. Lesley looked at the house, down the street to where the apartment made a monstrous outline against the morning sky.

"Rick, why do people want to live in such ugly places. And it smells bad—"

He nodded. "But all that's going to change. You know it, don't you?"

She gave a sigh of relief. Of course she knew it. The

change was beginning and it would go on and on until *here* was like *there* and the rule of iron was broken for all time.

The rule of iron? Lesley shook her head as if to shake away a puzzling thought. But, of course, she must have always known this. Why did she have one small memory that this was strange? The rule of iron was gone, the long night of waiting over now.

THE QUEEN OF AIR AND DARKNESS

Poul Anderson

The last glow of the last sunset would linger almost until midwinter. But there would be no more day, and the northlands rejoiced. Blossoms opened, flamboyance on firethorn trees, steelflowers rising blue from the brok and rainplant that cloaked all hills, shy whiteness of kiss-me-never down in the dales. Flitteries darted among them on iridescent wings; a crownbuck shook his horns and bugled through warmth and flower odors. Between horizons the sky deepened from purple to sable. Both moons were aloft, nearly full, shining frosty on leaves and molten on waters. The shadows they made were blurred by an aurora, a great blowing curtain of light across half heaven. Behind it the earliest stars had come out.

A boy and a girl sat on Wolund's Barrow just under the dolmen it upbore. Their hair, which streamed halfway down their backs, showed startlingly forth, bleached as it was by summer. Their bodies, still dark from that season, merged with earth and bush and rock; for they wore only garlands. He played on a bone flute and she sang. They had lately become lovers. Their age was about sixteen, but they did not know this, considering themselves Outlings and thus indifferent to time, remembering little or nothing of how they had once dwelt in the lands of men.

His notes piped cold around her voice:

"Cast a spell,
weave it well
of dust and dew
and night and you."

325

A brook by the grave mound, carrying moonlight down to a hill-hidden river, answered with its rapids. A flock of hellbats passed black beneath the aurora.

A shape came bounding over Cloudmoor. It had two arms and two legs, but the legs were long and claw-footed and feathers covered it to the end of a tail and broad wings. The face was half-human, dominated by its eyes. Had Ayoch been able to stand wholly erect, he would have reached to the boy's shoulder.

The girl rose. "He carries a burden," she said. Her vision was not meant for twilight like that of a northland creature born, but she had learned how to use every sign her senses gave her. Besides the fact that ordinarily a pook would fly, there was a heaviness to his haste.

"And he comes from the south." Excitement jumped in the boy, sudden as a green flame that went across the constellation Lyrth. He sped down the mound. "Ohoi, Ayoch!" he called. "Me here, Mistherd!"

"And Shadow-of-a-Dream," the girl laughed, following.

The pook halted. He breathed louder than the soughing in the growth around him. A smell of bruised yerba lifted where he stood.

"Well met in winterbirth," he whistled. "You can help me bring this to Carheddin."

He held out what he bore. His eyes were yellow lanterns above. It moved and whimpered.

"Why, a child," Mistherd said.

"Even as you were, my son, even as you were. Ho, ho, what a snatch!" Ayoch boasted. "They were a score in yon camp by Fallowwood, armed, and besides watcher engines they had big ugly dogs aprowl while they slept. I came from above, however, having spied on them till I knew that a handful of dazedust—"

"The poor thing." Shadow-of-a-Dream took the boy and held him to her small breasts. "So full of sleep yet, aren't you, littleboo?" Blindly, he sought a nipple. She smiled through the veil of her hair. "No, I am still too young, and you already too old. But come, when you wake in Carheddin under the mountain you shall feast."

"Yo-ah," said Ayoch very softly. "She is abroad and has heard and seen. She comes." He crouched down, wings folded. After a moment Mistherd knelt, and then Shadow-of-a-Dream, though she did not let go the child.

The Queen's tall form blocked off the moons. For a while she regarded the three and their booty. Hill and moor sounds withdrew from their awareness until it seemed they could hear the northlights hiss.

At last Ayoch whispered, "Have I done well, Starmother?"

"If you stole a babe from a camp full of engines," said the beautiful voice, "then they were folk out of the far south who may not endure it as meekly as yeomen."

"But what can they do, Snowmaker?" the pook asked. "How can they track us?"

Mistherd lifted his head and spoke in pride. "Also, now they too have felt the awe of us."

"And he is a cuddly dear," Shadow-of-a-Dream said. "And we need more like him, do we not, Lady Sky?"

"It had to happen in some twilight," agreed she who stood above. "Take him onward and care for him. By this sign," which she made, "is he claimed for the Dwellers."

Their joy was freed. Ayoch cartwheeled over the ground till he reached a shiverleaf. There he swarmed up the trunk and out on a limb, perched half hidden by unrestful pale foliage, and crowed. Boy and girl bore the child toward Carheddin at an easy distance-devouring lope which let him pipe and her sing:

"Wahaii, wahaii!
Wayala, laii!
Wing on the wind
high over heaven,
shrilly shrieking,
rush with the rainspears,
tumble through tumult,
drift to the moonhoar trees and the dream-heavy
    shadows beneath them,
and rock in, be one with the clinking wavelets of
    lakes where the starbeams drown."

As she entered, Barbro Cullen felt, through all grief and fury, stabbed by dismay. The room was unkempt.

Journals, tapes, reels, codices, file boxes, bescribbled papers were piled on every table. Dust filmed most shelves and corners. Against one wall stood a laboratory setup, microscope and analytical equipment. She recognized it as compact and efficient, but it was not what you would expect in an office, and it gave the air a faint chemical reek. The rug was threadbare, the furniture shabby.

This was her final chance?

Then Eric Sherrinford approached. "Good day, Mrs. Cullen," he said. His tone was crisp, his handclasp firm. His faded gripsuit didn't bother her. She wasn't inclined to fuss about her own appearance except on special occasions. (And would she ever again have one, unless she got back Jimmy?) What she observed was a cat's personal neatness.

A smile radiated in crow's feet from his eyes. "Forgive my bachelor housekeeping. On Beowulf we have—we had, at any rate—machines for that, so I never acquired the habit myself, and I don't want a hireling disarranging my tools. More convenient to work out of my apartment than keep a separate office. Won't you be seated?"

"No, thanks. I couldn't," she mumbled.

"I understand. But if you'll excuse me, I function best in a relaxed position."

He jackknifed into a lounger. One long shank crossed the other knee. He drew forth a pipe and stuffed it from a pouch. Barbro wondered why he took tobacco in so ancient a way. Wasn't Beowulf supposed to have the up-to-date equipment that they still couldn't afford to build on Roland? Well, of course old customs might survive anyhow. They generally did in colonies, she remembered reading. People had moved starward in the hope of preserving such outmoded things as their mother tongues or constitutional government or rational-technological civilization. . . .

Sherrinford pulled her up from the confusion of her weariness: "You must give me the details of your case, Mrs. Cullen. You've simply told me that your son was kidnapped and your local constabulary did nothing. Otherwise I know just a few obvious facts, such as your being widowed rather than divorced; and you're the daughter of outwayers in Olga Ivanoff Land who, nevertheless, kept in close telecommunication with Christmas Landing; and you're trained in one of the biological professions; and you had several years' hiatus in field work until recently you started again."

She gaped at the high-cheeked, beak-nosed, black-haired and gray-eyed countenance. His lighter made a *scrit* and a flare which seemed to fill the room. Quietness dwelt on this height above the city, and winter dusk was seeping in through the windows. "How in cosmos do you know that?" she heard herself exclaim.

He shrugged and fell into the lecturer's manner for which he was notorious. "My work depends on noticing details and fitting them together. In more than a hundred years on Roland, the people, tending to cluster according to their origins and thought-habits, have developed regional accents. You have a trace of the Olgan burr, but you nasalize your vowels in the style of this area, though you live in Portolondon. That suggests steady childhood exposure to metropolitan speech. You were part of Matsuyama's expedition, you told me, and took your boy along. They wouldn't have allowed any ordinary technician to do that; hence you had to be valuable enough to get away with it. The team was conducting ecological research; therefore you must be in the life sciences. For the same reason, you must have had previous field experience. But your skin is fair, showing none of the leatheriness one gets from prolonged exposure to this sun. Accordingly, you must have been mostly indoors for a good while before you went on your ill-fated trip. As for widowhood—you never mentioned a husband to me, but you have had a man whom you thought so highly of that you still wear both the wedding and the engagement ring he gave you."

Her sight blurred and stung. The last of those words had brought Tim back, huge, ruddy, laughterful and gentle. She must turn from this other person and stare outward. "Yes," she achieved saying, "you're right."

The apartment occupied a hilltop above Christmas Landing. Beneath it the city dropped away in walls, roofs, archaistic chimneys and lamplit streets, goblin lights of human-piloted vehicles, to the harbor, the sweep

of Venture Bay, ships bound to and from the Sunward
Islands and remoter regions of the Boreal Ocean, which
glimmered like mercury in the afterglow of Charlemagne.
Oliver was swinging rapidly higher, a mottled orange disc
a full degree wide; closer to the zenith which it could
never reach, it would shine the color of ice. Alde, half
the seeming size, was a thin slow crescent near Sirius,
which she remembered was near Sol, but you couldn't
see Sol without a telescope—

"Yes," she said around the pain in her throat, "my
husband is about four years dead. I was carrying our first
child when he was killed by a stampeding monocerus.
We'd been married three years before. Met while we
were both at the University—'casts from School Central
can only supply a basic education, you know—we
founded our own team to do ecological studies under
contract—you know, can a certain area be settled while
maintaining a balance of nature, what crops will grow,
what hazards, that sort of question—Well, afterward I
did lab work for a fisher co-op in Portolondon. But the
monotony, the . . . shut-in-ness . . . was eating me away.
Professor Matsuyama offered me a position on the team
he was organizing to examine Commissioner Hauch
Land. I thought, God help me, I thought Jimmy—Tim
wanted him named James, once the tests showed it'd be
a boy, after his own father and because of 'Timmy and
Jimmy' and— Oh, I thought Jimmy could safely come
along. I couldn't bear to leave him behind for months,
not at his age. We could make sure he'd never wander
out of camp. What could hurt him inside it? *I* had never
believed those stories about the Outlings stealing human
children. I supposed parents were trying to hide from
themselves the fact they'd been careless, they'd let a kid
get lost in the woods or attacked by a pack of satans
or— Well, I learned better, Mr. Sherrinford. The guard
robots were evaded and the dogs were drugged and when
I woke, Jimmy was gone."

He regarded her through the smoke from his pipe.
Barbro Engdahl Cullen was a big woman of thirty or so
(Rolandic years, he reminded himself, ninety-five percent of Terrestrial, not the same as Beowulfan years),
broad-shouldered, long-legged, full-breasted, supple of

stride; her face was wide, straight nose, straightforward hazel eyes, heavy but mobile mouth; her hair was reddish-brown, cropped below the ears, her voice husky, her garment a plain street robe. To still the writhing of her fingers, he asked skeptically, "Do you now believe in the Outlings?"

"No. I'm just not so sure as I was." She swung about with half a glare for him. "And we have found traces."

"Bits of fossils," he nodded. "A few artifacts of a neolithic sort. But apparently ancient, as if the makers died ages ago. Intensive search has failed to turn up any real evidence for their survival."

"How intensive can search be, in a summer-stormy, winter-gloomy wilderness around the North Pole?" she demanded. "When we are, how many, a million people on an entire planet, half of us crowded into this one city?"

"And the rest crowding this one habitable continent," he pointed out.

"Arctica covers five million square kilometers," she flung back. "The Arctic Zone proper covers a fourth of it. We haven't the industrial base to establish satellite monitor stations, build aircraft we can trust in those parts, drive roads through the damned darklands and establish permanent bases and get to know them and tame them. Good Christ, generations of lonely outwaymen told stories about Graymantle, and the beast was never seen by a proper scientist till last year!"

"Still, you continue to doubt the reality of the Outlings?"

"Well, what about a secret cult among humans, born of isolation and ignorance, lairing in the wilderness, stealing children when they can for—" She swallowed. Her head drooped. "But you're supposed to be the expert."

"From what you told me over the visiphone, the Portolondon constabulary questions the accuracy of the report your group made, thinks the lot of you were hysterical, claims you must have omitted a due precaution and the child toddled away and was lost beyond your finding."

His dry words pried the horror out of her. Flushing, she snapped: "Like any settler's kid? No. I didn't simply yell. I consulted Data Retrieval. A few too many such cases are recorded for accident to be a very plausible explanation. And shall we totally ignore the frightened stories about reappearances? But when I went back to the constabulary with my facts, they brushed me off. I suspect that was not entirely because they're undermanned. I think they're afraid too. They're recruited from country boys; and Portolondon lies near the edge of the unknown."

Her energy faded. "Roland hasn't got any central police force," she finished drably. "You're my last hope."

The man puffed smoke into twilight, with which it blent, before he said in a kindlier voice than hitherto: "Please don't make it a high hope, Mrs. Cullen. I'm the solitary private investigator on this world, having no resources beyond myself, and a newcomer to boot."

"How long have you been here?"

"Twelve years. Barely time to get a little familiarity with the relatively civilized coastlands. You settlers of a century or more—what do you, even, know about Arctica's interior?"

Sherrinford sighed. "I'll take the case, charging no more than I must, mainly for the sake of the experience," he said. "But only if you'll be my guide and assistant, however painful it will be for you."

"Of course! I dreaded waiting idle. Why me, though?"

"Hiring someone else as well qualified would be prohibitively expensive, on a pioneer planet where every hand has a thousand urgent tasks to do. Besides, you have motive. And I'll need that. I, who was born on another world altogether strange to this one, itself altogether strange to Mother Earth, I am too dauntingly aware of how handicapped we are."

Night gathered upon Christmas Landing. The air stayed mild, but glimmer-lit tendrils of fog, sneaking through the streets, had a cold look, and colder yet was the aurora where it shuddered between the moons. The woman drew closer to the man in this darkening room, surely not aware that she did, until he switched on a fluoropanel. The same knowledge of Roland's aloneness was in both of them.

*   *   *

One light-year is not much as galactic distances go. You could walk it in about 270 million years, beginning at the middle of the Permian Era, when dinosaurs belonged to the remote future, and continuing to the present day when spaceships cross even greater reaches. But stars in our neighborhood average some nine light-years apart; and barely one percent of them have planets which are man-habitable; and speeds are limited to less than that of radiation. Scant help is given by relativistic time contraction and suspended animation en route. These make the journeys seem short; but history meanwhile does not stop at home.

Thus voyages from sun to sun will always be few. Colonists will be those who have extremely special reasons for going. They will take along germ plasm for exogenetic cultivation of domestic plants and animals—and of human infants, in order that population can grow fast enough to escape death through genetic drift. After all, they cannot rely on further immigration. Two or three times a century, a ship may call from some other colony. (Not from Earth. Earth has long ago sunk into alien concerns.) Its place of origin will be an old settlement. The young ones are in no position to build and man interstellar vessels.

Their very survival, let alone their eventual modernization, is in doubt. The founding fathers have had to take what they could get, in a universe not especially designed for man.

Consider, for example, Roland. It is among the rare happy finds, a world where humans can live, breathe, eat the food, drink the water, walk unclad if they choose, sow their crops, pasture their beasts, dig their mines, erect their homes, raise their children and grandchildren. It is worth crossing three quarters of a light-century to preserve certain dear values and strike new roots into the soil of Roland.

But the star Charlemagne is of type F9, forty percent brighter than Sol, brighter still in the treacherous ultraviolet and wilder still in the wind of charged particles that seethes from it. The planet has an eccentric orbit. In the middle of the short but furious northern summer, which includes periastron, total insolation is more than double what Earth gets; in the depth of the long northern winter, it is barely less than Terrestrial average.

Native life is abundant everywhere. But lacking elaborate machinery, not economically possible to construct for more than a few specialists, man can only endure the high latitudes. A ten-degree axial tilt, together with the orbit, means that the northern part of the Arctican continent spends half its year in unbroken sunlessness. Around the South Pole lies an empty ocean.

Other differences from Earth might superficially seem more important. Roland has two moons, small but close, to evoke clashing tides. It rotates once in thirty-two hours, which is endlessly, subtly disturbing to organisms evolved through gigayears of a quicker rhythm. The weather patterns are altogether unterrestrial. The globe is a mere 9500 kilometers in diameter; its surface gravity is 0.42×980 cm/sec^2; the sea-level air pressure is slightly above one Earth atmosphere. (For actually Earth is the freak, and man exists because a cosmic accident blew away most of the gas that a body its size ought to have kept, as Venus has done.)

However, *Homo* can truly be called *sapiens* when he practices his specialty of being unspecialized. His repeated attempts to freeze himself into an all-answering pattern or culture or ideology, or whatever he has named it, have repeatedly brought ruin. Give him the pragmatic business of making his living and he will usually do rather well. He adapts, within broad limits.

These limits are set by such factors as his need for sunlight and his being, necessarily and forever, a part of the life that surrounds him and a creature of the spirit within.

Portolondon thrust docks, boats, machinery, warehouses into the Gulf of Polaris. Behind them huddled the dwellings of its 5000 permanent inhabitants: concrete walls, storm shutters, high-peaked tile roofs. The gaiety of their paint looked forlorn amidst lamps; this town lay past the Arctic Circle.

Nevertheless Sherrinford remarked, "Cheerful place, eh? The kind of thing I came to Roland looking for."

Barbro made no reply. The days in Christmas Landing,

while he made his preparations, had drained her. Gazing out the dome of the taxi that was whirring them downtown from the hydrofoil that brought them, she supposed he meant the lushness of forest and meadows along the road, brilliant hues and phosphorescence of flowers in gardens, clamor of wings overhead. Unlike Terrestrial flora in cold climates, Arctican vegetation spends every daylit hour in frantic growth and energy storage. Not till summer's fever gives place to gentle winter does it bloom and fruit; and estivating animals rise from their dens and migratory birds come home.

The view was lovely, she had to admit: beyond the trees, a spaciousness climbing toward remote heights, silvery-gray under a moon, an aurora, the diffuse radiance from a sun just below the horizon.

Beautiful as a hunting satan, she thought, and as terrible. That wilderness had stolen Jimmy. She wondered if she would at least be given to find his little bones and take them to his father.

Abruptly she realized that she and Sherrinford were at their hotel and that he had been speaking of the town. Since it was next in size after the capital, he must have visited here often before. The streets were crowded and noisy; signs flickered, music blared from shops, taverns, restaurants, sports centers, dance halls; vehicles were jammed down to molasses speed; the several-stories-high office buildings stood aglow. Portolondon linked an enormous hinterland to the outside world. Down the Gloria River came timber rafts, ores, harvest of farms whose owners were slowly making Rolandic life serve them, meat and ivory and furs gathered by rangers in the mountains beyond Troll Scarp. In from the sea came coastwise freighters, the fishing fleet, produce of the Sunward Islands, plunder of whole continents further south where bold men adventured. It clanged in Portolondon, laughed, blustered, swaggered, connived, robbed, preached, guzzled, swilled, toiled, dreamed, lusted, built, destroyed, died, was born, was happy, angry, sorrowful, greedy, vulgar, loving, ambitious, human. Neither the sun's blaze elsewhere nor the half year's twilight here—wholly night around midwinter—was going to stay man's hand.

Or so everybody said.

Everybody except those who had settled in the darklands. Barbro used to take for granted that they were evolving curious customs, legends, and superstitions, which would die when the outway had been completely mapped and controlled. Of late, she had wondered. Perhaps Sherrinford's hints, about a change in his own attitude brought about by his preliminary research, were responsible.

Or perhaps she just needed something to think about besides how Jimmy, the day before he went, when she asked him whether he wanted rye or French bread for a sandwich, answered in great solemnity—he was becoming interested in the alphabet—"I'll have a slice of what we people call the F bread."

She scarcely noticed getting out of the taxi, registering, being conducted to a primitively furnished room. But after she unpacked she remembered Sherrinford had suggested a confidential conference. She went down the hall and knocked on his door. Her knuckles sounded less loud than her heart.

He opened the door, finger on lips, and gestured her toward a corner. Her temper bristled until she saw the image of Chief Constable Dawson in the visiphone. Sherrinford must have chimed him up and must have a reason to keep her out of scanner range. She found a chair and watched, nails digging into knees.

The detective's lean length refolded itself. "Pardon the interruption," he said. "A man mistook the number. Drunk, by the indications."

Dawson chuckled. "We get plenty of those." Barbro recalled his fondness for gabbing. He tugged the beard which he affected, as if he were an outwayer instead of a townsman. "No harm in them as a rule. They only have a lot of voltage to discharge, after weeks or months in the backlands."

"I've gathered that that environment—foreign in a million major and minor ways to the one that created man— I've gathered that it does do odd things to the personality." Sherrinford tamped his pipe. "Of course, you know my practice has been confined to urban and suburban areas. Isolated garths seldom need private investigators.

Now that situation appears to have changed. I called to ask you for advice."

"Glad to help," Dawson said. "I've not forgotten what you did for us in the de Tahoe murder case." Cautiously: "Better explain your problem first."

Sherrinford struck fire. The smoke that followed cut through the green odors—even here, a paved pair of kilometers from the nearest woods—that drifted past traffic rumble through a crepuscular window. "This is more a scientific mission than a search for an absconding debtor or an industrial spy," he drawled. "I'm looking into two possibilities: that an organization, criminal or religious or whatever, has long been active and steals infants; or that the Outlings of folklore are real."

"Huh?" On Dawson's face Barbro read as much dismay as surprise. "You can't be serious!"

"Can't I?" Sherrinford smiled. "Several generations' worth of reports shouldn't be dismissed out of hand. Especially not when they become more frequent and consistent in the course of time, not less. Nor can we ignore the documented loss of babies and small children, amounting by now to over a hundred, and never a trace found afterward. Nor the finds which demonstrate that an intelligent species once inhabited Arctica and may still haunt the interior."

Dawson leaned forward as if to climb out of the screen. "Who engaged you?" he demanded. "That Cullen woman? We were sorry for her, naturally, but she wasn't making sense and when she got downright abusive—"

"Didn't her companions, reputable scientists, confirm her story?"

"No story to confirm. Look, they had the place ringed with detectors and alarms, and they kept mastiffs. Standard procedure in a country where a hungry sauroid or whatever might happen by. Nothing could've entered unbeknownst."

"On the ground. How about a flyer landing in the middle of camp?"

"A man in a copter rig would've roused everybody."

"A winged being might be quieter."

"A living flyer that could lift a three-year-old boy? Doesn't exist."

"Isn't in the scientific literature, you mean, Constable. Remember Graymantle; remember how little we know about Roland, a planet, an entire world. Such birds do exist on Beowulf—and on Rustum, I've read. I made a calculation from the local ratio of air density to gravity and, yes, it's marginally possible here too. The child could have been carried off for a short distance before wing muscles were exhausted and the creature must descend."

Dawson snorted. "First it landed and walked into the tent where mother and boy were asleep. Then it walked away, toting him, after it couldn't fly further. Does that sound like a bird of prey? And the victim didn't cry out, the dogs didn't bark, nothing!"

"As a matter of fact," Sherrinford said, "those inconsistencies are the most interesting and convincing feature of the whole account. You're right, it's hard to see how a human kidnapper could get in undetected, and an eagle type of creature wouldn't operate in that fashion. But none of this applies to a winged intelligent being. The boy could have been drugged. Certainly the dogs showed signs of having been."

"The dogs showed signs of having overslept. Nothing had disturbed them. The kid wandering by wouldn't do so. We don't need to assume one damn thing except, first, that he got restless and, second, that the alarms were a bit sloppily rigged—seeing as how no danger was expected from inside camp—and let him pass out. And, third, I hate to speak this way, but we must assume the poor tyke starved or was killed."

Dawson paused before adding: "If we had more staff, we could have given the affair more time. And would have, of course. We did make an aerial sweep, which risked the lives of the pilots, using instruments which would've spotted the kid anywhere in a fifty-kilometer radius, unless he was dead. You know how sensitive thermal analyzers are. We drew a complete blank. We have more important jobs than to hunt for the scattered pieces of a corpse."

He finished brusquely, "If Mrs. Cullen's hired you, my advice is you find an excuse to quit. Better for her, too. She's got to come to terms with reality."

Barbro checked a shout by biting her tongue.

"Oh, this is merely the latest disappearance of the series," Sherrinford said. She didn't understand how he could maintain his easy tone when Jimmy was lost. "More thoroughly recorded than any before, thus more suggestive. Usually an outwayer family has given a tearful but undetailed account of their child who vanished and must have been stolen by the Old Folk. Sometimes, years later, they'd tell about glimpses of what they swore must have been the grown child, not really human any longer, flitting past in murk or peering through a window or working mischief upon them. As you say, neither the authorities nor the scientists have had personnel or resources to mount a proper investigation. But as I say, the matter appears to be worth investigating. Maybe a private party like myself can contribute."

"Listen, most of us constables grew up in the outway. We don't just ride patrol and answer emergency calls, we go back there for holidays and reunions. If any gang of . . . of human sacrificers was around, we'd know."

"I realize that. I also realize that the people you came from have a widespread and deep-seated belief in nonhuman beings with supernatural powers. Many actually go through rites and make offerings to propitiate them."

"I know what you're leading up to," Dawson fleered. "I've heard it before, from a hundred sensationalists. The aborigines are the Outlings. I thought better of you. Surely you've visited a museum or three, surely you've read literature from planets which do have natives—or damn and blast, haven't you ever applied that logic of yours?"

He wagged a finger. "Think," he said. "What have we in fact discovered? A few pieces of worked stone; a few megaliths that might be artificial; scratchings on rock that seem to show plants and animals, though not the way any human culture would ever have shown them; traces of fires and broken bones; other fragments of bone that seem as if they might've belonged to thinking creatures, as if they might've been inside fingers or around big brains. If so, however, the owners looked nothing like men. Or angels, for that matter. Nothing! The most anthropoid reconstruction I've seen shows a kind of two-legged crocagator.

"Wait, let me finish. The stories about the Outlings—oh, I've heard them too, plenty of them; I believed them when I was a kid—the stories tell how there're different kinds, some winged, some not, some half-human, some completely human except maybe for being too handsome—It's fairyland from ancient Earth all over again. Isn't it? I got interested once and dug into the Heritage Library microfiles, and be damned if I didn't find almost the identical yarns, told by peasants centuries before spaceflight.

"None of it squares with the scanty relics we have, if they are relics, or with the fact that no area the size of Arctica could spawn a dozen different intelligent species, or . . . hellfire, man, with the way your common sense tells you aborigines would behave when humans arrived!"

Sherrinford nodded. "Yes, yes," he said. "I'm less sure than you that the common sense of nonhuman beings is precisely like our own. I've seen so much variation within mankind. But, granted, your arguments are strong. Roland's too few scientists have more pressing tasks than tracking down the origins of what is, as you put it, a revived medieval superstition."

He cradled his pipe bowl in both hands and peered into the tiny hearth of it. "Perhaps what interests me most," he said softly, "is why—across that gap of centuries, across a barrier of machine civilization and its utterly antagonistic world-view—no continuity of tradition whatsoever—why have hardheaded, technologically organized, reasonably well-educated colonists here brought back from its grave a belief in the Old Folk?"

"I suppose eventually, if the University ever does develop the psychology department they keep talking about, I suppose eventually somebody will get a thesis out of that question." Dawson spoke in a jagged voice, and he gulped when Sherrinford replied:

"I propose to begin now. In Commissioner Hauch Land, since that's where the latest incident occurred. Where can I rent a vehicle?"

"Uh, might be hard to do—"

"Come, come. Tenderfoot or not, I know better. In

an economy of scarcity, few people own heavy equipment. But since it's needed, it can always be rented. I want a camper bus with a ground-effect drive suitable for every kind of terrain. And I want certain equipment installed which I've brought along, and the top canopy section replaced by a gun turret controllable from the driver's seat. But I'll supply the weapons. Besides rifles and pistols of my own, I've arranged to borrow some artillery from Christmas Landing's police arsenal."

"Hoy? Are you genuinely intending to make ready for . . . a war . . . against a myth?"

"Let's say I'm taking out insurance, which isn't terribly expensive, against a remote possibility. Now, besides the bus, what about a light aircraft carried piggyback for use in surveys?"

"No." Dawson sounded more positive than hitherto. "That's asking for disaster. We can have you flown to a base camp in a large plane when the weather report's exactly right. But the pilot will have to fly back at once, before the weather turns wrong again. Meteorology's underdeveloped on Roland, the air's especially treacherous this time of year, and we're not tooled up to produce aircraft that can outlive every surprise." He drew breath. "Have you no idea of how fast a whirly-whirly can hit, or what size hailstones might strike from a clear sky, or—? Once you're there, man, you stick to the ground." He hesitated. "That's an important reason our information is so scanty about the outway and its settlers are so isolated."

Sherrinford laughed ruefully. "Well, I suppose if details are what I'm after, I must creep along anyway."

"You'll waste a lot of time," Dawson said. "Not to mention your client's money. Listen, I can't forbid you to chase shadows, but—"

The discussion went on for almost an hour. When the screen finally blanked, Sherrinford rose, stretched, and walked toward Barbro. She noticed anew his peculiar gait. He had come from a planet with a fourth again Earth's gravitational drag, to one where weight was less than half Terrestrial. She wondered if he had flying dreams.

"I apologize for shuffling you off like that," he said. "I didn't expect to reach him at once. He was quite truthful about how busy he is. But having made contact, I didn't want to remind him overmuch of you. He can dismiss my project as a futile fantasy which I'll soon give up. But he might have frozen completely, might even have put up obstacles before us, if he'd realized through you how determined we are."

"Why should he care?" she asked in her bitterness.

"Fear of consequences, the worse because it is unadmitted—fear of consequences, the more terrifying because they are unguessable." Sherrinford's gaze went to the screen, and thence out the window to the aurora pulsing in glacial blue and white immensely far overhead. "I suppose you saw I was talking to a frightened man. Down underneath his conventionality and scoffing, he believes in the Outlings—oh, yes, he believes."

The feet of Mistherd flew over yerba and outpaced windblown driftweed. Beside him, black and misshapen, hulked Nagrim the nicor, whose earthquake weight left a swathe of crushed plants. Behind, luminous blossoms of a firethorn shone through the twining, trailing outlines of Morgarel the wraith.

Here Cloudmoor rose in a surf of hills and thickets. The air lay quiet, now and then carrying the distance-muted howl of a beast. It was darker than usual at winterbirth, the moons being down and aurora a wan flicker above mountains on the northern worldedge. But this made the stars keen, and their numbers crowded heaven, and Ghost Road shone among them as if it, like the leafage beneath, were paved with dew.

"Yonder!" bawled Nagrim. All four of his arms pointed. The party had topped a ridge. Far off glimmered a spark. "Hoah, hoah! 'Ull we right off stamp dem flat, or pluck dem apart slow?"

We shall do nothing of the sort, bonebrain, Morgarel's answer slid through their heads. *Not unless they attack us, and they will not unless we make them aware of us, and her command is that we spy out their purposes.*

"Gr-r-rum-m-m. I know deir aim. Cut down trees, stick plows in land, sow deir cursed seed in de clods and in deir shes. 'Less we drive dem into de bitterwater, and soon, soon, dey'll wax too strong for us."

"Not too strong for the Queen!" Mistherd protested, shocked.

Yet they do have new powers, it seems, Morgarel reminded him. *Carefully must we probe them.*

"Den carefully can we step on dem?" asked Nagrim.

The question woke a grin out of Mistherd's own uneasiness. He slapped the scaly back. "Don't talk, you," he said. "It hurts my ears. Nor think; that hurts your head. Come, run!"

Ease yourself, Morgarel scolded. *You have too much life in you, human-born.*

Mistherd made a face at the wraith, but obeyed to the extent of slowing down and picking his way through what cover the country afforded. For he traveled on behalf of the Fairest, to learn what had brought a pair of mortals questing hither.

Did they seek that boy whom Ayoch stole? (He continued to weep for his mother, though less and less often as the marvels of Carheddin entered him.) Perhaps. A birdcraft had left them and their car at the now abandoned campsite, from which they had followed an outward spiral. But when no trace of the cub had appeared inside a reasonable distance, they did not call to be flown home. And this wasn't because weather forbade the far-speaker waves to travel, as was frequently the case. No, instead the couple set off toward the mountains of Moonhorn. Their course would take them past a few outlying invader steadings and on into realms untrodden by their race.

So this was no ordinary survey. Then what was it?

Mistherd understood now why she who reigned had made her adopted mortal children learn, or retain, the clumsy language of their forebears. He had hated that drill, wholly foreign to Dweller ways. Of course, you obeyed her, and in time you saw how wise she had been. . . .

Presently he left Nagrim behind a rock—the nicor would only be useful in a fight—and crawled from bush to bush until he lay within man-lengths of the humans. A rainplant drooped over him, leaves soft on his bare skin, and clothed him in darkness. Morgarel floated to the crown of a shiverleaf, whose unrest would better conceal his flimsy shape. He'd not be much help either. And that was the most troublous, the almost appalling thing here. Wraiths were among those who could not just sense and send thoughts, but cast illusions. Morgarel had reported that this time his power seemed to rebound off an invisible cold wall around the car.

Otherwise the male and female had set up no guardian engines and kept no dogs. Belike they supposed none would be needed, since they slept in the long vehicle which bore them. But such contempt of the Queen's strength could not be tolerated, could it?

Metal sheened faintly by the light of their campfire. They sat on either side, wrapped in coats against a coolness that Mistherd, naked, found mild. The male drank smoke. The female stared past him into a dusk which her flame-dazzled eyes must see as thick gloom. The dancing glow brought her vividly forth. Yes, to judge from Ayoch's tale, she was the dam of the new cub.

Ayoch had wanted to come too, but the Wonderful One forbade. Pooks couldn't hold still long enough for such a mission.

The man sucked on his pipe. His cheeks thus pulled into shadow while the light flickered across nose and brow, he looked disquietingly like a shearbill about to stoop on prey.

"—No, I tell you again, Barbro, I have no theories," he was saying. "When facts are insufficient, theorizing is ridiculous at best, misleading at worst."

"Still, you must have some idea of what you're doing," she said. It was plain that they had threshed this out often before. No Dweller could be as persistent as her or as patient as him. "That gear you packed—that generator you keep running—"

"I have a working hypothesis or two, which suggested what equipment I ought to take."

"Why won't you tell me what the hypotheses are?"

"They themselves indicate that that might be inadvisable at the present time. I'm still feeling my way into the labyrinth. And I haven't had a chance yet to hook everything up. In fact, we're really only protected against so-called telepathic influence—"

"What?" She started. "Do you mean . . . those legends about how they can read minds too—" Her words trailed off and her gaze sought the darkness beyond his shoulders.

He leaned forward. His tone lost its clipped rapidity, grew earnest and soft. "Barbro, you're racking yourself to pieces. Which is no help to Jimmy if he's alive, the more so when you may well be badly needed later on. We've a long trek before us, and you'd better settle into it."

She nodded jerkily and caught her lip between her teeth for a moment before she answered, "I'm trying."

He smiled around his pipe. "I expect you'll succeed. You don't strike me as a quitter or a whiner or an enjoyer of misery."

She dropped a hand to the pistol at her belt. Her voice changed; it came out of her throat like knife from sheath. "When we find them, they'll know what I am. What humans are."

"Put anger aside also," the man urged. "We can't afford emotions. If the Outlings are real, as I told you I'm provisionally assuming, they're fighting for their homes." After a short stillness he added: "I like to think that if the first explorers had found live natives, men would not have colonized Roland. But too late now. We can't go back if we wanted to. It's a bitter-end struggle, against an enemy so crafty that he's even hidden from us the fact that he is waging war."

"Is he? I mean, skulking, kidnapping an occasional child—"

"That's part of my hypothesis. I suspect those aren't harassments, they're tactics employed in a chillingly subtle strategy."

The fire sputtered and sparked. The man smoked awhile, brooding, until he went on:

"I didn't want to raise your hopes or excite you unduly while you had to wait on me, first in Christmas Landing, then in Portolondon. Afterward we were busy satisfying ourselves Jimmy had been taken further from camp than he could have wandered before collapsing. So I'm only telling you now how thoroughly I studied available material on the . . . Old Folk. Besides, at first I did it on the principle of eliminating every imaginable possibility, however absurd. I expected no result other than final disproof. But I went through everything, relics, analyses, histories, journalistic accounts, monographs; I talked to outwayers who happened to be in town and to what scientists we have who've taken any interest in the matter. I'm a quick study. I flatter myself I became as expert as anyone—though God knows there's little to be expert on. Furthermore, I, a comparative stranger, maybe looked on the problem with fresh eyes. And a pattern emerged for me.

"If the aborigines became extinct, why didn't they leave more remnants? Arctica isn't enormous; and it's fertile for Rolandic life. It ought to have supported a population whose artifacts ought to have accumulated over millennia. I've read that on Earth, literally tens of thousands of paleolithic hand axes were found, more by chance than archaeology.

"Very well. Suppose the relics and fossils were deliberately removed, between the time the last survey party left and the first colonizing ships arrived. I did find some support for that idea in the diaries of the original explorers. They were too preoccupied with checking the habitability of the planet to make catalogues of primitive monuments. However, the remarks they wrote down indicate they saw much more than later arrivals did. Suppose what we have found is just what the removers overlooked or didn't get around to.

"That argues a sophisticated mentality, thinking in long-range terms, doesn't it? Which in turn argues that the Old Folk were not mere hunters or neolithic farmers."

"But nobody ever saw buildings or machines or any such thing," Barbro protested.

"No. Most likely the natives didn't go through our kind of metallurgic-industrial evolution. I can conceive of other paths to take. Their full-fledged civilization might have begun, rather than ended, in biological science and technology. It might have developed potentialities of the nervous system, which might be greater in their species than in man. We have those abilities to some degree ourselves, you realize. A dowser, for instance, actually senses variations in the local magnetic field caused by a water table. However, in us, these talents are maddeningly rare and tricky. So we took our business elsewhere. Who needs to be a telepath, say, when he has a visiphone? The Old Folk may have seen it the other way around. The artifacts of their civilization may have been, may still be, unrecognizable to men."

"They could have identified themselves to the men, though," Barbro said. "Why didn't they?"

"I can imagine any number of reasons. As, they could have had a bad experience with interstellar visitors earlier in their history. Ours is scarcely the sole race that has spaceships. However, I told you I don't theorize in advance of the facts. Let's say no more than that the Old Folk, if they exist, are alien to us."

"For a rigorous thinker, you're spinning a mighty thin thread."

"I've admitted this is entirely provisional." He squinted at her through a roil of campfire smoke. "You came to me, Barbro, insisting in the teeth of officialdom your boy had been stolen; but your own talk about cultist kidnappers was ridiculous. Why are you reluctant to admit the reality of nonhumans?"

"In spite of the fact that Jimmy's being alive probably depends on it," she sighed. "I know." A shudder: "Maybe I don't dare admit it."

"I've said nothing thus far that hasn't been speculated about in print," he told her. "A disreputable speculation, truc. In a hundred years, nobody has found valid evidence for the Outlings being more than a superstition. Still, a few people have declared it's at least possible intelligent natives are at large in the wilderness."

"I know," she repeated. "I'm not sure, though, what has made you, overnight, take those arguments seriously."

"Well, once you got me started thinking, it occurred to me that Roland's outwayers are not utterly isolated medieval crofters. They have books, telecommunications, power tools, motor vehicles, above all they have a modern science-oriented education. Why *should* they turn superstitious? Something must be causing it." He stopped. "I'd better not continue. My ideas go further than this; but if they're correct, it's dangerous to speak them aloud."

Mistherd's belly muscles tensed. There was danger for fair, in that shearbill head. The Garland Bearer must be warned. For a minute he wondered about summoning Nagrim to kill these two. If the nicor jumped them fast, their firearms might avail them naught. But no. They might have left word at home, or— He came back to his ears. The talk had changed course. Barbro was murmuring, "—why you stayed on Roland."

The man smiled his gaunt smile. "Well, life on Beowulf held no challenge for me. Heorot is—or was; this was decades past, remember—Heorot was densely populated, smoothly organized, boringly uniform. That was partly due to the lowland frontier, a safety valve that bled off the dissatisfied. But I lack the carbon-dioxide tolerance necessary to live healthily down there. An expedition was being readied to make a swing around a number of colony worlds, especially those which didn't have the equipment to keep in laser contact. You'll recall its announced purpose, to seek out new ideas in science, arts, sociology, philosophy, whatever might prove valuable. I'm afraid they found little on Roland relevant to Beowulf. But I, who had wangled a berth, I saw opportunities for myself and decided to make my home here."

"Were you a detective back there, too?"

"Yes, in the official police. We had a tradition of such work in our family. Some of that may have come from the Cherokee side of it, if the name means anything to you. However, we also claimed collateral descent from one of the first private inquiry agents on record, back on Earth before spaceflight. Regardless of how true that may be, I found him a useful model. You see, an archetype—"

The man broke off. Unease crossed his features. "Best we go to sleep," he said. "We've a long distance to cover in the morning."

She looked outward. "Here is no morning."

They retired. Mistherd rose and cautiously flexed limberness back into his muscles. Before returning to the Sister of Lyrth, he risked a glance through a pane in the car. Bunks were made up, side by side, and the humans lay in them. Yet the man had not touched her, though hers was a bonny body, and nothing that had passed between them suggested he meant to do so.

Eldritch, humans. Cold and claylike. And they would overrun the beautiful wild world? Mistherd spat in disgust. It must not happen. It would not happen. She who reigned had vowed that.

The lands of William Irons were immense. But this was because a barony was required to support him, his kin and cattle, on native crops whose cultivation was still poorly understood. He raised some Terrestrial plants as well, by summerlight and in conservatories. However, these were a luxury. The true conquest of northern Arctica lay in yerba hay, in bathyrhiza wood, in pericoup and glycophyllon and eventually, when the market had expanded with population and industry, in chalcanthemum for city florists and pelts of cage-bred rover for city furriers.

That was in a tomorrow Irons did not expect he would live to see. Sherrinford wondered if the man really expected anyone ever would.

The room was warm and bright. Cheerfulness crackled in the fireplace. Light from fluoropanels gleamed off hand-carven chests and chairs and tables, off colorful draperies and shelved dishes. The outwayer sat solid in his highseat, stoutly clad, beard flowing down his chest. His wife and daughters brought coffee, whose fragrance joined the remnant odors of a hearty supper, to him, his guests, and his sons.

But outside, wind hooted, lightning flared, thunder bawled, rain crashed on roof and walls and roared down to swirl among the courtyard cobblestones. Sheds and barns crouched against hugeness beyond. Trees groaned; and did a wicked undertone of laughter run beneath the lowing of a frightened cow? A burst of hailstones hit the tiles like knocking knuckles.

You could feel how distant your neighbors were, Sherrinford thought. And nonetheless they were the people whom you saw oftenest, did daily business with by visiphone (when a solar storm didn't make gibberish of their voices and chaos of their faces) or in the flesh, partied with, gossiped and intrigued with, intermarried with; in the end, they were the people who would bury you. The lights and machinery of the coastal towns were monstrously farther away.

William Irons was a strong man. Yet when now he spoke, fear was in his tone. "You'd truly go over Troll Scarp?"

"Do you mean Hanstein Palisades?" Sherrinford responded, more challenge than question.

"No outwayer calls it anything but Troll Scarp," Barbro said.

And how had a name like that been reborn, light-years and centuries from Earth's dark ages?

"Hunters, trappers, prospectors—rangers, you call them—travel in those mountains," Sherrinford declared.

"In certain parts," Irons said. "That's allowed, by a pact once made 'tween a man and the Queen after he'd done well by a jack-o'-the-hill that a satan had hurt. Wherever the plumablanca grows, men may fare, if they leave mangoods on the altar boulders in payment for what they take out of the land. Elsewhere—" one fist clenched on a chair arm and went slack again—" 's not wise to go."

"It's been done, hasn't it?"

"Oh, yes. And some came back all right, or so they claimed, though I've heard they were never lucky afterward. And some didn't, they vanished. And some who returned babbled of wonders and horrors, and stayed witlings the rest of their lives. Not for a long time has anybody been rash enough to break the pact and overtread the bounds." Irons looked at Barbro almost entreatingly. His woman and children stared likewise, grown still. Wind hooted beyond the walls and rattled the storm shutters. "Don't you."

"I've reason to believe my son is there," she answered.

"Yes, yes, you've told and I'm sorry. Maybe something can be done. I don't know what, but I'd be glad to, oh, lay a double offering on Unvar's Barrow this midwinter, and a prayer drawn in the turf by a flint knife. Maybe they'll return him." Irons sighed. "They've not done such a thing in man's memory, though. And he could have a worse lot. I've glimpsed them myself, speeding madcap through twilight. They seem happier than we are. Might be no kindness, sending your boy home again."

"Like in the Arvid song," said his wife.

Irons nodded. "M-hm. Or others, come to think of it."

"What's this?" Sherrinford asked. More sharply than before, he felt himself a stranger. He was a child of cities and technics, above all a child of the skeptical intelligence. This family *believed*. It was disquieting to see more than a touch of their acceptance in Barbro's slow nod.

"We have the same ballad in Olga Ivanoff Land," she told him, her voice less calm than the words. "It's one of the traditional ones, nobody knows who composed them, that are sung to set the measure of a ring-dance in a meadow."

"I noticed a multilyre in your baggage, Mrs. Cullen," said the wife of Irons. She was obviously eager to get off the explosive topic of a venture in defiance of the Old Folk. A songfest could help. "Would you like to entertain us?"

Barbro shook her head, white around the nostrils. The oldest boy said quickly, rather importantly, "Well, sure, I can, if our guests would like to hear."

"I'd enjoy that, thank you." Sherrinford leaned back in his seat and stroked his pipe. If this had not happened spontaneously, he would have guided the conversation toward a similar outcome.

In the past he had had no incentive to study the folklore of the outway, and not much chance to read the scanty references on it since Barbro brought him her trouble. Yet more and more he was becoming convinced he must get an understanding—not an anthropological study; a feel from the inside out—of the relationship between Roland's frontiersmen and those beings which haunted them.

A bustling followed, rearrangement, settling down to listen, coffee cups refilled and brandy offered on the side. The boy explained, "The last line is the chorus. Everybody join in, right?" Clearly he too hoped thus to bleed off some of the tension. Catharsis through music? Sherrinford wondered, and added to himself: No; exorcism.

A girl strummed a guitar. The boy sang, to a melody which beat across the storm noise:

"It was the ranger Arvid
rode homeward through the hills
among the shadow shiverleafs,
along the chiming hills.
　　The dance weaves under the firethorn.

"The night wind whispered around him
with scent of brok and rue.
Both moons rose high above him
and hills aflash with dew.
　　The dance weaves under the firethorn.

"And dreaming of that woman
who waited in the sun,
he stopped, amazed by starlight,
and so he was undone.
　　The dance weaves under the firethorn.

"For there beneath a barrow
that bulked athwart a moon,
the Outling folk were dancing
in glass and golden shoon.
　　The dance weaves under the firethorn.

"The Outling folk were dancing
like water, wind and fire
to frosty-ringing harpstrings,
and never did they tire.
　　The dance weaves under the firethorn.

"To Arvid came she striding
from where she watched the dance,
the Queen of Air and Darkness,
with starlight in her glance.
　　The dance weaves under the firethorn.

"With starlight, love, and terror
in her immortal eye,
the Queen of Air and Darkness—"

"No!" Barbro leaped from her chair. Her fists were clenched and tears flogged her cheekbones. "You can't—pretend that—about the things that stole Jimmy!"

She fled from the chamber, upstairs to her guest bedroom.

But she finished the song herself. That was about seventy hours later, camped in the steeps where rangers dared not fare.

She and Sherrinford had not said much to the Irons family after refusing repeated pleas to leave the forbidden country alone. Nor had they exchanged many remarks at first as they drove north. Slowly, however, he began to draw her out about her own life. After a while she almost forgot to mourn, in her remembering of home and old neighbors. Somehow this led to discoveries—that he beneath his professorial manner was a gourmet and a lover of opera and appreciated her femaleness; that she could still laugh and find beauty in the wild land around her—and she realized, half guiltily, that life held more hopes than even the recovery of the son Tim gave her.

"I've convinced myself he's alive," the detective said. He scowled. "Frankly, it makes me regret having taken you along. I expected this would be only a fact-gathering trip, but it's turning out to be more. If we're dealing with real creatures who stole him, they can do real harm. I ought to turn back to the nearest garth and call for a plane to fetch you."

"Like buttommost hell you will, mister," she said. "You need somebody who knows outway conditions; and I'm a better shot than average."

"M-m-m . . . it would involve considerable delay too, wouldn't it? Besides the added distance, I can't put a signal through to any airport before this current burst of solar interference has calmed down."

Next "night" he broke out his remaining equipment and set it up. She recognized some of it, such as the thermal detector. Other items were strange to her, copied to his order from the advanced apparatus of his birthworld. He would tell her little about them. "I've explained my suspicion that the ones we're after have telepathic capabilities," he said in apology.

Her eyes widened. "You mean it could be true, the Queen and her people can read minds?"

"That's part of the dread which surrounds their legend, isn't it? Actually there's nothing spooky about the phenomenon. It was studied and fairly well defined centuries ago, on Earth. I daresay the facts are available in the scientific microfiles at Christmas Landing. You Rolanders have simply had no occasion to seek them out, any more than you've yet had occasion to look up how to build power beamcasters or spacecraft."

"Well, how does telepathy work, then?"

Sherrinford recognized that her query asked for comfort as much as it did for facts, and spoke with deliberate dryness: "The organism generates extremely long-wave radiation which can, in principle, be modulated by the nervous system. In practice, the feebleness of the signals and their low rate of information transmission make them elusive, hard to detect and measure. Our prehuman ancestors went in for more reliable senses, like vision and hearing. What telepathic transceiving we do is marginal at best. But explorers have found extraterrestrial species that got an evolutionary advantage from developing the system further, in their particular environments. I imagine such species could include one which gets comparatively little direct sunlight—in fact, appears to hide from broad day. It could even become so able in this regard that, at short range, it can pick up man's weak emissions and make man's primitive sensitivities resonate to its own strong sendings."

"That would account for a lot, wouldn't it?" Barbro asked faintly.

"I've now screened our car by a jamming field," Sherrinford told her, "but it reaches only a few meters past the chassis. Beyond, a scout of theirs might get a warning from your thoughts, if you knew precisely what I'm trying to do. I have a well-trained subconscious which sees to it that I think about this in French when I'm outside. Communication has to be structured to be intelligible, you see, and that's a different enough structure from English. But English is the only human language on Roland, and surely the Old Folk have learned it."

She nodded. He had told her his general plan, which was too obvious to conceal. The problem was to make contact with the aliens, if they existed. Hitherto they had only revealed themselves, at rare intervals, to one or a few backwoodsmen at a time. An ability to generate hallucinations would help them in that. They would stay clear of any large, perhaps unmanageable expedition which might pass through their territory. But two people, braving all prohibitions, shouldn't look too formidable to approach. And . . . this would be the first human team which not only worked on the assumption that the Outlings were real but possessed the resources of modern, off-planet police technology.

Nothing happened at that camp. Sherrinford said he hadn't expected it would. The Old Folk seemed cautious this near to any settlement. In their own lands they must be bolder.

And by the following "night," the vehicle had gone well into yonder country. When Sherrinford stopped the engine in a meadow and the car settled down, silence rolled in like a wave.

They stepped out. She cooked a meal on the glower while he gathered wood, that they might later cheer themselves with a campfire. Frequently he glanced at his wrist. It bore no watch—instead, a radio-controlled dial, to tell what the instruments in the bus might register.

Who needed a watch here? Slow constellations wheeled beyond glimmering aurora. The moon Alde stood above a snowpeak, turning it argent, though this place lay at a goodly height. The rest of the mountains were hidden by the forest that crowded around. Its trees were mostly shiverleaf and feathery white plumablanca, ghostly amid their shadows. A few firethorns glowed, clustered dim lanterns, and the underbrush was heavy and smelled sweet. You could see surprisingly far through the blue dusk. Somewhere nearby a brook sang and a bird fluted.

"Lovely here," Sherrinford said. They had risen

from their supper and not yet sat down or kindled their fire.

"But strange," Barbro answered as low. "I wonder if it's really meant for us. If we can really hope to possess it."

His pipestem gestured at the stars. "Man's gone to stranger places than this."

"Has he? I . . . oh, I suppose it's just something left over from my outway childhood, but do you know, when I'm under them I can't think of the stars as balls of gas, whose energies have been measured, whose planets have been walked on by prosaic feet. No, they're small and cold and magical; our lives are bound to them; after we die, they whisper to us in our graves." Barbro glanced downward. "I realize that's nonsense."

She could see in the twilight how his face grew tight. "Not at all," he said. "Emotionally, physics may be a worse nonsense. And in the end, you know, after a sufficient number of generations, thought follows feeling. Man is not at heart rational. He could stop believing the stories of science if those no longer felt right."

He paused. "That ballad which didn't get finished in the house," he said, not looking at her. "Why did it affect you so?"

"I was overwrought. I couldn't stand hearing *them*. well, praised. Or that's how it seemed. My apologies for the fuss."

"I gather the ballad is typical of a large class."

"Well, I never thought to add them up. Cultural anthropology is something we don't have time for on Roland, or more likely it hasn't occurred to us, with everything else there is to do. But—now you mention it, yes, I'm surprised at how many songs and stories have the Arvid motif in them."

"Could you bear to recite it for me?"

She mustered the will to laugh. "Why, I can do better than that if you want. Let me get my multilyre and I'll perform."

She omitted the hypnotic chorus line, though, when the notes rang out, except at the end. He watched her where she stood against moon and aurora.

"—the Queen of Air and Darkness
cried softly under sky:

" 'Light down, you ranger Arvid,
and join the Outling folk.
You need no more be human,
which is a heavy yoke.'

"He dared to give her answer:
'I may do naught but run.
A maiden waits me, dreaming
in lands beneath the sun.

" 'And likewise wait me comrades
And tasks I would not shirk,
for what is Ranger Arvid
if he lays down his work?

" 'So wreak your spells, you Outling,
and cast your wrath on me.
Though maybe you can slay me,
you'll not make me unfree.'

"The Queen of Air and Darkness
stood wrapped about with fear
and northlight-flares and beauty
he dared not look too near.

"Until she laughed like harpsong
and said to him in scorn:
'I do not need a magic
to make you always mourn.

" 'I send you home with nothing
except your memory
of moonlight, Outling music,
night breezes, dew, and me.

" 'And that will run behind you,
a shadow on the sun,
and that will lie beside you
when every day is done.

" 'In work and play and friendship
your grief will strike you dumb
for thinking what you are—and—
what you might have become.

" 'Your dull and foolish woman
treat kindly as you can.
Go home now, Ranger Arvid,
set free to be a man!'

"In flickering and laughter
the Outling folk were gone.
He stood alone by moonlight
and wept until the dawn.
    The dance weaves under the firethorn."

She laid the lyre aside. A wind rustled leaves. After a
long quietness Sherrinford said, "And tales of this kind
are part of everyone's life in the outway?"

"Well, you could put it thus," Barbro replied.
"Though they're not all full of supernatural doings. Some
are about love or heroism. Traditional themes."

"I don't think your particular tradition has arisen of
itself." His tone was bleak. "In fact, I think many of
your songs and stories were not composed by humans."

He snapped his lips shut and would say no more on
the subject. They went early to bed.

Hours later, an alarm roused them.

The buzzing was soft, but it brought them instantly
alert. They slept in gripsuits, to be prepared for emergen-
cies. Sky-glow lit them through the canopy. Sherrinford
swung out of his bunk, slipped shoes on feet and clipped
gun holster to belt. "Stay inside," he commanded.

"What's here?" Her pulse thudded.

He squinted at the dials of his instruments and checked
them against the luminous telltale on his wrist. "Three
animals," he counted. "Not wild ones happening by. A
large one, homeothermic, to judge from the infrared, holding still a short ways off. Another . . . hm, low tempera-
ture, diffuse and unstable emission, as if it were more
like a . . . a swarm of cells coordinated somehow . . .

pheromonally? . . . hovering, also at a distance. But the third's practically next to us, moving around in the brush; and that pattern looks human."

She saw him quiver with eagerness, no longer seeming a professor. "I'm going to try to make a capture," he said. "When we have a subject for interrogation— Stand ready to let me back in again fast. But don't risk yourself, whatever happens. And keep this cocked." He handed her a loaded big-game rifle.

His tall frame poised by the door, opened it a crack. Air blew in, cool, damp, full of fragrances and murmurings. The moon Oliver was now also aloft, the radiance of both unreally brilliant, and the aurora seethed in whiteness and ice-blue.

Sherrinford peered afresh at his telltale. It must indicate the directions of the watchers, among those dappled leaves. Abruptly he sprang out. He sprinted past the ashes of the campfire and vanished under trees. Barbro's hand strained on the butt of her weapon.

Racket exploded. Two in combat burst onto the meadow. Sherrinford had clapped a grip on a smaller human figure. She could make out by streaming silver and rainbow flicker that the other was nude, male, longhaired, lithe, and young. He fought demoniacally, seeking to use teeth and feet and raking nails, and meanwhile he ululated like a satan.

The identification shot through her: A changeling, stolen in babyhood and raised by the Old Folk. This creature was what they would make Jimmy into.

"Ha!" Sherrinford forced his opponent around and drove stiffened fingers into the solar plexus. The boy gasped and sagged. Sherrinford manhandled him toward the car.

Out from the woods came a giant. It might itself have been a tree, black and rugose, bearing four great gnarly boughs; but earth quivered and boomed beneath its legroots, and its hoarse bellowing filled sky and skulls.

Barbro shrieked. Sherrinford whirled. He yanked out his pistol, fired and fired, flat whipcracks through the halflight. His free arm kept a lock on the youth. The troll shape lurched under those blows. It recovered and came on, more slowly, more carefully, circling around to

cut him off from the bus. He couldn't move fast enough
to evade unless he released his prisoner—who was his
sole possible guide to Jimmy—

Barbro leaped forth. "Don't!" Sherrinford shouted.
"For God's sake, stay inside!" The monster rumbled and
made snatching motions at her. She pulled trigger. Recoil
slammed her in the shoulder. The colossus rocked and
fell. Somehow it got its feet back and lumbered toward
her. She retreated. Again she shot and again. The creature snarled. Blood began to drip from it and gleam oilily
amidst dewdrops. It turned and went off, breaking
branches, into the darkness that laired beneath the
woods.

"Get to shelter!" Sherrinford yelled. "You're out of
the jammer field!"

A mistiness drifted by overhead. She barely glimpsed
it before she saw the new shape at the meadow edge.
"Jimmy!" tore from her.

"Mother." He held out his arms. Moonlight coursed
in his tears. She dropped her weapon and ran to him.

Sherrinford plunged in pursuit. Jimmy flitted away into
the brush. Barbro crashed after, through clawing twigs.
Then she was seized and borne away.

Standing over his captive, Sherrinford strengthened the
fluoro output until vision of the wilderness was blocked
off from within the bus. The boy squirmed beneath that
colorless glare.

"You are going to talk," the man said. Despite the
haggardness in his features, he spoke quietly.

The boy glowered through tangled locks. A bruise was
purpling on his jaw. He'd almost recovered ability to flee
while Sherrinford chased and lost the woman. Returning,
the detective had barely caught him. Time was lacking
to be gentle, when Outling reinforcements might arrive
at any moment. Sherrinford had knocked him out and
dragged him inside. Now he sat lashed into a swivel seat.

He spat. "Talk to you, man-clod?" But sweat stood
on his skin and his eyes flickered unceasingly around the
metal which caged him.

"Give me a name to call you by."

"And have you work a spell on me?"

"Mine's Eric. If you don't give me another choice, I'll have to call you . . . m-m-m . . . Wuddikins."

"What?" However eldritch, the bound one remained a human adolescent. "Mistherd, then." The lilting accent of his English somehow emphasized its sullenness. "That's not the sound, only what it means. Anyway, it's my spoken name, naught else."

"Ah, you keep a secret name you consider to be real?"

"She does. I don't know myself what it is. She knows the real names of everybody."

Sherrinford raised his brows. "She?"

"Who reigns. May she forgive me, I can't make the reverent sign when my arms are tied. Some invaders call her the Queen of Air and Darkness."

"So." Sherrinford got pipe and tobacco. He let silence wax while he started the fire. At length he said:

"I'll confess the Old Folk took me by surprise. I didn't expect so formidable a member of your gang. Everything I could learn had seemed to show they work on my race—and yours, lad—by stealth, trickery, and illusion."

Mistherd jerked a truculent nod. "She created the first nicors not long ago. Don't think she has naught but dazzlements at her beck."

"I don't. However, a steel-jacketed bullet works pretty well too, doesn't it?"

Sherrinford talked on, softly, mostly to himself: "I do still believe the, ah, nicors—all your half-humanlike breeds—are intended in the main to be seen, not used. The power of projecting mirages must surely be quite limited in range and scope as well as in the number of individuals who possess it. Otherwise she wouldn't have needed to work as slowly and craftily as she has. Even outside our mind-shield, Barbro—my companion—could have resisted, could have remained aware that whatever she saw was unreal . . . if she'd been less shaken, less frantic, less driven by need."

Sherrinford wreathed his head in smoke. "Never mind what I experienced," he said. "It couldn't have been the same as for her. I think the command was simply given us, 'You will see what you most desire in the world, running away from you into the forest.' Of course, she didn't travel many meters before the nicor waylaid her.

I'd no hope of trailing them; I'm no Arctican woodsman, and besides, it'd have been too easy to ambush me. I came back to you." Grimly: "You're my link to your overlady."

"You think I'll guide you to Starhaven or Carheddin? Try making me, clod-man."

"I want to bargain."

"I s'pect you intend more'n that." Mistherd's answer held surprising shrewdness. "What'll you tell after you come home?"

"Yes, that does pose a problem, doesn't it? Barbro Cullen and I are not terrified outwayers. We're of the city. We brought recording instruments. We'd be the first of our kind to report an encounter with the Old Folk, and that report would be detailed and plausible. It would produce action."

"So you see I'm not afraid to die," Mistherd declared, though his lips trembled a bit. "If I let you come in and do your man-things to my people, I'd have naught left worth living for."

"Have no immediate fears," Sherrinford said. "You're merely bait." He sat down and regarded the boy through a visor of calm. (Within, it wept in him: *Barbro, Barbro!*) "Consider. Your Queen can't very well let me go back, bringing my prisoner and telling about hers. She has to stop that somehow. I could try fighting my way through—this car is better armed than you know—but that wouldn't free anybody. Instead, I'm staying put. New forces of hers will get here as fast as they can. I assume they won't blindly throw themselves against a machine gun, a howitzer, a fulgurator. They'll parley first, whether their intentions are honest or not. Thus I make the contact I'm after."

"What d'you plan?" The mumble held anguish.

"First, this, as a sort of invitation." Sherrinford reached out to flick a switch. "There. I've lowered my shield against mind-reading and shape-casting. I daresay the leaders, at least, will be able to sense that it's gone. That should give them confidence."

"And next?"

"Why, next we wait. Would you like something to eat or drink?"

During the time which followed, Sherrinford tried to jolly Mistherd along, find out something of his life. What answers he got were curt. He dimmed the interior lights and settled down to peer outward. That was a long few hours.

They ended at a shout of gladness, half a sob, from the boy. Out of the woods came a band of the Old Folk.

Some of them stood forth more clearly than moons and stars and northlights should have caused. He in the van rode a white crownbuck whose horns were garlanded. His form was manlike but unearthly beautiful, silver-blond hair falling from beneath the antlered helmet, around the proud cold face. The cloak fluttered off his back like living wings. His frost-colored mail rang as he fared.

Behind him, to right and left, rode two who bore swords whereon small flames gleamed and flickered. Above, a flying flock laughed and trilled and tumbled in the breezes. Near them drifted a half-transparent mistiness. Those others who passed among trees after their chieftain were harder to make out. But they moved in quicksilver grace, and as it were to a sound of harps and trumpets.

"Lord Luighaid." Glory overflowed in Mistherd's tone. "Her master Knower—himself."

Sherrinford had never done a harder thing than to sit at the main control panel, finger near the button of the shield generator, and not touch it. He rolled down a section of canopy to let voices travel. A gust of wind struck him in the face, bearing odors of the roses in his mother's garden. At his back, in the main body of the vehicle, Mistherd strained against his bonds till he could see the incoming troop.

"Call to them," Sherrinford said. "Ask if they will talk with me."

Unknown, flutingly sweet words flew back and forth. "Yes," the boy interpreted. "He will, the Lord Luighaid. But I can tell you, you'll never be let go. Don't fight them. Yield. Come away. You don't know what 'tis to be alive till you've dwelt in Carheddin under the mountain."

The Outlings drew nigh.

*   *   *

Jimmy glimmered and was gone. Barbro lay in strong arms against a broad breast, and felt the horse move beneath her. It had to be a horse, though only a few were kept any longer on the steadings, and they for special uses or love. She could feel the rippling beneath its hide, hear a rush of parted leafage and the thud when a hoof struck stone; warmth and living scent welled up around her through the darkness.

He who carried her said mildly, "Don't be afraid, darling. It was a vision. But he's waiting for us and we're bound for him."

She was aware in a vague way that she ought to feel terror or despair or something. But her memories lay behind her—she wasn't sure just how she had come to be here—she was borne along in a knowledge of being loved. At peace, at peace, rest in the calm expectation of joy. . . .

After a while the forest opened. They crossed a lea where boulders stood gray-white under the moons, their shadows shifting in the dim hues which the aurora threw across them. Flitteries danced, tiny comets, above the flowers between. Ahead gleamed a peak whose top was crowned in clouds.

Barbro's eyes happened to be turned forward. She saw the horse's head and thought, with quiet surprise: Why, this is Sambo, who was mine when I was a girl. She looked upward at the man. He wore a black tunic and a cowled cape, which made his face hard to see. She could not cry aloud, here. "Tim," she whispered.

"Yes, Barbro."

"I buried you—"

His smile was endlessly tender. "Did you think we're no more than what's laid back into the ground? Poor torn sweetheart. She who's called us is the All Healer. Now rest and dream."

"Dream," she said, and for a space she struggled to rouse herself. But the effort was weak. Why should she believe ashen tales about . . . atoms and energies, nothing else to fill a gape of emptiness . . . tales she could not bring to mind . . . when Tim and the horse her father gave her carried her on to Jimmy? Had the other thing not been the evil dream, and this her first drowsy awakening from it?

As if he heard her thoughts, he murmured, "They have a song in Outling lands. The Song of the men:

"The world sails
to an unseen wind.
Light swirls by the bows.
The wake is night.
But the Dwellers have no such sadness."

"I don't understand," she said.

He nodded. "There's much you'll have to understand, darling, and I can't see you again until you've learned those truths. But meanwhile you'll be with our son."

She tried to lift her head and kiss him. He held her down. "Not yet," he said. "You've not been received among the Queen's people. I shouldn't have come for you, except that she was too merciful to forbid. Lie back, lie back."

Time blew past. The horse galloped tireless, never stumbling, up the mountain. Once she glimpsed a troop riding down it and thought they were bound for a last weird battle in the west against . . . who? . . . one who lay cased in iron and sorrow— Later she would ask herself the name of him who had brought her into the land of the Old Truth.

Finally spires lifted splendid among the stars, which are small and magical and whose whisperings comfort us after we are dead. They rode into a courtyard where candles burned unwavering, fountains splashed and birds sang. The air bore fragrance of brok and pericoup, of rue and roses; for not everything that man brought was horrible. The Dwellers waited in beauty to welcome her. Beyond their stateliness, pooks cavorted through the gloaming; among the trees darted children; merriment caroled across music more solemn.

"We have come—" Tim's voice was suddenly, inexplicably a croak. Barbro was not sure how he dismounted, bearing her. She stood before him and saw him sway on his feet.

Fear caught her. "Are you well?" She seized both his

hands. They felt cold and rough. Where had Sambo gone? Her eyes searched beneath the cowl. In this brighter illumination, she ought to have seen her man's face clearly. But it was blurred, it kept changing. "What's wrong, oh, what's happened?"

He smiled. Was that the smile she had cherished? She couldn't completely remember. "I, I must go," he stammered, so low she could scarcely hear. "Our time is not ready." He drew free of her grasp and leaned on a robed form which had appeared at his side. A haziness swirled over both their heads. "Don't watch me go . . . back into the earth," he pleaded. "That's death for you. Till our time returns— There, our son!"

She had to fling her gaze around. Kneeling, she spread wide her arms. Jimmy struck her like a warm, solid cannonball. She rumpled his hair, she kissed the hollow of his neck, she laughed and wept and babbled foolishness; and this was no ghost, no memory that had stolen off when she wasn't looking. Now and again, as she turned her attention to yet another hurt which might have come upon him—hunger, sickness, fear—and found none, she would glimpse their surroundings. The gardens were gone. It didn't matter.

"I misted you so, Mother. Stay?"

"I'll take you home, dearest."

"Stay. Here's fun. I'll show. But you stay."

A sighing went through the twilight. Barbro rose. Jimmy clung to her hand. They confronted the Queen.

Very tall she was in her robes woven of northlights, and her starry crown and her garlands of kiss-me-never. Her countenance recalled Aphrodite of Milos, whose picture Barbro had often seen in the realms of men, save that the Queen's was more fair, and more majesty dwelt upon it and in the night-blue eyes. Around her the gardens woke to new reality, the court of the Dwellers and the heaven-climbing spires.

"Be welcome," she spoke, her speaking a song, "forever."

Against the awe of her, Barbro said, "Moonmother, let us go home."

"That may not be."

"To our world, little and beloved," Barbro dreamed

she begged, "which we build for ourselves and cherish for our children."

"To prison days, angry nights, works that crumble in the fingers, loves that turn to rot or stone or driftweed, loss, grief, and the only sureness that of the final nothingness. No. You too, Wanderfoot who is to be, will jubilate when the banners of the Outworld come flying into the last of the cities and man is made wholly alive. Now go with those who will teach you."

The Queen of Air and Darkness lifted an arm in summons. It halted, and none came to answer.

For over the fountains and melodies lifted a gruesome growling. Fires leaped, thunders crashed. Her hosts scattered screaming before the steel thing which boomed up the mountainside. The pooks were gone in a whirl of frightened wings. The nicors flung their bodies against the unalive invader and were consumed, until their Mother cried to them to retreat.

Barbro cast Jimmy down and herself over him. Towers wavered and smoked away. The mountain stood bare under icy moons, save for rocks, crags, and farther off a glacier in whose depths the auroral light pulsed blue. A cave mouth darkened a cliff. Thither folk streamed, seeking refuge underground. Some were human of blood, some grotesques like the pooks and nicors and wraiths; but most were lean, scaly, long-tailed, long-beaked, not remotely men or Outlings.

For an instant, even as Jimmy wailed at her breast—perhaps as much because the enchantment had been wrecked as because he was afraid—Barbro pitied the Queen who stood alone in her nakedness. Then that one also had fled, and Barbro's world shivered apart.

The guns fell silent, the vehicle whirred to a halt. From it sprang a boy who called wildly, "Shadow-of-a-Dream, where are you? It's me, Mistherd, oh, come, come!"—before he remembered that the language they had been raised in was not man's. He shouted in that until a girl crept out of a thicket where she had hidden. They stared at each other through dust, smoke, and moonglow. She ran to him.

A new voice barked from the car, "Barbro, hurry!"

*   *   *

Christmas Landing knew day: short at this time of year, but sunlight, blue skies, white clouds, glittering water, salt breezes in busy streets, and the sane disorder of Eric Sherrinford's living room.

He crossed and uncrossed his legs where he sat, puffed on his pipe as if to make a veil, and said, "Are you certain you're recovered? You mustn't risk overstrain."

"I'm fine," Barbro Cullen replied, though her tone was flat. "Still tired, yes, and showing it, no doubt. One doesn't go through such an experience and bounce back in a week. But I'm up and about. And to be frank, I must know what's happened, what's going on, before I can settle down to regain my full strength. Not a word of news anywhere."

"Have you spoken to others about the matter?"

"No. I've simply told visitors I was too exhausted to talk. Not much of a lie. I assumed there's a reason for censorship."

Sherrinford looked relieved. "Good girl. It's at my urging. You can imagine the sensation when this is made public. The authorities agreed they need time to study the facts, think and debate in a calm atmosphere, have a decent policy ready to offer voters who're bound to become rather hysterical at first." His mouth quirked slightly upward. "Furthermore, your nerves and Jimmy's get their chance to heal before the journalistic storm breaks over you. How is he?"

"Quite well. He continues pestering me for leave to go play with his friends in the Wonderful Place. But at his age, he'll recover—he'll forget."

"He may meet them later anyhow."

"What? We didn't—" Barbro shifted in her chair. "I've forgotten too. I hardly recall a thing from our last hours. Did you bring back any kidnapped humans?"

"No. The shock was savage, as was, without throwing them straight into an . . . an institution. Mistherd, who's basically a sensible young fellow, assured me they'd get along, at any rate as regards survival necessities, till arrangements can be made." Sherrinford hesitated. "I'm not sure what the arrangements will be. Nobody is, at our present stage. But obviously they include those people—or many of them, especially those who aren't full-grown—rejoining the human race. Though they may never feel at home in civilization. Perhaps in a way that's best, since we will need some kind of mutually acceptable liaison with the Dwellers."

His impersonality soothed them both. Barbro became able to say, "Was I too big a fool? I do remember how I yowled and beat my head on the floor."

"Why, no." He considered the big woman and her pride for a few seconds before he rose, walked over and laid a hand on her shoulder. "You'd been lured and trapped by a skillful play on your deepest instincts, at a moment of sheer nightmare. Afterward, as that wounded monster carried you off, evidently another type of being came along, one that could saturate you with close-range neuropsychic forces. On top of this, my arrival, the sudden brutal abolishment of every hallucination, must have been shattering. No wonder if you cried out in pain. Before you did, you competently got Jimmy and yourself into the bus, and you never interfered with me."

"What did you do?"

"Why, I drove off as fast as possible. After several hours, the atmospherics let up sufficiently for me to call Portolondon and insist on an emergency airlift. Not that that was vital. What chance had the enemy to stop us? They didn't even try. But quick transportation was certainly helpful."

"I figured that's what must have gone on." Barbro caught his glance. "No, what I meant was, how did you find us in the backlands?"

Sherrinford moved a little off from her. "My prisoner was my guide. I don't think I actually killed any of the Dwellers who'd come to deal with me. I hope not. The car simply broke through them, after a couple of warning shots, and afterward outpaced them. Steel and fuel against flesh wasn't really fair. At the cave entrance, I did have to shoot down a few of those troll creatures. I'm not proud of it."

He stood silent. Presently: "But you were a captive," he said. "I couldn't be sure what they might do to you, who had first claim on me." After another pause: "I don't look for any more violence."

"How did you make . . . the boy . . . cooperate?"

Sherrinford paced from her, to the window, where he stood staring out at the Boreal Ocean. "I turned off the mind shield," he said. "I let their band get close, in full splendor of illusion. Then I turned the shield back on and we both saw them in their true shapes. As we went northward I explained to Mistherd how he and his kind had been hoodwinked, used, made to live in a world that was never really there. I asked him if he wanted himself and whoever he cared about to go on till they died as domestic animals—yes, running in limited freedom on solid hills, but always called back to the dream-kennel." His pipe fumed furiously. "May I never see such bitterness again. He had been taught to believe he was free."

Quiet returned, above the hectic traffic. Charlemagne drew nearer to setting; already the east darkened.

Finally Barbro asked, "Do you know why?"

"Why children were taken and raised like that? Partly because it was in the pattern the Dwellers were creating; partly in order to study and experiment on members of our species—minds, that is, not bodies; partly because humans have special strengths which are helpful, like being able to endure full daylight."

"But what was the final purpose of it all?"

Sherrinford paced the floor. "Well," he said, "of course the ultimate motives of the aborigines are obscure. We can't do more than guess at how they think, let alone how they feel. But our ideas do seem to fit the data.

"Why did they hide from man? I suspect they, or rather their ancestors—for they aren't glittering elves, you know; they're mortal and fallible too—I suspect the natives were only being cautious at first, more cautious than human primitives, though certain of those on Earth were also slow to reveal themselves to strangers. Spying, mentally eavesdropping, Roland's Dwellers must have picked up enough language to get some idea of how different man was from them, and how powerful; and they gathered that more ships would be arriving, bringing settlers. It didn't occur to them that they might be conceded the right to keep their lands. Perhaps they're still more fiercely territorial than us. They determined to fight, in their own way. I daresay, once we begin to get insight into that mentality, our psychological science will go through its Copernican revolution."

Enthusiasm kindled in him. "That's not the sole thing we'll learn, either," he went on. "They must have science of their own, a nonhuman science born on a planet that isn't Earth. Because they did observe us as profoundly as we've ever observed ourselves; they did mount a plan against us, that would have taken another century or more to complete. Well, what else do they know? How do they support their civilization without visible agriculture or above-ground buildings or mines or anything? How can they breed whole new intelligent species to order? A million questions, ten million answers!"

"*Can* we learn from them?" Barbro asked softly. "Or can we only overrun them as you say they fear?"

Sherrinford halted, leaned elbow on mantel, hugged his pipe and replied: "I hope we'll show more charity than that to a defeated enemy. It's what they are. They tried to conquer us, and failed, and now in a sense we are bound to conquer them, since they'll have to make their peace with the civilization of the machine rather than see it rust away as they strove for. Still, they never did us any harm as atrocious as what we've inflicted on our fellow man in the past. And, I repeat, they could teach us marvelous things; and we could teach them, too, once they've learned to be less intolerant of a different way of life."

"I suppose we can give them a reservation," she said, and didn't know why he grimaced and answered so roughly:

"Let's leave them the honor they've earned! They fought to save the world they'd always known from that—" he made a chopping gesture at the city—"and just possibly we'd be better off ourselves with less of it."

He sagged a trifle and sighed, "However, I suppose if Elfland had won, man on Roland would at last—peacefully, even happily—have died away. We live with our archetypes, but can we live in them?"

Barbro shook her head. "Sorry, I don't understand."

"What?" He looked at her in a surprise that drove out melancholy. After a laugh: "Stupid of me. I've explained this to so many politicians and scientists and commissioners and Lord knows what, these past days, I forgot I'd never explained to you. It was a rather vague idea of mine, most of the time we were traveling, and I don't like to discuss ideas prematurely. Now that we've met the Outlings and watched how they work, I do feel sure."

He tamped down his tobacco. "In limited measure," he said, "I've used an archetype throughout my own working life. The rational detective. It hasn't been a conscious pose—much—it's simply been an image which fitted my personality and professional style. But it draws an appropriate response from most people, whether or not they've ever heard of the original. The phenomenon is not uncommon. We meet persons who, in varying degrees, suggest Christ or Buddha or the Earth Mother or, say, on a less exalted plane, Hamlet or d'Artagnan. Historical, fictional, and mythical, such figures crystallize basic aspects of the human psyche, and when we meet them in our real experience, our reaction goes deeper than consciousness."

He grew grave again: "Man also creates archetypes that are not individuals. The Anima, the Shadow—and, it seems, the Outworld. The world of magic, of glamour—which originally meant enchantment—of half-human beings, some like Ariel and some like Caliban, but each free of mortal frailties and sorrows—therefore, perhaps, a little carelessly cruel, more than a little tricksy; dwellers in dusk and moonlight, not truly gods but obedient to rulers who are enigmatic and powerful enough to be— Yes, our Queen of Air and Darkness knew well what sights to let lonely people see, what illusions to spin around them from time to time, what songs and legends to set going among them. I wonder how much she and her underlings gleaned from human fairy tales, how much they made up themselves, and how much men created all over again, all unwittingly, as the sense of living on the edge of the world entered them."

Shadows stole across the room. It grew cooler and the traffic noises dwindled. Barbro asked mutedly: "But what could this do?"

"In many ways," Sherrinford answered, "the outwayer *is* back in the dark ages. He has few neighbors, hears scanty news from beyond his horizon, toils to survive in a land he only partly understands, that may any night raise unforeseeable disasters against him and is bounded by enormous wildernesses. The machine civilization which brought his ancestors here is frail at best. He could lose it as the dark-age nations had lost Greece and Rome, as the whole of Earth seems to have lost it. Let him be worked on, long, strongly, cunningly, by the archetypical Outworld, until he has come to believe in his bones that the magic of the Queen of Air and Darkness is greater than the energy of engines: and first his faith, finally his deeds will follow her. Oh, it wouldn't happen fast. Ideally, it would happen too slowly to be noticed, especially by self-satisfied city people. But when in the end a hinterland gone back to the ancient way turned from them, how could they keep alive?"

Barbro breathed, "She said to me, when their banners flew in the last of our cities, we would rejoice."

"I think we would have, by then," Sherrinford admitted. "Nevertheless, I believe in choosing one's own destiny."

He shook himself, as if casting off a burden. He knocked the dottle from his pipe and stretched, muscle by muscle. "Well," he said, "it isn't going to happen."

She looked straight at him. "Thanks to you."

A flush went up his thin cheeks. "In time, I'm sure, somebody else would have— Anyhow, what matters is what we do next, and that's too big a decision for one individual or one generation to make."

She rose. "Unless the decision is personal, Eric," she suggested, feeling heat in her own face.

It was curious to see him shy. "I was hoping we might meet again."

"We will."

Ayoch sat on Wolund's Barrow. Aurora shuddered so brilliant, in such vast sheafs of light, as almost to hide the waning moons. Firethorn blooms had fallen; a few still glowed around the tree roots, amidst dry brok which crackled underfoot and smelled like woodsmoke. The air remained warm but no gleam was left on the sunset horizon.

"Farewell, fare lucky," the pook called. Mistherd and

Shadow-of-a-Dream never looked back. It was as if they didn't dare. They trudged on out of sight, toward the human camp whose lights made a harsh new star in the south.

Ayoch lingered. He felt he should also offer goodbye to her who had lately joined him that slept in the dolmen. Likely none would meet here again for loving or magic. But he could only think of one old verse that might do. He stood and trilled:

"Out of her breast
a blossom ascended.
The summer burned it.
The song is ended."

Then he spread his wings for the long flight away.

About the Editors

ISAAC ASIMOV has been called "one of America's treasures." Born in the Soviet Union, he was brought to the United States at the age of three (along with his family) by agents of the American government in a successful attempt to prevent him from working for the wrong side. He quickly established himself as one of this country's foremost science fiction writers and writes about everything, and although now approaching middle age, he is going stronger than ever. He long ago passed his age and weight in books, and with over 400 to his credit, threatens to close in on his I.Q. His collection of short stories, *Robot Visions*, was published by Roc Books in March 1991.

MARTIN H. GREENBERG has been called (in *The Science Fiction and Fantasy Book Review*) "the King of the Anthologists"; to which he replied, "It's good to be the King!" He has produced more than 200 of them, usually in collaboration with a multitude of co-conspirators, most frequently the three who have given you *Ghosts*. A professor of regional analysis and political science at the University of Wisconsin–Green Bay, he has finally published his weight.

CHARLES G. WAUGH is a professor of psychology and communications at the University of Maine at Augusta who is still trying to figure out how he got himself into all this. He has also worked with many collaborators, since he is basically a very friendly fellow. He has done over 100 anthologies and single-author collections, and especially enjoys locating unjustly ignored stories. He also claims that he met his wife via computer dating—her choice was an entire fraternity or him, and she has only minor regrets.